The computer d... points, and two of t... The controller tugged wire-framed spectacles from his hip pocket, perched them on his beak of a nose, and peered over to the display. His eyebrows rose slightly, then he turned to address Avery.

"Modern warfare is about communications as much as fire power," he began. "It isn't enough for the man in the field to learn of the enemy's strength. He has to report back what he knows and do it quickly. What we've built into Vulcan is the best model anyone has yet come up with to imitate the traffic of information sloshing around a battlefield.

"Suppose we want to build a bridge under heavy fire, or move in fuel supplies after the Russians have smothered an area with chemicals. Now, Vulcan knows how to handle these dilemmas. We've taught it steadily, all the time increasing the scale of combat, getting away from the eyeball-to-eyeball stuff and toward the total picture. The total picture is what were really aiming for, Mr. Avery."

The controller smiled appreciatively at the display, then faced Avery again. "Mr. Avery, what you see here today may seem like small beer. But you come back in about six months' time. You'll see whole cities frying then. Believe you me," he finished. "Believe you me."

SPY GAME

BY JOHN McNEIL

ZEBRA BOOKS
KENSINGTON PUBLISHING CORP.

ZEBRA BOOKS

are published by

KENSINGTON PUBLISHING CORP.
475 Park Avenue South
New York, N.Y. 10016

Printed in the United States of America

Prologue

The Operations Room was perhaps fifteen feet square and as sparsely furnished as a prison cell. Gradually, it had become just that to Major Colby. It was getting smaller, noticeably smaller, with the walls seeming to press ever closer in on him as the hours passed. There was no space to march about, as he so desperately needed: not enough room to swing a cat. So he settled instead for exercising his broad backside, shifting constantly in the uncomfortable metal chair beside his map table. He was always restless like that, cooped up, away from the action.

Through the window a chill wind was rippling a curtain of drizzle. Inside, the room was as oppressive as a greenhouse. The radiator was too hot to touch, with its valve firmly stuck in the fully open position. True to form, the ministry had allowed the window frame to be painted over so many times that no amount of pushing would budge it. The smoke from Major Colby's pipe hung in the air like steam over a tropical swamp.

He felt as if he were oozing water, melting away through every pore. His moist hands left a trail of damp patches on the table. Beads of sweat broke on his forehead, to trickle irritatingly down into the scraggy hedgerows over his eyes. His soaking shirt clung to his back, and when he raised an elbow just enough to sniff secretly at an armpit he grunted disapprovingly at what he discovered. The only part of his body that seemed dry was his mouth. Not bothering with a glass, he gulped down the last of the tepid water from a jug.

The major hunched over his map table, tracing again the route his tanks had taken, his forefinger moving slowly in their wake like a plump mourner following a funeral procession. The road was straight at first, a thin band of red striking out over a featureless white plain. After several kilometers it began to snake this way and that as contour lines bunched to block its path, then it made a bow to a patch of pale green woods, ducked under the striped black and white ribbon of a railway and doubled almost back on itself in order to take the laziest way up the looping curves of a hill. Over the crest there was a sudden downward gradient where his finger halted at a blue cross. He remembered jotting it there in grease pencil on the perspex sheet covering the map. Several hours ago, that must have been. Close by, an identical cross marked a second tank lost from his company. Since the surprise attack, there had been no radio contact from the crews, not so much as a whisper of static.

My God, he thought with a start: nothing since dawn.

He traced a detour away from the road, down the slope toward the sparse cover of a grove, swearing like a trooper under his breath when he encountered three more of those blue crosses in there. His finger stayed in the trees as if in fear of its safety while his eyes were more bold, daring to venture out. They scanned the valley to where the ground rose, on past the regular dotted trail of a farm track, up to a scattering of buildings.

"Bastards!" he muttered at the red triangles lurking there in a commanding position, as well defended as any soldier could wish.

His fingers made a sudden break for the road, just as his company had done earlier, moved quickly on, headed across a field, climbed and decended first one hill then another, then turned north onto the yellow of a meandering minor road. The major bent closer to the map, his dry tongue caressing his pipe as he reassessed with hindsight what had happened.

A school beside a crossroads, a narrow band of woods beyond that and a short distance farther the random blue shape of a lake. To its east, he brooded on an ominous gathering of red circles and triangles, then glanced back to the road, estimating the distance. The range was perfect for an RPG-7V, and the lake ideally hidden from the road by those trees. Colby had nothing but respect for the RPG-7V. Shoulder-held. Portable. Very bad news for tanks. Beside the road, a small cemetery of blue crosses recorded the outcome and he read his coded scrawl alongside: three Centurions caught as they made into a field; an armored personnel carrier within another fifty meters; two more Centurions some hundred meters on and well short of the safe cover of a hollow.

Now the pace of his journey quickened and he puffed on his pipe like a steam engine up an incline. Five uneventful kilometers later he finally caught up with the front of his column.

Front! he mused. Tattered tail end, more like.

Blue triangles marked the last-reported position of his forward platoon. They had halted a short distance off the road in the lee of a huddle of factory buildings, radioed back and said no more. Vanished off the bloody face of the earth. The major scouted the surrounding country, carefully reading the contours, the landmarks, the roads and the woods; searching out the likely places of concealment for artillery and rocket launchers. There *was* something there, something damned unpleasant. He could smell it.

"Got anything yet?" he asked gruffly over a shoulder. "Any radio messages?"

Young Franklin, sitting on the other side of the room, kept his eyes keenly fixed on his battery of display screens. "Not so much as a squeak, Harry."

"It's been a hell of a time," the major said.

"Nearly twenty minutes," Franklin noted.

Colby tapped the map impatiently, then drove his finger onward, pressing ahead as if to order his platoon forward whatever the consequences. Despite its evident dangers, the main road was now the only practicable route to his objective. If, that is, he was to get there this side of Doomsday! He traced it precisely, around bends, uphill, dipping down between fields, passing houses and industrial buildings and farms, moving recklessly fast across road intersections and over bridges; all the while his eyes darting this way and that in search of likely danger. He slowed as he reached the outskirts of Grimma, noting with concern the ever-growing numbers of red circles, triangles and squares, before cutting clear across the town in defiance of the regimented street plan. His finger came to rest at an airfield and he stared long and hard at a cluster of red symbols on the southwest perimeter.

The green field telephone gave a throaty rasp close to his elbow. With slow, deliberate movements he was encircling the red markings. Trapping them. Closing in for the kill. If only it were that easy!

"Yes. . . ?" he said, finally responding to the persistent bleat of the phone. He enjoyed keeping the lieutenant waiting. Jumped-up young sod!

"I've a message from the commander, Third Regiment," the lieutenant said, in a voice as smooth and objectionable as castor oil. "He reports a platoon of C Company under attack by two Mi-Twenty-four gunships. We'll have the grid reference for you in a twinkling."

Colby had no need to look to his map to remember where they were: over fifteen kilometers to the south of his own force.

"I've got enough on my plate as it is," he said irritably. "What's he playing at, telling me *his* problems?"

"Both gunships loaded to the gills with Swatter missiles, major," the lieutenant explained, and his voice had gone nasal now, as it always did when he felt knowledgeable. "*Very* nasty. And we've got no air support to take the bloody things out, not just now."

"I know that. Hell, I should know that better than anyone!"

"Well, if you could hurry it up a bit, that's the point of the message," the lieutenant said evenly. "If you could take out those SAMs at Grimma, major. Then we could get some aircraft back into this sector and blow those choppers away in no time flat."

Colby stared again at the red symbols beside the

airfield: six SA-2 surface-to-air missile launchers and an attendant radar trailer. Enough to have the boys in blue running scared, shit scared. Sitting on their asses in the warm while his men were having theirs blown off.

"I don't know if I still have anything to hit them with," he said flatly.

"Sir . . . ?"

"I haven't had a report from my column in over twenty minutes."

The lieutenant whistled his surprise

"Not a damned thing," Colby said. "They might just be bottled up. Or maybe I've got nothing left up there."

"I hardly think *that's* likely," the lieutenant said. "Apart from the tank radios, your crews should have their backpack transmitters, shouldn't they? It's probably just a spot of jamming, I'd say. Some fun and games with your communications."

Colby stabbed at the cradle to finish the conversation, a mental poke in the eye. "Very probably, general," he muttered into the dead receiver before slamming it down.

He resumed his interrupted progress over the map, having to stretch across the table to reach the far corner, so that his belt bit into his belly. Now he was airborne, only his eyes making the journey as he flew pell-mell over the countryside. Through Grimma and on, upward to the northeastern edge of the map, where a cobweb of converging roads on black overflowed off the margin. *Leipzig*. What was it, ninety kilometers inside East Germany? Damnit, he ought to know by now. Disdaining his ruler, he roughly measured the distance from the border with hand spans. Yes, ninety kilometers, give or take a few.

The telephone rattled again.

"I've got the latest weather report for you," the lieutenant said.

"Just the news I was waiting for!" Major Colby retorted with heavy sarcasm.

"Ah, could be useful stuff, major. Rain expected to ease in the next half hour. Wind forecast as rising to moderate, northeasterly."

"I'll send out the order to furl umbrellas!"

"That's not what I mean. Up here we have a sudden nasty feeling your armor's going to come under artillery bombardment as it hoves within range of Grimma. *That's* what I'm getting at."

"Don't you think I've already worked that one out?" Colby sounded more tired than peeved.

"Ah, but with chemical shells, that's the point, major. That's what just occurred to us. With the wind shifting like that, we have a feeling they might chance it."

"We're outnumbered four or five to one in this sector. There's no need for the fancy stuff."

"Well, they might nonetheless. Campbell-Jones asked me to suggest the possibility to you."

"Then you damned well suggest to Campbell-Jones there's a Soviet motor-rifle battalion moving on us downwind of Grimma! Tell him they're not in the habit of snuffing out several hundred of their own troops for each couple of dozen of mine they feel like dousing with Sarin."

"Hydrogen cyanide, more like," the lieutenant said through his nose. "But point taken, major."

11

"And while you're at it," Colby shouted, giving vent to his frustrations, "tell him I'm losing as many Centurions from shed tracks and blown engines as I am from enemy action. Tell him they don't need to go chemical or biological or even bloody nuclear as long as my armor isn't up to this top speed offensive he's ordered me to lay on."

"I'll tell him all that . . . sir."

The major held the telephone high above the table, subjected it to a withering stare and let go, to score a resounding hit on the cradle.

Franklin turned at the sound. "You're letting it get to you, Harry," he observed, as unfussed as ever.

The only reply was a noncommittal grunt. Colby felt his anger to be private.

"Maybe this'll galvanize you," Franklin chirped. "I've just had a report from Signals. Those tanks converging from Zeitz . . ."

". . . Almost certainly Russian, not East German," Colby said decisively, quite proud of not having to consult his map for the details. "Probably T-Seventy-twos."

"Confirmed," Franklin said with one of his birdlike nods. "Except that the first sightings seem to have underestimated the strength. Field HQ now reports an entire regiment from the Soviet Twenty-G Division at Jena."

Colby closed his eyes in agony and sucked frantically on his pipe. And I've got only two men and a dog in their path, he thought. How do we throw in the towel?

". . . Believed to be under the command of Colonel-Engineer Skubilin," Franklin added. "I'll see what we have on him."

"I wouldn't bother," Colby told him in a resigned voice. "Russian commanders are all much of a muchness. Damned bold when the odds are heavy in the favor. Piss awful when it's even-steven."

"I'll call up his file, just the same," Franklin insisted, and turned away to key in the request atone of his computer terminals, leaving Colby staring blankly at his back.

You bloody would, the major thought with feeling. You disrespectful pup, you scruffy young brat. *You damned backroom boy.*

This last was quite the most scathing oath of the three. For as far as the major was concerned, that's what Franklin was: a backroom boy. A chap who saw only statistics where he saw casualties and death. A chap who'd never seen action, never served his time in Cyprus, as Colby had, or put so much as a foot on the streets of Northern Ireland. A backroom boy in the classic mold, a boffin if ever there was one.

So the major kept young Franklin in his place by keeping as far away from him as the small room allowed. Mostly, Colby stayed at his end, using just his army maps and the colored pencils which he had at the ready, always perfectly pointed, on carefully ordered parade by the edge of the table. Everything else he needed was in his head.

In complete contrast, Franklin's corner was crowded with electronic equipment—with display screens and printers—and without it all he was helpless. Boffins were like that, Colby thought: useless if you pulled the plug on them. Lacking resource.

In truth, he needed Franklin more than he was ever

likely to admit and more than he hoped the young man suspected. The fact was, the major feared the computer more than an enemy with a leveled rifle.

Right now, the teleprinter, one of those expensive toys the lad had over there, was rattling away to itself.

"Jesus" Colby heard him say in a hushed tone. Then a far louder "Je-sus! Now *that's* heavy."

The major was sharpening his colored pencils one by one in a wall-mounted machine which wobbled precariously as he pumped the handle. His eyes had found their way back to the map, anxiously to the last-reported position of those Centurions.

"Message from Supreme Headquarters, Harry," Franklin said very soberly from the printer. "A nuclear strike on Frankfurt. A Scud B rocket, launched from the vicinity of Magdeburg. A whole cluster of other like-minded birds on the way. Target coordinates being computed now."

"Don't play silly buggers," Colby admonished in a friendly way. "Not now, old son."

"That's what it says here," Franklin persisted, and his manner was sufficiently grave to get the major scampering over, accidentally sending pencils raining down on the map as if in retaliation.

"It's a mistake," he judged after rapidly scanning the message. "It has to be."

"I don't think so somehow, Harry."

The major charged back to his table and snatched up the telephone. "Look here, this report . . . This business about a nuclear strike . . ."

"Ah, yes . . ." the lieutenant said.

"Well? Do we believe it or is it garbage?"

"I suggest you believe it, major."

14

"In that case, I want a word with Campbell-Jones."

"It's not a good moment. Sorry and all that but things are suddenly pretty hectic up here."

"Tell him I want a word, *sonny!* Tell him I insist!"

Colby heard the telephone thud carelessly onto a desk. A long wait ensued, with only the distant murmur of voices in the Command Room. It was impossible to work out what was being said, however hard he listened. Other phones were ringing, long and insistently, in the background.

The lieutenant was back at last, with much banging and scraping, to say, "Sorry, sir, but he says to let you know it *is* correct. We appear to have drastic escalation."

Colby waited for more.

"Sir . . . ?" the lieutenant squeaked.

"Is that *it?* Is that all he said?"

"Yup. If you want my opinion," the lieutenant offered nasally, "You're a good sixty kilometers inside their border. I'd say that's reason enough for them to up the ante, wouldn't you?"

The major dropped his head wearily into cupped hands for a moment's meditation. Then he stiffened, rose with determination from his chair and marched over to stand, hands defiantly on hips, behind Franklin.

"Get me a readout on all strategic missile sites in East Germany, and quick. Locations. Weapon types and numbers in place. Class of warhead. Range." Despite the resolute air, he had no idea yet what he would do with the information when it came. Not an inkling.

"Sorry," Franklin said weakly.

15

"What?"

"No can do, Harry. Look . . ."

The bank of display screens in the corner continued to flicker but they were now quite blank and Franklin's frantic jabbing at the keyboards was making no difference.

"Bloody thing's gone down again," he moaned. "The computer's gone on the blink again."

"You sure, old son?"

Franklin gave a helpless flap of the hands in confirmation.

"In that case, I'll stand you a pint." Colby was already turning in relief for the map table and his hastily abandoned pipe. "What do you say?"

They buttoned their coats in unison, turning the collars up against the biting wind. The major's was camel-colored, in heavy wool, with unfashionably wide lapels and two rows of wooden buttons down the front. Franklin's short raincoat barely reached to the knees and looked too thin for any but the lightest shower.

"It's pissing down," he said, looking pointedly at the major's umbrella.

"A spot of drizzle, lad," the major countered, and, keeping the umbrella tightly rolled, hoisted it to his shoulder like a rifle. "Nothing wrong with a drop of rain. A nice bracing walk through the Garden of England. Do you the world of good."

On a good day you could see Tonbridge Wells from the hill and beyond that the Weald of Kent. Now a stubborn sun painted rainbow hues on the droplets of thinning, drifting rain. The starkly red-bricked buildings of Fort Halstead huddled against the slope, staring gloomily with uncurtained windows down on the glistening roofs of Sevenoaks.

Major Colby splashed headlong through a puddle which the younger man chose to skirt, turned onto Penney Road and headed at a brisk trot for the mess.

"Bloody machine," Franklin grumbled still as he struggled to draw level. "Going down like that again. It did the same thing a couple of weeks back during the last game, remember? Right at a crucial point, too."

"Couldn't have come at a better time," Colby said with a shake of the head. "The game controller's lost his bottle. Must have. Drastic escalation indeed!"

"It does seem a bit extreme," Franklin said.

"Damned ridiculous, old son. We spend the best part of a week pushing armor and infantry east, twenty-four hours of simulated battle, fighting like grim death over every inch of damned ground. And then what? *Splat!* Nuclear warheads are dropping like locusts behind us. Who gives a tinker's cuss now about the odd few SAMs up at Grimma?"

"I wouldn't give up just yet, Harry. Not if I were you."

". . . And the other Blue commanders are all in the same pickle, you'll see. Complete bloody waste of time!"

"All the same," Franklin ventured meekly, "the controller *usually* knows what he's doing. You must admit he does, Harry."

"Tcha!" Colby snorted, and he forded another stretch of water to take a squelching shortcut over the grass to the mess.

As they sat, the waitress came crab-fashion between

17

the closely packed tables toward theirs, stirring the major's imagination as no young beauty could manage these days. He kept his sexual fantasies for other men's women now, like Franklin's bit of crumpet. For himself he sought only nostalgia, a good hard sniff with flared nostrils at the past. The waitress was sixty if she was a day, with streaked, iron-gray hair fashioned exactly as it must have been for the last quarter century. There were metal grips to hold it in place and her pinafore, which Colby assumed not to be civil service issue, was lace frilled. She had a curiously dated way of licking her stub of a pencil before taking the orders. So she always conjured up memories for him: of the late forties and of Lyons's Corner House and of a London now lost in his distant subaltern days, where you could still park where you damned well chose and still live in some style, even as a soldier.

"How are you today, my darling?" With excessive enthusiasm, he seized a hand to kiss it amorously.

"Major! Behave yourself!"

"She always plays so hard to get, doesn't she?" Colby said, nudging young Franklin across the table.

"There's brown Windsor soup or grapefruit segments. Roast chicken or fish pie. Trifle with custard."

"Soup and chicken," Colby said,

"Make that twice," Franklin said.

"Is Mr. Campbell-Jones here yet?" Colby asked. He couldn't spot the controller in the small dining room and he hadn't been in the bar.

"Not that I've seen."

"Be an angel and steer him this way when he comes, eh? Here first, mind."

18

She nodded agreement but he caught her hand again as she started her return to the servery.

"What about the Red commanders?" he asked in a low, confidential tone. "Have they turned up yet?"

"They're in there now. They arrived just before you." Her eyes strayed to the door leading to the adjacent dining area, where the officers commanding the opposing Red forces took what Colby derisively called their fodder. Strict seclusion was enforced between the two sides by the controller and his staff for the duration of each war game.

"Looking happy in there, are they?" Colby asked. "In a celebratory mood? Knocking back the bubbly? I'll bet they bloody are!"

"No, just the same as usual." The waitress was attempting, unsuccessfully, to tug her hand free.

"Look, if you should happen to overhear anything in there," Colby said, drawing her closer, "like . . . *intelligence.*" He relished the word, hissing it roundly in her reluctant ear. "How about letting an old friend in on it, eh?"

"Me? *I* don't go about listening to other people's business, Major Colby. Do you mind!"

"But if you should happen to . . . ?" With his free hand he stroked his ample mustache to increase his appeal.

"Well, as it's you, major . . ."

Smiling contentedly at the treaty, he released her. He demolished what was left of a large gin and tonic and embarrassed Franklin by leaning over to clasp a hand warmly on a shoulder.

"And that, Bob my old son, is how wars are won."

Franklin dropped his eyes to the small lager he was

toying with.

"You don't like losing, do you?"

"Who does?" Colby retorted with a ribald laugh. "My God, who does?"

"It's only a game, Harry."

"There speakest the true civil servant."

"But it is, though. Just a game. And that doesn't mean I'm knocking it."

"Now that, old son, is where you're wrong. It's a *battle*. Me, I don't give a stuff whether it's the real thing or simulated on a computer. It's still a battle, us against them, and battles are there to be won."

"You know, I can't work you out," Franklin said sadly, with a thoughtful shake of the head. "You complain about the facilities. You criticize the scenarios. You . . ."

"Analyze them," the major said in correction. "That's what I do. Subject them to soldierly scrutiny."

"Whatever. Half the time you dispute the outcomes of engagements with the controller. You haven't a good thing to say about the computer, not ever. Yet when Blue comes out badly it's like a death in the family. And I have to live with it all the working day."

The major sighed his disagreement. "Shall I tell you something, old son? I'm a gunner. I mean, that's what I'm trained to do and I'm dashed good at it, though I say it myself. Not counting a desk spell in Belfast, the last time I fired a gun in anger was in Nicosia. Now that's way, way back in the dim and distant. Try and imagine how I feel. Can you even begin to grasp what it's like? You're a . . . computer whatsit, right?"

"I've got a degree in computing science, yes, if that's what you mean." Franklin gave the major one of his sharp looks, eyes narrowed to show he wasn't taken in by the vagueness. The man always played dumb when it came to computers.

But Colby was undeterred by the stare. "Well, suppose you'd done that degree, all that study, and then . . . a big nothing. They don't let you near a computer, not properly, for twenty years. Oh, they let you look at the blasted thing, let you plug it in of a morning, grant you the privilege of polishing it up nicely once in a blue moon, but not use it as it *should* be used. Not for real, as it were. You'd be pretty cheesed off, am I right?"

"I know what you're trying to say, Harry." Franklin wriggled uncomfortably. He had a sneaking regard for the major but confessions always made him feel awkward.

"I was down at Bovington Camp," Colby continued, "down in sunny, quiet Dorset. Sitting on my bum at a blasted desk most of the time. Now and then, getting out to watch tanks churning up the firing ranges and worrying more about the cost of every shell than where it landed. Do you know what I could see looming up over the horizon? Ending my days administering the tank museum, God help me, showing holidaymakers around clapped-out Chieftains. No thank you very much. And then out of the blue came my letter of salvation." He began to trace words theatrically in the air. "A two-year tour of secondment to the Ministry of Defence. Assignment to the Royal Armaments Research and Development Establishment. Better known to one and all as Fort Halstead. Manna from heaven, that's how I saw it. The wife's always had a yen for Tonbridge Wells and I've got something to get

21

my teeth into again, something important."

"Two soups," the waitress said, plunking down bowls of thick brown liquid.

"Well, darling?" Colby asked expectantly.

"I'm still seeing to this side," she said, ducking quickly out of reach. "I haven't been in there again yet."

"I seem to have set the proverbial cat among the pigeons," Campbell-Jones declared with a self-satisfied smile. He took the chair next to Franklin and inspected his plate. "Chicken looks good." He cast around abortively for the waitress.

"A dashed stupid move, if you want my opinion," Colby grumbled.

"Now why on earth do you say that?" The game controller arched his eyebrows, affecting wounded innocence.

"Oh, come on, Howard! This started out as a bog standard land battle. You know as well as I do it would never go nuclear this quickly, not after only twenty-four hours."

"Tactical nuclear, maybe," Franklin contributed. "But strategic . . ."

"And why ever not, pray?" Campbell-Jones challenged. "There's one heck of a lot of blue armor pouring in at top lick over a hundred-and-fifty-kilometer front. Plus airstrikes on key military targets. British, German and American units. You can hardly say that won't shake the Kremlin up a trifle, now can you?"

"Not in twenty-four hours," Colby persisted. "We'd have a good three days of conventional warfare first.

Eyeball-to-eyeball stuff."

"That's always been my understanding too," Franklin said. "Red is supposed to be playing strict Warsaw Pact rules. No embellishments, nothing fancy. Just straight interpretation of what we know of their weapons and tactics."

"Correct," Campbell-Jones said emphatically, beaming a creased smile.

"You've lost me," Colby said.

The controller's beefy hand shot out to block the aisle as the waitress tried to squeeze by to another table. "Just the chicken, Doreen. I'll give the starter a miss." His rotund stomach was patted in explanation. "And I'll be over there with Brigadier Murdoch and the ministry chappie."

He turned back to wink slyly at the major. "Let's put it this way. Maybe, and I do mean maybe, we've just received word from appropriate sources that we ought to change our basic Red rules. Sources a good way east of the Channel, if you follow?"

"Aaah," Colby breathed, meeting his gaze knowingly.

"And you haven't heard me say that, all right? At least, not yet awhile." The controller struggled to his feet, his chair scraping a noisy protest on the polished parquet floor. "Had any radio problems today, by any chance, Harry?"

"You bloody know I have!"

"Well now," the controller mused, stroking his chin, "that could be nothing significant, I suppose. On the other hand it could be due to a fancy new Soviet gizmo we've just got wind of. Mounted on a . . . what? An armored personnel carrier, shall we say?

That's as much hint as you're getting. You'll have to wait for the postgame debriefing for the full story."

"In other words not long," Colby said sourly. "This whole shooting match should be over this afternoon. Another hour of game time at the most, that's what I reckon."

"Ah yes, I knew there was something else," Campbell-Jones said, striking his forehead at his absentmindedness. "I gather the computer's going to be out of action till after lunch tomorrow at the earliest. My chaps in the Command Room are pushing off home with my blessing. I suggest you people do the same. We're going to be running the game well into the evening tomorrow to catch up lost time. There are some very big wheels in Whitehall waiting with bated breath on the results of this one." He wandered off, threading his way between the tables to the largest, set apart to emphasize its importance, against a paneled wall with a photograph of the queen.

"I'll skip pudding, if you don't mind," Franklin said, slipping from his chair. "I think I'll stroll over and see what's up with the machine."

"You can't leave things be, can you," Colby remarked amiably. He was shepherding some very green processed peas into insipid gravy.

"Just interested, that's all, Harry. Anything wrong in that?"

"Horizontal entertainment, that's all that's lacking. When they can do that you'll be as happy as a sandboy."

"Eh?" Franklin said, mystified.

"One fine day you'll find a computer to dish up what that little experimental officer of yours provides." Colby jerked a spoon handle into an encircling finger and thumb. "Then you'll bloody settle down with it in a state of perfect bliss, won't you, old son?"

"There's no need to be crude," Franklin said primly and his face began to redden.

Chuckling, Colby watched him go out into the rain, still tugging on his raincoat as he passed the window with quick, short steps on his way back to the Assessment Branch building.

"Experimental," Colby said under his breath. "That's deuced appropriate."

The rain reminded him of Cyprus, as it so often did. A warm evening after an oven-hot day, the muggy atmosphere so thick you could cut it and a certainty of thunder you could feel on the skin. The three of them bumping over that excuse of a rutted track in the hills above Famagusta: Sergeant Collins beside him driving the Land-Rover and poor Tweety Nightingale spread-eagled in the back. Poor, dead Tweety, talking as always endlessly of nothing very much so that after a time you stopped listening and the voice became a distant buzz less interesting than the crashing suspension or the complaining creaks of the body. It was the talking, probably, which had made them careless: their eyes had simply turned off, much as their eyes had done. There was a bump little different from the rest, which might have been from yet another ridge gouged from the track. Then the flash, which for an instant he thought was the expected lightning. Then the thunder, but coming from under them, and he was flying upward, turning against the colors in deafened silence. It was sheer ballet, that's how Colby remembered it now, a time-slowed journey through the most beautiful pyrotechnic display he had ever seen, let alone *been* in. And after, he was just lying there, half in a ditch, staring like an imbecile at the Land-Rover and wondering what monstrous force could possibly have wreaked such havoc on it and what the mess was in the back where Tweety had been. Even as shocked reality was crowding in there was that second explosion only yards away; doubly terrifying because he could see it and feel the blast but not hear a bloody thing. Then Collins was pushing his tattered remains of a face close to his, mouthing words, and Colby, fool that he was, just lay there trying to read them. Suddenly all he cared about, above all else, was to know what the sergeant was saying—no, shouting. There came two more blasts which shook the earth and him on it, but still he went on reading. Then that glorious sense of achievement when he at last began to understand. It had been something about the bastards having one of our own mortars; firing on us with one of our own mortars, for fuck's sake. They would have been the last words the sergeant ever uttered and there had been no one there to hear them, not hear them properly. Even now, Colby thought that the saddest part of the whole sorry business.

The rain had come hours later, he never knew how long. But he could still recall it dashing on his face, bringing him round, and feel it as if it were there now, soaking through to every part of his body like a cooling balm. It was the wettest, most marvelous damned torrential downpour of his whole life.

Weather, he mused now, was a thing for God to

decide and Him only. Sometimes it was for you in battle and sometimes against; more usually preserving a strict neutrality and favoring neither side. But it wasn't for the likes of Campbell-Jones to conjure with on a whim, setting the wind speed and direction, turning the computerized rain on and off as he chose. Colby could forgive the controller for the nuclear rockets, any number of them. But not for playing God, oh no, not for easing the rain like that.

"Major?" It was whispered in his ear.

He spun round out of his reverie to find Doreen behind him, bending close and searching the dining room with caution. She spoke out of the corner of her mouth, like a spy secretly met, her eyes absently looking anywhere but at him as she placed his trifle and custard on the table.

"I've just been in there, listening."

"That's my girl."

"They're going to chance it, despite that out there." She nodded to the window, her voice barely audible above the fog of chatter filling the room. "They're off to the races for the rest of the day. Epsom."

1

That day the San Fernando Valley had been blanketed in smog and as sweltering under it as a desert. Malibu was cooler. A heat haze played with the automobiles on the Pacific Coast Highway. The ocean had settled for the evening into a slumbering calm and the merest suggestion of a breeze carried its sharp, salty smell inland to mix with the perfumes of hibiscus and honeysuckle and agave blossom. Martin Avery made a right turn into the shaded gully of Las Flores Canyon. The scents were stronger there, moist from the pulsing sprinklers which dusted the air with fine spray.

He stopped the car for a moment to glance again at the map Brokaw's secretary had given him: on heavy-weave paper and so beautifully printed to give the appearance of an old Spanish treasure chart that on first sight he had assumed it to be hand drawn. Las Flores Mesa Drive was the next on the right and after the turnoff the level became an upward grade into the foothills. Soon he was enjoying the exhilarating sweep from one tight twist to the next, cutting into the quiet like a rally driver, slowing to the occasional crawl to read the house numbers on the roadside posts. The houses themselves were low and mostly white, set behind trees or above verdant banks with cactus or blazing flowers, and anchored to face the ocean in their own generously watered seas of lush green. They became ever larger, ever farther apart and in progressively more sizable abutments of choice real estate carved from the hillside. The Pacific fell away below, sometimes to the front, mainly behind the car and only seen in blurred glimpses in the driving mirror. The land opened up as he rose, becoming wilder and less wooded, except close to the houses, and the dense ferns were amber in the setting sun.

Brokaw's house was the last and highest — well, it would be, wouldn't it? Avery thought — on a curve just before the road exhausted itself in overgrown land not yet invaded by the developers. A tall mast beside the turning loop carried a lazily stirring Star-Spangled Banner. The house sprawled on its own mesa, rising with the ground in a series of stepped buildings, to tuck into the hill. It was in white stucco, tanned now by the sun, which had eroded in places to reveal random stone walls. Elsewhere, the paint had flaked in the heat to uncover a history of coats in Mediterranean pinks and blues. The windows were darkframed with small panes, set well back into the shade of deep openings, some with wrought-metal cages. The shallow sloping roof of red clay tiles jutted out to form a porch over heavily carved doors blackened by perhaps a century of sun and rain. Vines jostled up to the shelter of the overhang. An ancient olive tree, reeking of oil, tottered in the center of a cloistered courtyard. Behind, at the corner of a wing where garage doors had been set neatly into the old stable, there was a low tower. Its mission bell could be seen glinting dully through the arched top. Avery recalled the curious talk back at the company when Brokaw had been building the place. That must have been all of three years ago.

He crunched up a graveled ramp onto the turning loop, circled the flag and parked his dusty MG beside two gleaming Mercedes—one a big saloon, the other a sports convertible with the soft top down. Why only two? he wondered. Where were all the others?

Brokaw was waiting outside, at the far end of a pool stretching almost to the very edge of the bluff. A low glassed fence guarded the steep drop to the property below and he leaned idly on the rail, basking in the last rays of the failing sun. He didn't bother to turn, merely raising a hand in greeting at the sound of the car door.

Avery ignored the winding path of stepping stones to the patio and scrambled up the grass bank. He swore, almost stumbling, as he realized that the president of Northridge Electronics was in a sweatshirt, faded jeans and a sweater.

"Why didn't you *ask!*" he muttered to himself. He had made the effort of changing for the occasion into a darkly unseasonal suit—the only one he had. Briefly, he considered snatching off his tie to hide it in a pocket, but Brokaw was finally swinging round even as the idea came to him.

The summons to the "Western White House" had been delivered only that morning. That's what the less reverent called these evening indulgences of Brokaw's —well out of his hearing, of course. In his five years with the corporation, Avery had met the president a bare handful of times, always at the Northridge complex in the Valley. Now, out of the blue, had come his first summons. Just the map and a curt note hoping he

30

could spare the time to stop by around nine, the wording suggesting there was a choice, which of course there wasn't. For a fleeting mad moment Avery had thought of replying—in suitable terms of regret—that it was inconvenient for him to come. Or even, damnit, just saying no. Brokaw was reputed to admire independence in his staff, wasn't he? To have a deep loathing of yes-men? Except, Avery had mused sadly, the man was unlikely even to miss him in the melee, so what was the point of the gesture? It was the thought of the famous White House food that had finally made up his mind: he didn't think he could stand a single day more of take-out hamburgers and tacos. Wherever Laura had gone this time, and whatever her faults, she was still a hell of a cook.

At least that was the reason he had given himself for agreeing to come, settling instead for the compromise of arriving a good half hour late to make quite clear he was unique in Northridge; that he was his own man and there was no thrusting eagerness to please about *him*. Already, seeing Brokaw out there alone, he regretted that hasty decision. Nothing was as the reports of these events had led him to expect. Where was the legendary array of al fresco seafood, served by the hired army of white-coated Mexicans? Where was the gossiping throng of company people, eyeing each new arrival to see who else was there and who was not? He noted the emptiness of the place and the silence and his pace slowed. It worried him suddenly, Brokaw being alone like that.

"I was beginning to think you'd miss it, you son of a bitch," Brokaw said brusquely, darting forward to catch him roughly by the arm, to steer him to the rail.

Avery mouthed an unheeded excuse.

"Would you just take a look at that . . ." Brokaw said. "Isn't that the damnedest thing you ever saw?" The annoyance passed as he gazed with proprietorial pride out over the Pacific. "Smartest thing God ever did on this whole earth, arranging for the sun to set like that, right on my doorstep. Every evening, just like that." His arms spread wide to orchestrate the happening.

The sinking red disk set a torch to the heavens. It spread like bushfire to the wisps of cloud and high into the smoky turquoise sky and across the glassy ocean to the foothills. The blaze was brief, dying to the smoldering embers of what might have been a million campfires out of sight beyond the razorsharp rim of the sea. It was all Brokaw's, and Avery was as profoundly envious as he was meant to be.

Brokaw patted his shirt over his heart. "Gets you right here, doesn't it?"

Without waiting for a reply he was off, padding past the pool to the house, to an outside bar stocked as extravagantly as a nightclub's. Two very large brandies were sloshed into oversized balloon glasses. It obviously wasn't his habit to ask.

"I come out here every evening," he said. "Every one without fail when I'm not away on business. I just sit alone for a while, unwinding. None of this meditation crap, you understand, just good, honest relaxation. You do anything like that? Anything to get work off your chest.

"When I get the time," Avery said. "Which means not too often right now."

"Some answer," Brokaw noted. "You're here a bare

coupla minutes and already I know how hard you work for me."

Signing Avery to do the same, he wheeled a lounger round to face the ocean. It was a hefty affair in white wood, with big rubber wheels and a mattress thick enough for a deluxe hotel suite, and he flopped onto it, looking for all the world like a bull seal beached beside the pool. As far as Avery knew, their ages were approximately the same. That made Brokaw no more than thirty-five and he looked ten years older. Avery couldn't make up his mind whether it was the appearance of maturity, to put it as kindly as he could, that had helped the man achieve so much so soon, or the precocious success that had aged him. Few men on the West Coast had made as much from electronics. Maybe Max Palevsky and a couple of others. But no one had made as much from automated office systems.

"You're wondering why I asked you up here," Brokaw said. "You're wondering why so badly, I could hear you coming clear from the highway."

"It did cross my mind," Avery said simply.

"I've got an assignment for you, okay? I asked around, read a few personnel files. You stuck out a country mile as the man I need."

"Brokaw took a moment to watch a flock of pelicans flap ponderously in slow silhouette just feet above the dimming orange of the sea, then turned unnervingly sharp blue eyes onto Avery.

"Carl Zell tells me you're the best systems designer in his division."

"That's kind of him."

"Is he right?"

"Yes, probably."

"He tells me you're the greatest stickler for detail he ever saw. If there's a flaw in a system you'll find it. If there isn't a problem but you *think* there is, all design work has to screech to a halt until you're satisfied. Is that fair comment, would you say?"

"I do the job you pay me for, the best I know how."

"That's the way I see it, too," Brokaw said benevolently. There may have been the ghost of a smile of encouragement but it was hard to be sure. His way of speaking reminded Avery of a ventriloquist: the perfect white teeth always on show and the lips barely seeming to move.

"Ever worked on a military project?" he asked.

"Never."

"Any interest in defense systems? Any out-of-hours dabbling in war games or stuff like that?"

"No. I thought you said you'd read my file?"

"They never tell the full story. I just wondered if there was something along those lines we hadn't got to hear about?"

"No. Does it matter?"

"On the contrary; it's what I hoped you'd say."

It was cooler on the hill than it had been on the highway and growing cooler still as night edged in. The breeze became bolder, ruffling the tangled ferns on the slope below the outcrop.

Brokaw shivered. "Want to go in? The show's about finished." He sounded suddenly bored with the view.

"I'd prefer to stay out awhile longer, if that's all right with you." It seemed to Avery good tactics to be seen to be decisive.

"As you like," Brokaw said, with the barest of

34

shrugs. "You're the guest." With a labored grunt, he eased sideways off the lounger and vanished into the house.

Moments later the pool lights came on and the bright blue water looked as heavy and still as molasses until insects appeared from nowhere to dance across, pin-pricking the surface. More lights came on in succession, flooding the patio and patterning the immediate hillside, and a tall oak that had brooded at the far side of the bell tower was turned to coral, etched in luminous pink against the darkening sky. It took Avery a time to realize it but the lights modulated continuously, changing colors, dimming in places and growing in intensity in others. It was all done by a microcomputer, he decided, a kind of silent *son et lumière*. It was tastelessly splendid and he couldn't take his eyes off it.

When Brokaw returned he was wearing a turtleneck sweater and leading a small procession. Behind him, pushing a food cart, came a squat Mexican woman in a domestic uniform far too short for her elephantine legs. Then a girl of perhaps twenty, with bare feet and in a kaftan of white toweling. Her blond hair was so pale that it, too, was almost white and her face was a cosmetics advertisement: the features frozen into a permanently surprised, vacant smile. the contrast with the maid was so marked Avery could almost believe the girl took her everywhere for added effect. She was made to seem ever taller and slimmer than she already was, and she comfortably matched Brokaw's six feet plus. Her very brown skin with its golden down might have been the finest of suedes against the mahogany leather of the Mexican.

They stopped by the bar and Avery was beckoned over as the maid plugged the cart into a wall socket.

"Carol Brokaw meet Martin Avery," Brokaw said.

"Hi, Martin," the girl said, tossing her head in welcome to spread the mane of hair and opening the smile yet wider. The actions seemed intended to suggest that she was an actress, and Avery felt that she probably was, at that.

"She just wanted to say hello," Brokaw said, his lips curling mischievously. "She really goes for you English guys."

"For *what?*" Avery exclaimed.

The big man issued a playful punch to his arm. "Just a joke, fella. She saw you arrive in that suit."

"And the little sports car," Carol explained seriously. "I said to myself, he's either English or from San Francisco. I wasn't sure which till Larry said."

"Boston, in fact," Avery told her. He noticed how she cocked her head slightly to verify the nuances in his speech, her eyes growing round and puzzled.

"You . . . !" she said accusingly to Brokaw.

"Same damned thing, for Chrissake," he retorted with a raucous laugh, and he punched Avery's other arm for good measure. "That's why I told her you were English."

Carol looked her visitor over, her gaze half lidded to make it plain there was nothing personal in the interest, it was simply the assessment of a hostess, a forensic curiosity that would never have been there but for the issue of his nationality. She felt that Larry had hit on an important characteristic of the man, but then Larry was quite terrific about people. There was a neutrality about Avery, nothing in his appearance to suggest where he came from, and little in his speech either, the East Coast accent being so slight as to be barely noticeable. She could recognize across a room the wide, open-faced look of her home state of Texas. She knew a breed of tall, bronzed men who were not merely American, not merely Californian, but as specific to a few miles of coast as the tortoises of Galapagos were to theirs. But Avery had none of that look of belonging to any place. It was the hair that caught the attention first, a sandy mop he might well have cut himself, with the rugged strength, the unruliness, of desert grass. Yet he himself was far from rugged. The skin was the kind that went with sandy hair, rather pale with a trace of freckles; so pallid in fact that she wondered how it stayed that way in the California sun. A week out by the pool would do wonders for him. Then again, it probably wouldn't change a thing. He was average in height and average in build, average in every department, really. It occurred to her that he was a man who could be in the house with her a month with Larry away and never make it with her, being neither handsome enough to get to first base the first night nor ugly enough to arouse her, given time. He was a chameleon—yes, that's what she would call him if he came often enough to justify one of her pet names—someone who would fade into the background wherever he was placed.

But the eyes weren't average. They met hers unwaveringly and without any sign of embarrassment at her increasingly close examination of him. Nor was there the suddenly preening self-confidence she could usually produce at will, gazing at men like that. It came to her then that the month might pass as she had thought, but because he wouldn't *try* to beat down her door; he was the type who would think that proved something important. The truth was, he could manage a stare every bit as distant and impersonal as hers, damnit.

The maid opened the top of the cart to reveal hot plates laden with more food than the three of them could possibly eat, then shuffled back into the house.

"Shit," Carol said, her hand flying to her mouth. "I hope you eat Mexican. Maybe I should've gotten lobster or something, you being from the east."

"I've lived in LA for five years now," Avery said. "Of course I like Mexican. In fact, it's been my staple diet for the past few weeks."

Her relief was beyond his expectations. She sagged visibly at the knees and let out a long, exaggerated sigh, her eyes closed and a hand fluttered over them. She *had* to be an actress, Avery decided. It was obvious why he had never seen her in anything.

"She doesn't do the cooking," Brokaw said. "Just the worrying. We've got books on how to worry in every cuisine known to man."

"Shut up, you," Carol said and she stood very close to him to tug reprovingly at his cheeks before wobbling them fondly.

"Unzip me, you old gopher."

He unfastened the kaftan and she shrugged it off, stepping out in the briefest of bikinis on a quite magnificent body. A determined look came into her eyes as she studied the pool, like an athlete preparing for a record jump. It was then that Avery noticed the very broad back and the well-developed upper arms.

"Have fun, you two," A half run and she made a perfect dive into the water, shattering its tranquillity. The men watched in silence as she swam two very fast lengths in a powerful, effortless style. At the sight of her body, Avery had begun to change his mind about her. Now his conversion was complete. If they still made swimming movies, he thought, she would be a sensation.

"She'll do that for hours," Brokaw said. "She does the exercise for both of us round here." He piled a plate high for Avery and contrived to get even more onto his own. Avery traversed the mountain of food, sampling it all: tacos, enchiladas, burritos, refried beans, several kinds of salad, and a sauce that proved to be every bit as explosive as it looked. It beat Taco Bell to-go.

"Best I ever tasted," he said, fanning his mouth.

Brokaw was back in his lounger, eating as if famished. The compliment was accepted with a nod.

"Isn't she terrific, though, he said, waving the tail end of an enchilada toward the pool. "That detective work with the car and all."

"It was a good try," was all Avery was prepared to say.

"Hell, it's better than that," came the retort. "Damnit, you're as English as they come in this neck of the woods."

Avery chose to make no reply. He almost said that a joke was a joke and this one had gone far enough, whoever Brokaw was. But then he saw how the man was sitting: on the very edge of the lounger this time, leaning intently forward. There was none of the look of idle conversation about him. Avery returned to his couch and adopted an identical pose, waiting while Brokaw worked his way well into his food.

"You spent a year over in England," Brokaw said when he was ready. "I read it in your file."

"At Oxford," Avery confirmed. "Some postgraduate studies in computing."

"That was after Harvard?"

"Yes."

"So why didn't you stay put, do the extra year there?"

"It's a long story."

"Then make it short. A quarter sheet summary on A-Four."

"My family are all lawyers, my father and two brothers. We go back through three generations of respectable, rock-of-the-community Massachusetts law practice. Nothing outstanding, just an old established partnership and one district court judge. So it didn't go down too well when I opted for a career in electronics, and that's putting it mildly. The year at Oxford was a gesture, I guess, a kind of penance for taking the wrong road in life."

"All of which means you know the country pretty well."

"I wouldn't say that, exactly."

"But better than anyone else at Northridge."

"Well, I guess so."

"And you like it over there?"

"Very much," Avery said.

Brokaw studied him relentlessly and eventually Avery gave him the pleasure of winning, glancing away to the pool. Carol was now swimming underwater, bathed in blue light. There seemed barely a ripple or a bubble, and she might have been a great bird soaring with economy of movement in a cloudless sky.

"What was our turnover last year?" Brokaw demanded.

"Two hundred million, wasn't it?" Avery said, dragging himself back with difficulty.

"Close. Two hundred and ten million. From what major markets?"

"Virtually any organization with a demand for office automation. Banking, insurance, retail and distribution . . . "

"Okay, okay. Now here's the crunch question. What percentage of our business was in military systems?"

"Well, none. How could there be any?"

"What would you call all that hardware of ours at the Pentagon?"

"Word processors. Just typewriter replacements to handle the flood of paper they push around up there."

"Then how about the system we've just put in at Fort Meade, Maryland? At the National Security Agency."

"Exactly the same, surely?" Avery was becoming increasingly bemused by the questioning.

"You wouldn't call it a defense system, then?"

"Not unless they're planning a war of words, no."

"You are so right," Brokaw said with feeling. "And if I allowed myself to lie awake nights worrying, that's what would do it. That bugs the hell out of me."

"Let me get this straight. Are you suggesting you want to get Northridge into the defense business?"

"Hole in one," Brokaw said, looking pleased.

"Why?"

"Isn't it obvious? It is to me."

"If I were an investment analyst," Avery said, "I'd judge Northridge as having a well-balanced and stable customer profile. I'd say the military market is volatile and shrinking. All the big defense contractors are diversifying as fast as they can into straight commercial markets. A corporation doing the opposite would look plumb crazy to me."

"Stick to systems design," Brokaw said. "You make a lousy financial expert. What you're forgetting is what half of Wall Street forgets. Those defense outfits you talk about are big, but big. And how do you think they got that way? By milking the fattest cow around. Sure, it's all cost plus or fixed margins, and Washington watches them like a hawk. I'd still like Northridge to be several times the size we are now on that kind of deal. One day, when we're as big as General Dynamics, I'll moan to the stockholders and promise to diversify back to where we started. For now, I'll happily settle for a back corner of the milking shed."

"With what?" Avery said. "One of our word processors painted army green?"

"With unerring perception you have just put your finger on the problem. Do you know how much it costs to develop a new avionics system? Or a ground guidance system? Or a battlefield information system?"

"I've no idea. Plenty, I would think."

"You bet. And we'd be starting from zero, with none of the right hardware on the shelf and no relevant experience. That sends the cost up to plenty times three. I don't like that kind of arithmetic. It makes the milk go sour."

"So?" Avery asked.

"So we buy in a ready-made product, what else?" It was stated as being obvious. "A war game system, for instance. What do you say to that?"

"If I knew what they did, maybe I could give you an answer."

"And if you ever want to make vice-president," Brokaw said, "it's time you learned to give opinions on matters you know fuckall about. What's wrong with telling me it's a great idea?"

"It sounds like a clever move," Avery agreed. It was said just to keep the man happy. He hadn't the slightest wish to make vice-president.

Brokaw demolished most of what was left on his plate, brushed the remains onto the patio and patted his stomach appreciatively.

"Ever come across a company called Quantek when you were over in England?"

Avery shook his head.

"Their mainstream work is avionics and communications systems. They're a sight smaller than we are but they could be our mirror image, as it happens. One hundred percent defense contracts and zilch in the business market. They've developed a computerized war game for the British Ministry of Defence. Name, Vulcan. Specification, terrific. The Pentagon's got nothing like it and they'll fall over their fat asses to buy when they see what it can do. Everything from infantry in trenches potting off rifles at one another to all-out global conflict. And nobody gets hurt in the process, that's the beauty of it."

"Why don't they buy direct from Quantek? In their

shoes, that's what I'd do."

"Good question," Brokaw said with approval. "I asked that myself. I've been nosing around Europe on and off for a year, seeing what there was in the shopwindow to build under license. Suddenly, there's Quantek beating a trail to my door and what looks to be a dream deal. It seemed too good to be true, know what I mean? So I did some checking behind the scenes. Their chief executive is a guy named Hurst. Everyone's favorite buddy. But he owns half the company and underneath he's as sharp a hard-nosed bastard as you'll find. At least he is on his home ground. When he comes over here he acts as if the whole country is Disneyland. Last year he charged into Washington waving folding money at everyone in sight: the brass hats, the government people, even the guy who cuts the grass, for all I know. Christ, he only tried the same kind of wheel oiling on the Pentagon that he used on Her Majesty's Government!"

"Tut, tut," Avery said with a smile. "And of course they were horrified."

"Done that way? You'd better believe it. Up there, you don't put crude oil on a couple of cogs in broad daylight. You need high-grade lubricant, the driving wheels and the darkness of the engine room. Know what I mean?"

Brokaw eased his way off the lounger again. The same grunt, the same sideways *plop* onto the patio. Over at the bar he poured clear liquid from a cocktail shaker into glasses with the rims already frosted with salt.

"You a marguerita fan?" he asked, coming back to tower over Avery.

44

"Well . . ." Avery began, but a glass was thrust into his hand regardless.

"Tastes better as a chaser, believe me. It purges the sting."

Well, it was different, Avery thought, starting with the brandy and now ending up with an apéritif. Perhaps that was how fashions started. Through ignorance.

Brokaw ambled to the pool's edge where he held another glass at arm's length, jiggling it to attract Carol's attention. Gathering speed, she rose from the water like a dolphin to take it.

"Amazing what you can train them to do," he said contentedly.

The girl floated on her back sipping the drink and as far as Avery could tell none of it had been spilled. Her eyes were on her husband's and his on hers. There was all the appearance of love but it probably wasn't that, Avery felt sure. It was mutual admiration and nothing more. And perhaps that was better than love; perhaps it kept going as long as looks or money lasted. In which case it would last a damned sight longer than any love he had known or was ever likely to. He ceased to see them, there by the pool, wondering instead where Laura had taken off to this time. Could be, back east to her parents. More probably, cruising north again along the coast to San Francisco, and beyond, picking up hitchhikers, giving them her inimitable come-on and delivering nothing. Few things turned her on more than that.

"Honey," Brokaw said to the girl, "tell Martin about that place in England."

"What place?"

"Swindon. You remember?"

"What a dump," she said, screwing up her face. "Next time I want that much fun I won't bother crossing the Atlantic. I'll fly up to Baltimore."

"Perfect for you, by the sound of it," Brokaw said, turning to Avery. "No distractions. Nice folksy people. Just the way you like it."

"Now hold on . . ." Avery started to say.

"Hold on nothing! I want you over there for a month. Longer if you can spin it out. Stick your nose into every corner of that system. Give me a long report every week and get them to type it. And I want to know straight off if anything nasty creeps out of the woodwork. I want an instant telex if you find so much as a screw loose on the video terminal."

"I've told you already," Avery said stoically. "What I know about war games would go on a postage stamp with room left over."

Brokaw sighed, pawing the air with impatience. "I want it that way, dummy. I want them to have to lead you through it like a freshman, however long that takes. I've already had our R and D people down in San Diego take the Vulcan specification apart line by line. I've had consultants in to give us an opinion on the military aspects. The system's terrific."

"Then what's the point of sending me?"

"That job you did on the new Archive-Fifty. That's what I want from you . . . an action replay, okay?"

"But that wasn't a war game," Avery insisted, with all the restraint he could muster.

Another sigh, this one long and distinctly pained. "You turned that design on its head. You had Carl Zell worried. You had the product committee worried.

Christ, you didn't know it but you even had me worried. It's a great product, but for a while there you had us all eating our hearts out and ready to ditch it. I want you to do that to our friend Hurst. Are you getting the picture yet?"

Avery stared, unable to reply. If Brokaw was saying what he thought he was . . .

"Kick the tires on that system," Brokaw continued, "and make damned sure he sees you doing it. I've already decided to buy but I want him stewing for a month thinking the deal is slipping away."

"That's a crappy assignment," Avery said, leaping to his feet. "The worst. And you know it."

"Since when was doing what you're best at crappy?" Brokaw said airily. "Look, I need time. There's a month's hard grafting to do up in Washington. Plus, I want Hurst's asking price slashed to ribbons. It's the most important assignment you'll be asked to do this year, okay? And the last, if you pass it over. You'd better believe it."

Carol was pulling herself from the pool, not bothering with the ladder.

"Say good-bye," Brokaw told her. "Martin's going."

"Keep away from the casinos and the cathouses," she said with her dazzing smile. "That's Sin City he's sending you to."

Her hair was silver in the light of a rising full moon. Her wet body was silver, with strands of platinum glistening on her legs. The house and the hillside were silver, dappled with the emerald and ruby of floodlights. The Pacific was lapping gently, its dark expanse streaked with mercury.

"Your wife . . . ?" Brokaw said as they reached the

MG. If the moon had intended to silver that it had given up at the sight of the dust.

"Laura," Avery reminded him.

"You want me to give her a call in the morning? Apologize for keeping you out late?"

"There's no need."

"I know women," Brokaw said confidentially. "The times you most need an alibi are the times you think you don't. Believe me. Hell, I should know that better than anyone."

"You don't have to bother, really."

"I'm glad to hear it," Brokaw said. "I don't want any pressures, any marital problems, clouding the issue. The stakes are too high. Do you hear what I'm saying?"

Avery nodded noncommittally, wondering how good the corporation grapevine was, how much Brokaw knew. Quite a lot, by the look of it. He was still there, staring after him with a piercing expression which said he missed nothing, as Avery headed down the hill.

2

The fields were the same green Avery remembered. They rolled in the same easy way to an horizon seemingly closer than anywhere else he knew. But everything else had changed. What doesn't in over twelve years? England was busier, dirtier, noisier.

Where he had once seen civilized aloofness in the people there was now a bustling indifference. Those things he had learned to wait for on his last visit took even longer now, exasperatingly longer: his bags were nearly an hour in appearing on the airport carousel and there was a barely moving line to change traveler's checks. The roads were full of German cars. The billboards shouted the virtues of Wrangler jeans, Marlboro cigarettes and Southern Comfort.

As for Swindon, Carol Brokaw had said it all. The place had meant something once, he had read, building most of the steam locomotives for the country's railways, when railways still mattered. Today, the new buildings trampled the old underfoot. The new roads tore their way through with little regard for the original fabric.

The company was in the outskirts, in a desert the planners presumably called an industrial zone. A sign on a high fence of wire mesh said simply, "QUANTEK LIMITED. Avionics. Mobile Communications. Computer Systems." A squat redbrick block house guarded the single break in the boundary wire. The buildings inside were like the town: untidy and characterless, with all the signs of hasty additions tacked onto every available inch of the site to take the growth. The only obvious sign that anything of note happened there was the electrically controlled barrier dropped across the entrance. But a glance over the parking lot at the front revealed silvered windows, one-way glass to prevent any view into the office and production areas.

A uniformed guard jumped into Avery's path, his hand up to augment the barrier and his eyes

49

swimming with suspicion. His ferret's expression said he would look under a nun's habit before letting her through.

"Mr. Hurst," Avery said, and that obviously cut the necessary ice, for the man vanished into his hutch, made heavy work of filling in a buff form, phoned through to announce Avery's arrival and then reemerged to issue a visitor's badge. It was to be worn conspicuously at all times, he warned with a ferocious look.

Hurst's secretary was waiting to lead the way even as Avery parked beside the doors to the main block. She suited the place: plain and dumpy in a shapeless flowered dress and so monosyllabic that he soon fell in behind to cut short the stilted conversation. She waddled ahead, up stairs in mottled marble, along blank corridors with a band of carpet which, if not yet threadbare, had seen better days, down a wooden ramp and then down stairs again, this time with rubber treads, working into the core of the premises until they reached Hurst's office.

It was as modest in size and appearance, as unprepossessing, as Avery was now expecting. There was a small teak desk, a meeting table also in teak and a scattering of chairs in comfortable tweed. On the walls, some not very large photographs in cheapish black frames: of soldiers with backpack radios, a swing-wing aircraft emblazoned with several European insignia, and hefty electronic equipment with the front panels removed to expose the circuitry. A single telephone was on the desk, which was completely bare of paper.

A tall fair-haired man sat by the window, staring

out through odd-looking binoculars. A cable ran from them to a small container rather like a portable radio, placed on the floor. The man jumped to his feet to grasp Avery's hand, warmly and firmly.

"Peter Hurst," he said. "You'll be Martin Avery." The eyes made the briefest of head-to-toe explorations, then skidded away.

"Glad to meet you, Peter." Avery's hand was still being pumped enthusiastically and the smile he was getting would have befitted a long-lost friend.

"Larry Brokaw told me all about you," Hurst said. "We're suitably intimidated." He finally released his grip only after inquiring solicitously about the flight and being reassured how easy the factory had been to find. Avery was then pressed into the chair which faced the window as he wondered exactly what it was Brokaw had said about him. The binoculars were held out for him to take.

"Do you know what these are?"

Avery eyed the cable and the container on the floor. "I'd be guessing."

"They're what we call image intensifiers. Night glasses, in other words. But these are rather special; they're our latest development for field use. Try the tree over there, the one up on the hill." Hurst indicated a gaunt skeleton of an elm. It came up clear and close in the glasses.

"Now press the button there." That was on the top panel of the battery pack and as Avery touched it red digits glowed at the bottom of the image.

"Two-five-one," he read.

"Meters," Hurst explained. "It's a laser range finder." He flicked a switch on the panel. "Now, do you see the aerial there?" He was pointing to an array of steel lattice work on the most distant of the factory roofs. Radar heads twirled slowly alongside.

"Yes."

"There's a long section of metal pipe at the base. Got it yet?"

"Yes." Avery homed in.

"Can you see what's at the far end?"

"A target."

"Is it clear?"

"Very."

"And now?" Hurst politely pushed the glasses away from Avery's face.

The pipe was perhaps ten meters long. It was impossible with the naked eye to see more than a meter or so into it; beyond that was pitch darkness.

"Clever," Avery said respectfully.

"Isn't it just. Now, one more thing. Try a window, any window." Hurst inclined his head toward the facing row of silvered panes and Avery focused on one.

"What can you see?"

"Only the sky."

"And now?" Hurst was adjusting a control.

Suddenly the office appeared in the glasses. The picture wasn't completely clear, as if viewed through gauze, but two men could be made out sitting at desks, one with his feet up, reading a newspaper.

"Impossible," Avery said. "Absolutely impossible."

With a contented expression, Hurst reclaimed his conjuring equipment. "The film on that window isn't one hundred percent reflective," he said. "And the lights are on inside the office. Just tune to the same spectral frequency and bingo!" The glasses were packed away in a molded carrying case pulled from under the desk. "This is going to be Quantek's next big money spinner, I hope. I'd like to see every serving British soldier issued with a set by the mid-eighties. We've got the size and weight right. I think we can get the price down to a suitable level, next."

"I'll have one," Avery said.

"It's not a sales pitch," Hurst said apologetically. "The reason for showing it to you is this, I'm afraid. Larry's telex about your visit arrived here late yesterday afternoon. You're here this morning. The Ministry of Defence procurement executives are expecting me in London this afternoon. We're reviewing several of our defense projects and that includes thrashing out the next stage of the development contract for Bush Baby here." He patted the case. "Do you see what I'm saying?"

Avery gave an affirmative nod.

"We tried to switch the meeting, but no luck. I do so *hate* appearing inhospitable. I'm sure you understand?"

"I'll be here a few weeks. Up to a month, probably. There's no hurry. You do what you have to, Peter."

Was there a sign of surprise or even dismay at the expected length of the visit? Avery felt there was. But Hurst's even tone when he next spoke gave nothing further away. He leaned against the edge of his desk, folding his arms and crossing immaculately polished shoes. Avery worked his chair round to face him.

"Anyway, how was that old rascal Brokaw when you last saw him?"

"As rascally as ever."

"And Carol?" Hurst asked. "How was she? Break my heart by telling me she was looking as fabulous as ever."

"Last seen swimming off into the sunset," Avery said.

Hurst smiled distantly at the thought, his eye on the toe of a shoe which he moved to catch the light. "They spent a few days with us at my place on their last visit. Did he say?"

Avery settled for a vague nod. The fact that Hurst didn't seem to be watching for it made it seem less of a deceit.

"I woke up one night and couldn't get back to sleep," Hurst said. "So I got up and wandered out onto the terrace. Maybe it was the sound of Carol in the pool that woke me, who knows. Anyway, there she was. Not a stitch on, playing in the water like a mermaid. A sheer bloody vision. She knew I was there, I'm certain, but she didn't say a word, didn't so much as look my way, and the next day she didn't mention it." His head moved slowly from side to side in wonderment at the memory.

"It has been known before," Avery said, with what he hoped was assurance. Whatever Brokaw had said to Hurst about him, it must have been quite a story. The welcome and the familiar chat showed that.

"As for Larry," Hurst said, "he's a streaker of a different sort, isn't he? Does that man move fast! To be perfectly honest, he's rather caught us on the hop, taking our offer up so quickly. Of course, I'm delighted he's taking Vulcan so seriously, absolutely tickled pink. But as for sending you over at such short notice . . . if I was the uncharitable type I might

54

almost conclude that was deliberate, to throw us off guard." Hurst's eyebrows arched and he contrived an inquiring look without actually seeming to glance at Avery.

"Everything Larry does is for a reason," Avery said.

"Quite so," Hurst acknowledged, the eyebrows climbing higher.

Clothes sat well on him. In fact, leaning against the desk like that, the legs elegantly crossed, he reminded Avery of the advertisements for suits he used to see at Oxford in magazines like *Punch*. Ads in which tall and slender men never walked or sat or engaged in strenuous activity. They simply leaned well back at a gentlemanly angle, looking indolent. All Hurst needed to complete the picture was a hunting dog.

"What's he like to work for?" he asked, with a flick of the hand to show how casual the question was. "Tough but fair, that would be my guess. How do you find him?"

"Yes, he's one of those," Avery said, feeling a desire to score a point back over Brokaw for the fairy story.

"Really?" That had the eyebrows working again. "But you're not saying which?" Hurst was amused.

"Uh-uh." Avery wagged his head in the leisurely way he was sure the other man would appreciate.

"What about this proposed Vulcan deal, then? Can I expect him to play fair? I hope you don't mind me asking?"

"I'd recommend plenty of guarded looks behind you. Especially if he suggests you negotiate in a dark alley."

"I can see you and I will get on splendidly," Hurst purred.

The creases at the corners of his eyes put him in his forties, but only just. The longish fair hair framed a rather too pointed face with the sharp nose of a fox but surprisingly full lips which had a tendency to pout. For all its angularity it was a disarmingly weak face, with no particular determination shown in the eyes: they bordered on the watery and wandered constantly, never staying on Avery for more than a few seconds before shying away. And that was deliberate, to give the impression of modesty, Avery decided after a time. It was a strangely disturbing brand of modesty, made more so by the fact that, recognizing it for the pretense it was, Avery still wanted to believe in it. And he wouldn't be the first to react to Hurst that way, he was sure. There was an undefinable charisma about the man, a feeling he would draw success to him like a magnet and charm his way out of trouble. Certainly, he was already drawing from Avery words he had no real intention of saying.

"I'll tell you what I've arranged, shall I?" Hurst said. "we've set an office aside for you over there." His hand flapped negligently to the window, at the block facing across the car park. "And I've assigned one of our best girls to fetch and carry for you. Coffee, typing, phone calls, whatever you have in mind. You'll find a file on the desk listing your main contacts here and what their connections are with Vulcan. Our hardware engineers, the software people, the army types who keep us up to date on the military angles. Of course, Larry assures me you're a one-man band and will need none of that. But the internal numbers are there, just to be on the safe side." He smiled knowingly.

"It sounds well organized."

"I'm glad you think so. It was like a three-ring circus here yesterday, getting it all sorted out. Now, as for Vulcan itself. There's only one development version at the moment. The Ministry of Defence have got it safely tucked away in one of their establishments. I've organized a visit there in the morning. It's down in Kent, actually. A rather pleasant drive, I think you'll find. And after that . . ." Hurst gestured expansively. "You're on your own and the ball's in your court. We'll do our level best to answer any questions you come up with. Let's hope we end up doing business, eh?"

Avery voiced his appreciation of the arrangements.

"What are you driving, by the way? A hired car, is it?"

Avery nodded. "A Ford."

"Can I have the keys? Do you mind?" A hand was extended in anticipation.

Avery fished for the keys, dropped them into the waiting hand and Hurst placed them beside him on the desk. He then produced two sets of car keys from a pocket. "Which do you prefer? A manual box or are you going to insist on importing lazy habits and wanting an automatic?"

"I have a stick shift back home."

"A man after my own heart." Hurst examined the tags on the keys, selected a set, and tossed it over. "It's one of our company Rovers. You'll find it a far nicer machine, more spirited. And don't worry about the Ford, we'll take care of that. Who did you get it from? Hertz?"

"Avis."

"I'll get them to collect. Now, where are you staying?"

"Nowhere yet I came here straight from Heathrow. I was planning to find a hotel downtown."

"And what would the arrangement be with Larry over that? Does he pick up the bills or are you on a per diem? Not that it's any of my business."

"A daily allowance," Avery said, curious to know where this was leading.

"Look, I'll tell you what, just between the two of us. I've got a weekend cottage a few miles away. A really comfortable place, up on the downs at Lambourn." Hurst spoke as if the idea had just come to him but another set of keys was already in hand from a pocket "I lend it to special clients now and then, mainly ministry people from London. They seem to prefer it to the local hotels. Quite why, I can't imagine." With an artful smile he threw the keys squarely into Avery's lap. "My secretary will tell you how to find it. There's a woman who comes in every day to clean, and an arrangement with a pub in the village to send meals over. Just give them a ring whenever you feel peckish. They do a splendid game pie, by the way."

There was a timid knock at the door.

"Come!"

The plump secretary peered in, holding up a hand and pointing urgently at her watch. "George is down in the car park," she said. "He's been here ten minutes."

"Look, I really am awfully sorry," Hurst said, slipping off the desk and shooing her away, "but I must make a move, I should have been gone by now. One of the MOD people is giving me a lift up to town.

It won't look at all good if I keep him waiting. What I've fixed up for you is this. My technical director, Dr. Corrigan, will take over from here. He'll show you your office and play host for the day. Patrick Corrigan, his name is."

With Avery in pursuit, he hurried along the outside corridor until they came to a place where it broadened sufficiently to take a desk and row of filing cabinets. A woman sat there typing, outside a door with the legend "TECHNICAL DIRECTOR."

"Is Pat ready for us?" he asked her.

She looked surprised. "I'm sorry, Peter, should he be?"

"This is Mr. Avery, from California."

The woman inclined her head pleasantly at Avery then glanced back to Hurst with a deep frown of concern.

"But I thought that had been changed. Patrick told me . . ." Her voice trailed away.

"Damn!" Hurst said. "Not again." He stiffened and turned for the door.

"He's got a visitor with him," she warned as he reached for the handle.

"Who?" Hurst demanded grasping it anyway."

"I'm sorry, he didn't say."

"Who didn't say?"

"Patrick. It was a meeting he arranged himself, only this morning." She had a small dark face and a suddenly helpless look.

"In place of *mine?*" Hurst said in disbelief.

Now she shrugged, unable to reply.

"Excuse me just a moment, would you?" Hurst said to Avery in a quiet, controlled tone. Then he tensed, his eyes blazing, and stalked into the room, slamming the door behind him. But it bounced off the lock with the impact, swinging slowly open again. It revealed an office furnished much as the one they had just left. Behind the desk sat a huge, bearded figure of a man who stopped in midsentence, scowling at the manner of Hurst's entrance. A younger man sat in front of the desk and he turned, baffled, at the commotion. There was a visitor's badge on his lapel.

"We seem to have a screw-up over diaries again," Hurst said with restraint, but clearly bristling with indignation. He seemed unaware that the door was still open.

"Really?" the big man said.

"I think so, yes."

The big fellow raised his hands lazily behind his head and stretched, in what Avery took to be deliberate provocation.

"I'm at a meeting, Peter," he said in a mock-tired way. "Or hadn't you noticed? Bloody bursting in like this!"

"I've got Avery outside, from Northridge. The chap you're supposed to be looking after, for heaven's sake." Hurst had dropped his voice to a frenzied whisper but it still carried out to the corridor. Corrigan's secretary jumped to her feet and started frantically for the door.

"*Stuff dat!*" The accent was Irish, rising with such unexpected suddenness, with such venom, to an almost hysterical pitch that a shudder ran down Avery's spine. The big hands crashed into the desk, threateningly clenched. "I'm pissed off, running fucking errands for . . ."

The secretary dragged the door shut and stood, wide-eyed, in front of it, her arms stretched across the frame as if to keep the sounds in. The words were lost but a jumble of violent disagreement still escaped past her.

"I'm Barbara Young," she said, to divert Avery. She was breathing deeply and her hands trembled. She dropped them to her sides to steady them.

"And what do you do round here?" he asked. "Referee?"

"Oh . . . that." She managed a feeble wave at the door as if it were nothing and went back to her desk. "They'll be friends again in a minute, you'll see. There's no real harm done." Her white face belied the words.

"How frequent are the bouts?" Avery asked, leaning across the desk with a smile he hoped would calm her. "Daily? Weekly?"

"What makes you think it's happened before?"

"The way you moved to that door says so. You've had practice, lady."

"With respect, you're mistaken."

"Now you are good," Avery said, with a reassuring wag of a finger. "I hope Bluebeard in there appreciates you."

She was able to return the smile at that. "Despite me not knowing who he's got in there with him?"

"Meaning there's no worse sin for a secretary?"

"Something like that."

"I think he'll get over it, don't you?"

It was a very attractive smile now. Avery would have described her as mature, for want of a better word. The wrong side of forty, he guessed, but wearing well.

And when she smiled like that, as the color flooded back into her cheeks, the years began to peel away. He would have liked to have known her a decade earlier.

"It's nothing personal, Mr. Avery," she said, her composure now fully returned and the manner assured. "Nothing to do with you. Please don't think that. It's just a . . . clash of personalities, two very forceful men."

There was a chair next to her desk and Avery settled into it, crossing a foot over a knee, his eyes expectantly on the door. The sound of argument had died away and there was an ominous silence.

"I'll put my money on the Irish heavyweight," he said, "I'd hate to be on the receiving end of that punch. I reckon Hurst will decide tact is wiser than valor."

"You're on," she said eagerly. "I think weight is a disadvantage against fast footwork."

"Whatever happened to employee loyalty!" Avery said with a grin.

Minutes later, Hurst slipped out of the room, his face an expressionless mask, but as he approached Avery he somehow tacked his familiar urbane smile onto it.

"Just a mix-up," he said airily. "These things do happen, don't they? Patrick will be out with you shortly."

Avery caught a triumphant glance from the secretary before he was drawn out of her hearing a distance down the corridor.

"Just keep off the subject of Vulcan, would you?" Hurst asked softly. "Let's put it this way. He was involved with the system in the early design stages.

Since then, for reasons I'd rather not go into, his participation in the project has been . . . phased out, rather. So it's not exactly his favorite subject, if you follow." The pale eyes were firmly fixed on Avery for a change and they drew a nod of understanding from him. "I'll be perfectly honest with you. If Larry hadn't taken me unawares like that yesterday I'd have done things differently. Hurried plans aren't always for the best, are they?" Hurst held out a hand. "I'll be back from London on Sunday. Perhaps you'd be good enough to join us for dinner?"

"I'd love to," Avery said, shaking the hand. He did all the work this time. It was limp and tired.

"I'll get my secretary and tell you how to find us." Hurst squared his shoulders and walked briskly off.

Avery rejoined Barbara Young and subsided into the chair. "I'm a lousy gambler," he said. "What the hell happened in there?"

"Let's call it a tie, shall we?" she offered magnanimously. "It usually is."

She brought him coffee as he waited. Half an hour passed. She brought more coffee and a morning paper—the *Herald Tribune,* a nice touch, he thought. He didn't really mind the wait; his senses had become dulled by jet lag and it was as good as a rest. But she became increasingly restless, obviously embarrassed for him.

"I'll remind him, shall I? I can't imagine what he's up to."

"There's no hurry."

"If you're sure?"

"It's quite all right, really."

Avery watched her as she typed, and made polite,

inconsequential conversation. She was suddenly out of patience, reaching for her telephone to press the button to the office and he could hear it *buzz* inside the door. She pressed again insistently, several more times.

"Fish!" she muttered crossly, rising to her feet and moving purposefully over to the office.

"Please . . ." Avery said. "Let's not start a second fight."

"Now *I'm* angry," she told him, opening the door. "Oh fish!" she said, more loudly now as she looked in.

When he came up behind her he saw that the office was empty.

"It looks as if your Dr. Corrigan dislikes Vulcan more than Hurst said," he suggested.

"It doesn't exactly bring a smile to his face," she admitted.

Moving in, he discovered a wide-open door to one side of the room. It led to a second room and from there, he assumed, there would be a way out into the maze of corridors.

"Useful things, secret exits," he said. He was too tired to care, to be annoyed.

"It really is impossibly rude," she exclaimed with feeling. "What can I say . . . ?"

Avery checked his watch and leaned, unfussed, against the wall as he made a mental calculation. "Let's look at it this way, maybe the guy's done me a favor. I left home in Sherman Oaks nearly sixteen hours ago and I don't sleep on airplanes."

He was later, and not that much later, to kick himself for taking the affair so lightly, for being his usual casual self and thinking it was just a silly quarrel. But he stifled a yawn now, his stomach still back in Los Angeles and his brain somewhere in the mid-Atlantic. "Do you know where Hurst's cottage is?" he asked.

"Lambourn, you mean?"

"I think that's the place he said."

"Yes, more or less."

"Why don't I buy you lunch and then have you point me that way for a few days' hibernation?"

"How can I say no?" she remarked, already heading for the desk outside and her handbag. "You must be the most even-tempered man I ever met."

"I can think of plenty who'd disagree with that," Avery said. And he closed the door without so much as a further glance back.

3

A line of racehorses trickled along the lane, necks drooping and flanks steaming after a workout of the downs. Avery slowed to the same leisurely pace behind them. The stableboy to the rear signaled him by but he was in no hurry and chose to stay back, following. Around a bend the heads were suddenly lifting and the ears beginning to prick. The horses turned and clattered up an incline into a cobbled yard. There were more stables along to the right and yet more a distance to the left. The fields behind bristled like brushes, and a clouded sun cast kind light on the chalky earth laid bare by the recent harvest.

Avery drove on through the village, back out onto the Downs. Hurst's cottage was a good half mile past Upper Lambourn, well away from the other houses. He found it down a narrow private lane, set in a bowl of an acre or so which cut into a steeply rising fold of stubble. Rooks argued shrilly in a copse to one side, partway up the field.

Hurst referred to it as a cottage, Avery supposed, because it was in the country and had a rustic look. He would have called it a house, and it was a fairly large one at that. It was Hurst's private side, his apology for Swindon. There was a graveled forecourt spacious enough for several cars, then a well-trimmed lawn up to a door not quite vertical under a timbered porch. Bright windows looked across the lane to a covert. Russet roof tiles stained with lichen tumbled to eaves darting with house martins; under them more tiles cosseted the upper story, above red brick walls with the texture of home-baked bread. Driving in was a homecoming, a return after too long away to the familiarity and welcome of a place where he had never been before. Some houses did that to you.

He parked the Rover in the double garage and let himself in through the internal door to the hall. It was almost of a size suited to a small manor, with broad stairs lined with portraits leading to a landing where a solemnly tapping grandfather clock broke the silence. The door to the living room was immediately facing.

It was a man's room, with a strong, masculine look and smells of wood and leather. But it had been masterminded by a woman, something told him. The walls were hung with sporting prints and old guns:

66

flintlocks and dueling pieces, a blunderbuss with the mouth of a trumpet, a long-barreled rifle last used against the Boers. In pride of place over the open fire was an eighteenth-century print of a racehorse; the scene in the background was probably of the Lambourn Downs, looking scarcely different from the way he had seen them today. Beams spanned the ceiling and the honey-toned floor was spread with good if not especially precious oriental carpets. Books in muted leather jackets filled an alcove, with the look not of having been bought by the yard but of being individually chosen over time, then read and read again. The chesterfield and club chairs were in ample buttoned hide. Picture frames were gold leaf worn with age. The gun metal had a deep, dead luster. Brass shone cheerfully among the browns and dark reds. Avery discovered the Danish hi-fi and the Japanese color television hidden away, as well they should be among such Englishness, behind pine doors.

Outside at the back he came across a cache of logs and he carried in an armful to make a blazing fire, although it was pleasantly mild and not yet four in the afternoon. Lying on the carpet, staring into the flames, took him back to his teens, to a time that might have been a hundred years in the past. There had been a log fire just like this at the vacation home in Chatham, out on the scorpion's tail of Cape Cod. The house there had been in white New England clapboard, not the brick of this one, though the book-lined walls and the tangy smell of burning wood were much the same. But the atmosphere had not been the same; invariably as crowded in the fall as a courtroom with half the Averys in Massachusetts and the talk all

67

of legal battles lost and won and obscure precedent. Except, that is, when the family had gone their various ways: back to Boston, out walking, to fish off Hyannis, to retire upstairs and sleep off the Sunday afternoon claret. Then, left alone by the fire, Avery had felt as relaxed and near contented as he ever seemed able to be. He was that way now. Los Angeles and Laura and Carl Zell were six thousand miles away. And Brokaw, thank God. The logs snapped and shifted restlessly, rocketing sparks up the chimney. He was still watching, still staring in with empty thoughts as the fire subsided into graying embers.

He showered and climbed between cool sheets in the largest of the upstairs bedrooms. His limbs were leaden. The last he remembered was the harsh cries of the rooks as they circled the roof, diving away into the sleep of the dead.

4

It took three cups of very strong black coffee to begin to revive Avery in the morning, an excellent blend of dark-roasted Colombian beans from a large canister in the farmhouse-style kitchen. From habit, he tried the television as he took a simple breakfast. The screen was a void of neurotic speckles and the set hissed on all three channels: he had forgotten the civilized hours of British broadcasting. So he reveled instead in the near silence: the slow, restful clank of the clock in the hall and the unaccustomed sounds of the countryside. Then a horn was sounding insolently from the lane outside and the rooks were stirring to cry their protests. The car had approached so quietly he hadn't heard it come.

If he had had his wits about him, he would have known beforehand the kind of chauffeur Hurst would send to drive him to Fort Halstead. He would have predicted her fiery red hair, the generous figure, the immaculate, businesslike look of an airline stewardess. At least, once having caught sight of her through a window, he was sure his guess would have been close.

"Tracy Jackson," she called, on seeing him. "Your carriage awaits."

He might have predicted the type as well, if he had thought to. Some well-groomed women carry "Keep Off" signs; this one invited attack. The hair shouted out to be tousled, the clothes to be disarranged, the body to be tumbled in the hay. Then again, perhaps he was still half asleep and not yet seeing straight. As he crossed the lawn toward her, scattering dew, she wasn't really that kind; not much like it at all, come to think of it. The hair was dramatically lit by the bright, slanting rays of the early sun and there was a certain boldness in her stance, hand on hip, by the car. But as they shook hands all that remained of the provocation he had imagined was a vestige of flirtatiousness in the smile.

"Now, you're not going to be standoffish, are you?" she said bossily. "You're riding up front with me."

"It's where I'm used to," Avery said. "Front seat, left-hand side."

But try as he might, he would never have predicted

that car. He had sensed a dichotomy in Hurst's behavior and had believed he was beginning to understand it. Now he realized he did not. On the one hand there was the understated, almost shabby, nature of the company premises; on the other, the sophistication of the guest house. It was as if there was a sober business style that the man felt it necessary to adopt but from which he was trying to escape, anxious to demonstrate whenever he could that the real Peter Hurst was far from ordinary, far from drab. But the car was an escape into orbit, a grand gesture that went way over the top. It was a silver Rolls-Royce Corniche convertible, filled inside with the same exotic aromas of wood and hide as the living room. Except that these smells were undeniably newer.

"It's Peter Hurst's," the girl explained, urging the Rolls eastbound onto th M-4 highway. "Since he's up in town today he thought you might like to travel in comfort."

"Indeed," Avery murmured, playing with the joystick beside him to power the seat into the most sybaritic position.

"You must be important," she said, turning her head to him and letting the car find its own silent way for a while.

"So it would seem. And you?"

"I'm just playing chauffeur for the day. I'm on the marketing side at Quantek."

"Meaning what exactly?"

"Meaning I help to persuade important people like you to buy our electronics." A radiant smile. "And if you want to know, I much prefer Americans to the usual run of Arabs. Yuk! Greasy types with the manners of camels and as many hands as an octopus."

"Let me hazard a guess," Avery said after looking her over and considering her precise, very English, accent. "Educated at Roedean, probably. Then a brilliant degree in electrical engineering from somewhere like Girton. That's if they teach engineering there. Then an expensive year doing nothing very much in Zurich or Berne. Am I warm?"

She laughed uncontrollably, wagging her head. "Actually, I dropped out halfway through a business studies course at Slough Tech. Do you know Slough? I don't think so, somehow."

"No," he confirmend.

"Don't bother, take it from me."

She settled for a sedate passage in the middle lane, adjusting the cruise control to a fraction over the legal limit.

"Try the glove compartment."

On a clipboard with a pen dangling at the ready from a coil of plastic, Avery found a form printed on green paper. After quickly scanning a summary of the Official Secrets Act, he added his signature to verify that he was now aware of its provisions.

"They'll need that at the fort," she said. "If you want to be shown what they play at."

"How about a nice simpleminded introduction now, before we arrive?"

Another laugh. "You, sir, have to be kidding. Shall I tell you the only thing I learned at Slough before I chucked it in? The difference between marketing and selling. To sell a product, you need to know something about it. To market it, you don't. Vulcan's a closed book to me."

Avery turned in the deep seat to watch her drive. "So who's complaining?"

The Royal Armaments Research and Development Estalishment was set well out of sight of the busy Sevenoaks Road, thronged at that time of the morning with commuter traffic bound for London. There were two security barriers, the first set some distance down the private entrance road from the main gate. A slow-moving member of the Kent constabulary searched the trunk for explosives.

"I ask you," Tracy said loudly to Avery, "do we look like the IRA?"

The barrier was swung up and she slid the car regally forward to the next obstacle.

"All out," she told him, then leaned closer to whisper, "and don't use any words longer than *cat* or *mat*. They once recorded an IQ greater than a hundred in there." She nodded to the gate house. "They had to get a hundred of the guards together to do it."

Just as she predicted, the constable behind the counter was a burly country soul with an accent so thick Avery could barely understand half of what he said. The contents of Avery's briefcase were first examined closely. Then their names and the car number were checked and double-checked against a dog-eared list. A directory was then searched for the contact she gave, with the correct page being passed over twice. The number was dialed with infinite slowness, the man peering short-sightedly at each digit before being prepared to insert his finger. It was the finger of a gardener, broad and blackened, with a torn nail.

"Are you cleared to go in unaccompanied?" he asked the girl when the brief conversation was done.

"Afraid not."

"You'll need a messenger, then."

A bell on the counter was heavily thumped several times.

"The bells! The bells!" the girl uttered in a strangled croak close to Avery's ear. He looked at her as if she was mad. "You'll see," she said quietly.

The messenger was some minutes in coming. His skin was as wrinkled as a dried peach, one foot dragged uselessly behind him, and as he led them outside his remarks on the weather echoed flatly through a cleft palate. He scrambled into the Corniche to sit grandly in the back, directing her with jabs to the left or right shoulder, although Avery could see she knew the way. They drifted in and up the hill, past a straggle of buildings with the military look of barracks, past high sheds with hangarlike doors, around a grassed mound prickling with barbed wire, between newer constructions in concrete and brick whose windows were shuttered in crisscrossed metal like old elevator doors. She parked close to a sign that said "D BRANCH. Assessment." The messenger sat stubbornly where he was until a tall, gray-haired man appeared from a side door and intruduced himself as Howard Campbell-Jones. Only then did he consent to scramble out.

I'll have it when you're through, darling," he said hollowly to the girl, caressing the winged lady on the radiator. Then he limped away over the grass.

"Peter Hurst asked us to make it open house," Campbell-Jones told Avery. "What is it you want to see?"

"The works, the whole thing."

Tracy handed over the signed green form. "How about the usual visitor's tour, Howard?" she suggested.

"We'll see what we can do." Campbell-Jones held open a door to the building and followed them in as she confidently forged ahead.

Down a bare, cream-painted passage, they came into a spacious, high hall of a room, full of activity. There were no side windows, that was the first thing Avery noticed. It was lit, dully but evenly, from skylights let into the ceiling above exposed girders. The skylights were shuttered. At a dais against the far wall several men sat at desks, studying display screens. Perhaps another dozen men, with a token sprinkling of young women, sat or stood in the well of the room. Most were keying in data as they watched more displays; some were using telephones. The room seemed full of telephones. One was ringing now as they entered, and a young man reached for it without much evidence of urgency, "Yes, Field HQ?" he said in a mannered drawl. His hacking jacket was in a tweed remarkably similar to that worn by Campbell-Jones. In fact, surveying the scene, Avery found that most of the men were in jackets like that, as if it were required dress, except for two up on the dais who wore identical army uniforms. He didn't know the rank but it would be high, to judge from the quantity of braid. Brigadier, at least, he thought.

Printers were adding their chatter to the general buzz of conversation. Yet more screens lined a wall, filled with ever-changing columns of figures. A far larger display presented what appeared to be a simplified version of a map, all straight lines and patches of color. Even as he watched it, a red circle began to flash in an area of green, and that seemed to be the cue for a hurried conference up on the platform. There were two digital clocks on the wall. One gave the correct time as 0920; the other was showing 0435 and the sign above said that was *Game Time*. A huge map dominated the room, hanging at an angle from the roof trusses to face the dais. It covered an area of Central Europe extending east into Poland as far as Warsaw and taking in Budapest to the south.

"We call this Command Room," Campbell-Jones explained. "I'm the game controller and this is where I keep a friendly eye on the hostilities."

"I'll tell you what it reminds me of," Avery said. "Those operations rooms in the Battle of Britain movies. Except that they always had big horizontal map tables and a swarm of girls pushing counters around."

"Same thing here, once upon a time," the controller said. "We used a great, three-dimensional terrain model. Damned near the size of a squash court, it was. We had to squint along pointers to decide whether one tank had line of fire to another. The arguments that caused, I can tell you! Vulcan has made my life happier and easier, thank you very much."

He steered them to a corner away from the action, to sit them on chairs which he drew into a circle. "Take over, would you, Ted?" he called over to the dais. "I'm going to be tied up for a while." One of the men raised a hand in acknowledgment and transferred to the largest desk, in the center of the platform.

75

"Now, where would you like me to start?"

"How about explaining the whole point of the excercise first," Avery asked.

"You mean, why have war gaming at all?" Campbell-Jones raised bushy eyebrows in polite astonishment.

"Humor me," Avery said.

"Very well, if you wish." The controller hooked a toe around the leg of a spare chair to pull it closer, lifting his feet up to sprawl more comfortably. There was a hole in the sole of one of his suede shoes.

"War gaming is as old as conflict itself," he began. "The principle is the same as it ever was. The difference is that it's become damned complicated these days, modern warfare being what it is. Put simply, the U.K. has men and equipment. So have our allies. And so, bless their thick woolen socks, have our friends in the Warsaw Pact. The objective here at the fort is to see what would happen should we ever have to use our forces in anger. Our job is to measure how effective any particular device or weapon is likely to be and to discover how best to use it. As you might guess, a great deal of background research has to be carried out before we can even begin a game like this. And there are field trials, of course. As far as the other side is concerned, we learn what we can from a variety of sources." A broad, knowing wink accompanied that. "I'll give you an example, shall I? Suppose the Russians were to fire an antitank gun at one of our next-gereration MTB Eighties from a range of six kilometers. What's the chance of a hit and what's the damage likely to be? It doesn't matter what hardware we're deploying in a game: armor, support units, radars, aircraft, whatever. We have to know the conditions under which each piece can be detected and what it takes to knock it out. And that detailed information has to go into the computer. Are you with me so far?"

"Of course," Avery said.

"To run a game, we need two types of chap in here. Soldiers, naturally, to play out the tactics. They're the people who have to fight the battles for real, after all. So it's their show, in a manner of speaking. The rest of us, the civil servants like yours truly, are here just to look after the technical side for them. We're the men behind the scenes, as it were, nursing the performance along."

"Howard's an SPSO," Tracy interjected. "A senior principal scientific officer. That's getting pretty high in the establishment pecking order."

"How kind of you, m'dear," the controller said. He took in the room with a generous sweep of the arm. "In here, we know everything, Mr. Avery. Not a piece moves, not a gun gets fired, without we see it. I like to think of myself as God, if you won't misunderstand me. This is my little universe, and nothing, but nothing, escapes my beady eye. Not so much as a single APC under camouflage net."

"APC?" Avery asked.

"An armored personnel carrier," the controller elaborated, with a barely concealed sniff. "Now, down that way we have the Blue side rooms." He aimed a thick finger at a door to the left of the dais. "There are ten rooms, meaning we can play up to ten independently commanded Blue units. And t'other way are the corresponding Red rooms." His thumb jerked over a shoulder. "Same story there: ten soundproofed rooms, all kept locked during play. The only outside contact the officers have is by telephone, via us. On the screens and printers they have in there with them they can see only what the computer decides to tell them. Now, here's the crucial point. I've said that we have a complete picture of the battle in here. But the soldiers in the side rooms don't have any such thing. As in real combat, they only know a part of the story. Each officer, Blue or Red, will only know of the existence of an enemy piece if one of his units has spotted it or if someone else in another room has and has bothered to report it. Yes? If a commander orders a shell to be blasted off over a ridge, he'll only learn of the damage if he's posted an observer or if he whistles up a reconnaissance flight and HQ feels in an obliging mood. How are we doing so far?"

"Just fine," Avery said.

"I suspect a trip to the side rooms will make it even clearer," Tracy said helpfully.

"Of course," Campbell-Jones agreed. "We'll stroll along to one in a tick. But let's consider the computer side of the game first. Developing Vulcan was a joint effort. I don't know whether that was explained to you at Quantek. Here at RARDE we posed the questions and suggested some of the solutions. Peter Hurst's bright young men in Swindon came up with the definitive answers. Broadly, I'd say there are three ways in which the resulting system is regarded as rather special in gaming circles. The first is the means by which we represent a map inside the computer. That isn't easy, believe you me."

"I know," Avery said.

"We've managed it pretty successfully, I would say. If there's so much as a tree between an observer and his target, Vulcan makes sure he doesn't get to see that target. If there's an unmetaled road and it's been raining, the speed at which a supply truck can proceed along it is reduced accordingly."

"Very clever," Avery said, adding a nod of approval. His knowledge of the subject came from a book read on the flight from Los Angeles; the only book which Lisa, his secretary, had managed to find at such short notice. But it was enough of an introduction to tell him that what Quantek had achieved was considerable.

"Let's move on to point number two," Campbell-Jones said crisply. "Modern warfare is about communications as much as fire power. It isn't enough for the man in the field to learn of the enemy's strength. He has to report back what he knows and do it quickly. What we've built into Vulcan is the best model anyone has yet come up with of the ways in which information sloshes around a battlefield. Think of it like this. A battalion commander in Blue Room One happens across a convoy of SS-Sixteen missiles. Nasty beasts, if Reds gets to fire them. So he reports back to base. In real life, the time from first sighting to the shit hitting the fan at HQ is going to be ten minutes, shall we say. So Vulcan imposes that delay on the message. Every scrap of intelligence is treated in the same way. More than that, some messages get garbled and a few are even lost, just as they would be in the heat of battle." A mischievous smile lit the thin face. "We have our own little fights as a result, I can tell you. Down in the mess at lunchtimes."

The computer display chart was suddenly flashing at several points and two of the printers started up in unison. The controller tugged wire-framed spectacles from his top pocket, perching them on his beak of a nose to peer over to the display.

"I'll need to get back to the grind, by the look of things," he murmured thoughtfully. "We seem to have some of the brown stuff striking the fan blades right now. Funny that. I didn't expect any developments for another half hour at least. Red's got prematurely trigger happy, that's what it must be." He rose to his feet, slipping the glasses away again as if ashamed of them. "To round off on the third and final point," he said, rather hurriedly. "Vulcan is what we call heuristic. I take it you know what that means?"

"Sure," Avery said. "It means it's a self-learning system. You can teach it to play better as time goes by."

"Precisely," the controller beamed. "Now, the big problem with a pan-European war is likely to be this. It'll be sheer chaos, a regular dog's dinner of limited local engagements and strategic conflict on the grand scale. We'll have tanks slugging it out on the ground, fighters filling the skies, and nuclear rockets going off all over the Continent. And the rockets won't settle the argument by themselves, take my word for it. If we tried to play out a situation like that without the computer doing most of the work, we'd need a thousand side rooms and the entire chiefs of staff of NATO. So here's what we've done. We fight out several variations of tank battle under a variety of conditions. Vulcan stores away the tactics and the outcomes. Next we switch to a different aspect, to bridge building under heavy fire, say, or to the movement in of fuel supplies after the Russians have smothered an area with chemicals. Now Vulcan knows how to handle that situation. And so on, do you follow? We teach it steadily, all the time increasing the scale of combat, getting away from the eyeball-to-eyeball stuff up to the total picture we're after: the view the generals will have inside their cosy bolt holes. What you see here today may look very small beer, Mr. Avery, but you come back in six months' time. You'll see whole cities frying then, believe you me. I'm quite looking forward to it."

Campbell-Jones started at a brisk pace across the room, urging Avery and the girl to follow. "I've arranged for you to sit in with Harry Colby," he said as they reached the door to the Blue wing. "He feels in need of a bit of company, poor chap. You can give him a hand if you feel so inclined. I'm sure you'll learn more that way."

"Count me out," Tracy said, tucking a hand under his arm. "Howard's taking me for coffee as soon as he's sorted this latest bit of excitement out."

"Tea, m'dear, tea," Campbell-Jones said, patting the hand. "I wouldn't wish the fort's coffee on Moscow."

5

Side room Blue Three was full of smoke; a strong haze
that didn't quite have the smell of cordite but was just
as acrid. As Major Colby came spluttering through it
toward him, his arms, like windmills, flailing the stuff
away, Avery fancied that there must have been times
when he had looked like that under enemy fire. One
side of the face was uncannily smooth and pale against
the mottled beetroot of the rest. It seemed as if a great
flap of flesh had been lifted up then slapped roughly
back in place. There was a curious, twisted smile as a
result, with the lips pulled back from the yellowing
teeth at one corner of the mouth. The major clamped
them onto a pipe as he came, perhaps to make them
less noticeable. The good cheek was liberally covered
with hair which thickened over the upper lip into a
nicotine-stained mustache. His eyeballs bulged, like
those of a bulldog.

"Don't mind if I smoke, do you, old son?" he asked
after the introductions had been made and the
controller had retreated, locking the door behind him.

"Not at all," Avery said, his eyes already beginning
to water.

"I won't beat about the bush," Colby said. "Any
other day you wouldn't get the friendliest of receptions
in here, and that's letting you have it straight. There's
quite enough going on as a rule to keep me running
around like a blue-assed fly, without visitors cluttering
the place up. But my right-hand man's gone AWOL.
So if you're prepared to make yourself useful, we'll get
along just fine." He was patting the back of a chair
that faced a bank of display screens.

Avery thought it diplomatic to take the seat. "I'll do my best for you, major."

That got him the twisted smile as the pipe was thrust his way.

"Pipe of peace, you might say," the major muttered. "The circumstances being what they are. Did they tell you what we're up to this time?"

"Not in detail."

"It's a fishing expedition into East Germany, really. Some mobile detection devices pushed over the border under cover of darkness. Radars, infrared cameras, image intensifiers, the usual fancy gubbins. The commandos took out a border patrol north of Coburg to get us in. The trick now is to see how far we can penetrate without further engagement. I've got my lot nearly twenty kilometers, almost up to Saalfeld. That may not sound far in four and a half hours of game time, but it's good enough for me."

Colby resumed his seat under the only window, to run a finger over his map table. "It's pretty routine stuff, as a matter of fact. Not like the last game a couple of weeks back. Then, all hell broke loose. Nuclear warheads, chemical shells. We retreated licking our wounds and leaving the door open for Red to push in clear up to Baden-Baden. A right poke in the eye, that was, for the forces of good." He was soon lost in deliberation over the map.

There was a checklist of terminal commands in a clear plastic cover, on the table beside Avery, and a brief set of explanatory notes on the reverse. He began keying in instructions and to his pleasant surprise was rewarded with a flickering response from the displays. It was quite simple, he decided, and became sufficiently bold to press a key marked "OWN UNIT STATUS." A screen blinked, cleared, and then produced a brief summary at the top.

"You've got two APCs and two Land-Rovers with an infantry detachment, is that right?"

"Spot on," the major acknowledged, without looking round.

"And a Fruitbat. What in heaven's name is that?"

"Lips are sealed, old son. Highly secret. But it squeaks in the dark and listens. That's all I'm saying."

"Aah," Avery murmured.

One of several telephones rang, next to the major's elbow. "All right, all right," he snapped into it. He turned, covering the mouthpiece. "Can you put instructions into that thing yet, do you think?"

"You mean enter data?"

"Of course that's what I mean," Colby said with mounting impatience. "They're hustling me, do you see? My next move is overdue."

"Sorry, I'm still learning how to get a readout."

The bulbous eyes regarded Avery sadly. "You'll have to do it for me up there," he said into the phone. "My Yankee pal isn't *au fait* yet." His nose pressed close to the map. "Tango Four and Tango Five down to fifteen kilometers an hour. Bearing unchanged. Got that? And I want X-ray Nine to hold station with Fruitbat directed at that barn across the valley. What? Yes, of course, *that* barn. I've got a nasty feeling about it." For some reason he sniffed contemptuously as he slammed the phone down.

"What did you mean just then?" Avery asked. "About someone going AWOL?"

"Each side room has a resident technical Johnnie,"

84

Colby said. "Mine's a fellow called Franklin, a scientific officer here. The best of the bunch, if you ask me, but don't tell him I said so. He didn't show this morning, didn't so much as ring in to say sorry. Looked as right as rain yesterday, too." He came over, touching the side of his nose meaningfully. "The fellow's shacked up with a bit of stuff from the Command Room. A real goer, if you ask me. Well, she's not in, either, today, get my drift? The call of nature proved stronger than the call of duty, that's what happened. And the best of luck to them, but it's deuced inconvenient for me, that's all I can say." Colby eased himself onto the table beside Avery. "Been in the Command Room yet?"

"Just now."

"As full of scientists as a convention, wouldn't you say?"

"Pretty busy, yes."

"I asked Campbell-Jones for the loan of one, just for the day. You'd think he could spare one from that clutch, wouldn't you? The hell he could. I'm a man short but he's a woman under strength, so he says. So tough titty on me." The major rested a hand on Avery's shoulder. There was a discolored patch on that, too, extending out of sight under the cuff of his checked shirt. "Are you a fast learner, would you say, old son?"

"So I'm told."

"Good man. I'm depending on it."

"Well?" Tracy asked expectantly as the door was unlocked.

"Absolutely fascinating," Avery said, gulping in the

fresh air outside like a swimmer coming up from the depths. He had forgotten how smoke-laden the room was, so engrossed had he been.

Colby thumped him on the back. "A military genius, this chap," he said. "Take my word for it. He trickled my men past a Red patrol without them turning a hair, just like that." One palm slid graphically over the other. "A soldier to the manner born." His arm came around Avery's shoulder as they walked along the passage. "Stick around, old son. We'll give the Communists a black eye or two, eh?"

The girl was ahead of them and she glanced back, a teasing expression on her face. "You sound like Errol Flynn in Burma."

"I feel like it," Avery said. "I haven't enjoyed anything as much in years."

The well of the Command Room was virtually deserted, with most of the civil servants already away to lunch. Campbell-Jones was still on the dais with the two officers and a man who hadn't been there before: he wore a dark suit, and Avery was sure he would have noticed that in the room earlier. They huddled together, talking quickly with much gesturing. The screens were all blank now, turned off until play resumed. It occurred to Avery that he had yet to be shown the computer, which was presumably in a nearby room. It would be nothing special, he was sure, a computer room much like any other, but he ought to ask for a visit just to round off his tour. Perhaps after lunch.

The desk tops were awash with manuals and charts and a plethora of ruled forms part filled in with penciled figures. Most had little room to spare with all

86

that paper piled so high around the terminals. He moved to the nearest of the desks to take a closer look at what kept the scientists in there so busy. The complex, multicolored graph he picked up was headed "MTB-80 *versus* T-72." Quick examination suggested that it gave the degrees of damage the two opposing tanks could inflict on one another at different ranges. As he put it down, he noticed a handwritten title on one of the files that littered the desk. It said *R.J. Franklin, D Branch,* and across the top was a red *CONFIDENTIAL* stamp.

"Why don't you people push on ahead," Campbell-Jones called over. "We're still cooking mischief for this afternoon."

"Come on, Errol," Colby shouted to Avery, jerking his fingers toward his mouth. "Chop, chop."

Lunch was a battle relived, a bitter engagement fought again from memory. It served to divert Avery's attention from a steak pie which he was to liken on the journey back to meat-flavored jelly encased in burnt blotting paper. The major's pie was left to grow cold, not because it wasn't to his liking but because he had more important matters on his mind. The plate was gradually pushed to one side, then the salt and pepper as he made his advance into the hills of Cyprus. No sooner had Avery crossed his knife and fork over his barely touched meal than the major was eagerly thrusting it away to claim the ground. A different, faraway look entered those staring eyes and he had an eloquence when he talked of combat that captivated his audience. As he began, Tracy cast amused half smiles at Avery from behind a hand and her foot tapped his under the table at crucial points of the narrative. Her manner soon changed, the smiles fading to sober, absorbed interest as Colby spoke of the rain, torrential bloody rain it was, and what it was like to find yourself still alive after death had taken you by the throat, thrown you down, and cast its dark cloak over you. Avery even thought there was a tear in her eye as Colby told of his men being covered and carried away. Then, and only then, he said, had he allowed himself to be driven back to Famagusta. He had insisted on climbing into the truck unaided. It was nothing more than a gesture, he said, but it hurt like buggery. A man had to show what he was made of when he had just survived two chaps lost for no reason, no damned reason at all.

"And that's how I got this," he said simply, touching his left cheek. "The spoils of war, you might say."

"Did you get a medal?" Tracy asked solemnly.

His head shook vigorously at the very idea. "After driving into an ambush, like rats into a trap? Not bloody likely. And if one had been offered, I couldn't have taken it. Not under the circumstances."

Campbell-Jones came bustling into the mess, cast around for them and headed their way at a pace, pushing chairs aside in his hurry. He touched the girl on the arm. "Can you spare me a second, Miss Jackson? Just a word in your ear. Do you mind?" he asked the others. She was led quickly away through a side door.

Colby gave his crooked smile, tapping his nose as he had before. "Something's afoot," he declared. "Something of a *personal* nature, wouldn't you say?"

Avery laughed. "Very probably. I guess Peter Hurst

88

has to keep the civil servants here happy in one way or another."

"He might include the army in his largesse," the major said morosely.

Tracy Jackson rejoined them after an interval, sitting down very straight-faced. "Howard wants to be diplomatic," she told Avery. "He's asked me to break it to you. To put it bluntly, it won't be comfortable for them if you stay around this afternoon. I don't think he's heard of the Atlantic Alliance." This last was said sorrowfully.

"You don't say." Colby was staring at her with rapt interest, but her eyes remained on Avery.

"Apparently they have something top secret in mind as the game unfolds. Howard won't tell me what, but it seems an American on the sidelines would cramp their style."

"Aha!" Colby cried, slapping a thigh. "I bloody *knew* it! I knew it was all too simple to be true. Didn't I tell you it was too quiet to make sense?" He clasped Avery's hand beseeching agreement.

"More or less," Avery said, remembering no such thing.

"Exactly." Colby folded his arms in triumph.

"So, I'm not wanted, is that it?" Avery asked the girl.

"It rather appears that way, I'm afraid."

Avery looked at his watch. "Don't worry about it. I've seen enough for the time being."

"That's really considerate of you. Howard hoped you'd see it that way."

"But I'll need to go back for my briefcase. It's still in the side room. I kind of assumed we'd be going back."

"Well . . ." she began doubtfully.

But Colby was leaping to his feet. "So we are, so we are." He bent to take her hand paternally. "Get Howard to see you to the gate, sweetheart. I'll bring my comrade in arms here down to join you as soon as we've picked up his case."

"She's let the cat out of the bag, hasn't she," he remarked with glee as they took the road back to the Assessment Block.

"Has she? I thought she gave very little away."

"Surprise, old son, that's what she's blown: the element of surprise. Now I'm on my guard, do you see? I haven't the faintest what they're going to hit me with, but I *do* know I'm going to be clobbered. The controller's boobed. He's given the game away."

"Pity I won't be around to see it," Avery said with genuine regret.

"But you'll be back? You'll be coming again?"

"I very much hope so."

"I'll tell you about it then, don't worry. I'll let you know how it all pans out."

The Command Room was filling up and the screens were on again. The diagrammatic map on the big display was different to that shown in the morning. Avery stopped to compare it with the suspended map, curious to learn what part of Europe would be the focus for the afternoon's events. But the diagram was far too general and there was no way of telling.

Colby noticed his interest. "Grab a pew," he suggested. "I'll fetch the case." He hurried off.

Avery glanced around. The scientists were all together, grouped in a corner and talking in urgent whispers. As others drifted in they moved across to join the debate. There was something in the air, Avery sensed suddenly, noticing the secretive way they drew together. One of the men caught his eye as he was speaking, hesitated, then dropped his voice to continue. His gaze wandered, just for an instant, before he closed up into the circle, and Avery followed the look. Just in front, off the aisle, was Franklin's desk. Avery stared at it, subconsciously starting toward it, but several of the group in the corner were turning to watch him. Instead, he thrust his hands idly into his pocket and moved away, glancing up to the overhead map. But he had already seen enough. It was the desk that was causing the excitement, he was sure. That was the reason he was being bundled out of the place. It was completely bare now. The drawers had all been pulled out and cleared.

"Franklin's girlfriend," he said to Colby as they approached the main gate. "What did you say her name was?"

"Valerie something or other. Val, that's all I ever call her."

"But you don't remember the surname?"

"Not really," the major said. "A pretty wisp of a thing, she is. Body as thin as a rake, but accessible-looking. Do you know the sort?"

"Don't we all!"

"Too damned right, old son," Colby said with a grin. He clenched a fist, tensed a forearm, and jerked it upward.

6

The Corniche made a stately descent of the lane at Lambourn. Tracy Jackson drew up beside the house and cut the engine.

"Your mansion, sir," she said, tongue in cheek and with a sweeping gesture. "It's all part of the service."

Avery smiled his thanks but walked around to her window, making clear he had no intention of inviting her in. That seemed to throw her slightly and she tugged the driving mirror round to straighten her hair. Not that it needed it.

"Tomorrow's Saturday," she announced. "And there's plenty to see around here. Marlborough. Bath. The White Horse of Uffington, up there on the Downs. Have you heard of it? The ancient Brits are said to have done it, cutting the turf so the chalk shows through."

"Sounds a bundle of fun," Avery said flatly.

"Oh, I don't now. You might be pleasantly surprised." She crossed one shapely leg over the other, easing her skirt up.

"And that would be part of the service, too?"

"Do you have to put it like that?" she protested with a frown.

"I'm sorry," Avery said. "It's just that I don't want any hard sell out of hours, not over my weekend."

"Who said that was the idea?" she demanded. She took her time resetting the mirror, thinking. "We could wander further afield if you like," she proposed then, her eyes firmly on his to gauge the reaction. "There's always Stonehenge. Most of our overseas visitors like to be taken there. It was the world's first computer, as a matter of fact. Did you know?"

"I had heard, yes." Avery stared her out.

"And it was *British*. How about that, Mr. Martin Avery?"

"But it took the Americans to make the idea work," he said. "Awkward stuff, stone."

She glanced back again, her manner growing chilly. "I said I wasn't too good at selling. It seems I was right."

"Honestly, I appreciate the offer but I already have plans. Some other time, maybe?"

"That's up to you." She took a visiting card from her handbag and wrote a number on the back. "You can reach me here if you change your mind."

"Thanks for the drive, anyway. You're my favorite chauffeur." He kissed his fingers and touched them to her cheek. "Those civil servants we saw today. Will they live close to the fort?"

"Fairly near, I should think. Why?"

"Just curious. Back in LA journeys to work can be fifty miles or more."

"Not there," she said. "Not out in the country like that."

Standing on the lawn, he watched her turn the Rolls, pause to give him a long, puzzled stare, then shake her head sadly and move off. The car climbed slowly up the incline until it was lost in the trees. Then he heard the tires squeal as it reached the upper lane and caught a flash of silver through the hedges as she hurtled away.

"Some other time," he repeated to himself as he entered the house. "But under my conditions and someplace else. Not here, not at Peter Hurst's bidding and certainly not with him footing the bill for services rendered. No way!"

Besides, there was this Franklin business. Avery needed to be alone, to think it through. It had bothered him for the entire journey back and it troubled him still. Perhaps it had been nothing. Perhaps the controller had told the truth and that was all there was to it. There must be at least a dozen good reasons why that desk had been cleared. For all he knew, Franklin had been suddenly promoted or demoted or pushed off sideways to another branch of the fort. Why should an amiable old buffoon such as the major be told the score? But suppose, just suppose, it hadn't been like that. Suppose Franklin was gone, that he had pulled up stakes and taken off into the blue yonder, and half the country's defense secrets with him, Fruitbat and Vulcan included. Because if Vulcan was involved, so was Northridge. And in that case, like it or not, so was he.

He went out for a fresh supply of logs, made an even bigger fire than yesterday and sat, pondering what to do next, as it built steadily into an inferno and billowing smoke raced up the chimney. Nothing, he decided, not now. There was nothing to be done until tomorrow.

He awoke with a start. It was dark now and the room was lit only by the flames, which licked slowly over what was left of the wood. He got stiffly to his feet to gaze from a window. The night was pitch black, starless and moonless, with the facing trees barely discernible in that faint flicker from the room. It was a country night, well away from any city. Los Angeles was never like this, the electric glow always reaching far up into the heavens to fend off the darkness. He went into the hall to open the back door and peer out, shivering in the inrush of cold air. It was the same there. The field rose in a scarcely visible sweep, little paler than the sky it touched. Avery shivered again. This place wasn't just quiet, it was dead. It wasn't just a distance from the village, it was positively isolated. And there had to be a reason. Why? Because there just had to be, that was why. Hurst was the kind of man who has a reason for everything.

"Hell!" Avery exclaimed on a sudden thought. "You bloody bet he has!"

He burst back into the living room, switching on all the lights and blinking at their brightness. Hardly aware yet of what he was doing, he unscrewed both end caps from the telephone to look inside. All was as it should be. But of course, it would have to be. With defense people staying at the house, the telephone would be too obvious, the first place they would look in a routine search. He took down a picture next, to find nothing behind it but an unfaded patch of wallpaper, seemingly as startled as he at the unexpected light. Another picture came down, then another, then one of the guns. It was infectious. He worked his way round the room, examining every object on the walls. For what? For a hole, he told himself. For wires. For a microphone. What else was the house for? My God, why hadn't he considered that before, instead of being seduced by its comfort and not seeing it for what it really was. For what it had to be.

"Slow down," he told himself sternly, "or you'll miss

95

it, whatever it fucking is. Take it easy, very easy."

He pulled a carpet to one side, crawling on his knees to examine the floorboards. They were just floorboards. In nice, old wood, beautifully grained and lovingly waxed. Anyway, who ever put microphones under the floor! The sound of footsteps would be deafening. He turned to the book alcove, stripping each shelf in turn to discover only dust. The television, then. Of course; with all those wires and the power supply conveniently on tap. But pulling it forward he could see only the wire to the point on the skirting, and the aerial lead. It would be a stupid place, anyhow, now he came to consider it more carefully. With the set on and that high voltage in there, the interference would be dreadful. No one in his right mind would put a mike in a television set. And the same went for the record player and the speakers. That would be a certain way to blow the hell out of eavesdropping eardrums!

So he gave up the living room as a bad loss, conceding defeat. It was there somewhere, he was sure, right under his damned nose. But only specialized equipment would find it. The kind of electronic bug detectors the security people most certainly had at RARDE. At Quantek, too, come to that, secretly kept in one of those godawful buildings.

The attic, then. That was a thought. There had to be an attic. Wasn't that where transmitters were usually hidden? He ascended to the upper hall, to see a folding ladder up by a ceiling hatch. As he hauled the ladder down, the hatch helpfully opened itself. No, he decided with a sigh, there would be no bugging equipment up there, not with access as easy as that. A moment's hesitation and he was climbing up anyway.

The switch was just inside on a rough timber beam, and the shadows cast by a single bare bulb patterned the sloping underside of the roof. His hands bit into dust around the hatch; otherwise it was undisturbed, laying thickly over the joists. Nobody had been up there in years. He stayed where he was at the top of the ladder, looking around. Tea chests brimmed with oddments. Yellowing newspapers spilled from a heap loosely bound with coarse string. A doll stared glassily back at him from a jumble of toys against the quietly hissing water tank. Then he was smiling as it dawned on him that all this stuff dated from before the place was a guesthouse. And it had been Hurst's own residence then; the sports equipment told him that as surely as if it could speak. It was everywhere: a history of weekend pursuits taken up on a whim and just as quickly discarded. Almost every kind of racket and bat known to man. A perfectly good set of golf clubs in what had been a rather splendid leather bag, now spotted with mildew. Over in a far corner he could just make out an exercise bicycle and beside it a rusty contraption with a masssive spring and what looked to be a hinged arm. His curiosity aroused, he clambered in and worked his way over the joists for a closer look. With difficulty, the rust flaking off in his hand, he forced the arm down and it locked against a release lever. It was a clay-pigeon launcher. But the shotgun used with it wouldn't still be there; he knew that without a further glance. It would have been an expensive handmade job, far too good for even Hurst to leave behind. Right now it was probably decorating his new study wall. Climbing down, Avery slapped the dust from his clothes, coughing as it rose in a cloud around him.

More logs were tossed onto the fire and he settled beside it again, hypnotized by its restless motion. He recalled with distinct embarrassment that he had done all this before: exactly the same kind of unfounded search with precisely the same result. That had been at his own house in Sherman Oaks, some three years back. It had started simply enough, as those things usually do, with a telephone call that Laura ended abruptly as he came into the room. Several nights had then followed when she was back very late with no explanation, none that he could believe. So he had searched their bedroom, naturally. And finding nothing remarkable there he had gone on to search all the other rooms, the entire house. For what? He couldn't remember now. A photograph, probably, or letters or a scrap of evidence such as a visiting card with a name he didn't know. He had found none of those.

So he had taken a day off. What else was a man to do when his wife was two-timing him? Laura hadn't seen him as he waited down the road in his car, hadn't so much as turned her head when she drove by. He had followed, carefully keeping his distance as she cut across to the San Diego Freeway and made her leisurely way to Sunset. Then along Sunset to Beverly Hills and a two-hour wait outside her hair salon. She was coming out again then, looking almost like the cover girl she had always believed she should be, getting into the Pinto and heading, more quickly now, back along the boulevard. Her car sped ahead, just in view, under an azure sky he could picture still, under the tall palms and past the crisp apartment blocks. A quick flit in convoy along the freeway to Santa Monica, a turn to follow the coast and they were soon coming into Marina Del Rey. She had parked outside Martha's apartment, rung the bell and stood there for a time, her hand impatiently drumming on the door. *Just her goddamned sister!* But still he stayed out there in the MG, watching her on the balcony, unable to tear himself away as the wind slapped the cables against the masts of the bobbing yachts. After a while she was coming down and back into her car to drive off, slowly now, more thoughtfully. Avery had tucked in behind as she headed back the way she had come, to Santa Monica. There she had left the Pinto, bought a veritable armful of magazines and a can of Coke and meandered onto the beach, aimlessly kicking sand. Her shoes came off and her cotton jacket; she turned to face the sun, loosening her shirt. Then she had read and dozed and read some more and all the time Avery watched from the shelter of the pier.

And that had been that. The next day was the same; a different route, a different beach but the same damned nothingness, the same empty squandering of time. Carl Zell had rung that evening, angrily demanding to know where Avery was and what in hell's name he was doing, leaving the team high and dry. So there was a forced end to that episode, to acting the gumshoe under the palms and over the Pacific sands in the time-honored way. Yet nothing had been quite the same since. He may not have discovered what he first feared but he had chanced on something else, something altogether more disturbing.

An affair he could have forgiven, there was purpose in passion. But vacant hours, the idle wasting of lonely days—that he had never been able to accept or forget. Where was the sense in it?

Shoes off, he padded across the room in his socks to the hi-fi, thinking to play some music. Hurst had thoughtfully provided a little of everything, a disk for every taste. Classics. Avant-garde. Jazz. Pop. Sinatra, lots of Sinatra. Avery closed his eyes and pulled down the record his hand chanced upon. He didn't bother to look at the cover, simply taking the record from the sleeve to place it on Hurst's nice Bang and Olufsen turntable.

"Fool!" he cried out at himself, instantly mesmerized by the playing arm. "Microphones have magnets. So do those heads!"

The compact stylus head came easily off the arm and he tested it against the heavy metal frame of a mirror. It stuck there, staying securely in place as he removed his hand.

"Now we're getting somewhere," he breathed excitedly, picking it carefully off. There were glass tumblers in a liquor cabinet beside the records. He chose the smallest and placed the head inside.

It seemed to him then that the corner to search was obvious and had been all along: over where three leather club chairs were grouped beside the brass-bound trunk that carried the telephone. He quickly cleared the wall of pictures, throwing them roughly onto the carpet, and ran the tumbler across, keeping the magnetic head to the front, against the wallpaper. Suddenly it twitched. He stopped, holding his breath, going a short way back to test that part of the wall again. Now the head positively jumped, clinging to the paper, and when he took the glass away it stayed there, some five feet from the floor and right above the telephone. Avery charged to the kitchen for the sharpest knife he could find.

The microphone was just under the surface, beneath the patterned wallpaper and barely covered by a skin of plaster. It was a tiny thing, a cylinder little bigger than a transistor. But it *was* a microphone. Slender wires trailed behind as he eased it out. He tucked it carefully back and folded the paper in place as well as he could, wetting it with spittle to help seal it down. With a hammer fetched from the garage, he repositioned a picture slightly to hide the place.

He could understand why, of course. All those defense people who stayed at the house, no doubt discussing what they thought of Quantek and planning their next moves in the negotiations for whatever contract Hurst was after; in all probability talking about the competition's prices, while they were at it. The sheer nerve of it, the audacity, appealed to him. He just had to be careful himself now, that was all.

The big upstairs room was almost feminine with its flowered paper and chintz curtains and the silk-shaded china lamps. Only the bed showed a masculine hand, sheer chauvinist fantasy. And what a bed! A bed with a vast brass frame, all thick railing and baroque knobs. A deep and wide half-acre plot of a bed. Now what was that there for? As if he didn't know! Avery suppressed a grin as he climbed in and heard the squeaked complaints from old and probably

101

much exercised springs.

His eyes closed. It was as quiet outside as a churchyard. The trees creaked and in the distance an owl called as it quartered the fields in search of prey. Then Avery was sitting bolt upright again, his hand clawing in the darkness for the light switch. A moment to stare at the wall behind him and he was leaping from the bed, running two and three steps at a time down the stairs for the tumbler and the stylus head.

The head gripped the wall in the first place he tried. This time there was no need for the knife. The microphone was slap bang in the center of the bed frame, just inches above the pillows.

"Peter Hurst, you're a dirty old man." He had to smile, though, in spite of it all. But he merely thought the words, stopping himself just in time from saying them aloud.

7

Avery rose early and took breakfast on the lawn. The dewy fields lent their fragrance to a cool breeze. The clouds were moving aside to uncurtain the sky. The sun shafted through the trees and the leaves trembled as they bathed in it, rustling with satisfaction. The black rooks cawed shrilly from their high bare elms. Nothing made them happy.

He backed the Rover from the garage, turned for

the lane then stopped abruptly, muttering at himself. Returning to house, he changed from the jeans and sweater he was wearing into his only suit, a white shirt and a tie. Just to be on the safe side, he told himelf. On the way back to the car, he collected his briefcase from the hall.

He followed the route to Kent the girl had taken the previous day, but continued past Fort Halstead, driving down into Sevenoaks where he left the car in a Council parking lot. The post office was along the crowded High Street and full of slow lines and weekend gossip. A child sprawled on the floor, pushing a toy car. Avery stepped over him to the side counter, to a stack of telelphone directories next to the kiosks. Now, he thought, which one? More to the point, was the guy going to be in any of them anyway? The major had only said he was shacked up with the girl, with Valerie. He hadn't said in whose place. Damn the man for not remembering her name. And yet there was the entry in the very first book he tried, the Sevenoaks volume. *R.J. FRANKLIN.* With an address he took to be a village close to the town. Easy as pie, Avery thought, and waiting until a kiosk was free he went in to dial the number.

A woman answered, a young woman.

"Is that Valerie?" Avery asked.

There was a silence, and Avery, suspecting nothing, cheerfully repeated the question.

"Who the hell is that?" the woman demanded frostily.

"You won't know me. I'm just calling to . . ."

"Is this some kind of joke, is that the idea? One of Bob's dirty bloody jokes?"

"I'm sorry?" Avery said. Suddenly he heard the cry of a child in the background and closed his eyes in disbelief.

"You tell them from me they deserve one another," the woman shouted, her voice breaking with emotion. "Have you got that, whoever you are? They deserve their grotty little love nest. I'm staying put." The line went dead.

Colby, you old buffoon, Avery's racing brain complained, you might have mentioned he was married! He stood, staring in a daze at the telephone and wondering how he could have been so dumb, why that possibility had never for a moment occurred to him.

A matron with an iceberg for a face and a shopping cart in tow rapped a coin on the glass. Avery jumped at the sound, swiveled his head to disconcert her with the broadest smile he could muster, then turned back to the kiosk mirror to straighten his tie.

"Ah well," he said to himself, "it looks like Plan B, after all."

All was quiet at Fort Halstead. There was no movement inside the boundary fence, not a single person in view, and only one car, parked at the verge by one of those great, windowless sheds. The same guard was on duty in the gate house: the gardener. The man whose hands looked as though they spent every available hour buried deep in rose bushes and compost. Why were they always referred to as *green* thumbs? Avery wondered. A newspaper lay on the counter, open to the sports pages, a chipped mug of thick brown tea beside it. He was shoveling in spoon after spoon of sugar as Avery entered. His flat policeman's cap with its checkered band was on a cupboard and Avery did not like the look of that, not one bit. He had remembered the man only as a gardener, as a simple peasant, and forgotten what he really was.

"I was here yesterday," Avery said, finding the resolution to stride to the counter and set his briefcase down with a *thud*. "Remember?"

The man peered myopically at him, "Ah, yes," he said after heavy thought.

"I have an appointment with Mr. Franklin." Avery glanced helpfully at the establishment directory, on a string beside the telephone.

"It's Saturday," the gardener responded, taking to his chair.

"I know."

"A bit unusual, isn't it, sir? If you don't mind me saying. A meeting on a Saturday?"

"That's the whole point," Avery said cheerfuly. "We wanted a quiet get-together, a few hours' peace up at D Branch."

"Franklin, you say? D Branch?"

"That's right."

The callused hands moved at last to the directory, to thumb the pages. *He doesn't know,* Avery breathed in relief. The security guys haven't told him yet. They're still keeping it under wraps and that means it's big. Either that or there's nothing to tell.

The gardener dialed as slowly as yesterday and listened for a time. He held the receiver to his eyes to urge a reply then listened again. "There's no answer from 'um," he said. "Nobody up there. I thought as much, to be honest. I've seen nobody from D Branch pass through today and I've been on since six."

"I'll hang around," Avery said. "He'll show, I know he will."

There was a tubular chair to one side, its plastic seat torn and the stuffing showing through. The upright back pressed hard into his spine.

"Suit yourself," the gardener said, returning to his paper and bending close to mark it with a pencil.

The clock on the wall moved on twenty minutes, to 10:40.

"You've made a mistake, haven't you?" the man declared, furrowing his brow to read it. "He won't be turning up, not now. Not on a Saturday."

"He'll be along all right," Avery said confidently. "But he's an unpunctual son of a bitch, old Franklin. Always was and always will be."

"Can't abide that," the gardener said. " 'Tain't right to keep people waiting. Not when there's an arrangement."

"Don't let it bother you. I'll hang on awhile." Avery delivered an easy smile, leaned back and crossed his legs, trying to look comfortable.

The man shrugged his big shoulders and hunched again over his *Sun*, tapping the pencil to it. After some minutes of deliberation he was lifting the telephone receiver, to dial rather more quickly than he had before. "Red Planet," he said decisively, after a brief exchange of pleasantries. "The two thirty at Kempton. Two quid on the nose." A glance at Avery when the call was over, the ruddy face screwed up with the effort. "Are you a racing man, sir? If you'll forgive the question." He was tucking the pencil

106

behind an ear.

"Hardly."

"A real good 'un, Red Planet. You mark my words. A near certainty, as certain as they come. A quid or two mightn't come amiss if you fancy chancing your arm."

Was that a hint? On second thought, almost definitely not. That heavy hand was back on the telephone in readiness. Avery politely declined the invitation, getting up to stretch.

"He won't be coming and that's a fact," the gardener said.

Avery resumed his seat, crouching forward to stare with profound boredom at the scuffed woodblock floor.

The clock hand jerked to 11:25. Christ, was that all? It seemed like two o'clock, at least. Avery decided it was time to make his move.

"Look," he said, walking to the counter, "something's obviously gone wrong. You can see that. Don't you have his home number here, or his address? He gave them to me but I've left them behind. How was I to know the guy wouldn't come!"

The man shook his head ponderously. "That's as may be."

"I really ought to call, to find out what happened. It won't keep till Monday, that's the problem." Avery leaned over, lowering his voice. "It's an important defense matter, I can't stress that too highly. Britain and America. NATO."

"Couldn't help you even if I wanted to," the gardener said, still shaking his head. "I've only got the internal numbers. What would I be doing with home numbers?"

"Back home they keep a list at the gate," Avery challenged. "In case of emergencies at the plant. Christ, you never know when you're going to have to get hold of a guy in a hurry."

"Not here, sir," the gardener said phlegmatically. "That's not our way. Oh, no."

"But there must be a list *somewhere* in the establishment!"

"I dare say. But not here, not with me."

"Your internal list, then. May I see it?" Avery was already reaching for the directory.

"It's classified," the man snapped, banging his hand down over it. He could move surprisingly fast when he wanted to. "How many people work here, the names, that's all restricted information."

"What's *your* name?" Avery demanded sternly.

"Roberts, sir. Constable Roberts." From habit, the man stood stiffly to attention as he said it.

"Very well, constable, tell me about this." Avery grabbed for the telephone, lifted it bodily and shook it under his ripening strawberry of a nose. "Are private calls allowed on this? Are you allowed to make wagers on duty? Like hell you are!"

"Now just a minute . . ." the gardener mumbled, his cheeks deepening to scarlet. A network of fine veins throbbed darkly across them.

"A trade, that's all I want," Avery said more quietly and put the telephone down. "A quick look at the staff list for D Branch. Christ, what harm will that do? I was up there with them yesterday! A trade, and I'll forget I ever heard of Red Planet."

The man just stared lamely for a time then

108

wandered away, hands clasped behind him, to his peephole window overlooking the entrance. "The weather's holding up," he said over a shoulder. "The running should be good up at Kempton." He stayed there, assessing the sky and presenting his broad back.

It only took a moment for Avery to find what he was after. All the women in D Branch were clearly listed as Miss or Mrs. And only one had the initial V.

Avery strolled to the door. "Kempton?" he said. "Never heard of it."

There was a phone booth not far from the fort, just along the road toward London. Avery looked in the Sevenoaks directory for *V. ASHTON*. He found a single entry, with an address in the town. There was no way of knowing whether the subscriber was male or female. He dialed the number.

"Hello?" The answering voice was timid. The kind of voice he could well imagine coming from a wisp of a girl, a girl with a body like a rake.

"Hallo?" she asked again.

"Is that Valerie? Valerie Ashton?" The question was asked with some trepidation.

A slightly puzzled, "Yes."

"My name is Gardner. You won't know me."

"What do you want?" She was instantly on the defensive.

"It's about this Franklin business."

There was a long, troubled pause and when she finally spoke the words tumbled out in a rush. "I can't tell you anything I haven't already told the others."

"I'm sorry but it's important. I've got some questions of my own."

109

"Can't it wait?" she pleaded. "I'm feeling all washed up, exhausted by the whole affair. Don't you people understand? Why can't you leave me alone? Why?"

"I'm sorry," Avery said again, but very softly now. "I'm afraid it really won't keep. I'll come over now, if you don't mind."

8

Mayfield Avenue was not the smartest street in Sevenoaks, not by a long shot. Avery drove down it slowly, searching for number 43. Behind crumbling brick walls with a brow of bedraggled hedges, the houses rose like unwelcoming chapels. They would be turn of the century, he guessed, in yellow brick long since gone muddy and with a smattering of carved stone to dress up the windows. Steep steps climbed to forbidding arched doors with stained-glass panels. The high slate roofs pointed in prayer to the sky.

He parked some way on from the house when he found it, using a miserable porcupine of a tree to shield the Rover and its number plate from the door. Five bell pushes congregated under the porch amid a tangle of wires. From the one marked "ASHTON" a wire looped openly across the outside wall to the immediately adjacent window. The curtain there moved as he rang.

If nothing else, Major Colby had an accurate turn of phrase. The girl who came to the door was every bit as thin as he had described, quite remarkably so. Her creased cotton dress hung limply over a flat-chested body, and from the slanting hem legs like matchsticks dropped to slippers. She was without makeup or stockings, and a less likely *femme fatale* he could hardly imagine. Possibly, her normal appearance would be presentable enough, even pretty in an odd kind of way; all bright-eyed and with the chirpy attraction of a sparrow. Quite conceivably that had appealed to Franklin. Some men went over board for the skinny type. But right now the only sparrow she resembled was one hunched disconsolately in a downpour, and the face was white from lack of sleep, the brown eyes dead and red-rimmed.

"Marty Gardner," Avery said, extending his hand.

She took it with a sullen nod and ushered him without enthusiasm to a door just along a hall dingy in creams and greens. The flat they entered was small, little bigger than a bedsitter, and gloomy due to half-drawn curtains that she made no attempt to pull back. Nothing in the cramped living room was new. The carpet was certainly secondhand; so were the lumpy settee under the window and the two monstrous armchairs, which looked rock hard. A cane rocking chair filled a corner and the shelves behind it bulged from forays into what must have been every junk shop in the county: clocks, art deco statuettes, china ornaments and books with tattered covers. But they had all been restored with care and what he was sure must have been much effort. The chairs had been recovered in a tastefully bright fabric. The rocker was stipped to the wood so that the only remaining evidence of the thick varnish it had acquired over time was to be seen in the crevices of the curling arms. The clocks with wooden cases were sanded and waxed and the brass counterweights of another flashed proudly as it swung this way and that under a glass dome. To one side, he could see through a curtain to the shambles of a tiny kitchen. The sink overflowed with unwashed dishes and pans.

She waited silently as he inspected the room as if that were normal, to be expected of him. "You weren't here with the others," she said, finally deciding he must have seen enough.

"That's right," he replied.

"What has all this to do with the American's?" She cocked her head and he could see a glimmer of the perkiness, the lurking sharpness he had sensed at the door. "You *are* American?"

"Your name is Valerie Ashton," he stated very formally. "You are employed at the Royal Armaments Research and Development Establishment. You work on war games, in the Vulcan Command Room. All correct?"

She nodded listlessly. "Yes, but . . ."

"Then you deal with NATO weaponry, including U.S. equipment. Does that answer the question?"

"I suppose so. Please forgive me, I just had to ask."

"Of course. May I?" Avery motioned with his head to the settee, since she showed no sign of inviting him.

"I'm sorry, go ahead. It's just that I'm dog tired. I don't mean to be rude."

"I promise not to take a minute more than I have to." Avery chose a corner of the settee, opened his wallet to the notepad at the back and produced his pen. The girl sat rigidly in a facing armchair, her hands gripping the thin knees so tightly the knuckles showed white.

"Well?" he said. "Tell me about it?"

"What part? What more do you need to know?"

"Let's start at the very beginning, shall we? When did you first realize he had gone?"

"On Thursday night. Bob dropped me off at the fort that morning. He went on, he didn't say where. When I returned here after work he wasn't back. And when he still hadn't shown by midnight . . ." She dropped her head into her hands.

"But you didn't report him missing till yesterday. Not till nearly lunchtime." Avery was guessing, from what he had observed at the fort, but when she raised her face to him he could see he was right.

"At first, I thought he'd gone back to his wife."

"At Godden Green," Avery interposed quickly.

"Yes. His suitcase was gone, you see, and his toilet things. What else was I to think?"

"But then . . . ?" Avery prompted.

"Later, during the night, I went through what he'd left behind. Just being sentimental, I suppose. It all looked so final, you see, him dropping me at the fort gates and taking off like that, not even saying good-bye. There was no blazing row, nothing to drive him away in a temporary huff. He was simply gone. So I went through his drawers." Her eyes flickered to a door by the kitchen alcove. That would be the bedroom in there. "It took me a while to realize it but his passport was gone. That frightened me."

"You still took your time reporting it," Avery pointed out. "You didn't let on first thing in the morning. You didn't turn up at the fort. You kept quiet for several more hours. Why?"

"I just did, that's all. I was upset, in a turmoil. Do I need more reason than that?"

Avery gazed inquiringly at her, chewing on his pen in his best investigative manner. That caused her to glance furtively away.

"What else was gone?" he asked quietly. "What papers did he take?"

She agonized before admitting, "His files. His technical notes. But you know all that."

"Including material on Vulcan?"

"Yes. How many more times do I have to go over it!"

"Here?" Avery said, trying not to show his astonishment. "He kept notes like that *here?*"

"Oh for heaven's sake, be realistic! He was simply conscientious. There was no more to it than that. Bob cared about his work. He did a good job at the fort and he couldn't simply pack his bags at five and drift off to the local like the others. So he sometimes put in extra hours here. He never brought back any classified material, just the odd few notes on parts of the system he was specially interested in."

"All right," Avery said. "So you finally got around to reporting his disappearance."

"Yes. I finally did, as you put it."

"To the security people at the Establishment?"

"No, to the branch superintendent, Bob's boss. *He* notified security. I thought you'd know that." There was a sudden trace of suspicion in her manner.

Avery glanced down, importantly making notes in his little pad. "Keep going," he said brusquely.

"He ordered me to sit tight. Not to go out, even to

114

the shops. To touch nothing and talk to no one. Not till Special Branch came."

"And what did they have to say about the missing papers, the Vulcan files?"

"Exactly the same as you. What were they? What had he taken with him?"

"And they didn't believe you either, did they, Miss Ashton? They didn't accept your story about there being no classified information her."

"Well . . ." She was staring fixedly at the floor.

"Well they didn't, did they?" Avery shouted at her. She cringed so helplessly at that, raising her hands to cover her ears, that he hated himself for doing it. He hated how easy it was to do.

"You know what I told them," she answered feebly, bending forward to pick a match from the carpet. "There was nothing here with a classification higher than restricted. He didn't keep secret documents here." She lifted her head to meet his eyes defiantly. "Well, he didn't. He would never have broken the ministry rules, not Bob."

"Only bend them a bit," Avery retorted.

"They all do from time to time at the fort. Who doesn't, when it suits them? But his intentions were good, I promise you."

Something in her voice told Avery she was telling the truth. At least, the truth of what Franklin had led her to believe.

"All right, Miss Ashton, I'm convinced," he told her gently. "What did they do next?"

"The flatfeet? Took me through all the usual background, as they insisted on calling it."

"Bob's political affiliations?"

"Yes."

"The evening meetings he went to? What newspapers he read?"

Her eyes locked tight and she nodded her head silently.

"And you told them what, Miss Ashton?"

"Oh, for goodness' sake!" She leapt up, waving her hands about in exasperation. "You bloody well *know* what I said. Do we have to keep on and on and on?"

"I'm only doing my job," Avery insisted.

"I'm sorry," she muttered, clasping the hands before her as if they had life of their own and needed restraint. But her feet remained their own masters. She couldn't keep still. "Look, would you care for a drink? Or coffee?"

"Coffee would be great, thanks."

She pushed through the curtain into the minute kitchen. "My God, look at it," he heard her say. "Just look at it. I'm in a mess." There was the sound of a running tap.

He followed, holding the curtain aside. "The affiliations, Miss Ashton," he reminded her.

"Oh, yes, the bloody affiliations." She made him wait while she finished filling the kettle, cleared a space for it on the cluttered counter beside the sink and plugged it in. "He reads the *Guardian* and the *New Scientist,* as every good boy should. He doesn't give a stuff for politics, not two hoots, left or right or center. He doesn't go out secretly in the evenings. He doesn't meet men in trenchcoats under station clocks." The galloping flow of words stopped as she fished distractedly in the cold, gray sink water for two mugs which she ran under the hot tap. They were then

116

merely shaken before the instant coffee was spooned in. "All he does . . . did, is stay here and talk to me, or watch television, or lie on the bed and do calculations half the night. Bloody homework for the same ministry that's now hounding him. Have you got all that down, mister? In your little book of clues, I mean?" She jerked around, her eyes blazing and a vivid tinge of red smudging the otherwise deadly white cheeks.

"Take it easy," Avery said.

His outstretched hand was brushed aside with a shudder. "Don't! Please!"

It seemed wise to retreat to the settee. Behind the curtain, the girl was slamming cupboard doors, carelessly moving jars, dragging open a drawer.

"When did Bob move in?" Avery asked in a conversational tone.

"Here?"

"Yes, here."

"Twenty-third of April," she recited. "God, that's not even six bloody months, is it? I always predicted it wouldn't last a full year out. I had an instinct about it, a premonition."

"Why was that?"

The curtain billowed out as she swept back in with two steaming mugs. Avery's she placed by his elbow on a small carved table. She then resumed her chair, sitting more alertly than before, even showing a trace of interest as she gazed over to him. Being alone for a short time, having a simple chore to occupy her mind, seemed to have worked wonders.

"Why?" she echoed, brushing a trailing lock of hair from her forehead. "I'll ask you a question for a

117

change. Have you ever had an affair, Mr. . . . ?"

"Gardner."

"Well have you, Mr. Gardner? Have you ever had a bit on the side?"

"Let's say yes, for the sake of argument."

She threw back her head for a hollow laugh. "For the sake of argument," she mimicked sarcastically, now swaying her head to taunt him. "You people! In the back of your car, was it? In your place or hers? In a sleazy hotel room? Or should I say *motel* room?"

"What are you trying to tell me?" Avery asked, suddenly concerned by the wildness in her face.

"It doesn't matter where, do you see," she replied with a drooping resignation. "An hour here, an hour there. That isn't enough once it gets serious. You want more than a quick grope followed by an apology for the impending departure into the night. And it's never because the wife is waiting, is it? There's always a plausible reason, a clever excuse."

"I know," Avery murmured sympathetically.

She sipped her coffee in silence, staring with sad, wide eyes at the rising steam. "Before he finally moved in here," she said then, "Bob learned to joke about it, about his reasons for pushing off. He had to go by midnight or his car would turn into a pumpkin, that's what he used to say. He almost had me believing him, too." She laughed thinly, still watching the steam. "Suddenly one day he was out there, on the doorstep with his case. I was so happy I can't tell you, over the moon." The last of the coffee was gulped down and she lifted wistful eyes to him. "Except that *I* was the wife then, in all but name. Entitled to the regulation once-a-week grope and no more. You don't think of that in advance. Well, did you ever think of that, Mr. Gardner, in the sweat and passion of your motel room? For the sake of argument, I mean?"

"Oh, yes," Avery said. "I thought of that."

"Clever you." She struggled to her feet from the hard depths of the chair, starting toward him. "More coffee?"

"Thanks, but I'm fine."

"Do you mind if I do?"

"Go ahead."

She darted back into the kitchen and the kettle began to rumble. A cupboard door banged and a spoon rattled against china.

"Where is he now?" Avery called.

Her head pushed through the curtain. "You tell me! You're the people with a man at every airport, with half of Interpol examining every bloody incoming passport. How the hell should I know, sitting tight here!" She withdrew abruptly, to reappear shortly with the mug steaming once more. This time, she perched on the arm of the chair, propping herself against the back.

"Where do you *think* he is? That's what I meant," Avery explained. "You must have a theory."

"Does it matter?" she spat, rearing her head.

"It just might. I'm prepared to hear you out, anyway."

She studied him closely, biting her lip, before answering. "Look, I've been going with Bob for close on two years," she said, leaning forward to demand his belief. "He lived here for five of those months. I know him, Mr. Gardner. I know him better then any of his so-called friends up at the fort and far, far

119

better than those flat-footed twits from Special Branch. No, I don't know where he is, but I know where he *isn't!* He isn't in bloody Moscow. No way is he in Moscow. I'd have suspected if he was planning a move like that. Defection, my eye! I'd have seen it coming a mile off."

"But you didn't, did you," Avery reminded her quietly.

She could find no reply to that, gazing glumly into space. He felt it was time to leave; he had learned all there was to learn. She perked up considerably as he got to his feet.

"Have you a photograph?" he asked. "One I can take with me?" He imagined that to be the correct line, the way intelligence men ended a session like this.

She pointed to a crammed mantelpeice over the gas fire, where a circular mirror hung above a funereal clock in black marble. "I did have, over there." He could see a space where he guessed it had been. "Batman and Robin took it."

"*Who?*"

She was still capable of a wan smile. "I don't remember their names. The fearless duo who came yesterday to take the place apart. The insensitive bastards!"

Placing her mug on the floor, she stood, straightened the flimsy dress and then drifted over to the fire to check her face in the mirror, pulling the cheeks down with bony fingers to stare into the eyes. "God, I look like something the cat dragged in. You woke me when you phoned, did you know that? I didn't get an ounce of sleep last night."

"I'm sorry," Avery said genuinely.

"I've got a photo album in the bedroom. I'll see what I can find for you."

"I'd be grateful."

She went through the door next to the kitchen, leaving it half open, and Avery could just see into a tiny room almost filled by the unmade bed. Silly young fools, he thought. How could they ever have believed an affair could survive a room that small, a flat this cramped? She was right: it hadn't stood a chance from the moment Franklin moved in. He would have gone sooner or later, espionage or not.

The small photograph she handed Avery was a typical holiday snap, poorly composed and slightly out of focus. A young man in rugged hiking clothes posed somewhat self-consciously against a tree. There was water in the background and a large pleasure boat cruising past.

"That's Windermere," she explained. "The Lake District. It was taken last year on what is euphemistically called a stolen weekend."

Avery peered closer, giving a sudden start. The face, what he could see of it, was strangely familiar, and yet not.

"Was Bob at Oxford?" he asked, frowning as he tried to place it.

"No, London University. Imperial College."

"But was he *ever* at Oxford, even for a short while?" Even as he asked he realized the man was too young to have been there during his year.

She shook her head, looking puzzled. "I didn't know him in his student days. But no, I don't think so or he would have said. Why?"

Avery pushed behind the settee to the window, to see the snap in better light. "Haven't you got a better picture?" he muttered, racking his memory. "This is dreadful."

"It is rather."

Avery froze at that, then swung round on her, glowering fiercely. She had sounded altogether too pleased, too emphatic in her agreement. "Don't play games with me, Miss Ashton," he bellowed, waving the snap under her nose. "Digging up the most godawful shot you can find! You can do better and you damned well know it! I want the most treasured photo you've got. Crisp and clear. Or do I have to search that bedroom for myself?"

She went very limp, as though all the life had drained from her body. "I'll see what I can find," she said mechanically, her eyes quite dead again.

She was back almost instantly with a larger photograph; too quickly to have needed to hunt far. "I asked Bob to get it done for me," she said, thrusting it into Abery's hands. "I'm lousy with a camera." Then she moved away to fuss with the clocks in the corner.

Avery turned the picture this way and that, staring intently at the face. It was a well-lit and stiffly composed studio shot and as he regarded it closely the memory started to crystallize. He put a hand over his eyes to hold it. "Hell, yes," he murmured as it all came back to him, and he shook his head and dropped the hand. The girl had a handkerchief in her hands now and was dusting the domed clock, but she was watching him anxiously with veiled eyes.

"Let's go back to Thursday morning," he said in an

ominous tone. "Let's go over that part one more time. He dropped you at the fort?"

"Yes."

"And then what? He went on where?"

"I haven't the faintest."

"And you didn't think to ask!"

"No, why should I!"

"Sit down, Miss Ashton," Avery ordered roughly.

Meekly, she obeyed, twisting the handkerchief in her hands.

"I'm not Special Branch," Avery said thunderously. "I'm not flat-footed and I'm not fucking stupid. *Where did he say he was going?*"

"For God's sake, how many times do I have to tell you? I don't know. And I'll thank you not to swear, not here, not in my house."

"Then I'll tell you where, shall I?" Avery said, bearing down on her. "To Quantek, that's where. To Swindon."

"How did you . . . ?" She stopped in the instant, glancing away and wishing she had bitten her tongue off.

"We're better informed than Special Branch," Avery said softly. "Let's leave it at that."

"Yes, you're right. He went to Quantek. But that's all I know and that's the truth."

"He went there to see Dr. Corrigan, right?"

"Yes. At least, that's who I think he said."

"How many times before had he been there?"

"Never, and that's the honest truth, so help me," she said, looking up at him pleadingly. "He had no reason to go to Swindon. If there was any matter to take up with Quantek it was always done at the fort.

123

The ministry foots the bills, don't you see. Let the damned contractor come to us, that's the attitude. But never Dr. Corrigan. I've never seen him at RARDE, not once."

"Then why did Bob go to Swindon on Thursday?" Avery demanded. "The very same day he vanished off the face of the earth! Tell me that, Miss Ashton? The suspense is killing me."

She drew herself up and stared up at him with a suddenly summoned composure. "This may come as a surprise to you, Mr. Gardner," she said evenly, "but I do not live, eat, and breathe war games. Bob does, but I do not and I have no wish to. There was a house rule around here. No talk of Vulcan at home. No gossip about the people at the fort. No chat about computer programs, nothing like that. If two people work together and live together one of them at least has to draw the line, to drop the shutters when the shop closes. Can you get that into your thick skull?"

Avery gave her a slow, understanding nod of the head. The sentiments had a ring of truth and came from the heart.

"*Intelligence* people!" she said scornfully. "That's a bloody laugh! Oh, yes, he dropped me off. Yes, he told me he was going on to see Dr. Corrigan. But no, I didn't ask what for. And shall I tell you why? Because I didn't bloody give a damn. I didn't *want* to know."

"Okay, okay," Avery said, holding up a hand in submission. "I believe you."

She was moving decisively to the door, feeling in command of the situation after her outburst. "And now, if you're quite finished . . . ?"

Avery paced over to her. "I can see what he saw in

124

you," he said, bunching a fist and striking it gently against her cheek. "You're a real fighter. I hope you get him back, truly."

Her eyes went suddenly moist. "I hope so too," she said in a choking voice.

Outside, there was a game of cricket in progress in the road, with a bald tennis ball and a carton for a wicket which the wind insisted on shifting to disconcert the bowler. Avery stood at the top of the steps, raking the parked cars. None were occupied. No men waited against lampposts or lurked behind the hedges. Nothing looked other than normal, than dully suburban.

If you're going to play this spy game, he told himself, you'll have to get smarter. You'll have to learn to look *first*.

Reaching the Rover, he placed the key in the ignition but just sat there, not yet switching on. The memory came flooding back again. Hurst bursting in through an office door. That big Irishman, Corrigan, behind the desk with challenge and perhaps even hate in his eyes. And a young man with a visitor's badge turning to see what was happening. The face in the photograph.

And where are *you* now, Dr. Corrigan? Avery wondered. One minute you're in that office with Franklin, the next instant you're both gone. Christ, have you fled the coop too?

9

From its commanding position at one end of Chilton Folliat, the Hurst place, Bridge House, kept a benevolent if squirely eye on the village. The road shied away from its high gates to hump over the stone arches from which the house took its name. The bridge spanned a river full of swaying tresses of reed and fat trout, which wended its unhurried way on to Hungerford.

It was a country seat in the true sense, a gracious Regency residence. It seemed taller than it was wide, giving an upright look, an undeniable air of superiority. The roof had the unevenness of age and the mellow walls were resonant with history and ivy. Through the dusk, light fanned from every window onto the broad drive, glinting on the Rolls-Royce strategically placed for best effect in front of the portico. Another car, a big Ford, was parked in the shadows.

There was a double-height hall, a living room known as the library, a dining room and a breakfast room, but Avery was disappointed to hear there was no luncheon room, although in fine weather tea could be taken in the Greek folly in the garden known as the summer house. There was a fine galleried study reputed to be by Robert Adam, a smoking room, a snooker room, a three-car garage and extensive wine cellars. The house needed not one kitchen but two, the largest in order to cater for the frequent dinner parties of twenty or more. Then there were the ten bedrooms, the majority with dressing rooms and bathrooms *en suite*, the sauna and the gymnasium with solarium. Apparently there were also other rooms too numerous to name, or unnamed, or as yet undiscovered after three years' occupation. Outside, the terrace overlooked a swimming pool, an ornamental pond, a tennis court, a rose garden, and lawns as smooth as a billiard table sweeping down to the river with its hundred yards of fishing rights, the whole extending to some three and a half acres. Much of this Avery learned from Hurst before he was even out of the hall and the rest was to emerge during the evening. It was said not in any obvious display of ownership but as a helpful introduction for the first-time visitor, with just enough supporting history to make it bearable. It was, Hurst remarked in an aside as they entered the library, difficult to know quite what to do with it all, modern living being so intrinsically *compact*. Avery expressed his sympathy at the problem.

Tonight was clearly to be an intimate affair: only two others waited in the enormous room. Hurst introduced his wife, Halina, a pleasant, rather plain woman in early middle age whose husky and seductive French accent Avery found to be easily her most redeeming feature.

"And this is George Ballantine," Hurst said, taking him to the roaring fire, where a stocky, balding man of some fifty or so years stood warming his back. "He's a big noise in the Ministry of Defence, a man of some influence. His friends call him an old war-horse, don't they, George?"

Ballantine responded with a neutral grunt and shook hands with a grip so viselike that Avery took a second look at the short, pot-bellied figure, wondering where the strength came from.

"He's one of my clients," Hurst said in a stage whisper. "That's why you'll see me shamelessly buttering him up over dinner."

"That'll be the day," Ballantine said.

"It really is decent of you to give up your Sunday evening like this," Hurst said. "To be perfectly honest, I had an ulterior motive in asking you over. George was one of the defense committee that drafted the original specification for Vulcan. The idea is for you to pump him dry on how the final product turned out. To take up references on us, as it were."

"That's fine by me," Avery said.

"Vulcan?" Ballantine said, shrugging his shoulders. "It's neither the best system I've ever seen nor the worst."

"And here I am fondly believing you're a friend," Hurst said, not seeming especially bothered by the lukewarm comment.

"Going to be around long, are you?" Ballantine asked.

"A month, I think," Avery said.

"It took us a year to decide what we wanted the blasted system to do," Ballantine said. "And then Quantek were another two years developing it. If you can come to grips with three years' work in a single month of poking around, I'll take my hat off to you."

Avery was handed a scotch on the rocks and guided into a deep armchair. Ballantine continued to hog the fire. Hurst chose to sit cross-legged at his wife's feet, looking like a guru in his white cotton trousers, white shirt without a collar and white moccasins worn without socks.

"How's the visit been so far?" he asked.

Avery regarded each of the men in turn. There had been no mention of a missing defense scientist in the Sunday papers, not even a brief item tucked away on an inside page, and he had bought every one. "Intriguing, if nothing else," he replied, choosing his words with care. "A drama in two acts. In Act One, your Dr. Corrigan vanished before I so much as met him."

A hearty laugh came from the man by the fire. "Think yourself lucky, Mr. Avery! He damned near wrecked a meeting room at the ministry a couple of years ago. At the start of the Vulcan contract, if I remember rightly. His idea of making a negotiating point was to smash a chair against a wall. I kid you not. So now he's *persona non grata* at our hideaway in New Oxford Street. They won't have him through the door, and who can blame them!" Seeing Hurst scowl, he raised his glass in appeasement. "Don't take it to heart, Peter old man. You still got the contract, didn't you? That must say something about our opinion of Quantek."

"Is he all right?" Avery asked. He watched Hurst especially as he added, "I couldn't help wondering, with him vanishing into thin air like that."

"Patrick?" came the carefree answer. "Gosh, I should imagine so. He never seems to disappear for long."

"Worst bloody luck!" Ballantine murmured, and he drained his glass and began to gaze longingly at the drinks table.

"You said *two* acts," Hurst noted, looking apprehensive. "Does that mean there's more bad news?"

"For Act Two, the scene switched to Fort Halstead," Avery said. "I was in and out of the place with barely time to take a breath."

"Really?"

"I was bundled out. I'm getting the distinct impression I've wandered into the wrong play."

"Is this true, George?" Hurst demanded. "Don't your colleagues down in Sevenoaks have any manners!"

"It's no use glaring at me like that," Ballantine said, wriggling his backside against the blaze. "And I think *bundled out* is coming it a bit strong. There was an unavoidable change of plan, that's all."

You bet there was! Avery thought.

"The people at the fort had no choice, do you see? When the order comes down from our masters, ours is not to reason why. There was an urgent need to assess some plunder, that's what they told me."

"Plunder?"

"Treasure from the East. Information from a well-wisher."

"Maybe, but I got the distinct impression there was rather more to it. I sensed a problem just as I left."

"That doesn't surprise me a bit," Ballantine replied distantly, his eyes hopefuly back on the drinks. "War gaming is like that, dashed unpredictable."

"What sort of problem?" Hurst asked. "Something you saw obviously bothered you."

Avery decided to back off. "I can't put my finger on it," he said. "It was no more than a feeling."

"But about *what?*"

Avery simply spread his hands. His probing was

130

evidently leading nowhere: Hurst seemed genuinely baffled and Ballantine was totally unperturbed.

"I'll tell you what," Hurst offered. "We'll have a return engagement as soon as possible. George, when will they be fit to receive visitors again at the fort? When will this silly cloak of secrecy be lifted?"

"Soon. No more than a week, I should think. I'll give you a shout."

"Don't take their rude behavior personally," Hurst said to Avery. "They won't let any of my staff in either, when they use Vulcan for the big-league games, not even the people who developed the bloody thing! Christ, they won't even let *me* in!"

Ballantine was now blatantly holding his empty glass up, turning it against the light, looking with mournful glances from it to the bottles displayed on the table by the wall. But Hurst chose to ignore the hint. "George, what exactly do you get up to behind those locked doors? Total destruction of Europe?"

"Don't be so melodramatic, old man," Ballantine answered, with an air of finality that said the subject was closed.

Far away, the doorbell sounded and Halina held up a chubby wrist to peer at her watch. "Late again!" she snapped. "I told you he'd be late!"

Hurst jumped to his feet and kissed her lightly on the forehead. "Be nice if you can," he asked, taking her hands. "As a favor to me, huh?"

No sooner had the door closed behind him than Ballantine was scampering for the drinks table to fill his glass to the brim. He took a long, grateful draft then beckoned Avery with a jerk of the head and strode to the far end of the library, well away from where Halina continued to sit, pretending not to notice.

"Do you really want my opinion of Vulcan?" he asked in a conspiratorial tone, standing close.

"Naturally."

"I wasn't prepared to voice it with Peter Hurst in earshot. Why? Because I've no intention of making the man even more insufferably bigheaded than he already is. Nice bigheaded, mind, but nonetheless bigheaded for all that."

He looked out of place and ill at ease in the grand room, like a policeman drawn by duty into intimidating surroundings. His suit was modest and overdue for replacement, going baggy at the knees and with the seat noticeably shiny as he had walked ahead. The tie was soup-stained and probably regimental. The uncommonly sharp eyes, set deep in dark hollows, gave the lie to the general appearance. One could all too easily be fooled into taking him for a simple, bluff Englishman, Avery decided. He was almost certainly a *shrewd,* bluff Englishman.

"I can sum up what I think of Vulcan in three quick points," he said. "First, there's nothing like it anywhere else in the world. Not over the Pond where you come from, nor the other side of the Curtain. Second, it does exactly what we expected of it. Quantek has done an outstanding job, absolutely first rate. Third, and this is the important point, experience so far is that Vulcan will enable the army to evolve strategies they never before believed to be feasible. That's the acid test, Mr. Avery. Is it going to change this country's appoach to a future war? And the short answer is yes."

132

"Can you give me an example?"

"Of a new strategy?"

"Yes."

"In other words, what were they doing at the fort on Friday? You're busting a gut to know."

Avery laughed. "Yes, I guess that's the question."

"Then you can easily guess my answer!"

"But what you've just said is also the official ministry view?"

"Straight down the line."

"Then I'll pass your comments on to Larry Brokaw at Northridge. They're most encouraging."

"I'm glad to hear it. This poor little land of ours needs all the foreign earnings it can get."

Ballantine downed the rest of his scotch, smacked his lips and headed back for more. Avery returned to his chair by the fire, to receive a friendly lecture from Halina on the varied past adventures of the room and the problems of finding craftmen willing to restore its elaborate plastered ceiling. No one wanted to work anymore, not these days.

The door flew open with a crash and Corrigan was framed there, in an ancient creased dinner jacket and a black tie worn over an ordinary striped shirt. He seemed even larger, if it were possible, than on first sight in his office at Swindon. Halina cringed as the door rebounded from the paneled wall. Seeing the Irishman, Avery almost choked on his drink.

"A state visit, that's what it is," Corrigan announced with a low, jesting bow. "A state visit to bloody Toad Hall." He swept over to the fire with Hurst fussing behind. "And who have we here?" he boomed, narrowing his eyes to survey the gathering. "Ah yes,

Toad himself." He looked down his nose at Hurst. "And the little Mole over there." He blew a kiss to Halina, sitting with a stern expression, in her plain black dress. "And Badger, of course." This to Ballantine. "Where would we be without Badger to complete the trio? Long time no see, George. Still snuffling around in those dark, secret tunnels of yours?"

Ballantine confined himself to a grave nod.

"You *are* going to behave tonight, aren't you, Patrick?" Halina said with concern. "We can't afford you when you don't."

"Since when was there anything *you* couldn't afford, darlin'," Corrigan retorted, wafting her another kiss. He then inched toward Avery, bending close with curiosity. "And this, now? What would this one be? Friend or foe?"

Avery introduced himself solemnly, still getting over his surprise at the unexpected arrival.

"I've heard of you," Corrigan responded, giving Avery a hard shove in the chest. "The Quiet American, no less. The man of whom it was said: they also serve who only sit and wait." He held out a huge hand. "Pat Corrigan. The villain of the piece."

"For God's sake say it," Hurst urged. "Let's get it over with."

Corrigan bent even nearer. Close to, his face resembled the surface of some distant fiery planet: red and cratered, with the dark hair clawing its way through like undergrowth to mat into the heavy beard. "I owe youse an apology," he said, "that's what the fella's trying to tell me. I shouldn't have stood you up last Thursday. I offer my deep, my humbled and

134

my sincere plea for forgiveness. No offense meant, Mr. Quiet American."

"And none taken," Avery said, to make the peace.

"I only invited Patrick to apologize," Hurst said. "It was the least I could do in the circumstances." He glanced craftily at Corrigan as he added in another of his stage whispers, "He knows damned well he'd never be here otherwise."

"All right, you've had your pound of flesh," Corrigan said, pushing his way to the fire to warm his hands with much rubbing. "The deed's done and the Hursts can sleep easy in their beds again." He inclined his head to speak into Ballantine's ear. "The fella just sat there, George, that's what my girl said. Just sat outside my office not saying a bloody word and me long gone. Jesus Christ! Where's the Glenmorangie, Peter? Let's have a toast to patience. It's a rare virtue in these troubled days."

Hurst exchanged frowns with his wife. "I thought you were back on the wagon? Siobhan promised me you were."

"Tcha!" Corrigan swung round, jostling Ballantine. "That was yesterday! Today's the Sabbath." He made a lopsided sign of the cross.

"Just a small one, then," Hurst said with reluctance, and he went hesitantly to the drinks table. But Corrigan hurried after, to tilt the bottle and fill the tumbler to overflowing. He raised it to Avery, splashing whisky onto the carpet. "To patience and forgiveness."

Avery smiled weakly and lifted his glass in reply. Corrigan finished his drink in two rapid gulps and twisted back for more.

"Patrick!" Halina protested.

He peered over a great shoulder, pointing skyward. "It's the Sabbath, Halina my dark beauty. The Lord's resting up there and won't see a thing. And I'm not likely to tell him."

The dining room was a pavilion. Through a slender framework of arches against the walls, trees and ferns could be seen on all four sides, in a medley of greens on silk. A willow-pattern lake washed to the windows and herons rose in a flock to the ceiling. A tablecloth that Halina said was nearly one hundred and fifty years old provided a perfect foil for Georgian silver and Spode china. The lace was delicate and pure white except at Corrigan's elbow where it resembled a bandage over a violent wound. Corrigan had just spilled his burgundy, his fine drop of buggery as he insisted on calling it, and he was getting drunker by the minute. If he *was* a spy, Avery thought, it was only a matter of time before he gave himself away in his increasingly wild speech. He watched the man avidly, waiting, barely hearing the irrelevant dinner party conversation of the others as they strove to ignore the antics.

Ballantine finished gnawing on a pheasant wing which he had held to pick to the bone. "If I were at home now," he said to Avery, "I'd be eating chicken. And that's if I were lucky." He licked his fingers and put his head to one side in silent question.

"And I'd probably be making do with a McDonald's and a thick shake," Avery told him.

Corrigan contributed a belch and to Halina's distress uprighted his toppled goblet and proceeded to

136

refill it.

"Wealth's a wonderful thing, isn't it, Mr. Avery?" Ballantine said with a sly glance across to Hurst.

"It has its place," Avery said.

"Peter's got too much fucking wealth," Corrrigan spluttered as he drank. "And here's my struggling with the mortgage."

"On a damned big house, I might say," Hurst snapped.

"Now ignore him and listen carefully, Peter," Ballantine said. "What I was leading up to is this. One of these fine days I'm going to jack it all in at the ministry. I'm going to kick over the traces and start a business of my own." He winked at Avery to enlist him in the joke. "Follow your excellent example and become a gentleman tycoon, that's what I'll do."

"You don't say," Hurst remarked coolly, cupping his chin in his hands.

"Making military systems, naturally," Ballantine went on. "Selling overpriced kit to underpaid cretins like me. There's no better way to make a quick bob or two."

"Quite," Hurst said, now pursing his lips.

Corrigan stared blearily across the table at the man from the ministry. Halina began surreptitiously moving the wine bottle out of his reach while his attention was diverted.

"D'you want my advice, Badger?" he said. "Forget the military market. Forget the crappy British army and their crappy little war games. I'll tell you where the real money is going to be. In home computers, that's where. In tiny machines so cheap everyone will have them by the ton. In the living room, to play

137

with. In the kitchen, for perfect meals without having to raise a finger. For a share of the profits, I'll advise you how to go about it. What do you say, Badger? Do we go into business together selling cheap little computers?"

"I wouldn't dream of poaching you from Quantek," Ballantine said sarcastically. "Where would they be without you!"

"Now hear me out, Badger Ballantine," Corrigan said. "Your friend Toad here had the bright idea of pushing me into a corner called technical development. Out of harm's way, wasn't that the idea, Peter? Well, I haven't been idle in there. I haven't been pissing your money into the wind like you keep telling me!" He thumped the table. "We're taking Quantek into home computers, that's what my research says we must do."

"You already know my opinion on that subject," Hurst said flatly.

"Do I indeed!" Corrigan glowered and his chair creaked as he rocked back to delve deep into a trouser pocket. "Where is the bugger?" he muttered, feeling around. "Don't get excited, darlin'," he said to Halina, "it's only this." The result of the search was held high, concealed in a bunched fist. "So, we're supposed to just sit back and let the opposition carve us up, are we? Well this little fella is about to make every bloody piece of hardware on our factory floor obsolete." Now he tossed the object onto the table in front of Hurst. It was encased in plastic and the size of a small cigarette lighter, with a bank of minute electrical connectors at both ends. There was a fraught silence, with Hurst staring daggers at

138

Corrigan and Ballantine prodding the device as if it would bite.

"You can't stop progress," Corrigan snorted at length, and he rose to grab the wine bottle. After filling his own goblet he made an uncertain progress around the table, topping up the others.

"*Please* be careful!" Halina squealed.

"It's a microprocessor," Avery told Ballantine. "We use exactly that model in our office systems."

"I'm not *totally* uninformed on technology," Ballantine protested.

"Clever little fella, isn't it?" Corrigan said, slumping back into his chair. "A computer with a built-in memory. As small as that and costing as little as fifteen dollars in the States. If Peter would give me my head I could have Quantek turning them out by the million in a few years' time. I could get the manufacturing cost down to a matter of pence. Pence, Badger! Think of all the things you could do with a little fella like that."

"It's going to be a cutthroat business," Hurst said wearily. "Let someone else take the risk. If we need micros, we'll continue to buy them in just like now. We'll stick to what we know best, okay?"

"Defense systems!" Corrigan sneered. "Jesus bloody Christ!"

"That's what pays our salaries, Patrick," Hurst said, turning his face in disgust to the ceiling. "That's what keeps your mortgage going." Avery had the impression that his hands, which were hidden by the tablecloth, were tightly clenched.

"You're a bloody fool," Corrigan said, struggling to his feet. The glasses and cutlery rattled as he leaned across to Avery. "Do I have your permission to leave the table, O honored guest? Too much talk and too little fucking common sense aren't my idea of a quiet Sunday evening!" The words were badly slurred.

Avery glanced to Hurst and received a mute nod. "You're excused if you wish, doctor," he said. "I'll continue to campaign on your behalf, shall I?"

"God save America," Corrigan said with a shaky salute. He stopped at the sideboard to tuck an unopened bottle of burgandy under his arm then swayed out of the room.

"That wasn't the drink talking," Ballantine declared with a sad shake of the head. "There's a man under severe pressure, if every I saw one. A volcano about to erupt."

"*About to . . .?*" Halina said, her eyes on the stained tablecloth.

"I'll have a quiet word with him tomorrow," Hurst promised. "Get him to take a few weeks off in the sun. It won't be the first time." He looked over to Avery, resignation written on his face. "I'm sorry about all this, Martin. It was a ghastly mistake asking him. I should have know better."

"You never said a truer word," Ballantine muttered grimly.

"Don't worry about me," Avery said, with a strained smile to dispel the gloom. "I look on it as an education. I've always wondered about dinner in English country houses. Now I know."

Coffee was served in the library by a motherly cook who was warmly congratulated on the meal. Hurst produce a box of Havana cigars and the men sat puffing contentedly, gazing with full stomachs into the fire. It was like Lambourn, Avery thought, but larger and older and more opulent. The gilt-framed pictures on the walls were oils with the dark patina of time. There were many valuable books in the shelves that reached to the high, vaulted ceiling with its plaster stalactites. The fire strobed rosy light onto the burnished yew furniture. Corrigan was nowhere to be seen.

Hurst suddenly thought to look round for him. "Did you hear Pat's car, by any chance?" he asked the others.

"Don't!" Halina exclaimed, her hand flying to her throat. "He'll kill himself, sloshed like that."

"That's what he's hoping," Ballantine muttered under his breath. Hurst made as if to go to the door, but Halina leapt up to touch his arm. "I'll go," she volunteered quietly.

When she had left on the search, Hurst commandeered the fire, standing much as Ballantine had done earlier, drawing silently with closed eyes on his Romeo y Julieta.

"You're from California, I gather?" Ballantine said, turning to Avery.

"Yes, Los Angeles."

"Where the sun always shines."

"Well, when it can penetrate the smog."

"All I've seen of the States is Washington. I've been there twice. No, I lie, three times. I've never made it to California, but not for want of trying." Ballantine shifted in his chair to laze an arm over the back. "It's full of crazies and strange sects, so I hear?"

"We seem to have our share of them, yes."

"Then you'll be thoroughly used to displays like tonight's, I dare say. Used to men high on drugs or alcohol who think they can change the world?"

Avery merely swayed his head in agreement.

"I wouldn't hold it against Peter Hurst, not if I were you. One bad apple doesn't mean the whole blasted basket is rotten, does it?"

"I'll reserve judgment," Avery promised. He looked up to see that Hurst had discreetly presented his back while Ballantine made the apologies. There seemed to be something in his hands, undergoing close scrutiny. It was suddenly dropped into the flames, to flare briefly and explode with a subdued *pop* like a dud firework. The microprocessor? Avery wondered. He couldn't remember Corrigan taking it and he was sure it hadn't still been on the table when they left the dining room.

"Peter!" Halina was standing in the door, her face pale and strained. "I think you'd better come."

Hurst went to her without a word. Ballantine got up to follow, crooking his finger excitedly to bid Avery to join in. "Drama," he whispered in passing. "I smell death or damage."

With the men close on her heels, Halina hurried across the high hall and through a facing door. They crossed an anteroom full of buttoned leather chairs, which Avery assumed to be the smoking room, and stopped in a huddle just inside the room beyond. It was spacious and shadowy, with a look redolent of the twenties: all mahogany panels and heavy velvet drapes. The only light came from the inverted trough over the snooker table, onto Corrigan as he lay slumped on the green baize, a cue in his hand and

142

muttering to himself. The cloth was ripped in several places as if slashed by a knife. There were snooker balls all over the floor. Hearing them enter, Corrigan staggered to his feet, took a wild swipe at the only ball remaining on the table and tore another gaping rip in the baize. Then he collapsed, out like a light.

"Oh, my God," Hurst said, frozen to the spot in horror. "Oh, my God, my lovely table."

"Out!" Halina shouted, jabbing furiously at the door. "He goes out of my house *now*."

"Never to return," Ballantine said in Avery's ear. "Want to bet, old man?"

Avery was staring at the wine bottle, which had fallen from the wooden rim of the table to dump its contents, what little had been left of them, in an ugly spreading pool.

Hurst finally summoned the resolve to uproot himself and stalk over to give the inert man a timid prod in the ribs. There was a groan but no movement.

"He can't drive," he said, shaking his head. "Not like this."

"Out!" Halina screamed. "Out!"

On a sudden impulse, Avery stepped forward. "Leave it to me, Mrs. Hurst. I'll drive him home for you."

"That's wonderful," she said with a sigh of relief. "I can't tell you how grateful I am."

"You won't, you know," Hurst said firmly. "Not with him like this. I won't allow it. If he wakes up in your car you'll *both* end up dead!"

Pulling back one of Corrigan's eyelids, Avery gazed like a doctor into a red-veined, unseeing eye. "The worst is over by the look of it," he judged. "It'll be quite all right, Mrs. Hurst. I won't take no for an answer."

"He lives just this side of Bath," Hurst said. "That's miles too far out of your way."

Avery folded his arms to show his mind was made up. "Get some coffee," he told Halina. "Black and very strong." A drunk man, he was thinking, could be easier to interrogate than a sober one. A damned sight easier . . . if he could be kept awake.

Ballantine was now doing his own medical examination of the bloodshot eye. "Bath, you say, Peter? Look, you won't know Bath, Mr. Avery. Why not leave the removal job to me? There's no point in putting yourself out. The man's hardly made your evening a pleasure as it is."

"Where are you staying?" Avery asked pointedly.

When Ballantine made no reply he repeated the question to Hurst.

"Here with us," Halina said, when her husband also maintained an obstinate silence. "Just for the night."

"Then it's crazy for you to go out specially, George," Avery said. "I have to drive back to Lambourn anyway." He turned to Hurst, his arms still determinedly folded. "Just give me directions to Bath, would you? Period."

10

Corrigan lolled in the passenger seat, breathing erratically and dead to the world. After some minutes of solo conversation, Avery swore and pulled in to the side of the road to open both front windows wide. Then he drove quickly to create a rush of cold, reviving air. A few miles farther on Corrigan stirred and let out a low moan.

"You're in safe hands," Avery said.

With effort, Corrigan pried open his eyes and stared, first at Avery, then around the car, then out into the dark blur of the passing countryside. "The man himself," he said dully. "The Quiet American, no less."

"The same," Avery said.

Corrigan thrust his face out of the window into the buffeting slipstream for a full minute. "Jesus Christ," he said, shanking his head furiously as he pulled it back in.

"Feeling bad?" Avery asked.

"Me? Never! I've got pure alcohol flowing in my veins." Corrigan tussled with the seat lever to force the seat back into the rearmost position. His eyes closed again and he curled up with a vacant smile, his shoulder against the door. "No one came to play," he complained. "Jesus but you're an unsociable bunch."

"You and Peter Hurst don't seem to get on," Avery said.

"Are you ever a perceptive fella!" Corrigan replied, slapping the side of his head hard to bring himself around.

"Why don't you?"

"Why don't I what, sunshine?"

"Get on with Hurst?"

"Because he's a prize fart. Tonight you have had the questionable privilege of dining with one of the world's great piss artists."

"Then why stick around?"

Corrigan's face contorted, going an even deeper shade of purple as he struggled to sit upright. "Because we are what is laughably known as partners." He finally gave up the attempt and slumped back.

"Then break the partnership," Avery suggested.

"And leave him with all the fool's gold! What have you got in that ginger head of yours, empty space?"

"Aah," Avery murmured, as he peered into the headlights for a sign to Marlborough.

"Did anyone ever tell you about the dog?" Corrigan tore off his dress tie to open his shirt to the waist. "A true-life shaggy dog story. That'll show you the kind of fella we're up against." He breathed deeply, smacking his exposed chest.

"What dog?"

"The notorious Alsatian. The . . . what do you Americans call them?"

"German shepherds, you mean?"

"Dear God, isn't that American all over," Corrigan said, with a beseeching plea to the sky. "Never use one word when two will do." He shivered and wound up his window. "Shut that bloody hole, for Chrissakes. You'll give me pneumonia." His arm pressed into Avery's face as he stretched over, trying to do it himself.

"I can manage!" Avery yelled, quickly obliging.

"He used to bring it into the office," Corrigan said with a toothy leer. "A great hulking brute of a dog."

"Who, Hurst?"

"Sure, Hurst. The Saint Francis of Swindon, who else! It used to lie there under his desk, slobbering from opening time to nightfall. Jesus Christ, who ever heard of a dog in an office!"

"So?"

"So it turns out to be a fucking wolf in disguise. Don't Alsatians look like wolves to you?" Corrigan shuddered at the memory.

"There is a resemblance, now that you mention it." Avery had turned at a crossroads after picking up the first sign to Bath. On the wider main road he could have traveled more quickly but he dropped back to an easy pace to spin out the journey.

"The bastard had a real go at me one day, sank its fangs into my ass. It bit my girl twice, once in a very private place. It even went for his own girl. Jesus, what a brute! She refused to go into his office after that. The only one it never took a hunk out of was holy Saint Francis himself. He finally had it put down, gassed to death."

"I'm not surprised."

"Aren't you indeed," Corrigan said with a sneer. "But it wasn't dispatched for eating people, that's the twist in the tale. How does that grab you for a denouement?"

"You've lost me," Avery said.

"We got up a petition." Shakily, Corrigan traced words with a finger over the car roof. "We the badly damaged undersigned are not prepared to be eaten alive in the course of our work. Was that heeded? The fuck it was! Dracula continued to lurk under the desk and half of Quantek lived in terror. Until . . ." He strained over to whisper in Avery's ear. ". . . Until it started to go bald. *Now* do you see?"

"Dracula you mean?"

Corrigan lurched back and gave a leaden-headed nod. "It started losing fur by the handful. It ended up looking exactly the wild thing it was. Like a . . . moth-eaten hyena. Then, ah yes, *then* the blessed Saint Francis finally consented to give it the chop."

"I presume there's a moral there somewhere?" Avery suggested.

"You bet your boots there is, sunshine. The bloody thing could have gone on till kingdom come, sinking its mad fangs into people, and Saint Francis wouldn't have given a stuff. But the moment it didn't look so pretty anymore . . . the moment it wasn't an *asset* . . ." With a long-drawn gargle, Corrigan sliced a finger across his throat. "The fella's nothing but show, that's what I'm saying. A bloody dilettante." The effect of telling the tale took its toll. He puckered his eyes tight shut and wedged himself between the seat and the door in an attempt to sleep.

"Tell me about Vulcan?" Avery asked, when a sidelong glance said it was now or never.

"What about it?"

"I'd just like your opinion."

"I am uninvolved in the enterprise, as they say. Off the project. Disinterested and disillusioned. Out in the bloody cold. Ask Saint Francis for *his* opinion, friend. He'll give you a rosy picture."

"But you must have views of your own! Hell, it's one of your biggest contracts! You're a director of the company, aren't you?" There was no answer and Avery turned to find Corrigan rapidly drifting back into a stupor. He swung the wheel violently to rock the car. "*Well, aren't you?*"

Corrigan's head struck the door post. "Whatsat?"

"Forget it," Avery said angrily.

"Vulcan is . . . just a succession . . . of board failures," Corrigan mumbled, as if talking in his sleep. "One . . . after . . . the other."

"And I suppose you're the only man on the board whose conscience is clear?"

"You said it, darlin'."

Avery stole another quick look. "And how about Franklin? Where does he fit in?"

"*Saint* Franklin?" Corrigan said in a puzzled mutter. His head dropped suddenly onto his chest.

Avery tried rocking the car again but to no effect. Corrigan slept, snoring loudly, all the way to Bath.

His big house was rambling and ugly, so ugly that it seemed successive occupants had given up the task of trying to make the best of it, letting it slip into genteel decay. The headlights picked out gray walls as welcoming as an institution and peeling brown paint on the woodwork. The gaunt turret pushed up to the sailing moon. Overgrown rose bushes straggled like barbed wire into the short drive, scratching the sides of the Rover as Avery drew in.

"Home sweet home," he announced with heavy irony, but Corrigan snored on. So he left the car to try the bell. A single light showed through the fanlight over the iron-studded front door. After some time a woman came, staring into the shadows at him and rubbing her eyes. She wore a robe hastily donned over a long nightdress.

"Mrs. Corrigan? Siobhan Corrigan?"

She nodded sleepily.

"I have your husband in the car. I'm Martin Avery."

She peered around him to the Rover and scowled. "Bring him in, then." Turning on her heel, she went through a door just along the hall. A light came on in the room there, brightening the drive.

"Thanks!" Avery said. Returning to the Rover, he slapped Corrigan's face hard, eventually managing to stir him sufficiently to get him into the house. The woman was waiting at the foot of the stairs as they struggled in, to show the way silently up to the main bedroom. With Corrigan snoring within moments of being laid out on the bed, Avery looked to his wife, who leaned mutely against the door. When she made no move to help, he shrugged and pulled off the shoes.

"Don't bother with the rest," she uttered curtly.

"I might as well while I'm at it."

"He'll neither care nor thank you," she said, promptly leaving the room. He followed her down to the living room. It was bright and clean, so spotless it looked almost as if no one ever used it; quite the reverse of what he had expected from the outside apearance of the place. The style was rustic and austere, more suited to a croft than a house in town.

Once in there, Mrs. Corrigan relaxed and her tense facial lines smoothed away. "You're most kind," she said. "Are you a friend?"

"In a way. We . . . met for the first time last week. I was with him at the Hursts' tonight."

"New friends are always the best." Her hands tucked into her robe pockets as she looked him over, her tongue lolling provocatively from the corner of her mouth. It was a very Irish face, he thought, open and honest, with wide green eyes that seemed far away even when they turned on him. She was quite wrong in that house. She should be out in the meadows of Kerry or gazing the day long at the Atlantic breakers. Her voice rose and fell in soft cadences.

"Can I get you coffee to see you on your way?" she asked. "I can't offer anything stronger." The thin shoulders twitched. "We don't keep any here. You probably can guess why."

"I prefer coffee anyway. Hot and black." He took a severe-looking chair as she went to busy herself in the kitchen.

"I hope you don't mind me saying this," he remarked cautiously when she was back with the tray, "but your husband seems to be under some strain."

She met his gaze squarely. "Are you being helpful or plain rude?"

"Just making a friendly observation, Mrs. Corrigan."

"Strain?" she said, rolling it around her tongue. She said it once more, listening to the sound. "Yes, that could be a polite word, now I come to think of it. I'll try it out on the man himself over breakfast."

"Is it recent?"

She gave a strangled laugh. "Since he and Peter Hurst started that blessed company, that's how recent."

"But worse lately, perhaps?"

"He hasn't touched a drop in over a year, if that's

what you're after. If you ever mean to be an old friend, don't judge him by tonight's performance."

"He started again on the stuff on Thursday," Avery guessed. "Am I right?"

She sat, to stare ahead as she thought about it. "Yes, very likely. He was back late. Or was that Wednesday? Anyway, there was one night when he was back after midnight and much the worse for wear. But what business is it of yours, pray?"

"None, I guess I'm just playing amateur psychiatrist."

She leaned forward, clasping her hands. "Are you with Quantek? God, I didn't think to ask and here I am spilling the beans on the man."

"No." He looked her straight in the eye. "I've nothing to do with Quantek."

"He ought to be out of that company, well out. It's no good for him. He could sell his share, come back to Ireland and get a good academic post at Trinity. That's what I'd like him to do. Oh, God, how I wish he would."

Avery oberved a respectful silence as she gazed absently into space, presumably constructing a better future.

"Do you know a Bob Franklin?" he asked then.

"No, who would he be?"

"Just a guy. Has Patrick ever mentioned him?"

She sucked pensively on the rim of her coffee cup. "No, I don't think so."

"Not even on Thursday night?"

"Not even then."

Avery finished his coffee and prepared to leave. "I'd better be off, Mrs. Corrigan. You should be back in bed."

"Siobhan, please. If you ever come again, call me Siobhan."

"Agreed." He smiled warmly and pointed to his empty cup. "Have plenty of that on hand in the morning, huh?"

She tilted her head back for a peal of laughter. "You really don't know him, do you!"

"Hardly at all."

"He has a constitution of an ox. That man will be up again within a couple of hours, no more, and looking none the worse for his adventures. And then while I'm sleeping soundly he'll be over in his nursery as usual, playing through the night." Seeing that Avery hadn't understood, she drew him to the window on the garden side of the room, pulling back the curtain to point out. *"That's* the nursery. He doesn't like me calling it that." In the darkness he could just discern the outline of a hulking outhouse, perhaps old stables or a studio. "The man keeps his toys there, all his gadgets. She threw him a questioning glance. "Are you in computers?"

"Not exactly. My line is office equipment."

"Tell me now, is that a mad business too? Do *you* have to let off steam by playing like a child?"

"I prefer grown-up games," he answered with a grin. "Would you mind if I looked?"

"Help yourself." From under the stairs in the hall, she chose a key from a collection strung out on a board, handed it over and gestured to the back door.

"Aren't you coming?" he asked.

"Would you just listen to the man! What would I be doing, traipsing around the garden in my night clothes at one in the morning!"

Blinking in the sudden, overbright glare of the fluorescent tubes angled against the roof, Avery found himself in a very high studio, some twenty-five feet square. The big sloping window was roughly painted over. Lavatory-white tiles covered the walls to shoulder height and above that the graying paint flaked and dusty cobwebs sagged from the rafters. The floor was stone flagged and his footsteps echoed as he moved in. He stopped short, turning slowly and emitting a low whistle at what he saw. It was an electronic fairyland, a playroom for an obsessive man-child. Against the walls, new benches were lavishly equipped with tools and jigs for component assembly. There were three separate minicomputer installations, one linked by a snaking tangle of cables to an electric train set laid out on a massive table in the center of the room. The computer obviously controlled both the signals and the many trains now immobile under the vaulted roof of the miniature terminus. Another computer was connected via an array of homemade printed circuit boards to a hi-fi amplifier and thence to a loudspeaker. He found the main switch and juggled the controls on the computer panel. The speaker hissed and crackled and the computer lights blinked insanely. He continued to fiddle and a strange, high-pitched tune suddenly issued from the speaker. After some bars he guessed it to be "The Rose of Tralee," relayed by the computer in a piercing, unnatural sound quite unlike any he had ever heard. Grimacing, he shut the system down. There was a great deal more equipment in the studio and its purpose was obscure on cursory examination.

Maybe they weren't just playthings! he thought with a start, and he searched under the benches, then looked up to the rafters, then tapped some of the stone flags with a screwdriver to see if they perhaps concealed an opening. *A transmitter,* he was thinking. Somewhere among all that hardware there was surely a transmitter? But if there was, it was well and truly hidden.

Siobhan Corrigan was waiting patiently in the hall, on a rush-seated wooden chair and now sipping a glass of warm milk.

"Satisfied?" she asked. "Have you had a good play too?"

"It's just about the best-equipped private laboratory I've ever seen," Avery said.

"And so it should be. The man spends enough of his hard-earned money on it."

"What does Peter Hurst think of his hobby? Half of those tools in there have *Quantek* stamped on the handles!"

"Peter? Tush!" She flapped a hand to show how little she cared. "It's no business of his and I doubt if he ever suspects."

"I thought you'd say that," Avery murmured.

"It's harmless and childlike, wouldn't you agree? But Peter Hurst would see it as child*ish* and there's a big difference. I don't think he'd understand, somehow."

"I'm sure you're right," Avery said.

11

Avery's temporary office at Quantek was plain and utilitarian: just a desk and two chairs, and a glass-fronted bookcase which had been cleared for his arrival and refilled with chunky reference manuals on Vulcan. Some texts on war gaming and land battle tactics had thoughtfully been included. The carpet finished the regulation twelve inches short of the walls, which declared it to be an office intended not for managers but for lesser souls. The window had a far from inspiring view, overlooking the parking lot and the gatehouse, and beyond that the road to the town center. Over the road, glimpsed between a row of warehouses in clumsily plain concrete and glass, were open fields rising to a hill spiked with spidery elms and the odd contrasting oak in full leaf. The main office block was close by, running at right angles to one side of the parking lot. Its mirrored widows were pale and blank, as if merely painted over, and seemed to reflect nothing very much.

Avery got there early the next day and set the door catch to lock himself in. Pushing both chairs to the window, he made himself as comfortable as he could, slouching in one with his feet stretched out on the other. The first to arrive was Hurst, ever the dutiful employer, not in the Rolls, which was presumably never flaunted at the factory, but in a Rover identical to Avery's. He stopped in his marked space right next to the main entrance and walked briskly in. Some quarter of an hour later, just before nine, a procession of cars lined up at the barrier for quick scrutiny by the guard, and weekend adventures were exchanged in the open air before the drivers dispersed their various ways to the sprawl of buildings. Then came the late stragglers, parking in haste and untidily, to head away at a trot. When men were late, Avery noticed, their briefcases weren't carried by the handles; they were tucked under the arm, often with a raincoat bundled over them to add to the general look of Monday morning disarray.

Corrigan came last of all, a little after nine thirty. Driving yet another of the ubiquitous Rovers, he barged into the reserved space next to Hurst's, squealing to a halt only just short of the wall. He dug behind the seat for a battered case but then, being Corrigan, didn't hurry off like the others. He took his time by the car, stretching languorously as he gazed about, around at the buildings and up to the sky, sniffing to test the weather. There wasn't the slightest sign of a hangover.

Avery went to the bookcase for a selection of manuals and returned to his vantage point at the window. Keeping a wary eye on Corrigan's car, he spent almost two hours in rapid passage through the books, sketchily adding to his knowledge of Vulcan. On occasion he felt a dawning fascination at the methods Quantek had adopted to make the war games as true to life as possible. But each time he resisted the temptation to delve deeper, his attention always drifting back to the Rover. Somehow, he was sure, Corrigan would decline the period of leave Hurst had promised to impose. If, that is, Hurst would choose to say anything at all about the previous night; in the cold light of day a further confrontation would almost certainly not be to his liking. And the assumption seemed to be correct. Mid-morning came and went and still the Irishman had not emerged from the building.

Shortly before noon, Avery snapped his fingers on a sudden inspiration, jumping up for his folder of company contacts. The main list was no help but there was an appendix entitled "Other Areas of Interest" and a short search revealed that the optics division was headed by a Mr. J. Garston. Avery dialed the internal number and the secretary put him through.

"I'm over here for a few weeks, evaluating Vulcan," he said, after introducing himself.

"Talk of the devil," Garston said chirpily. "Mr. Hurst's memo on your visit is in front of me at this very minute."

"Am I right in assuming that your division handles the Bush Baby project?"

"Absolutely."

"Peter Hurst gave me a demo last week. I was very impressed."

"If only every Monday started with flattery! You've made my week."

"I was wondering, Mr. Garston, is there any chance you'd be interested in a U.S. license? I think that little toy of yours would go for a bundle back home."

"That's for the marketing boys to decide. My job stops with the finished goodie, Mr. Avery. No glamorous lunches, no juicy commission on sales. It's the story of my life."

"But what's the possibility? Can you say?"

"At a guess, marketing will jump at the idea."

"That's what I hoped. Look, could I possibly

borrow one to play with for a while? I'm not an optics expert, but if it still seems as good the second time round I'll alert the right people back in California."

Garston clicked his tongue dubiously. "You'll have seen the Mark Two, I imagine?"

"If that's the latest version, yes."

"All the prototypes are with the ministry and the army, I'm afraid. Can it wait a few weeks?"

"I'll be long gone," Avery said.

"Then how about an obsolete Mark One, to be getting on with? I'm up to my ears in the things."

"Does it have the spectral frequency feature?"

"Absolutely. The main difference is that it weighs a lot more. It's a beast to lug around, frankly."

Avery allowed himself to be persuaded. "I don't want to hassle you," he said, "but can I have one now?"

"Not to use off the premises," Garston pointed out sternly. "We'll have to go through a whole rigmarole if you want to cart it off somewhere. Bureaucracy gone mad, if you ask me."

"Then I'll have to test it right here, won't I?"

"Done. Tell me where they've parked you and I'll send a technician over with one straight away."

Through the glasses, as if behind a screen of muslin, Corrigan sat with his back to the window, tapping a pencil on his desk and gazing steadily at the opposite wall. For half an hour he did nothing else, and apart from the nervously ticking hand he was virtually motionless. Was he plain worried? Avery wondered. Or making plans? Or just sweating out a thumping headache, bravely hidden from the world? His

159

secretary brought in aspirins and a coffee but they were left untouched, the coffee growing cold as the preoccupied thoughts continued. There were no visitors and he made no telephone calls. Suddenly, he shook his head vigorously like a dog leaving water, lumbered to his feet and turned to the window to stare out. He stood there for some minutes, looking straight over to where Avery sat watching, or so it seemed. At first, the relentless stare made Avery flinch, momentarily doubting the protection of the mirrored glass. *Was* the damned window mirrored? He hadn't thought to check from outside. But then he eased again as he saw the empty expression on Corrigan's face, as close in the magnified image as if he were standing only inches away. The man wouldn't have noticed him even if there was plain glass in that window! He simply stood there with a slack stance, frowning and vacantly staring out, a hand drumming a tense rhythm on his side. Boy, are you ever a troubled guy, Avery thought. What did you tell Franklin last week? Or more to the point, what did he tell *you,* sunshine?

In an instant, Corrigan was spinning away, rummaging in a drawer for his car keys, snatching up his case and dashing from the office with a rough slam of the door which shook the pictures on the wall. Stopping only to conceal the Bush Baby in the deepest drawer of his desk, Avery made his own quick exit to the parking lot. Even as Corrigan turned onto the road, his tires yelping under fierce acceleration, Avery was backing out in pursuit.

By the time he cleared the barrier, there were already two other cars between him and the fast-

160

moving Rover. He edged out over the center line to keep his quarry in view, but stayed well back, happy to be hidden. "Just like old times," he murmured with a private smile.

All four cars slowed slightly for a crossroads, increased speed again to travel in loose formation to a roundabout and then Corrigan began to draw rapidly clear, driving wildly in the direction of the nearby highway. Avery leap-frogged the Citroën ahead of him and tucked in behind a Ford Granada. With the Rover still pulling away, he closed up on the Ford, waiting his chance to pass, but a line of oncoming cars forced him to cut back in and he cursed as the Rover was lost around an approaching bend.

"Move it, move it," he said uselessly to the Ford. That made it slow down if anything, its brake lights flickering as it took the curve at an unnecessarily cautious pace. The driver wore a hat and drivers with hats always took bends too slowly. They did *everything* with infuriating slowness—Avery knew that. It was British folklore. He flashed the car to hurry it but the man in the trilby responded by throttling back even more.

There was a gap in the stream of vehicles coming the other way, not really enough to overtake in safety but Avery dropped a gear, swung out, scraped by the Ford and swayed recklessly back in the moment he was past.

The first of the oncoming cars swerved in fright and blared its disapproval of the maneuver. The driver of the Ford added his opinion with furious flashes of his headlights.

"Too bad, friend," Avery said, as he put his foot to

161

the floor to make up the lost ground. But now the Ford joined the chase, accelerating after him with the lights still signaling unspeakable oaths in Morse. Avery wound down his window and replied with a slowly wagging V sign, inverted to show his disdain. At that, the man instantly dropped well back, as if so offended he wanted no more part in the race.

"Damn right, too," Avery muttered through clenched teeth. "This is a man's game."

There was a nasty moment to come. The road unwound, to run almost straight for at least a mile, and the Rover was nowhere in sight. He took the car up to over a hundred, rode out the next long bend and breathed a hefty sigh as he made contract again. Corrigan's brake lights were glowing in the distance as he slowed for the wide rotary leading to the highway. Avery followed him onto it, heading west. Bath, he said to himself. The guy's going home. And that means the nursery!

Corrigan was moving like the wind, as fast as the Rover would go. But after only a few miles he suddenly braked hard and darted in from the outside lane. Avery could soon see why. Ahead, a roof-mounted cluster of lights betrayed a police patrol car traveling at seventy precisely, with a log jam of vehicles beginning to pile up behind it. So he braked too and cut into a space several cars back from the Rover. He was able to relax then and revel in the chase. He wasn't likely to lose the man now, not on a highway.

Corrigan screeched into his drive and let himself into the house. By day it was less ugly than Avery remembered but still desperately unattractive. Windows in a hodgepodge of shapes and sizes were scattered in haphazard fashion across the somber facade. A mess of pipes trailed like black spaghetti down beside the door. Two children's cycles lay where they had been dropped on the balding, dusty grass of the front garden. The battlemented tower looked to be an ill-fated attempt to turn the place into every Englishman's dream of a castle.

Avery parked a safe distance farther on and walked back slowly, casually glancing about to assess the lay of the land. He could see no other pedestrians and there was a lull in the light traffic that used the street as a shortcut to the center of the city. Corrigan's house was set well apart from its immediate neighbors but another, almost a reflection in its turn-of-the-century starkness, faced it across the road. No cars stood in the drive there but he had no way of knowing whether there might be anyone at home. Too bad, he thought with a shrug and, passing Corrigan's open gate, he ducked through a break in the limp front hedge. Somewhere, a dog barked. From the side of the house a high wall of crumbling brick took a wayward path to the boundary of the site. Halfway along it a tree offered the prospect of limited cover so he made for that, jacking himself up the wall with a foot against a low stump. He was just in time to see Corrigan going through the ungainly performance of unlocking the outhouse while simultaneously trying to balance both the briefcase and a plate of sandwiches. The door closed behind him and the only window, the big studio skylight, gave no view into the place. Brushing off the damp moss he had picked up in the scramble, he returned to the car to wait.

An hour later almost to the minute, Corrigan sauntered out, reversed from the drive and began to retrace his tracks, obviously heading back to the factory. Avery turned to tail him as before, keeping a good distance back now that he was sure of the route. It was a notably sedate trip this time, with none of the frenetic pace of before. Whatever the man had been up to in the studio had settled his nerves no end.

The Irishman coasted down the on-ramp to join the highway, keeping to the inside lane at a steady sixty and content to let the rest of the traffic stream past. Avery did the same, widening the gap to nearly half a mile. The tires whistled on the concrete highway and the engine burbled remotely. The wind slipped almost silently over the car, only hissing where it tussled with the outside mirror. There was a weak sun and the other cars, once past, sped ahead on a road as straight as a die, blurring and shimmering as they were gradually dissolved in their own haze.

He was vaguely aware of a BMW seeming to slow fractionally . as it drew alongside, with the front passenger glancing his way. It spurted and pulled in sharply just in front. The passenger turned in his seat to stare back, saying something to the driver. A heavy truck with a trailer began to thunder by. Without warning, the BMW's stop lights glared and it was barking fiercely, with black smoke pouring from locked, screaming tires.

"What the . . . ?"

In a pure reflex, Avery hit his brakes. Even as he did, he caught a glimpse in the mirror of another car right behind, bearing down fast.

"Shit!"

Blocked by the truck from swerving out, he went the only way he could: sending the car sliding sideways onto the hard shoulder, fighting to regain control as the tail wagged madly to either side. The BMW immediately swung across to shut the door on his intended way past. Then the car on his tail bobbed in, too, and as he skidded to a ragged halt it closed up to bottle him in. His hands began to tremble at the unexpected suddenness of it all. Angrily, he watched the Rover dwindle into the distance but instantly forgot it as the reversing lights in front of him blinked on and the BMW inched back until its bumpers locked against his. That done, the two men inside simply sat there, not moving, not even turning. Behind, a door slammed and he stared grimly ahead, tightly gripping the wheel, as someone approached, only the legs and ample stomach visible in the mirror. The man strolled up on the inside, one hand tucked in a pocket, as if intent on nothing more startling than to inquire the time of day. The side door clicked open and he slipped into the passenger seat.

"Do you mind telling me what this is all about?"

The voice was subdued and matter-of-fact. It was George Ballantine.

12

A favorite party game of the Averys' was an exercise in masochism known as Stoics. It was played regularly at Christmas and Halloween and on other occasions when the adults were of a mind to punish the children in the name of self-improvement. It was a game with no real rules to speak of except that a single cry of fright or pain was sufficient to cause the offender to drop out in disgrace. There were no winners, only the sometime loser, and the less said thereafter about him or her the better. The idea was for the children to disperse around the house and garden and then to scare one another if they could, in any way they could, or to inflict very minor injuries such as the classic move of "the pin in the ass." More serious attacks, such as might cause bruising or draw blood, were considered *infra dig*. There was no explicit rule forbidding them, it was more that the players were on their honor to show civilized manners. The point of it all? Well, it was said to be an excellent preparation for life: to instill an iron will against adversity and to help develop coolness in the face of surprise. Martin's father, Hamilton Avery, attributed at least one infamous courtroom victory to the youthful training. That had been the time that slippery eel of a DA, MacPherson, had sprung the eleventh-hour shock of a torn photograph found under the carpet in the defendant's car trunk. He, Hamilton, hadn't so much as blanched, as the tactic so obviously intended he should, but had launched an immediate poker-faced counterattack. The defendant had still gone down for fifteen to twenty but Hamilton hadn't been seen by the jury to turn a hair, and that was the crucial thing. Victory, he often said, was as much a matter of *behavior* as of actual outcome.

As for Martin, he hated the stupid game. When he was old enough to have an opinion worth heeding, he used to point out a possible consequence which seemed to have occurred to no one in its two-hundred-year history. It was, he suggested, as likely to send you through life in constant dread of being leapt on from every dark corner as to teach courtroom-style nerve; to produce a reflex covering of the ass with the hands at the first scent of danger from behind. That was dismissed as fanciful.

Whatever, there were times when Avery discovered in himself a steel resolve that surprised him more than the surprise that provoked it, although whether that was in any way due to his childhood cavortings in shady corridors and closets in Boston he never knew. Now was just such a time. His hands were suddenly steady on the steering wheel and he turned a deadly cold eye on Ballantine.

"In Act Three, the plot thickens," he said. "A bunch of lunatic cowboys force me off the road. Why didn't you settle for a friendly wave in passing, George? I'd have gladly stopped for you without all this stupid drama."

"I'm still waiting for an answer," Ballantine insisted doggedly.

Avery played dumb.

"You were tailing a director of a company supplying secret defense systems," Ballantine said. "And you're not a British national. I'd say an explanation is in order."

167

"Oh, that!"

"Yes, *that,* Mr. Avery."

"I could ask exactly the same of you, George. It looks like a case of great minds thinking alike. A single hunted bunny with two tails."

"Cut the comedy," Ballantine retorted, his mouth tightening into a singularly unamused line.

"I know what *I* was doing," Avery said. "I'd be interested to hear your reason for following our Irish friend." He narrowed his eyes to peer through the window and feigned disappointment. "Well, he's gone! Escaped from both of us. Now how the hell did that happen!"

"Let's get this straight. We were after *you,* Mr. Avery."

"You and the lone rangers." Avery inclined his head to the BMW.

"Dr. Corrigan noticed a strange car pursuing him . . ."

". . . A Rover," Avery interjected. "A Quantek Rover."

"One of thousands like it on the road! He tried to give it the slip but it clung like glue, that's what he said. Then, while he took a quiet lunch in the bosom of his family, unwelcome eyes intruded. Someone shinned up his garden wall to pry, if you don't mind." Ballantine's eyes were ablaze and he thrust his round, moon face close. "For Chrissake, man! Corrigan did the only thing he could: he raised a full-scale security alert. On Sundays, he can bust up every snooker table in town and I don't give a bugger. On weekdays, what he does and who takes an unnatural interest in him is of national concern. Got it?"

Avery turned away, trying not to show how foolish he felt. The BMW was still there embracing his front bumper but the men were now looking back at him with expressions of granite.

"It's all a misunderstanding," he said bravely, deciding to continue the smoke screen.

"Come now, you can do better than that!"

"But it is. When Corrigan arrived at the factory this morning, I assumed he'd have at least a word of thanks for me. Hell, I hauled the man off home in the early hours, George, you know that. Well, I'll be honest. When he didn't bother to make contact I got angry. Then later, around lunchtime, I got to thinking that maybe I was being too tough on him. It can't be easy to face a man who's put you to bed in a state like that. So I strolled across to his office for a friendly chat, to clear the air for him. His secretary told me he'd gone home for lunch. So . . ." Avery gestured the rest with a hand, smiling his innocence.

"Except that you didn't ring the doorbell in the usual way when you got there! You followed the traditional California habit of peeping over his wall. And when that got you nowhere you mounted a surveillance!"

"He was obviously working over sandwiches in his outhouse, so I decided to leave him alone." Even as he said it, Avery was aware how weak the explanation must sound. "I thought I'd nail him as he came out again. But he was off like lightning before I had the chance."

"Thirty-mile-an-hour lightning," Ballantine said in somber correction. "We were there too, by then."

"He was still too quick for me. I was in bed very

169

late, remember?" Blearily, Avery fanned his eyelids to add conviction.

Ballantine sighed his disbelief. "I know a tail when I see one."

"And you must see plenty, behind that desk at the ministry!"

"I've been around, laddie. Don't push your luck!"

"What you saw was Corrigan on his way back to Quantek," Avery said, sticking to the story. "And me behind doing the same. Two minds with but a single thought: a pleasant afternoon in sunny Swindon."

"Where *did* they dig you up," Ballantine said with a disgusted droop of the head. "Why couldn't they send over a normal analyst, a man who minds his own business."

"Admit it, George," Avery said cheerfully, "you're oversuspicious. I think last night's excitement has turned your mind. You're smelling trouble where none exists."

Ballantine regarded him in icy silence, pulling on his lower lip. Then he opened the car door and swung out his legs, leaning back to wag an admonitory finger. "You're a guest in this country, Mr. Avery, and don't you forget it. You're welcome to be as damned inquisitive as you like with computer listings and instruction manuals. But keep your nose out of private matters, okay? Drunk or sober, Paddy Corrigan's little odysseys are no affair of yours. Otherwise you're liable to have a door slammed in your face in the departure lounge at Heathrow. Got that?"

Avery made an acquiescent nod. "Loud and clear, George."

Without a further word, Ballantine marched back

to the passenger seat in the car behind and the driver started the engine. As if on a signal, the BMW went off like a slingshot down the hard shoulder, suddenly cutting clear across the highway through barely adequate gaps in the traffic, to disappear at high speed in the outside lane. Avery shrugged his shoulders sadly at the sight. "Cowboys," he murmured. "Nothing but a bunch of cowboys."

Ballantine's car was more circumspect. It backed away and the driver waited patiently, his signal lights flashing, for the road to clear. As it cruised past, Ballantine's head was down, intent on some notes he seemed to be making. The car trundled off in no great hurry, making no attempt to catch the other half of the posse.

"Well, how about that!" Avery exclaimed as he watched it into the distance. He had been too anxiously trying to avoid a collision to notice it properly at first, and then too engrossed with Ballantine. It was a dark red Ford Granada and the driver wore a trilby.

You were following him before I was, George, he realized. No damned wonder you blew your top when I suddenly got into the act. And since when did nice, portly civil servants with desk jobs spend their days the way you do!

13

Corrigan, it seemed, was a creature of habit. Waiting at the window, Avery watched him arrive in much the same thrusting manner as the previous morning, as late as ever. He came just on nine thirty, well after the main influx of staff. There was a similar ritual beside the car: a defiant stretch of the arms for anyone who might be looking, a yawn of boredom, a frown for today's sky because the clouds masked the sun, and then the same strutting entry to the building. Avery switched on the Bush Baby and trained it in readiness on the office across the parking lot.

Corrigan paused in the doorway, to toss his briefcase the length of the room onto the desk. It bounced, skidded over the surface and dropped slowly off the far edge. For that, he awarded himself a rueful thumbs-down sign. His secretary was promptly following him in with a steaming mug and as soon as it was safely put down he made a lunge for her bottom. She arched her back, twisting like a bullfighter to avoid the charge, and threw a solemn-faced comment over a shoulder as she beat a hasty retreat to the door. A pursed mouth from Corrigan as it closed, another inverted thumb and a shrug to tell himself he didn't care. He then settled at his desk to work at a frantic rate through the day's correspondence. Drinking the coffee with one hand, he sorted the papers with the other, scattering them about with what seemed at first to be total abandon. But a rough order soon became apparent as several untidy piles began to spring up all over the desk. Within minutes, he summoned more coffee with a prod on the intercom button and a barked order. Whatever he said to his girl as she brought it in produced a look of scorching severity and a second hurried exit. It was definitely not his day. Having drained the mug, he threw his feet on the desk and reclined back at what looked to be an impossible angle; he turned his eyes to the window and restlessly scanned the heavens as he spoke into a pocket Dictaphone. Then came several protracted telephone calls, with his hands thrashing the air and his face as mobile as if there were someone there to appreciate the emphasis his eyes and his brows and even, at times, his ears were meant to lend to the conversation. By now he was in need of yet more coffee. This time when his secretary came in he confined himself to a joke. She turned at the door for a tale of her own and he pounded the desk with delight, his head flying back for a roar of laughter. The coffee was gone in a few gulps and he reached again for the Dictaphone.

And so it went on—an everyday office routine writ large. Nothing done that didn't happen in a million other offices across the country, yet nothing done quite as others did it. Avery finally tired of the theater and put the Bush Baby down. He tried instead to interest himself in his books on Vulcan and battles, but that proved to be a short-lived activity. Very soon he was pushing his chair round to the window again, irresistibly drawn back to the office over the way. But when the glasses dissolved the reflective film he stiffened, crouching well forward as if to get closer.

"Damn," he said softly.

In the interval, Corrigan was a changed man. He was over at the window now, gazing out with the same

173

unseeing look of yesterday. After some minutes of that, he slumped at his desk, brushed a stack of papers aside and stared down. At anything in particular, or just at the blank desk top? Seeing only his back, Avery was unable to tell. What the hell had happened in those few lost minutes? Avery was furious that he had abandoned the watch right at the vital moment. Had there been a visitor? Had he called someone? Had someone perhaps called him? He kept the glasses in close-up on Corrigan and the man scarcely moved in an age.

"You're plain dumb!" he suddenly said, and he lowered the glasses to scan the windows of the office block without their help. From there he turned his attention to the stretch of road passing the gatehouse. Only some fifty meters of it was visible; the view was cut off to one side by the wing Corrigan occupied and to the other by the corrugated roof of the shack housing the service department. Raising the glasses again, he panned to the windows at the road end of the building. At the very corner of the top floor he found what he was after: the windows were small and set high, and just showing through them were the melamine partitions of a lavatory. But male of female? He kept watching to settle the question, his tongue clicking in satisfaction as a man's head came toward a window, turned about and sank from view.

Avery must have washed his hands three times before he was finally alone there. Then he went to the end cubicle and climbed on the toilet, to look out of the high slit of a window. The view of the road was even better than he had hoped. He was next to the end wall of a building that ran nearly to the boundary of the site, so the road passed almost below, stretching ahead for perhaps two hundred meters before being lost from sight behind a warehouse close to a bend. Toward the bend, parked cars lined the curbs to both sides—probably the overflow from the busy factories there.

"Good morning, George," he said contentedly. The nearest of the cars was a Ford Granada, facing the Quantek gate. The windscreen darkly reflected the sky and it was impossible to see whether there was anyone inside, but he didn't need to see. Ballantine would be waiting in there, and the man with the trilby. No doubt about it.

He tried to judge what the view would be from Corrigan's office. But no, the Granada would definitely not be visible; the roof of the service block got nicely in the way. And Ballantine, now he came to think about it, was surely too old a hand not to have thought of that. So what in hell's name *was* bothering Corrigan? Ask, Avery told himself. Why not ask?

He drove from the gate, heading in the opposite direction to the Granada, and took four right turns in succession, to rejoin the road well behind where it sat waiting. He left the Rover there, just after the turn, and approached with caution. The two men in the car had their heads down and were too involved with something between the front seats to see him come. Snapping open a door, he slid into the back.

"Do you mind telling me what this is all about?" he said with a grin, to Ballantine's astonished face. The man at the wheel was so startled by the door that he knocked over a miniature chess set, sending the pieces flying.

It was to be some time before Ballantine thought to do the honors and introduce the man with the hat as Mulholland, and Avery never did find out his first name. He was a thin individual of around thirty, with a cockney accent which he managed at times to hide. He was very nattily dressed in an almost white linen suit, and the hat wasn't exactly a trilby now that Avery could see it closely. It was soft-brimmed and in cream suede, and in a style sufficiently out of fashion to be back in again. A pair of dark glasses with thin gold frames protruded from his top pocket and as he leaned back over his seat, the first of the two to recover, Avery wished he had them on. The pale gray eyes held naked hate.

"Why don't you take a running jump?" he snarled.

"Now, George, is that nice?" Avery said. "When you did this to me yesterday I laid out the welcome carpet."

"Just piss off," Mulholland hissed.

"Let's get this straight, shall we?" Avery said, ignoring him. "Today, *I'm* following *you*."

At that, Mulholland puffed up his chest, squared his shoulders and showed every sign of leaping over into the back, but Ballantine stirred at last and put out a restraining hand. The pallid eyes flickered one more time over Avery before Mulholland twisted away in a sulk, sinking into his seat and pulling the hat brim well down over his face. A muffled obscenity drifted back.

"Look, this isn't your show," Ballantine said through his teeth. "Be a good lad and run along. Someday I'll tell you the story."

But Avery sat tight. "You lied to me yesterday,

176

George. You were after Corrigan, not me. And you're after him again now."

"I won't say yes and I won't say no. Where does that leave us?"

Avery put his head to one side and met the furious gaze with defiance. "It leads the three of us here, doesn't it? Waiting for the good doctor to lead us to Franklin."

Mulholland slowly pushed himself up to stare in awe over the seat, his hat suddenly askew. Ballantine lost his powers of speech again."

"Well, George?" Avery asked.

"Look, prick . . ." Mulholland started to say, but that brought the older man back to his senses. His fingers snapped, demanding silence, and he opened his door.

"A word in your ear, Mully," he growled. "A private word." His head bobbed toward Avery. "Do you mind? We won't be a minute."

"Be as long as you like. I'm not going anywhere."

Ballantine walked his driver a good distance along the pavement, where they argued, heads together, gesticulating at one another, with Mulholland constantly glancing in anger toward the car. The quarrel was quickly over: they returned slowly like strangers, a little apart, and Ballantine waited at the curb as Mulholland climbed back behind the wheel.

"Just *watch*, Mully," he ordered, pointing to the factory. Then he opened the rear door and sat beside Avery, jamming himself in the corner to take a long, hard look.

"I suppose there's no point in my saying Franklin who?" he finally said.

"Hardly."

"What else do you know?"

"Ut! Ut!" Avery said, with a firm shake of the head. "First, you're going to tell me about the Jolly Green Giant in there. I want to know why you're after him."

"Ut! Ut!, to coin a phrase," Ballantine said, and they sat staring in silence for a while, each willing the other to yield.

"There was a buzz from the front and Mulholland lifted a phone from the dash.

"Hold it!" Ballantine shouted at him. "Let's agree on this," he pleaded to Avery. "You find yourself a quiet corner for a few hours. What do you say? I give you my word I'll fill you in on the essentials later today. Over a cozy dinner, if that suits you. But let's leave it at this for the present. Corrigan has no connecton with Vulcan. For God's sake, man, you know that!"

Avery clucked his refusal again. "But *Franklin* has, George. He high-tailed it from the fort with a bagful of your precious secrets. If you don't want Northridge to suddenly lose interest in Vulcan, you're stuck with a passenger."

Ballantine resumed the cold, lengthy scrutiny before giving Mulholland the nod. The phone crackled and Mulholland said "Yes" several times and "Uh-uh," then another eager "Yes" followed by a closing "Out." He bobbed his head round, pushed up the hat, wrinkled his reptile eyes and gave Ballantine the kind of nod in return that Avery wasn't supposed to see, or to understand if he did.

"We obviously have some action at last," Avery said.

"There's going to be a meet," Ballantine confirmed with a regretful sigh.

"Corrigan and Franklin?"

"Correct."

"Guvnor!" Mulholland shouted, in protest at the admission. But Ballantine silenced him with delicate flicks of the hand, as if brushing off an insect. "Franklin has just called Corrigan," he explained, with a subconscious nod at the factory.

"With a time and place," Mulholland added from under the hat. "And they're going to have company they haven't bargained for."

Avery gestures at the phone. "Your communications are a bit slow, George. Corrigan had that call all of twenty minutes ago."

"You don't say," Ballantine murmured, sagging in his seat. His face betrayed a sudden veiled respect.

"Yet you were aleady here waiting before it happened. Well before."

"We were, how shall I say, expecting something of the kind."

"Like yesterday?"

"Correct again." The stare was instantly steely. "Except that if contact had been made then, you'd have blown it to high heaven with that harebrained driving of yours! And if Corrigan had spotted you . . ."

". . . Which despite what you said, he obviously didn't!"

". . . If he *had*," Ballantine continued grimly, "You'd be back home in the smog by now. Or sampling the delights of Her Majesty's hospitality. Take your pick!"

Avery folded his arms to fend off the threat. "Does Hurst know you tap his phones?"

"He's a defense contractor," Ballantine said with a wicked gleam. "He knows it can happen." Leaning forward, he rapped Mulholland on the shoulder. "How long have we got?"

"It's all set for one. And I'd guess it's just under the half hour from here, maybe a bit less."

Ballantine frowned over his watch, his lips moving in slow calculation.

"Which gives us an hour or so to kill," Avery said, to help out.

"What a life!" Mulholland muttered, and he sank deep into the recesses of his seat, propping the hat over his eyes.

"Do you play chess, Mr. Avery?" Ballantine asked, his smooth, round face lighting up at the thought.

"Now and then."

"Good at the game, are you?"

"So I'm told."

"Splendid." Ballantine rubbed his hands in anticipation. "Mully here is a dead loss. He delivered another sharp jab to the driver's shoulder. "Be a good chap and pick up those pieces. There's an international challenge match in the offing."

He was an excellent player, strong in attack and prepared to take risks. Somehow, Avery had expected it of him. He cornered Ballantine's queen, only to see it slide out to freedom by a backdoor route he hadn't noticed, and he was then totally unable to reconstruct how it had got there. Mulholland dozed soundly, oblivious of the battle.

"This is the only war game for me," Ballantine said,

moving a bishop to a most unholy position. "It's the oldest, you know, and still the best."

Avery agonized over his predicament. "Is it money or conviction?"

"The two bad lads, you mean?"

"Sure."

"One of each, would you believe. We're not certain yet but that's the way it looks."

"With Corrigan as the one they have to pay, presumably." Avery plumped for moving his remaining knight to threaten the queen again.

"Try again."

"Really? He talked a lot about money the other night. Seemed obsessed by it."

"He was *criticizing* wealth, Mr. Avery, not wanting it for himself." Ballantine bowed low over the chessboard. "Frankly, they baffle me, people like that, stupid men who think they can create the world they want by slipping the Russkies the odd secret. I mean, I can understand the other thing, selling what you know for money. Does that surprise you? Shock you, even? I see it as a straight barter, no complications, no high expectations. It's probably a damned sight less damaging to the nation than the big-time tax dodging we all turn a blind eye to. But as for men who betray their country for some half-baked political ideal . . . they're the worst kind, the dangerous ones. They're the ones who can screw up the balance of power and not even know it." He hovered his queen before dropping her in the sanctuary of a corner heavily guarded by his two rooks.

"And which country is he supposed to be betraying, George? Corrigan's Irish."

"That makes it worse," Ballantine said with profound gloom. "They've lived off us like leeches for centuries. And what thanks do we ever get from them!"

Avery thought it best to leave that little local difficulty alone. He gazed down to the board, then sharply back to Ballantine. One of the rooks that now saved the queen from certain annihilation had been two squares away only moments ago. He was sure of it.

There was a buzz from the front of the car, too quiet to be the telephone. Mulholland started slightly then wriggled his way up the seat, fiddling with his wristwatch to turn off the alarm. The three men tensed and stared in mutual silence at the distant gate. From somewhere, Mulholland had produced a pair of folding binoculars and he aimed them to examine the cars leaving the site. A siren blast heralded the lunch break and a steady stream began to issue, some heading away, the rest passing them with never a second glance. Mulholland churned the engine, cocking an ear to see if the idle note was to his liking. Barbara Young drove by in a scarred Renault, liberally caked with mud that seemed to have been left there in preference to the dents and scratches that would otherwise have showed.

"That's his secretary," Avery said.

"Good man," Ballantine murmured.

14

It was almost a repeat of yesterday's chase but faster. Considerably faster. Mulholland slid the Ford tail-out through a chicane, barely keeping pace with the Rover.

"*Steady*, Mully!" Ballantine said, clinging grimly to his passenger strap.

The road unkinked and far ahead Corrigan was hopping past a goods van, to be lost from sight as he pulled in beyond it. Mulholland bore down fast, hugging the tailgate and waiting his moment to follow.

"I'm going to lose the bugger," he complained. "He's got a liter more than us." He made a sudden break for it, forcing an oncoming motorcyclist onto the shoulder to avoid a collision.

"The saints preserve us," Ballantine muttered, covering his eyes.

"I get a distinct feeling of *déjà vu*," Avery said.

Mulholland half turned with a victorious smile. "That's this game all over," he threw back. "Always the bloody same. Half the time we're sitting around doing nothing, watching other guys doing nothing. Then, when the action comes . . ." His fingers cracked. "They've got cars with more damned poke than we have." He floored the accelerator on the long straight run to the highway.

"And the game is what, exactly?" Avery asked, a subversive edge in his voice.

"Keeping the country safe," Ballantine said.

Without seeming to slow, the Rover charged onto the elevated rotary over the highway, cutting right across the bow of another car.

"Is it Bath, George?" Avery asked. "Is that the rendezvous?"

"Use your head, man!" Ballantine retorted.

"He won't be going anywhere much, if he doesn't watch it," Mulholland said.

With the Rover heeling over, Corrigan ignored the first ramp, circled on past the westbound ramp and kept going, to emerge the way he had just come, traveling straight back toward them.

"What the. . . ?" Mulholland exclaimed, instantly easing off.

"Keep rolling," Ballantine ordered. *"And get your bloody face down!"* he yelled at Avery, pulling roughly at his jacket to drag him to the seat as the Rover shot by.

They made the same full circuit of the rotary and turned back onto the road to Swindon. The Rover was stationary a quarter of a mile along, its inside wheels propped on the shoulder.

"Pull over," Ballantine said.

"Here?" Mulholland queried. "It's bloody exposed."

"Here!"

The Ford was bumped over the curb and onto a grass bank, to come to a halt close in to a fenced wood. They could still just see the Rover around a clump of trees. And that, Avery observed, meant that Corrigan could surely see them too, if he had a mind to glance in his mirror.

"I thought you said it was a half hour's drive," he said.

"This isn't the place," Mulholland said angrily.

"Then what is it?"

"Can't you shut this twit up, Guvnor?"

"Just cool it, would you?" Ballantine requested, quietly but firmly. He took the opportunity to return to his seat at the front and the first thing he did was to fasten the seat belt, pulling it very tight. There were no belts at the back.

"The glasses!" he said with an outstretched hand, and Mulholland retrieved the tiny binoculars from a cubby under the dash. Ballantine homed in on the Rover and then tried the road, turning to check behind them for good measure. There was a single house in sight, set close to the road not far beyond where Corrigan waited and he examined each of the windows in turn before giving judgment with a baffled shake of the head.

"We're sitting ducks," Mulholland said.

"So?" Ballantine asked harshly. "What do you suggest we do?"

"Nothing, Guvnor. Nothing."

They sat in strained silence for a full five minutes, with Ballantine expectantly aiming the binoculars at every passing car in case any signals were exchanged. Avery could see only Corrigan: simply sitting there, his unmoving back betraying nothing, in just about the most open position he could possibly have chosen. The Granada was none too far behind, there for all to see despite Mulholland's attempt to use the cover of the trees. He could detect not the slightest flicker of interest from the drivers who sped by.

"Something stirs," Ballantine said suddenly. Avery peered around the hat, to see Corrigan taking advantage of a break in the traffic for a squealing U turn. The next moment he was roaring past, back to the highway.

"Crazy!" Mulholland said.

"Don't you believe it," Avery said. "We've just been rumbled."

"Well, what are you bloody waiting for!" Ballantine bellowed, slapping the dash in his impatience. "Move it!"

"He'll get stopped," Mulholland predicted in a tone of despair.

"The boys in blue will have him." The Rover was a rapidly dwindling speck in the distance, moving at something approaching a hundred and twenty. The Ford was losing the battle, at full stretch with its speedometer needle wavering just over the hundred mark.

"You've got the place staked out, of course?" Avery said.

Neither of the other men responded but Ballantine perhaps wriggled a shade uncomfortably at the suggestion.

"You're kidding!" Avery said in amazement.

"Back home, you'd have a full motorcade on the job, I suppose!" Ballantine countered.

"How should I know? But yes, I guess so."

"We'll get the bastard," Mulholland muttered. They were on a downhill section and he somehow succeeded in wringing an extra five miles an hour from the engine. His mouth was determinedly set and his hands tugged on the wheel to urge the car faster. He wore black leather driving gloves Avery hadn't noticed before, perforated across the backs. At some stage, most probably as they sat waiting, he had donned his dark glasses.

Mulholland gave no signal that he intended taking the service road. Without warning, he sliced between two trundling trucks and then stamped on the brakes as they careered into the narrow, curving entrance to a service area. The sign said the place was Leigh Delamere. They had seen no trace of the Rover in at least three minutes.

Like a stalking tiger, he cruised the crowded parking lot, taking each of the ranks in turn, his eyes darting beadily to either side. He stopped abruptly at a white Rover to stare at the number plate, gave an exasperated sigh and resumed the search. As they turned at the end of a line to double back, headlights flashed from a stationary BMW with two men inside.

"You're a habitual liar, George," Avery said, clicking his tongue in rebuke.

"Maybe," came the retort, "but I'm not the fool you take me for."

"*Voilà!*" Mulholland said, nodding his head to a Rover, abandoned at a crazy angle across two parking spaces.

"Get well clear, Mully," Ballantine said. "And I want line of sight into that building."

Mulholland found a handy observation point not far from the entrance to the cafeteria.

"Glasses . . . ?" Ballantine said. When he had them, he avidly scanned the big windows. Avery could see a row of fully occupied tables behind the windows and what looked to be a line at the counter beyond, but little else.

"Aah," Ballantine murmured. "One large Irishman. Very sober. Sitting alone and with his head going like a Yo-yo every time someone comes in."

187

"The condemned man ate a hearty meal," Mulholland said, easing back into his favored slouch, with the hat tipped over his brow. "Motorway coffee and raw fingernails."

"What does Franklin drive?" Avery asked.

"Ride, more like," Ballantine answered. "A Kawasaki. But since it presently resides in a police pound at a certain airport, forget it." The binoculars were forced on Mulholland, who grudgingly sat up again to take over the watch. "Another quick game of chess, Mr. Avery?" Ballantine suggested, with an inviting twitch of the eyebrows. "I fancy we have a wait ahead of us."

"I'm not up to your tactics, George," Avery said diplomatically.

Ballantine sighed. "Pity."

"I think he's sussed you," Mulholland said. "And a bloody sight quicker than I did."

"All right, Mully," Ballantine retorted. "A progress report will suffice."

"He's onto the second course. Yogurt and fingernails. The man's a bundle of nerves."

Avery tried again to catch sight of their man but to no avail.

"Hurst knows about this too, doesn't he?" he said. He's known for several days."

Ballantine turned to give him a cold stare. "Meaning what?"

"That I've just worked out that business at his house the other night. A strange way to carry on, wouldn't you say? Inviting a one-man disaster to perform in front of a multi-million-dollar prospect." Avery paused for an unnerving smile.

"Go on . . ."

"That was for your benefit, not mine. A chance to study the suspect at close quarters."

"You're forgetting something, aren't you? I already knew the man well."

"But you hadn't seen him in almost two years. You as good as said so."

Ballantine glanced away. "It's plausible," he conceded at length.

"Except that the wrong man got to drive him home," Mulholland muttered fiercely, his eyes fixed on the cafeteria.

"I'm beginning to think our American friend makes a habit of that kind of thing," Ballantine said.

"Damn!" Mulholland dropped the binoculars and snatched at the ignition key, to start the engine. Corrigan had appeared at the cafeteria door and was eyeing the parked cars.

"He's dumped you, laddie," Ballantine murmured.

The Irishman's face was a picture of rage as he made for his car to finish the search in comfort. With the Rover moving slowly between the serried ranks, Mulholland slipped out ahead, taking to the highway. Through the rear window, Avery saw the Rover hesitate at the foot of the service road for a dawdling car with a caravan. Then it was off again, shooting over to its familiar place in the outside lane and blasting lesser vehicles from its path with imperious flashes of the headlights. Mulholland couldn't resist another pointed reference to his inadequate horsepower as he took up the chase.

"We need the two point eight for capers like this."

"It might have been another false stop," Avery said helpfully.

"Never. The meet's off. Aborted."

"It certainly looks that way," Ballantine concurred, and both men fell into a sullen silence.

After some minutes, they unexpectedly began to gain ground as the Rover slowed and pulled over. It left the highway, made an uncharacteristically modest progress around an elevated rotary and descended to the other road to start back the way it had come.

"Crazy," Mulholland said again.

There was perhaps a mile of leisurely travel in the slow land before a puff of oily exhaust issued from the Rover and it was moving out yet again, accelerating to well over a hundred.

"We have lift-off, folks," Mulholland said, fondling the wheel. He held to the center of the road, keeping the car in his sights.

"He's heading back to Quantek," Avery suggested. Want to bet?"

"Where did you find this fucking wet blanket?" Mulholland demanded of Ballantine. There was a weary shrug in reply.

To the front, a long line of traffic straggled in the middle lane, balked by a truck with a heavily laden trailer. Corrigan began to overtake. A Mini popped out just ahead of him, its indicator blinking a forlorn plea to be let through. But Corrigan had no intention of giving it leeway. He maintained speed, bearing relentlessly down on the tiny car.

"Bully!" Avery said.

Miraculously, the Mini discovered a space and dived in to escape. The stop lights on the Rover

190

flashed erratically, for no obvious reason since the lane was now clear. The nose dipped under the braking and the car slowed. Corrigan's head was suddenly nowhere to be seen.

"Mully!" Ballantine shouted, making a grab for the dash to brace himself.

The Rover mounted the divider, spraying sparks from the armored barrier. It bounced away, hit the truck and rebounded, to scrape for some distance along the barrier, its wheels hopping wildly on the uneven curb.

"Oh, my God," Avery said.

The Rover made an abrupt change of direction, cutting a swath through the frantically scattering column of vehicles. It took a glancing blow from the truck, shuddered as if winded and plowed across the hard shoulder, into the bank. The hood was lost on the way, crushed under the enormous wheels and left spinning along the road with cars swerving to miss it. The trailer jackknifed into the barrier, buckling it as if it were tin and leaving smashed crates strewn in its wake.

With considerable coolness, Mulholland had stabbed at his hazard indicators in the early throes of the pile-up. Skillfully, he threaded his way to the hard shoulder, stopping short of where the Rover lay on its side under a rising pall of smoke. A single wheel still turned slowly, wobbling, thrashing the ribbons of a torn tire against the bodywork. Like a wound, a jagged furrow was ripped across the grassy slope. Pausing only to snatch up the binoculars, he leapt out and began scanning the steep banks to either side of the road.

"Youthful enthusiasm," Ballantine said, seeing Avery's puzzled look. "But that won't be how they did it. The best sniper in the world can't shoot round a moving lorry." At which, he left the car to trudge to the Rover. Avery kicked open his door but sat for a moment to control the shake that threatened his knees. The smell was one he would remember always: a blend of scorched rubber and tortured metal and burning oil. And fear—he was sure he could smell even that; an all-pervading sense of panic and blind fright. Drivers sat frozen in their damaged vehicles. The traffic in the oncoming lane was slowing for a prurient gaze at the carnage.

He hesitated as he reached the wreck, took a deep breath then strode manfully to the front. Ballantine was already backing away after the briefest of stares through the shattered windscreen.

"I wouldn't," he advised, but Avery looked anyway, to spring back at the first glance, his stomach heaving. The top of the head was gone and a sticky gray mass seemed still to be pulsing under the blood.

Ballantine put a protective arm around him and led him back to the Ford, where Mulholland was giving a helpless shrug after his scrutiny of the surroundings.

"The manner of his passing was that of his living," Ballantine said irreverently, with a gesture at the road. Dazed drivers were emerging at last, shaking their heads and feeling their limbs in wonder. Blue lights began to flash on the horizon and the rising and falling bay of sirens was carried on the wind.

"See they keep their clumsy hands off," Ballantine said, jerking a thumb at the Rover.

"Sure thing," Mulholland said.

"I want it taken apart, is that clear? Down to the last nut, if need be. I want to know how it was done."

Mulholland nodded with enthusiasm, in his element.

"And *who* did it," Avery added, as he allowed himself to be pressed into the passenger seat.

"We did it, Mr. Avery," Ballantine said soberly. "You and I."

Avery stared.

"The moment we began trailing him, we marked him out as a liability. For all I know, you personally signed the death warrant with that mad chase yesterday."

"Sorry, George," Avery muttered.

"Don't say it to *me*, laddie," Ballantine said, with a solemn nod toward the wreck. He rapped on the car roof. "What channel is the BMW on today?"

"Five," Mulholland said. There was a plastic ID card in his hand, ready for use on the police. He pushed the dark glasses up his nose, to reinforce its authority.

Ballantine took the driver's seat. "I'll get them to take over. When the road's clear, I'll shepherd you home, Mr. Avery. Well away from all this." He said it with emphasis.

Avery made no response, his wide eyes glued to the shattered car.

"You're an amateur, trying to mix it with professionals," Ballantine told him with evident disgust. "A pain in the bloody neck. Corrigan there was another amateur and look where it landed him, the poor bastard." A quaver in the voice suggested he was more shaken than he was prepared to admit.

193

"What about Franklin?" Avery thought to ask.

Ballantine's hard eyes narrowed to slits. "I had assumed he was just another amateur. This would suggest otherwise, wouldn't it?" He lifted the phone and punched the channel selector.

15

Avery was driving too fast for his own good. It was night, so dark he could see nothing beyond the feeble light from the headlights, not even the glimmer of a star. There was a road of sorts, at least he thought so, a wriggling ribbon of track which buried itself like a worm in the blackness ahead. It changed direction so constantly, so unexpectedly, that his hands were kept working at the wheel to stay the course. It was uncannily like playing one of those fairground coin machines for would-be racing drivers. He was so addicted to them he had one at home. But however hard he tried, however many tries he had, he always spun off the circuit before the time was up. As he did now. A particularly vicious bend came at him out of the night and he reacted just too late. The track vanished but it made no difference. The car simply shot off into the unknown, smoothly and in total silence. For some reason, his hands dropped of their own accord to his sides, leaving him to gaze helplessly at the writhing wheel, and when he attempted to raise them again they felt like lead. A horn blared a warning and his foot jammed under the brake pedal. The horn became a scream, much nearer. But from what and from where? He stared in horror as the hood suddenly started to buckle, against nothing. It crumpled and tore away, bouncing back over the roof. The engine disintegrated with awful slowness before his eyes, cracking and melting without a sound. Then he was being lifted as if by an invisible hand, tracing a graceful arc toward the windscreen. Yet all he could think of was the equation for the arc. Perhaps knowing it might save him. *What the hell was it?* Something to do with a moving body colliding with an immovable mass. His head hit the screen and his skull began to cave in, shaping to the tough glass as it bulged outward, refusing to shatter. There was an equation for that too, for the deformation of the head. There must be. But his brain was squashing to a mindless pulp and he realized it was too late to work it out, ever. Strange to note how he felt no pain, just an infinite sadness. The top of his head went, sliced off by the window frame and the horn let out a final blast, a savage bray of triumph. Turning over and over, the car was sucked down into the blackness of the grave.

He sat upright with a start, to find sunlight streaming into the bedroom. But the horn was still there, a seemingly endless din which must be heard half a mile away in the village. Through the window, the rooks glided like vultures against the sky, for once shocked into silence.

The Rolls-Royce was below on the forecourt, its soft top down to let in the new day. Hurst had his seat reclined right back and his feet on the horn ring. He hopped out as he saw Avery peer down.

"Country life and all that," he called up. "I thought you might fancy a spot of exercise?" He jogged on the spot, elegantly turned out in a poloneck and hacking jacket, silk, by the look of it, with leather trimmings. Fawn riding breeches were tucked into high boots.

"Never miss it," Avery mumbled, stealing a look at his watch. He had expected the man to show up sooner or later, to pour his personal brand of smooth oil on the troubled waters. But *this* soon? At six in the morning? A social call, it was not.

"Jeans and a sweater will do," Hurst shouted. "Any old thing, really. Got any sturdy boots with you?"

Avery mouthed a reply.

"Take your time getting ready. I won't bother to come in." Hurst began to prowl the lawn, checking his gardener's precision with the mower.

"My God, you look awful," he said cheerfully, when Avery emerged after the hastiest of preparations. "Like underdone pastry." His eyebrows arched at the sight of Avery's track shoes. "We shan't need the car," he said with a resigned shrug and another downward glance. "It's just up the lane." So he left the Rolls there, the top down, the keys still dangling in the ignition, and set an energetic pace toward the village. The sun was low over the Downs, beginning to climb. Mist fled before it into the gullies.

"Terrific, isn't it?" Hurst filled his chest with fresh air and beat on it with his fists. "Enjoying it here?"

"Apart from today's dawn chorus, very much."

"I knew you'd like it. Didn't I say you would?"

Their destination proved to be the nearest of the local stables, to the back of the field behind the cottage. To reach it, Hurst turned down a side lane, vaulted a style and crossed a paddock. A stableboy greeted him with respectful familiarity and led two magnificent thoroughbreds into the yard. Already saddled, they rapped the cobbles in their eagerness to be off, snorting vapor and showing their teeth. Avery circled them, keeping his distance.

"I took it for granted you could ride," Hurst said. "We can always find you something tamer?"

In answer, Avery chose the largest of the pair, mounted with ease and took the reins. He deliberately reared the horse to show his control. The lad backed away, looking apprehensive.

"Okay, so you ride," Hurst said. "But that's my favorite you've grabbed for yourself, just so you know. Silicon Chip." He made a long face at the horse he was left with before swinging up. "He's here in training for me. If he doesn't pay for his keep with prize money, my accountant goes berserk. So watch how you handle him, for Chrissake!"

"Just the one?"

"Two, actually. This is Memory Module. He specializes in coming fourth." Hurst pulled one of the horse's ears. "Did you hear that, you lazy beast?"

"Keep a tight rein," the stableboy advised Avery. "He goes like the clappers." His eyes were riveted on the track shoes.

"What's with the crazy names?" Avery asked. "Are you trying to force up the odds?"

"Just flying a lonely flag for the computer business," Hurst said. "Someone has to." With a hefty tug, he wheeled his mount for the gate. An easy trot along the lane to a nearby bridlepath, then he dug in his heels to lead at a canter out onto the rolling Downs. Reaching a ridge, he reined in and stood in the stirrups to chart the way ahead. In a thoroughly good mood by now, Avery stopped beside him and drank in the panorama. The hedgerows switchbacked to the horizon. Upper Lambourn was slumbering below them in a crumpled quilt of fields. Thin purple strands spiraled up from several of the chimneys into the still air.

"In the far-off days they called that smoke," Avery said, pointing. "Now it's pollution. There's progress for you."

Hurst smiled. "My word, a romantic no less."

"I guess I am."

"And in more ways than one. Or so George Ballantine would have me believe. You're an incurable seeker after adventure, that's his opinion.

"We shared a thrill or two yesterday, if that's what he means." Avery had known it couldn't be long before Ballantine figured in the conversation.

"An unpleasant business by the sound of it," Hurst said evenly.

"At the time. In retrospect, I see it as more sad than anything."

"Yes, that too. I'm sorry you got dragged into it."

"I *chose* to be involved, Peter. Didn't Ballantine tell you that, while he was at it?"

"He did, as a matter of fact," Hurst said with one of his fleeting stares. "That's why I decided it was time to get my own oar in, before you jump to a wrong conclusion. I wouldn't put it past you." His horse was prodded into a cross-country stroll and Avery spurred his to fall in alongside.

"Patrick was a fool," Hurst said. "He got in way over his head and paid the price."

"Some price!"

"In the immortal words, I'm shaken but not stirred. To my dismay, I find I was harboring a spy in the camp. I'm not going to shed crocodile tears over his death, however nasty it might have been."

Avery was disturbed by the lack of sentiment. "Might have been!" he echoed angrily. "It was an assassination, for God's sake."

Hurst frowned. "Between you, me and the gatepost it probably was. But I'd be grateful if you wouldn't use that word so freely. I have the reputation of my company to consider."

"And a very messy death to explain away!"

"I think we can rely on George to pull some strings. How does a highway accident sound?"

"Not very original."

"They happen, Martin. They happen."

They skirted a field, both horses straining to be given their heads.

"You knew Corrigan was a risk," Avery said.

"Not that kind of bloody risk, I didn't!"

"But you sure as hell knew he was unstable. One of life's walking wounded. It beats me why you kept him on."

"He owned a slice of the company," Hurst recited mechanically.

"A nominal share, surely? You could have twisted his arm to sell out."

Hurst hauled so roughly on the bridle his horse reared, with a whinny of protest. When it settled, he leaned over to fondle Silicon Chip's mane. "You're sitting on ten thousand guineas' worth of racehorse," he said softly. "Old-fashioned money or not, that's a dickens of a lot."

"Je-sus," Avery breathed.

"What I mean is, I'm not exactly short of bread."

"I had noticed."

"I've got property, paintings, equities. Then there are these four-legged extravagances. Since I was so high, I've wanted a racehorse of my own. Now I've got two. For the rest, I don't much go in for philanthropy. In this country, a businessman has to cling for grim death onto the miserly pittance the taxman leaves behind. But the occasional charity is expected of a man in my position and I sometimes oblige. Shall I tell you one of them?"

Avery shrugged, feeling he was being diverted. "Whatever paves the way to a knighthood? How should I know?"

Hurst glared. "Our late lamented friend, Patrick! We started the company together and he was a tower of strength in those days. Well, towers have a habit of crumbling, I discovered. But I'm not one to forget a debt, not even when it's long since been repaid. *That's* why I kept him around, on twice the salary he would have got anywhere else. And how does he treat me in return?" Eyes blazing, Hurst took it out on the horse, digging his heels visciously into the flanks to gallop away over a ridge.

Avery trailed behind at little more than a trot. There was a suggestion of a stumble at a rut and he caught his breath at the thought of a broken leg. Silicon Chip felt twice as fragile now he knew its value. In his own time, he ran Hurst to ground a few furlongs on, taking a breather beside an ancient earthworks.

"Does Larry Brokaw know about this?" he was asked. "About the Corrigan incident?"

"Not yet."

"I'd rather he didn't. I hardly need to explain why."

"Hardly. I don't see it going down too well at the Pentagon. It might make the system we offer look a little shopworn."

"It was espionage involving RARDE, you do realize that, Martin? They were after the secrets Vulcan handles, not details of the system itself."

"That reassures me no end!" Avery retorted.

"But they blew the operation prematurely. If they'd held out for another six months it might have been a different story. But right now, you could pick up virtually every fact the fort is feeding into Vulcan from a basic army manual. What Franklin stole couldn't have been worth a nickel."

"Then why did he run?"

"Search me. I'm not privy to Ballantine's innermost thoughts. He tells me the bare minimum of information, on a strictly need-to-know basis. You've seen that for yourself."

"Corrigan, then? What was his part in the enterprise?"

Hurst stared resolutely into the distance.

"Oh, come on, Peter," Avery insisted. "He worked for you. That gives you a right to know, don't kid me."

Hurst eyed the sky in search of inspiration. "All right," he said at length. "I'll lay my cards on the table. I'll tell you all that George has told me, not that it amounts to much. But he'd have my balls for garters if he ever got to know. He's been doing an exhaustive check on Patrick's recent movement. Last night, he had the factory practically taken apart. The upshot is that Patrick had no access to papers on the Vulcan project in the two years he's been off it."

"As far as you know!"

Hurst tossed his head adamantly. "No, for sure. Our controls on document issue are watertight. It must have been some other aspect of our work they were after. I let Patrick have a hand in several other defense contracts, God help me. Lesser projects, that's why I thought it was safe."

"And you already know which one took his fancy?" Avery guessed. "You've been told."

Hurst hesitated. "The night wasn't exactly wasted, let's put it that way. George and his boys do a thorough job."

Avery worked his horse forward for a searching look at Hurst's face. "And it's no damned business of mine, is that it?" he suggested when he was offered no further explanation.

"I wouldn't put it so bluntly, Martin. It's simply a question of need-to-know. You're here to cast your eyes over one project, and my problems with Patrick and his pal concern another one altogether. It was no big deal, I promise you that. He got only minor secrets, snippets of information. Can't we please let it rest there?"

"You're asking me to take a lot on trust."

"I suppose I am."

Avery scratched his head. Did the guy *always* get his own way? he wondered. He heard himself say, "What the hell! If you can trust me with this walking gold mine I guess I can reciprocate."

"I hoped you'd see reason."

"It's not done as a favor to you," Avery retorted, anxious to retain some vestige of self-respect. "If you must know, I hardly slept last night. I'm haunted by the thought I might be partly to blame for what happened on that highway."

"Then it's a favor, nevertheless," Hurst said coldly. "In my time, I've lost plenty of sleep myself over that man. At least you've helped put an end to that."

He turned his horse for home, threw down the gauntlet with a challenging jerk of the head and set off at a spirited gallop. But Avery made no serious attempt to give chase, conceding an easy win. It wasn't diplomacy, nor was he any longer worried about the horse's vulnerable legs. It was his own legs which help him back. By now, they ached like the devil.

Hurst lingered with him over morning coffee in the cottage kitchen. The pot sang quietly to itself on an Aga stove that wouldn't have looked out of place in a bakery.

"One more thing," Avery said. "What's George's job? I mean his real job?"

"Does it matter?"

"Sure it does. You introduced him as uncle dependable, the man from the ministry. It turns out he does something more devious."

"He's in intelligence," Hurst replied.

"That's obvious, now."

"He runs a unit which gathers defense information from what we call the other side. They monitor radio transmissions, eavesdrop on military exercises, all manner of tricks. Sod it, Martin, I don't know the full details myself and my company supplies him with the communications kit he uses. People like Ballantine play their cards close to their chests."

"So I've noticed."

"But I do know this, at least I've deduced it. His unit is the main source of Red data for the Vulcan war games."

"Which means he has a backroom job? He's a desk mandarin running a network of intelligence sources?"

"That's how it looks, yes."

"Then what's he doing riding shotgun, getting personally involved in surveillance operations?"

"Protecting his interests, I should think," Hurst said, losing his patience. "Making damned sure the information he works so hard to get doesn't leak back where it came from."

"Okay, I'll buy that. Is he with the Ministry of Defence or not? I don't know how these things work over here."

"Didn't he tell you himself, in your travels together?"

"He's none too talkative when we're driving," Avery said.

"Quite so." The corners of Hurst's mouth flickered upward.

"Well, is he or isn't he?"

"More or less, so I've been led to believe."

"You're one hell of a helpful guy!" Avery said.

With a spoon, Hurst traced ripples in his coffee. "And George is right about you," he suggested distantly. "You're bright, very bright. You're obviously an unusually quick thinker. You're probably wasted in whatever narrow technical slot Larry Brokaw has you wedged in. You're vegetating there, for all I know. But you've stumbled on a grubby little conspiracy and it's gone to your head. You've already fatally tripped one poor sod with your clumsy feet, on your own admission. Isn't it high time you left well alone?"

Avery smiled stiffly. "I'll try, Peter. Since you ask so pleasantly."

"Let's hope you succeed, for all our sakes." Hurst nodded a slight good-bye and started for the hall door. "When did you last ride?" he inquired, turning. "Some time ago by the look of it."

"Ten years at least. That's what the bruises tell me."

"Well, any time you feel like more practice, let me know. I'll arrange it with the stable."

"Only if they can lay on something a bit cheaper. I'd feel safer."

Hurst peered down his long nose. "So would I, Martin. So would I."

16

Peter Hurst was many things, a mixture, like most men, of good and bad, but he was no liar. He was a man who shaded the truth when it suited him, but don't we all? A man, one would guess, who spent more of his time doing just that—shading the truth without actually bending it, subtly shifting the facts to his advantage—than most of us need to or have the energy for. But he was never a liar; he had no reason to be. Usually, he could draw on his charm to persuade you that night was day. And when that failed he would smile disarmingly and confess: yes, you're right. Have a good meal on me and ignore it, would you? Borrow my cottage and do me a favor in return. Have my house and my wife and my precious racehorses, and forget what you saw or heard. Just as long as we stay good pals.

But he *was* a fool. So thought Avery as the Rolls purred away up the hill, into the blinding sun.

Franklin had kept papers on Vulcan back at his flat, that was a fact. And Corrigan had been in contact with Franklin. So much for watertight document procedures! He could have got any information he wished from his contact at the fort: on the system itself, on the weapons they were studying, on the results of the war games. Couldn't Hurst see that? Yet all he cared about was keeping the scandal from Brokaw when the real danger was staring him in the face.

Corrigan was far from what Hurst wanted to believe, Avery thought: a man passing odd snippets of information. Very far from it. He was at the very center of events, the key to the story. Whatever the goddamned story might be.

He bided his time. The news of Corrigan's accident caused the expected excitement at the factory. There was shock but no great surprise. It was sadly inevitable with that mad driving of his, that was the judgment.

The ripples spread and died within days.

During those days, Avery worked diligently at what he had been sent to do, and made sure people knew it. He arrived early and went late, leaving only when the patrolling guard stood pointedly at the door, jangling a bunch of keys a jailer would have envied. The manuals moved from the bookcase to crowd the desk. He spread intricate circuit diagrams wide on the floor, lying beside them to probe their meaning. He went through his list of contacts, asking questions, calling the most senior Vulcan staff more than once so they would be in no doubt of his interest.

Hurst dropped by several times, popping his head round the door just to say hello. He would take in the activity and soon withdraw. I'd better leave you to it, he would say, it's good to see such industry. Avery wrote his first report to Brokaw, making a few carping criticisms of the system design but no mention of Corrigan. With satisfaction, he noted how the girl who typed it produced two copies but gave him only one. Hurst's visits became less frequent, then ceased. They met only in the rambling corridors, exchanging little more than smiles, each busy in his own different world.

Barbara Young was at her desk outside Corrigan's old office, typing without enthusiasm. She was pleased to see him, she said, and looked as if she meant it.

"I'm just copy-typing till my luck changes," she explained with a gesture to an intimidating pile of longhand notes. "They can't seem to find anyone I can work for. All the managers are happy with their present secretaries, damn them."

207

"Are you over the shock yet?" Avery asked.

Her reply was perky, to conceal her sadness. "Not really. I still catch myself pouring two coffees. Silly things like that." But her eyes alighted on the office door and she shivered, very slightly. "I wish they'd move me somewhere else. I have asked, more than once."

"Can I take a look, just for a minute?"

"Morbid curiosity?" she asked accusingly.

"I was there when it happened. At least, not long after."

"So I heard." Quantek had an efficient grapevine.

"I thought I recognized the car, what was left of it, so I pulled over."

"Don't!" Her shoulder shook.

"Well . . . ?" He nodded to the door, considering the explanation sufficient.

"Oh, go on then," she said with a sigh. "I'm not the bloody guardian at the gates anyway." She followed him in and sat on the desk to watch. Her presence cramped his style and perhaps she intended it should. He felt unable to touch things, to search the drawers and the cupboard in the corner, and was forced simply to look around.

It was an office similar to Hurst's but with small personal touches to make it more comfortable, less like a waiting room. The family snapshots were still on a side cabinet, under a crayon drawing done by a child; the youngest of the Corrigan brood, Barbara said as he peered at it. The orange leather chair was Patrick's own, she explained, so was the wastebasket in lurid green plastic. The office manager had got on his high horse when they appeared and demanded they

208

go straight back again, company rules and all that, but Patrick had told him to get lost.

"Peter Hurst said his room was searched," Avery remarked, when he had seen as much as he could.

She was surprised that he knew. "By the security men, yes. Not the company guards, two men from London. The heavy mob, we call them."

"Do you remember their names?"

"Do people like that have names! I thought they had numbers and lived in filing cabinets."

"What reason did they give?"

"To *me?*" she retorted. "They're not accountable to me! I was the doormat, something to tread over in the stampede through the place."

Avery fixed her with an inquiring look, refusing to let it rest there.

"Oh, something to do with some secret papers Patrick had on loan," she admitted. "It was nothing sinister, no big deal. He obtained them through the proper channels and they were all signed for three times over." She glanced down at the desk, fidgeting with a paperweight. "The ministry needed them back in a hurry."

"That's what they said?"

"Yes, that's what they said."

"The very afternoon of the accident?"

A mute nod.

"And all through the night?"

"So I gather. They were still at it when I left."

"Some hurry!" Avery said.

"Some quantity of paper," she said, opening a desk drawer to reveal its bareness. She pulled out another, equally empty. It was Fort Halstead all over again,

Avery said to himself. What the devil did they do with all that paper when they carted it away?

"The whole office?" he asked, scratching his head.

"And the filing cabinets outside. Everything except my personal effects."

Avery tried the cupboard to satisfy himself, and it couldn't have been more empty.

"I don't know about you but I have work to do," Barbara said hurriedly, perhaps feeling she had talked too much. She ushered him out and returned to her typewriter, picking at the keys. He took the chair beside her desk and watched her remorselessly, as she had just watched him. It was taken passively, only a stiffness in the typing, an occasional fumble with the paper, showing her discomfort.

Why, he wondered, did women you were just getting to know look so completely different each time you saw them? She was smaller than he remembered and older-looking, except for the eyes which altered so often as to defy description; innocent one minute, youthfully alert the next, then suddenly as vacant as those of an aged woman with nothing to live for but memories. The sharp lines on her face were etched as much by experience as by time; she struck him as one who had known her share of problems. A divorce perhaps, or just the strain of dealing with Corrigan every day? A glance at her left hand found no ring yet she was too attractive, at least she had been, never to have married.

"I enjoyed that lunch we had," he said.

"Me too." The work stopped and she looked up in expectation.

"I was wondering, how about dinner?"

"It's the logical next step."

"Tonight, or is that too little notice?"

She gave a slow nod. "I think I can fit it into my crowded diary."

"When and where?"

"If you don't mind me looking like this, why not straight from here?"

"That's fine by me."

"You've come to my rescue, actually. My old Renault is being patched up for the umpteenth time. I was wondering how to get home. This little lot will keep me going till seven and the girl who gave me a lift in is the type to push off at one second past the siren."

"Let's say seven, then. I'll arrive on a big white charger."

She caught his eye. "Tell me honestly, Martin. Is it me you're inviting or Patrick Corrigan's ex-secretary?"

"Do you mind which it is?"

"Not if the meal's good and the conversation amusing. I ceased thinking too deeply about male motives some years back." She gave a shy smile, stating a fact rather than baring her soul.

The restaurant, in Bath, was her suggestion. Given a choice, Avery would have preferred anywhere but Bath, to avoid that highway journey, but she described the place in such glowing terms he felt it would be churlish to refuse. It was far from cheap, she said, but well worth the trip. The statutory few minutes in the ladies' room before they left Quantek had done wonders for her. The hair was sleeker, the lips fuller. The plain office suit was brightened for the evening with a silk scarf that had appeared at the neck.

Such was the effect that stretch of road had on him that as soon as he joined it Avery's eyes went automatically to the mirror. Headlights were strung out behind him in the darkness like bright, slowly moving stars, all of them much the same, all following.

"How long have you been with Quantek?" he asked, giving up the search as a bad job.

"Fourteen years, would you believe."

He whistled. "And how long for Patrick?"

"Most of that time."

"With not a medal to show for it."

She smiled ruefully. "Not a one."

"He was involved with the Vulcan project at one time, so I heard."

"At the beginning. He was the technical brains on the team."

"Until he was eased off it?"

She maintained a faithful silence.

"Why was that, Barbara?"

"Can't we change the subject, please? Don't spoil my evening."

"Am I straining your loyalty?"

"More than a little, and you know it."

"That's some company you work for," Avery said. "The reward for long service is an empty desk in a lonely corridor. No boss, no obvious prospects. Whose damned interests do you think you're protecting?"

Her head dropped. "Perhaps Patrick's. Who else can, now?"

"You seem to be forgetting," he said more

persuasively, "I'm not one of the heavy mob from London."

"You might as well be!" she countered. "I was watching you in that office today, like a hound on a scent. How do I know what you were after!"

"If I knew myself, I'd tell you," Avery said. "Believe me I would."

She was startled.

"I'm just an ordinary systems designer, Barbara. Like a dozen others you work with at Quantek. But I've walked slap bang into the middle of something over here, and it stinks. I don't know what it is, but for my sins I've decided to find out. Does that make it clear?"

"Yes and no."

"You must have had a lot of respect for Patrick or you wouldn't have stuck around for the best part of your working life."

She confirmed with the faintest of yeses.

"Suddenly, what do you find? Before he's even laid out on the morgue slab" (she shuddered and turned away) "the security guys are crawling all over his office. They don't tell you why but they don't need to. You know bloody well what the implication is."

"Yes, I can read between the lines," she agreed after some thought.

"So put the record straight. Tell me your side of the story. Defend the guy if you must. I've got an open mind."

She examined her conscience and his plea made sense. "Why not," she uttered remotely. "You asked why he was taken off Vulcan?"

Avery nodded.

"It was for quite the silliest reason, really. He got into an argument with one of the scientists at the fort. He could be so pigheaded. I'm sure it was nothing, just a design detail. I'm no technician, how should I know what it was? But the dispute dragged on for days. The fort wanted a particular feature and Patrick would have none of it. Things escalated and came to a head. Finally, Patrick blew his top and as good as punched the man. Can you imagine, coming to blows with a civil servant under the very eyes of the ministry? In one of their own offices! Well, that was it. He apologized the next day, wrote all manner of letters eating humble pie, an that wasn't easy for him. But the damage was done."

"Hurst would have handled it differently," Avery suggested. "There are more diplomatic ways of getting what you want."

"Oh, yes, that bloody man would have," she said with surprising bitterness. "Trouble sees him coming and dives into the shadows, out of his way."

"And that's all there was to it?"

"That's the whole story. Silly, wasn't it? He never could control his temper, not over what he saw as a matter of principle."

"And he had no more to do with Vulcan?"

"Nothing whatsoever. The fort didn't want him around and he washed his hands of it. Let the project sink, he said, he was confident it would without him. When it turned out to be such a success his pride was hurt but he kept it hidden."

"Did he ever again see papers on Vulcan?"

"No."

"Details of the war games at the fort?"

"No."

"Well, did he sit in on any of the project meetings?"

She was becoming puzzled. "Not a one. Don't you believe me or something?"

Avery produced his trump card. "Then why did Franklin visit him?" The play was greeted in silence and he turned to see she hadn't understood. "The young man who was with him on my first day over here. The guy from Fort Halstead."

"Oh, him! That embarrassing business. I haven't the faintest idea what that was about."

"Patrick didn't explain it to you?"

Her head shook vigorously. "No, sir, he did not."

"Did you ask?"

"Ask Patrick?" she said with sudden amusement. "He told you things in his own good time or not at all."

They drove without speaking for a while. The mirror said the road behind was almost clear. The only pair of headlights in sight was definitely dropping back, making no attempt to stay with him. They dwindled and were soon gone, eclipsed by a bend.

"I've got a few final questions, miss," Avery said, in a ponderous Scotland Yard accent.

She laughed. "As long as it *is* only a few."

"That last day in the office . . ."

The laugh died in the instant. "What about it?" she asked fearfully.

"How was he that morning? Worried, would you say?"

"Not in the least. Why should he be?"

"You're quite sure?"

"No, of course I'm not sure. But I don't know of

215

any reason he had to be worried so it's a fair assumption he wasn't." The answer was edgy; he was close to trying her patience.

"He had a telephone call, correct?"

"Several, I should think," she said with dignity. "He still had friends in the company. More than that man Hurst, I'll tell you that for nothing. There were plenty who needed his advice. Most days there would be a host of queries: on projects he was involved in and even those he wasn't."

"I'm thinking of one call in particular," Avery said. "The call from Franklin."

"But he didn't call, not that day or any other." She noted his surprise and explained, "There's no direct line to the office. All calls have to come through me."

"I'm told he rang," Avery said doggedly.

She gave the matter more thought. "Well . . . he might have, but I wouldn't swear to it. There was a rather mysterious call. Personal, that's what the man said, and he wouldn't give his name. He *did* sound youngish, now you mention it."

"And you still insist Patrick wasn't worried after that? Try to think."

She shook her head.

"Nervous, then? On edge?"

"No, not even that." She issued an anguished sigh, warning him to drop the questioning.

"Soon after the call he left unexpectedly and drove off," Avery said, regardless. "What reason did he give you?"

The persistence brought another long sigh and a subdued answer. "I spent some time on another floor, at the photocopier. When I got back he was gone. He

216

left no note, no word to say where or why. I was his secretary not his bloody keeper. It wasn't the first time it had happened and I had no reason to think it would be . . . the last." There was a catch in the voice and she turned her face away, pressing her nose to the side window. The fields were ghostly in the shifting light spilling from the highway. Long shadows from the isolated trees swept like black searchlights along the hedges.

"I do have other interests besides the company," she said coldly after some time. "I'm a Shakespeare freak, if you care. The only decent thing about Swindon is that it's a comfortable drive from Stratford. I get up there whenever I can. You owe me a visit, by the way. I've been clocking each question up on my meter. One more peep from you about Quantek, just one, and it will be *two* visits, best stalls."

"So tell me about Stratford," Avery said with a smile. "I know when I'm beaten."

Her conversation became animated; she turned in her seat, her hand resting lightly on his, to describe the season's productions. *Coriolanus* was the best, she said. The Romans all togged out in black leather, can you imagine? The words were lost on Avery as he thought only of her earlier answers. How could Corrigan not have been worried, deadly worried? A call from a defector with half the country's police on his trail, an arrangement to meet in secret, and she said he wasn't concerned! Avery had seen for himself how the man was: those empty stares through the window, the crazed drive, that agonized wait in the cafeteria. He had seen them together, Corrigan and Franklin, and seen the guy explode when Hurst burst in. How could she work for him so long and know him so little? She didn't really remember, that's what it must be. Or she didn't *want* to remember, to think back on the final day of those fourteen long years. Who could blame her?

"You're doing just fine," he heard her say. "Keep on like this and we'll end up in Wales."

Just in time, he swerved across the highway, clipped the curb to the service road and turned south to Bath.

Coffee back at the cottage was her idea. Having heard so much about the place, she said, it would be crazy to pass up the opportunity for a look, a quick nose around. So as Avery lit the fire she toured the living room picking up objects, rearranging ornaments, with the half-curious, half-superior air of a woman drawn into an exclusive shop and not wishing to admit the prices are beyond her. Then she settled in front of the fire before it was properly ablaze, praising his boy scout skill, holding her hands to its warmth and nodding that he join her.

The courtship was swift, done with such restraint that Avery's hand was on a breast before their lips ever touched. Closing her eyes as he stroked, she stretched out on her back, raising her arms languorously above her head. Looking down, fascinated by the way her mouth curled, he unbuttoned first the jacket then the shirt. They had still yet to kiss.

"Don't do that," she said, showing her white teeth. His hand moved in, over a nipple which encouraged him on. "Don't do that unless you mean business."

He had one of the smaller bedrooms in mind, because of the hidden microphone. Maybe they hadn't

218

bothered to bug all of them. But she discovered the big brass bed. Her shoes lay discarded on the stairs and she stood in the doorway pointing, the shirt draped carelessly over a shoulder and the skirt awry.

"There, lover. There." Her head shook slowly as if in awe of its challenge.

Both hungry for too long, they devoured each other. She was athletic, adventurous, downright outrageous; the best for longer than he cared to remember; perhaps the best ever.

"You're disgusting," she murmured with satisfied agony. "Deliciously disgusting."

She had no idea about the microphone just inches from her head, listening to every word. How could she guess that it spurred him on? He had feared inhibition as they entered the room. How would he keep her quiet? How would he stop that damned ancient bed from creaking and rattling like a rusty old steam engine? But it wasn't like that. My God, far from it. No, sir, he thought, it was not one bit like that. If the walls had ears then the bloody ears might as well burn! They stirred him to action, extracting an inspired performance such as a keen audience can wring from an actor, surprising even him. He pictured the microphone and it grew ever larger. He *became* a microphone, probing her deeply, listening avidly for every sound: gentle interior whispers, smoothly caressing murmurs of flesh, more urgent damp rustlings (how did dampness make a noise, such a noise?) and, later, her suppressed cries, her choked snatches of breath among many breaths. Never before had Avery realized that lovemaking was so loud, such a cacophony of bodies, such exciting orchestra.

He rolled away as if wet from a bath, the soaking hair straggling down over his face. It was pitch black in the room because she had wanted it that way, perhaps being sensitive about a no longer young body. Why? he wondered. It was no miracle but it was nothing to be ashamed of. His hand reached out to trace it as she sat with knees tucked under her chin, her face toward him. When he had explored her fully she fell on him.

"Revenge," she hissed.

At some stage they dozed, cradled together with the ears taking a well-earned rest in the wall above them. He awoke to discover her gently untangling herself, to sit on the edge of the bed. In the darkness, she reached unerringly for the light switch and then left for the bathroom on the far side of the landing. When she returned she drew him onto her, the light not seeming to bother her now. A quick shower had made her body refreshingly cool and firmed it for action. There was a provocative tautness to the skin.

"You've been here before," Avery said, stiffening. He felt oddly slighted, a man deceived.

"Don't be silly," she said.

"Those doors out there all look the same yet you knew which one." And more than once, he thought. The light switch said so.

Her eyelids batted but she held his gaze.

"Peter Hurst!" he exclaimed. "Christ Almighty, you and Peter Hurst!"

Angrily, she pushed him away and retreated across the bed, biting her thumb. "Don't be so bloody thick," she said amidst sighs and headshakes. "I wouldn't have that man near me if he was the last on earth."

He stared.

"It was Patrick," she said, closing her eyes. "This is a company house, not Peter Hurst's. It was his but he sold it back for tax reasons." She drew the quilt over her body, up to her neck, and lay regarding the ceiling. "We worked together for fourteen years, Martin. It can happen. Perhaps it had to happen."

"Sure," Avery said coldly. "A big, thrusting boss. Larger than life. You were swept off your feet."

"You wouldn't understand. It wasn't sex and it wasn't hero worship, far from it. I knew his failings, every one, like they were warts on his face."

"No sex!" Avery said. "You came up to the bedroom to *talk?*" He spoke with contempt, imagining that gross Irishman pawing her; her small, very white body. It robbed him of a prize he had held for mere hours.

"I didn't say there was *no* sex. I said it wasn't sex. Who knows what it was. Mutual support, maybe? I was the only person Patrick didn't need to pretend with, I suppose. Sometimes when we came here he would just flake out and sleep, holding me. He knew I wouldn't mind or think less of him for it. At other times we would just sit downstairs by the fire and he'd talk the night through and I'd just listen. I've never known such a talker, such stories. He had stolen the Blarney Stone, he would joke, and kept it hidden in his hip pocket. When he was with me the company feuds took on a different light. He could lose a fearful boardroom battle and do you know how he'd describe it to me? Peter Hurst twitched his Pinocchio's nose as he lunged in for the kill, things like that. All the rancor went and he could see the funny side. He had an observer's eye for detail."

"And you?" Avery asked. "What was in it for you?"

"You'll laugh."

"Try me."

"Watching him take failure square on the chin," she said simply. "You look at Peter Hurst and you say, there goes success, what a man. But Patrick was the fading star, the man who hadn't made it and never would. Who admires failure? Well, I do. Success is easy, it nourishes you for more. Failure is the toughest thing in the world. I admired him for the way he faced up to it."

"And you loved him?" Avery guessed.

"Yes, I loved him," she admitted. She sat quietly thinking back for a while then shook her head to throw away the memories. Roughly pushing the cover from the bed, she turned to him. "Do I have to lie here by myself for the rest of the night?"

"Why should I help you forget," Avery said harshly.

She came to him. "Because I'm asking. Ever so nicely."

You're a conceited fool, Avery told himself as she lay, finally, asleep in his arms. A blind, overbearing, unthinking idiot!

He had barely met Corrigan. One evening together, a few hours of spying through those binoculars, and he was convinced he knew him. Yet she was the real expert. She had know him for all those years, really known him. Ye gods, she had slept with him without making love! Passion depended on ignorance, as theirs had done tonight, on curiosity, on newness. But merely to sleep with someone, that called for knowledge, for mutual understanding. Oh, yes, she had known the man all right.

Corrigan wasn't worried by that telephone call, that's what she had said. Okay, so now he could see that she must be right and he had been wrong. But where did that leave matters? Either Corrigan was the coolest cucumber in history or he had no reason whatsoever to feel threatened. And cool, he was not.

Avery thought back, trying to remember what he had seen: the man standing at the window with that strange, lost look on his face. Yes, it made sense now he knew better. Franklin had phoned and Corrigan was baffled. *He simply did not understand the call*. And then the ensuing drive: the sudden turn back toward the factory, the unexplained wait at the side of the road. Yes, that made sense too. Corrigan was confused because the meeting mystified him. He changed his mind on the way, turned back, then had second thoughts, probably deciding: why not see it through? He was that kind of man.

Avery stroked Barbara's hair. "Thank you, darling," he said. "You've helped enormously. Now it's ten times less clear than before."

She stirred at his touch, half opening her eyes. "What?"

He kissed her forehead.

"What's the time?" she asked drowsily.

A press on the button of his watch and the digits glowed. "Three thirty-nine, precisely."

"It can't be! My husband will kill me!" She sat bolt upright, fluffing her hair with urgently combing fingers.

Avery recoiled. "Now you tell me!"

Her eyes were as innocent as a child's as she brought

223

them close, pressing her nose to his. "You didn't ask, did you?" At which, she leapt from the bed in search for her clothes.

It was four by the time Avery dropped her off, halting short of the house at her request, for discretion's sake. It was an ordinary street in a barren outpost of Swindon, no longer town but hardly country yet. One end ran into a road of small shops, the other pointed to scrubby fields.

Yes, she said on the journey, her husband had guessed about Patrick and pretended not to know. Patrick wasn't a threat, you see. Who in their right mind would see him as a threat? "But you, my love," she said. "I do not see him tolerating you. Oh, no."

She touched a hand to his lips and hurried from the car, wincing as the slam of the door cut into the silence, and giving no backward glance in the street. Avery noted the gate she entered and cruised slowly past after a minute or so. It was a plain, semidetached house, quite small, closely hemmed in by others so alike one would be hard pressed to tell them apart. The back of a dressing table filled an upstairs window, framed by fussy net curtains. He should have stopped at the corner, he thought, and not come into the street. At the cottage, she was a temptress, a woman of the world. Swallowed by the nondescript house, she was suddenly a suburban secretary once more, a wife. Were there any bicycles in the hall, or a pram even? He hadn't thought to ask that either.

There was a phone booth in the shopping center and he made a collect call to Los Angeles, to Lisa, his secretary. Charge the call to Northridge, he said, it's business. Right now, he would rather not consider how he happened to know her home number from memory.

"What time is it there?" she said.

"Don't ask!" Avery said. He let her inquire about England, answering as briefly as she would allow. Then he said, "I want you to do something for me. Who's the project manager on the system we're putting in at Fort Meade?"

"Fort Meade?"

"The National Security Agency."

"Oh, *that* Fort Meade. No can say, sweetheart. This is home, not the company records office."

"Then find out, Lisa!"

"If you insist."

"And when you've found out, ask him for a contact in the agency. Don't say why, just ask. Got that so far?"

"Uh-uh."

"Then call the contact and ask him for a name in England. I don't care who or at what level. All I need is a way in and I can take it from there."

"Take what from where?" she asked uselessly.

"A name and a phone number will do. And if a whisper of this gets back to Larry Brokaw, you're fired."

"Terrific," she said. "You're two weeks gone without a word and your first call is to threaten me with job attrition."

"Don't call me, I'll call you," Avery said. "Tomorrow evening at around eight, your time. That gives you less than twenty-four hours."

17

David Sherman ducked his tall frame through the bathroom door and flapped in his bare feet across the ice-cold linoleum. They were truly enormous feet—no others he had ever seen remotely matched them for size—very broad and with fleshy webs between the toes. To make matters worse they were quite flat and tended to splay outward as he walked, looking so like white flippers when bare that he kept them covered in public as if they were disfiguring birthmarks. They made for effortless swimming but he no longer swam; he was too painfully conscious of them out of the water. Saunas were out of the question, however badly he needed to sweat off his excess weight.

He plonked them on the weighing machine and tore his eyes from them to watch the needle swing wildly before stabilizing at just under the three-hundred-pound mark. There goes breakfast again, he thought, and lunch. Not that it would make much difference. Sometimes he felt his body was taking him over, growing ever upward and spreading at the waist whether he ate or not, whether or not he took his evening jog in Hyde Park. Six foot five he might be, but three hundred pounds! No wonder he was known as the Hulk.

He chased a razor over his face, showed a brush to his teeth and lumbered back to the bedroom to dress. Then the monastic breakfast, a single black coffee, no sugar, in the sparse living room as he gazed around with satisfaction at its emptiness, at its perfect embodiment of his chosen way of life. He had two chairs because he and his woman of the moment had to sit somewhere, his being large and sagging. Against a wall he had tacked some shelves which groaned under his books—volumes on history and international trade, so many political treatises on Russia and Eastern Europe that one could be forgiven for assuming him to be a revolutionary in the making, a row of mathematical texts preserved in memory of his years at Princeton. A rickety table beside the shelves; one had to have a table. Then over in a corner a portable TV, not because he ever watched it but because people expected to find a TV in every flat; they might become overly curious about a man without one and Sherman had no wish for visitors to wonder about him, to think twice about what he might be. And that was the room, give or take a few trinkets. Possessions were an encumbrance, a millstone holding you down to one place, and a corrupting influence if you weren't on your guard; furnish a room to create an image and you could all too easily end up molded to it. So no possessions, no unnecessary furniture. Sherman needed to be free, to travel at a whim and to be what the agency required him to be. Today, a stalker in London. Tomorrow, who could say? Back at Fort Meade in ten years' time, in the prime of his forties, secure in one of those vast offices and with a house and family in nearby Laurel—only then perhaps might he start to accumulate furniture. But not a moment before.

Soon he was turning off Bayswater Road into the quiet enclave of Kensington Palace Gardens, nodding good morning to the porter in his kiosk. It was a longer way round than his usual walk to the Listening Post, taken several times a month for a routine inspecton of the hardware. On the corner stood the brutal new concrete fortress of the Czechoslovak Centre and he surveyed the aerial array slung across at the back: like an elongated lobster pot with the wires strung over big metal hoops. Nothing new there. He slowed as he came to the Russian embassy. Russia was his speciality; it was their traffic that occupied his days, their attachés and visitors he stalked in search of incoming agents. Only television aerials could be seen on the roof; the big stuff, the medium-wave lattice, was out of sight at the back and the top security traffic was transmitted from elsewhere using roaming dishes. This month they had rigged up a microwave link on the embassy's residential block on the heights of Highgate Hill and the next location was anyone's guess. There would be the usual two- to three-day hunt before the agency or the British tracked it down.

The Gardens opened to one side to a meadow in the center of the city—Palace green, with Kensington Palace resplendent beyond. He looked with respect at the Norwegian embassy, not that their hardware was much in evidence but because the Nordics were just about the most reliable source in town right now. Their tiny U.K. intelligence squad was currently rated among the best; an inspired group of listeners and manipulators, with burglars who came and went, so the circuit gossip had it, without a trace. Yes, their traffic could be very useful. The Chinese, not so. He strode past their mansion with barely a glance. Two Mercedeses were leaving, packed with smooth yellow faces tunicked to the neck, and the irony of the street struck him as it so often did on these morning detours. Here were great houses originally built for the cream of English capitalists and now they were occupied with obvious relish by the Communists, the Marxists, the Maoists and the rest of their ilk. Exclusiveness hung in the air like expensive perfume.

It was a few minutes short of nine. The transmitters along the Row would be silent or sending only spasmodic messages of a routine nature. The hours after midnight were the peak, when the airwaves were cleanest and interference at a minimun. An early morning walker would hear none of it, of course; the only sounds would be from the rowdy embassy binges. But the night air would be full of traffic, with the transmitters and receivers going full tilt while the professional listeners in the nearby streets bent over their consoles and their tape recorders turned, capturing as much of the mêlée as they could.

He crossed the road at the Rumanian embassy for a good honest stare back at the roof. Now there was an aerial to beat them all: a huge horizontal lattice of metal tubes displayed unashamedly between the high chimneys. A status symbol and damn-all else, Joel Henderson called it, a one in the eye for the eastern bloc Joneses up the Row. It was used, and not that frequently, for purely consular messages of no great interest. A curtain stirred at an upper window and he gave a cheery wave before crossing back. Then he took the side alley beside the embassy and cut through to Church Street.

Listening Post Three, referred to simply as LP-3 on the agency paperwork, was in a smart avenue some streets to the west of Embassy Row, at an optimum distance for listening. Place the eavesdropping antennae too close and there were blind spots and

229

local distortions; move too far away and new distortions crept in. The airspace was too damned crowded, that was the trouble: the underground trains, the winding motors for office elevators, even the passing cars, all threw in their squeaks and crackles to make life harder for listeners.

The house took its place with ease among the others in the tree-lined street, with its spick white stucco, the trim laburnum at the front, its air of affluent innocence. Other houses close by blinkered their interiors with venetian blinds, why should this one be an exception? And the rocking horse in an unshuttered attic window was a nice homely touch. The house next door had blinds too, but in a different color. Who could tell from the outside that they were knocked together to form cramped but usable office spaces?

Sherman hurdled the low front wall and loped up the stairs. A chat to the entry phone and the latch buzzed, then a run up four flights, which left him panting, and he was in his eyrie, in his transient cubbyhole at one end of traffic correlation.

"Our Russian friends had a slack night by all accounts," Henderson said, dropping a page of computer output onto the desk. "Seventy-three messages out, fifty-nine in. First analysis suggests only one of interest to you."

"*One?*" Sherman repeated. "I might as well go home now."

"A bevy of electronics engineers en route from Kiev to Sao Paulo. A one-week stopover here. Sound promising?"

"I'll take a look-see," Sherman said. Left to it, he

made a rapid excursion through the names then pondered the itinerary listed for London. No, he thought, nothing there. Maybe he'd organize a spot check during the stay to make sure they were all still together and keeping to the schedule, and a set of photos for the records, but it called for no more than that.

He stood at the window, wondering how to fill the day. Behind him the typewriters chattered and the telex machines rat-tatted beween bouts of rest, responding to the stations in Brussels, Bonn, and The Hague. He pulled down a slat to peer over the gardens to the rear. Immediately below, the yard of the agency houses was almost filled by a greenhouse; canvas sunshades prevented a view in to the receivers and the auxilliary generator. Beyond it, the garden ran between two houses situated on the next road and a billboard bridged the gap. It was unusually deep for a billboard if any passerby thought to dwell on it, some five feet thick to take the hidden antennae. The cables were well hidden, running within the supporting scaffolding and through underground conduits to the glasshouse. The advertisement on the far side was for Smirnoff vodka. That little touch of Henderson's was a good one, he thought, almost as good as his with the rocking horse.

Henderson made the rounds again just after ten, stopping at each desk in turn to discuss progress.

"Well?" he asked.

"It's clean," Sherman said. "A twenty-four-carat visit. No undertones, no overtones."

"My feeling exactly," Henderson said and he put his

231

head close. "So now time hangs heavy and idle hours loom? We'll put that straight, won't we? I've got a conundrum for you to solve." Then he turned tail for his den a floor down, assuming Sherman would follow.

"The oddest thing has happened," he said from behind his desk. "I've just had a call out of the blue, a guy I've never met nor heard of. Name of Avery, does that ring any bells? He says he's American and certainly sounds it."

Sherman shook his head.

"He says he's over here on a business trip and he's chanced on an espionage conspiracy." Henderson narrowed his eyes. "He refuses to say how he got my name and number. I ask him if this alleged conspiracy involves the U.S. and he says no, not directly. What do you make of it so far, Hulk?"

"It doesn't feel right."

"There's more to come. I insist on calling him back as a crude check on his credibility and guess what, he's in a phone booth in the middle of nowhere. Then he clams up. He won't elaborate on the story, not till we meet face to face. No dice, I say, I must have some token of good faith. Which gets me one name. It involves Franklin, he says, Franklin from Fort Halstead. What does that do to you?"

"A British defense establishment? That's way out of my orbit, Joel. But the suggestion of a meeting stinks to high heaven. It's a ruse to flush you out. It's ham-fisted and obvious, but what else could it be?"

"That was my immediate reaction, too. So I give him a polite brush-off. If it doesn't involve Uncle Sam, I say, why don't you go tell the British. It sounds like their can of worms. Now, here's where it gets interesting. They already know, he says, I thought you people would like to be in on the act." Henderson paused, searching Sherman's face.

"That's some bait," Sherman said at length.

"Isn't it, though."

"Except that it isn't traffic territory."

"You know me, I'm all for law and order and agency protocol," Henderson said piously. "But one fine morning I get a call from a stranger and there's an outside chance it may be pure gold dust. I'm not about to hand it over to Grosvenor Square. Not when I've got an experienced stalker with time on his hands."

"I don't operate on Americans," Sherman countered.

"Today you do. Give it a going over, use your intuition and report back. But don't follow through, Hulk. Just tell me whether or not it's genuine." Henderson slid a sheet of memo paper across. "That's the number of the booth. He promised he'd wait and I get a strong feeling he will."

Sherman stopped at the door with a dawning smile. "You're a sly fox, Joel. You want ammunition, to get your own back on the British over the Iraq business."

"The thought had crossed my mind," Henderson said.

The connecting door to the adjoining house led to the one-man elevator to the basement. It was the home of the Beach Combers down there, the group mainly composed of bookish young women who scanned newspapers from every European capital and every last scrap of intercepted traffic to glean incidental information. Most was recorded and cross-referenced then never seen again. But some of it proved useful in triggering a fruitful train of thought, in filling in gaps, in helping to complete the pictures the Listening Post existed to paint.

Arthur Rand was at his table in the corner, his computer terminal to one side and the microfilm reader to the other.

"Does the name Franklin mean anything to you, Art?" Sherman asked. He had to stoop under the low ceiling.

Rand shook his graying head. "What's the context?"

"Fort Halstead."

"That's the RARDE place in Kent. What else do you have?"

"That's it."

With a soulful sigh, Rand turned to his terminal and began a dialogue on the keyboard. Sherman saw him enter the name *FRANKLIN*.

"What's the time frame, Hulk? Recent? Distant past?"

Sherman replied with a shrug.

"No sweat. If it's in there, we'll find it. It'll just take longer, that's all."

Even as Rand spoke, lines of text began to fill the screen.

"*Very* interesting," the old man muttered, pushing his bifocals to the top of his head and reading with his nose only inches away. "A scientist working on war games who took to his heels and vanished east."

Sherman felt his heart beat faster. "With any information of ours on him?" The head was blocking his view.

234

"Not to speak of, at least that's what it says here. They had some data on U.S. weapons at the fort but nothing you couldn't pick up from the bookshops in the Charing Cross Road."

"When did he run?"

"Just coming up to three weeks ago."

"Did it make the papers? I don't remember seeing it."

"Nope. The British kept it quiet. They reported to us via the usual liaison channels. No American connotations, they said, hands on hearts. We were being told as a matter of courtesy."

"Is that likely to be true, Art?"

"God only knows, with M16. You're as familiar with those people as I am. Too many leaks in the past two decades, too much sensitive U.S. date slipping through their clumsy fingers. They've become as touchy as hell every time it happens again. But no, I'd make book this one's straight. Franklin was a very small fish and Fort Halstead is hardly a pond we need to watch too closely. The record coding says Grosvenor Square took a sniff and marked it for archives."

"If it was kept so quiet," Sherman mused, "how would an ordinary guy over here on business get to know?"

"He shouldn't have."

"Just what I'm thinking."

"My name's Sherman," The Hulk said into the phone. "Joel Henderson has been briefing me on your conversation."

"About goddamn time," Avery complained. "I've been kicking my heels in here for well over an hour."

"I gather you have some recent news on Franklin?"

"Yes." There was a finality to the reply.

"But not till we meet, is that it?"

"Yes."

"Well, our feeling is it might be worth pursuing. Did you have a fee in mind?"

"No," Avery said primly, "I'm just doing my job as Joe Citizen."

"I see," Henderson murmured with a private frown. "What's your passport number, Mr. Avery?"

It was given, then his place of residence, but Avery flatly refused to part with the name and address of his employer.

"That's neither here nor there," Shreman said. "I can get it from the IRS in Los Angeles."

There was a silence before Avery said in a subdued tone, "Northridge Electronics, Devonshire Street, Chatsworth. And I don't want them to hear about this, is that clear?"

"Why not?"

"Because I don't, period. If you people can't guarantee discretion the relationship ends here."

"They won't get to hear," Sherman assured him. "Now, how soon could you be in London?"

"Two hours, I'd guess. Three at the outside."

"Let's settle for three this afternoon, huh? That gives you ample time." And me too, Sherman was thinking. "Do you know the Round Pond in Kensington Gardens?"

"I can find it."

"We'll meet there."

"How will I recognize you?"

"Just be there. I'll pick you out in the crowd."

"North or south side?" Avery asked, with what sounded to be sarcasm.

"West, naturally," Sherman answered.

He shouted for Jane, the section gopher.

"Here's a name, address, and passport number, kid. I want a fax of the passport photo wired from Washington within the hour. Then check with Fort Meade whether we have any record on him. Then try Sacramento. I want a full listing of his California police files if there are any, down to the last traffic violation."

"Any particular offense in mind?"

"Hoaxes against authority," Sherman said.

18

A stiff breeze sprang through the trees in Kensington Gardens to scamper across the broad expanse of the pond, crinkling the water and bending the sails of the model yachts. Above, a brother wind played havoc with the kites.

Sherman made a wary progress round the perimeter, tossing bread to the ducks. The most likely candidate was the gangly individual over on a bench by the keeper's hut, looking all the while at his watch. Presenting his back, Sherman checked the facsimile photograph. Yes, it was Avery all right, even though the picture gave no indication of the ginger hair and he was older. Well, it was a 1974 photograph.

Sherman made for the hut and was spotted as he came, his gait shambling and devoid of the coiled-spring alertness he could inject into his body when he wished. From a repertoire of Shermans he chose the backwoodsman, the ponderous-moving, ponderous-thinking fellow from way out of town. Size had its uses; whoever thought instinctively of small people as stupid?

"Dave Sherman," he drawled, seizing the free corner of the bench. "Pleased to make your acquaintance." Avery merely nodded, looking him over the way men always did on first sight, more than a little intimidated and politely trying not to show too much astonishment at his height and the sheer volume of flesh.

"You look just as I expected," Sherman said. "A clean-living systems designer with only two freeway speed violations to man an otherwise honest life."

"Efficient," Avery said, scratching an ear.

"We do our best. The post office over here does its damnedest to balk transatlantic communications but we seem to get by."

"I'm disappointed in you, though," Avery said. "I expected a button-down shirt at least, and a gray-flannel suit with a vest." His eyes made one more tour of the worn cord pants and the grubby windbreaker with the lumberjack pattern.

Sherman cleared his pocket of bread, lobbing a crust to the pond to start a squabble among a flock of waiting geese. "So tell me the story," he invited.

"Here?"

"What's wrong with here? Out in God's fresh air, surrounded by peaceful English folk walking their dogs. You want a soundproof room and a polygraph?"

"If you must." His eyes holding Sherman's with an almost disconcerting directness, Avery first described the empty desk at the fort and his interrogation of Valerie Ashton. If it was an invented tale, Sherman thought, it was the most offbeat he had ever heard.

"You actually quizzed the girl?" He said. "And she *let* you?"

"Personal charm might have something to do with it," Avery said, smiling.

"We were told the whole news item," Sherman said to deflate him, and regarded his fingernails one by one.

"By who?"

"Who cares who? Through the normal processes of liaison, that's who. It was a purely domestic matter, a nuisance to the British with no Stateside connotations."

"Now where have I heard that before?" Avery retorted.

"You know differently?"

"I didn't say that. What did they tell you happened to Franklin?"

"He's gone to earth in Hungary, at least that's where the trail went cold. First a motorcycle dash to Lydd airport in Kent, then two airplanes on a zigzag route to Budapest; a regular Cook's tour. We did our own routine follow-up on receipt of the report and it didn't raise an eyebrow. He's a dead file at the agency."

"Then I suggest you open it again. It could just be he's zigzagged all the way back."

"Come out with it," Sherman said. "Let's have the

rest of the story."

"Did they tell you about Corrigan, your friendly liaison sources?"

"Who's Corrigan?"

"So they didn't?" Avery said with a broad grin.

"Then you'd better," Sherman suggested, and he held an impassive face as the chapters unfolded then stared for an age at the pond while he tried putting the pieces together in his mind. It sounded genuine and it sounded big.

But Avery's part in it disturbed him; he got everywhere a mite too easily, and conveniently knew all the right questions but none of the answers. What would Henderson think of it? he wondered. That it was just about the best contructed bait he had encountered in a long time, that's what he would say.

"It might have been an accident with the car," he suggested. "Who says it wasn't?"

"Ballantine for one. And Mulholland guessed it was a sniper. Except it couldn't have been, of course." Avery modestly looked away at the ducks, anchored patiently nearby. "Even the best sniper in the world can't shoot around a moving truck."

"Would you credit that?" Sherman said, wagging his head in amazement. "Now that's what I call heavy, real heavy."

"Well, did they tell you?" Avery asked again, to receive a wry smile in answer. "So the liaison procedures only operate for small fry? Not for the serious stuff, the assassinations."

Sherman stared at his fingernails again; one of them bothered him and he bit it to shape. If this wasn't being told to me on a park bench, he considered, by a smart-ass who sets my teeth on edge, what would I make of it? If it had come in as an intercepted report from monitored British traffic, what would I think of it then? That it was almost certainly the real goods, he decided, that's what, and we'd pull out the stops to find out more.

"What do you know about SIGINT?" he asked. "Signals Intelligence?"

"Nothing."

"But you know that's the agency's main role over here?"

"No."

Sherman stared. I'm over here as part of what we call the UKUSA Agreement," he explained. "Put simply, that means we pool information with the British and they play ball with us. Over there," he gestured toward Embassy Row, "half the diplomats in London talk their hearts out and we try to hear what we can. Down in Sloane Street there are the Danes and beyond them the West Germans. And, and, and. There's plenty of useful talk in the air, do you get the picture?"

"What has this to do with Corrigan?"

"All, and nothing. The agreement's a sham, a political pretense written on the wind. When the British latch on to a secret worth having they sit on it. At this very minute they're hedging the pound against the dollar on the back of some choice information on future oil price movements picked up from the Iraqis. They have better ears than we do in Baghdad, do you follow? We'd like to know more, you bet your boots we would, but we're being stalled."

"So?"

"So it would help some if we caught them out on a blanket job over this Corrigan affair, an outright cover-up. You might just have handed us a king-sized stick to beat over their stubborn heads. For which, much thanks." Sherman gave his big country-boy smile, a slow-witted look of pleasure, all the while regarding Avery closely.

"The idea was that you'd take this more seriously," Avery said with contempt. "If I'd thought for one minute you'd simply use it for power games I wouldn't have bothered!" There was a self-righteous anger surfacing in those pale eyes, a total lack of understanding of the agency's world, perhaps of any real world, Sherman thought. A guy from the intelligence community would never have taken it like that. There was a reflex acceptance of double-play that became ingrained in intelligence people, it was their one common language. Sherman had it, it was in his blood. Yes, Avery was real all right. Sherman rose to his full height, the meeting over as far as he saw.

But Avery remained glued to the bench. "There's a quid pro quo," he said quietly. "A fee of sorts."

"Such as?" Sherman felt the suspicion inching back in.

"I want two things in return from you, Mr. Sherman. Two details my personal resources won't run to."

"And here am I fully convinced you can see through walls and hear everything," Sherman said.

"Whatever. First there's the car. It's curiosity, I guess, but I'd appreciate your ideas on how it was done. It happened right in front of my eyes yet I'm damned if I can work it out."

"Buggered brakes? I know it's corny but it's effective at the right place and time. Or a shot from the Mini you mentioned?"

"No." Avery shook his head emphatically. "The brakes were working. And I saw the body; he wasn't shot."

"I'll see what we can do on that one. It could make for some interesting field research."

"And then there's the plot itself. I want to know why; what they were after and what they got."

"That's a tall order. I'm not sure I can make any commitment."

"The need-to-know doctrine?"

"The agency is strictly in the listening business," Sherman said, repeating a favorite cautionary phrase of Henderson's "It's not our practice to broadcast."

"To an audience of one? And don't forget who put you onto the story."

Sheman bit another nail as he pondered, making a lopsided job of it. "Okay, let's agree on this," he said finally. "If I can, I'll give you an off-the-record briefing. But I must reiterate, there can be no firm promises." He stooped to present his hand. "I'll call you when I have news."

"Not at Quantek, you won't. Nor at the cottage."

"Perhaps you're right," Sherman agreed, and recited a number for Avery to memorize; a pigeonhole number, there was no danger in passing it on. "That will always find me. And if I want you I'll phone, give a wrong Oxford number and ring off. Call me back as soon after as you can."

On Kensington Road he caught a cab to Harrod's, pushed quickly through the crowds to a far entrance and took a second cab to Bayswater. From there he walked to the post, loitering in a bookshop on the way to make certain he had no tail. Avery seemed all he said he was but one still didn't take chances. There were plenty who would like to know where Listening Post Three was this year.

Art Rand punched the keys on his terminal for ten whole minutes, roaming through his files.

"No Corrigan," he said, turning with a shrug.

"That's no surpise," Sherman replied.

"A car accident, wasn't that what you said?"

Sherman nodded, taking care to mind his head.

"Then it should have made the newspapers?"

"Highway pile-ups are ten a penny, Art."

"Let's have a look, anyways." Rand made his way across the basement vault to a row of card files.

"Don't you cross-reference everything on the computer?" Sherman asked.

"What for? We qualify all inputs for likely future relevance. Less than twenty-five percent warrant a computer entry." Rand began pulling out drawers, thumbing the index cards. With a triumphant smirk he was soon swooping on a card and he then went to a distant cabinet for another. They led him to two clippings in the bound press files: from the *Daily Telegraph* and the *Sun,* both dated October 15.

"They don't tell us anything new," Sherman observed. "Ten vehicles involved according to the *Telegraph,* fifteen in the *Sun*. Three people detained in hospital. One dead, our Dr. Corrigan."

"Both mention Quantek, that's how they came to be clipped." Rand was squinting at an index card. "It's a

List X company."

"List X?"

"Cleared to secret level by MOD Procurement Executive. Quantek supplies defense systems to the army, Hulk. More to the point, they're contractors for SIGINT equipment to Government Communications Headquarters in Cheltenham."

"Are they indeed?" Sherman breathed. "GCHQ, our old friends and rivals. The very bunch with the lid on the Iraq story." He belted Rand fondly on the back. "Joel is going to love you, Art."

Rand adjusted his glasses, almost knocked off by the hearty slap. "I presume eagle-eyed Lucy over there saw the mention of the company and dived for her scissors."

"But it still didn't make your computer."

"Why should it have?" Rand said defensively. "A run-of-the-mill accident, an unfortunate death. Where's the indication of a darker side?"

"Where indeed?" Sherman concurred, patting his back again from a great height to console him.

From his cubbyhole on the top floor he called Quantek and asked for the transport manager.

"David Sherman," he announced. "N.S. Insurance."

"Well, Mr. Sherman?"

"I've got a deal you won't believe. We can slash your fleet insurance costs and, catch this, give you improved injury cover at one and the same time. What say we meet? How's your schedule for tomorrow?"

"I'm quite adequately covered, thank you."

"They all say that. Wait till you hear the details of

245

what we can offer."

"Do you provide buildings policies?" the man asked with weary disinterest. "Plus employee life cover and pensions?"

"No, just fleet insurance."

"We have all aspects of our company operations under an unbrella scheme. I have no intention of parceling parts of them out to fly-by-nights. What outfit did you say you were with, again?"

N.S. Insurance," Sherman said. "Can I ask who handles your group policy?"

"I don't see the relevance."

"To go in my report. I have to say why I've made no sale. Help a guy, would you? It's only statistics."

"Guardian Royal," the manager said.

Sherman telephoned Guardian Royal. It was about the Quantek account, he explained, a question on the motor policy. After two transfers of extension he was talking to a clerk in the motor department.

"Are you with Quantek?" she asked.

"No."

"Then I can't tell you a thing, can I? It's company confidential."

"I'm with N.S. Films," Sherman said. "We need a crashed Rover for a scene in a movie. I heard Quantek had one."

"Could be," she admitted.

"Then why don't we make a deal? You tell me the value on your books and I'll add some. We'll pay more than you'll get from a scrap dealer. I mean, what's a few hundred dollars on a movie budget?"

She left the telephone to examine her files. "It's pretty grim," she said on returning.

"Exactly what we need, sweetheart, a real wreck."

"Our assessor puts the present value at five hundred. That's pounds, not dollars."

A very reasonable fee for Avery's story, Sherman decided quickly. That's how he would justify the expenditure to Henderson. Buy the man off with part of what he wanted; tell him the mechanics of the accident and tell him nothing else. It should be sufficient to keep him quiet.

"Is it sold?" he asked.

"Not yet." She lowered her voice to confide, "There was some trouble with the police. They wanted an examination to make sure it was roadworthy; in case of a prosecution, I suppose. We've only just had it released to us by the Home Office."

"Can you tell me where it is?"

"Not this minute, but I can find out." She took his number to call back. "What's the name of the film, by the way?"

"*Gold Dust,*" Sherman improvised.

He yelled for the gopher and told her to arrange a car transporter, to be ready at a moment's notice.

"Where do they modify our special cars?" he asked. "Is it an inside job or contracted out?"

"There's a big auto workshop at Chicksands. Very well equipped, so they say."

"Could they do a postmortem?"

"On a *car?*"

"Sure, on a car."

"I would imagine so, if you get the right authority."

"Find out for certain, kid."

No, he thought, let's start with Ballantine and his sidekick. Back he went to the next building and into

247

the elevator, down to find out what tidbits the ever helpful Art Rand had stored away on that machine of his.

19

Why did you do it? Avery asked himself, and the feeling of anticlimax gripped his stomach like hunger. But the deed was done and there could be no going back on it. The pack was in full cry now—the professional agency bloodhounds—and there would be no calling them off until they cornered their quarry. They had all the resources denied to him, of course; spy hunting was their business. Sherman was far from being the dimwit he pretended, and he had electronic toys and skilled people, the full might of the National Security Agency, to help him in the chase. Since when had Sherman ever had to resort to a phonograph head to detect a hidden bug? What did the English call it, a Heath Robinson contraption? My God, he thought, I'm only over here a matter of weeks and I'm already falling into the English habit: cobbling together cheap solutions from whatever bits and pieces come to hand and then being ridiculously proud of it.

Damn that man Sherman, he *could* be a prize fool and still get by; the electronics would do it all for him. He must have thousands of dollars' worth of sophisticated devices at his beck and call, and teams of hard-nosed specialists ready to do what he asked.

He had only to lift a telephone and give the word. Send me up a bug detector, would you? Follow that car, we mustn't be seen. Could you possibly kill a Russian for me, he's being a bloody nuisance? But make it clean, now, be sure it looks like an accident. Take a leaf out of the Soviet handbook and do it the way they did to Corrigan.

Staring out of the window across the compound to the Irishman's old office, watching the sun glint on the obstinate glass, Avery felt an envy of Sherman which turned first to dislike and soon to a near hatred which he knew to be irrational but which he was quite unable to shake off. So what was to be done now? Zilch, he told himself, aching with frustration. You had the ball and in a weak moment you passed it to that great oaf from the Appalachians or wherever. What the hell *can* you do? Knock on the agency door and ask for it back? Damn, damn, damn.

"It's a good view from here," Barbara said loudly in his ear, making him jump. "Such a pity about the mirrored glass." He hadn't heard her come in.

It was only a joke about the glass, she said quickly on seeing his troubled face; she recognized that idle look, the signs of work getting on top of you. He needed a break.

"Come to lunch," she invited, patting a plastic box under an arm. "Nothing in the Fortnum and Mason league, just sandwiches and two cans of beer. Take me to the park."

He jumped up willingly. "Where?"

"Hurst Park," she said with a smile. "One of the great playgrounds of Europe."

It was shoe-horned between the radar assembly

sheds, a piece of open ground which had miraculously escaped the rash of building covering the rest of the site. Everyone called it Hurst Park, she explained, even the great man himself, ever since old Drummond from Avionics had claimed it as his own, had the balding grass rollered and planted some spindly shrubs at Quantek's expense. (Drummond ran the Gardening Club, and when he wasn't wandering the offices with packets of seeds at discount was to be seen pottering in the park; he never seemed to do work as such, not proper work.) She found a place in the sun and settled Avery beside her, spreading the beer and sandwiches on a newspaper as if for a country picnic.

A cold front promised from Iceland had made fools of the weather men by heading instead for the mid-Atlantic, leaving the way clear for a few glorious days of Indian summer. Under the cloudless blue sky it almost could be taken for a park, Avery agreed kindly, with the staff out in their droves to lap up the sun while it lasted and the sparrows hopping round them for morsels. Women from the wiring shop sat in a circle making half-heard comments about the men and giggling like convent girls. It might have been high summer but for their heavy cardigans. Swindon women still clung to the fashion, Avery noticed, and some of the men wore them too, under their suits.

"Isn't this what new lovers do?" Barbara said. "Sit in the sun and whisper secrets? That's Agnes over there, Peter Hurst's secretary. What wouldn't she give to know that we're lovers."

Avery smiled and blew a discreet kiss.

"Not that you bloody care," she said. "A stud you may be, a romantic you're not. Three days and not a

250

word. No phone call with sweet nothings, no flowers. Why couldn't you think of flowers, Martin?"

"Not so long ago," he said obliquely, "Peter Hurst was accusing me of being a romantic. Accusing me, Barbara. You can't both be right!"

"What does he know of people?"

"I'll bring you a flower tomorrow, a single red rose for your desk. Just enough to set Agnes thinking without making it obvious."

"Be sure you do." She popped the rings from the beer cans and passed him a cheese sandwich.

"Can I ask you a question?" Avery said. "And try not to get mad." She stiffened, guessing the subject. "It's about those men in Patrick's office, the heavy brigade."

Her eyes closed and she swayed angrily. "I had something to tell you about Patrick, as a matter of fact, but it's suddenly gone clean out of my head. You might have waited five more minutes before resurrecting him. What's the point," she questioned herself aloud, "of taking a new lover to help forget an old one if the bloody man won't let you?"

Avery allowed her a brief respite, drinking his lukewarm lager and taking in the activity around them. Eventually she urged him to get on with it, if he *must*. He had known she would.

"Well?" she asked, drumming a hand on her knee. "Do I have to sit here all afternoon waiting for the other shoe to drop?"

"You said Patrick had some secret papers? The heavy boys came to reclaim them."

"I seem to remember saying something of the sort." She gazed sadly into his eyes and added, "Lover."

"I'd like to know what they were, what projects they related to."

"Wow-ee," she breathed, lifting her face to the sky.

"Just the project names, Barbara, only the names."

She stared at him in astonishment then anxiously around at the nearby groups on the grass, wondering if they had heard.

"Why?"

Avery stalled, shaking his beer can to be sure it was empty before returning it neatly to her lunch box. He wanted to trust her, to tell her the whole story, but the act of faith was beyond him. Why? For no damned reason at all, he told himself, it just was. Maybe he'd tell her tomorrow, maybe next week but not now. Each of us, he thought, has only so much trust to give in a lifetime and whenever you part with some only to have it betrayed it is gone for good, the precious stock is diminished. He had already given and lost more than he could afford to lose. He felt he had too little left and that must last him the rest of his days.

"Trust me," he said. "I'll explain it all one day, I promise." That's right, he thought, turn the tables on her. If a woman wants trust let her earn it, let her give some first.

She continued to stare for some time then gave a sniff he did not understand. "This is the classic way of getting defense information, did you know? Seduce and squeeze, it's called. We had a lecture on it once. Beware of strangers with loving eyes and foreign accents. *You've* got a foreign accent."

"Give, lady," he said with a smile. "Don't make me report back that the seduction was wasted."

She looked away, not finding that funny. "He had

no papers on Vulcan. I told you that."

"And I believed you."

After glancing around the area again she moved closer, cutting lines into a patch of exposed earth with a can tab as she spoke, watching the aimless doodles, not him.

"There were some papers on Bush Baby. Do you know what Bush Baby is?"

"Yes. And for your peace of mind, I've been shown one, quite officially."

"He had those for years, a regular collection in his filing cabinet, his big ministry-approved hideaway with the combination lock."

"I don't recall seeing that."

"It was in his office." She shrugged as she said, "The heavies carted it away. Then there was a file on Knapsack. That's the field radio system."

"The backpack radio?"

She nodded sparely.

"Go on," Avery said. "I don't see radios as important enough to bring security people running all the way from London. And they didn't come because of Bush Baby either. It's a clever toy but hardly a strategic secret."

"And that's the lot."

"It wasn't born yesterday. *What else did he have, Barbara?*"

"Classified secret, you mean? Nothing else."

"That you know of."

"Nothing, period. I had access to all his drawers, even to that secure cabinet. I knew the combination. They were the only secret papers, I swear, just those two projects."

"And yet the security officers cleared the office completely. They took every last scrap. What the hell were they after?"

"I told you, they didn't take me into their confidence." His perplexity seemed to delight her, the scribbles in the earth became wilder. "That's why I didn't take them into mine."

"About what?"

"About something even Patrick didn't know."

"So tell me."

"I was going to. That's why I suggested lunch; one of the reasons, anyway. But now I'm not so sure. You're only interested in me for what you can learn about Patrick."

"I think you're terrific," he said softly. "A little volcano. I'll make it two roses, two every day till I leave."

"Bloody man! Why do I always fall for men who can't even *pretend* to care?" She fluffed her hair with her fingers and it reminded him of a song from *South Pacific*. Did women know what their subconscious gestures conveyed? He reached out to tickle the end of her nose, eventually extracting a reluctant smile.

"Patrick was a whirlwind," she said with a shrug, "you'll be familiar with that side of him. He was a hurricane, force ten. I'd type some work for him, leave it half finished and uncorrected while I went to the loo, then come back and find it gone. It was *maddening*. He would change appointments and not tell me. Some days he wouldn't show up and I'd be forced into my secretary-defending-the-boss routine, lying through my teeth for him. But I told you, he'd say the next day, I told you I had that meeting up in

London with thingammy—it must have slipped your mind. And he'd give me one of his daft smiles as if forgiving me for his sin. Grr!" Remembering the habit could still stir her to fury: she struck the ground with a clenched fist and her mouth tightened. "You need a defense against hurricanes, Martin, some form of storm shuttering. Mine was down the corridor with Agnes." A slight nod toward Hurst's secretary, eating a solitary lunch in the shade. "Do you understand what I'm leading up to?"

Avery caught his breath. "I'm beginning to get a glimmer."

"I had an unofficial lease on one of her filing drawers. It was my secret and hers, a place for me to leave typing and notes away from the Irish gales. I haven't looked there for over two weeks, not since the accident. I'd no reason to. But I was bored out of my mind this morning so I went along for a natter with Agnes, anything to pass the time. 'Don't think me heartless,' she said for openers, 'but can I have my drawer back now? I don't suppose you'll have any more need of it, not having a boss to hide things from.' " Barbara stared daggers across the open space. "She and Hurst deserve one another."

"And you found . . ."

"I cleared it out then and there, to shut her up." She paused, watching him. "I came across Patrick's diary. I'd forgotten it was there."

Avery waited, saying nothing.

"I used to do a once-a-week diary purge, Martin. Patrick called it my Mother Hen act. You know, making sure he had his appointments sorted out, that I had my own record of when and where and with who. Have you ever tried answering the phone from an irate client, not knowing where your boss is that day? No, of course you haven't."

Get on with it, Avery thought. For God's sake, give. "What did you find?" he asked without urgency.

"I hadn't noticed it when I put it away there. A slip of paper in the diary, a list of dates and numbers—I think they're times. They mean absolutely nothing to me. They're not even in Patrick's writing.

Avery held out a hand.

"I don't have it with me," she said, feigning shock. "If it's important, do you think I'd hand it over to one of the seduce-and-squeeze merchants in front of half of the company! I left it upstairs."

Hauling her roughly to her feet, Avery demanded, "Show me," and made at speed for the main block, leaving her standing there, straightening her skirt and brushing off the strands of grass. The wiring women lapsed into silence, turned to follow her progress after him and then constructed whispered theories. It was a quarrel, they said, he touched her hand, did you see? Who is he, anyway? someone thought to ask. A Yank, another said, I heard he was a Yank. For some reason that began the giggles again. By the time the tale reached those who had been unwise enough to miss it by lunching in the canteen, Avery had as good as made love on the grass.

Stopping only for a glance at the scrap of paper, Avery returned it to the diary and placed that in his briefcase. Then he insisted on leaving the factory, driving some distance away and taking several turnings, until finally drawing in at the side of the road in open country. He gave no explanation for the drama and she asked for none but there was excitement in her eyes. The secrecy gave the paper an importance she clearly relished.

It was a sheet of plain foolscap, a list of handwritten dates with what seemed, as she had suggested, to be times.

"Do you use foolscap at Quantek?" he asked.

"No, only A-Four," and she repeated that she did not recognize that writing.

He stared at the list. 14 July, 1200. 24 July, 2200.

"Ten o'clock? Rather late for a meeting," Avery suggested.

"Too late for Patrick," she agreed. "Long ago he used to work all hours but not recently."

5 August, 1200.

"He was on holiday then," she recalled, "motoring through Greece."

"Suppose he just told you that's where he was?"

"I had several postcards, he always sent me postcards. From Athens, Corinth, and some other places I can't remember. And he had a complexion like a boiled lobster when he got back. Is it that hot in Russia? No, he was in Greece, all right."

21 August, 2000.

She took the diary and turned the pages, then searched Avery's face before admitting shyly, "I was with him that evening. See that circle around the date? That was to remind him of an evening with me. Just a circle, no name. He was the soul of discretion, my Patrick."

"And you kept the appointment?"

"Sometimes he forgot. I never did."

"How about that night?"

"We had dinner in Newbury. I remember it clearly."

3 September, 0400.

"Who meets at that time of morning?" Avery mused. "And for what possible reason?"

"Who says they're meetings?" she asked.

"What goes on at Quantek at four in the morning?"

"Cemeteryville. Sleeping guards and rats scavenging at the back of the canteen. What else *can* happen?"

That night, back at the cottage, he spent hours worrying over the list, comparing the dates with the diary and finding no clue to the puzzle. Perhaps the paper was of no significance after all, he began to think. Why, if it meant anything, would Corrigan have left it in his diary for his secretary to find? Who could guess what wild reasons the man had for his actions?

The telephone rang, a rare event during his stay there. It was a man asking for an Oxford number and the accent was passably English.

"Sorry, wrong number," Avery said. Snatching up his coat he went to the garage for the Rover and drove off in search of a telephone booth.

20

Sherman had a *penchant* for park benches. This one was beside the busy road on the northern fringe of Hyde Park, with the Marble Arch just visible through almost leafless trees. He kept Avery waiting well past the appointed time before staggering into view in a sweat-stained track suit and dusty running shoes. His head lolled as he came, he panted with great gulps like a stranded fish, and tributaries of perspiration coursed down his scarlet face.

"Exercise," he explained needlessly as he collapsed beside Avery. "Jesus." He buried his face in his hands, his body heaving. When he finally regained his breath he drooped his arms wearily over the back of the bench, thrust out a leg and nodded to what Avery thought must be the largest track shoe Adidas had ever made. "They should print a government warning on the soles: jogging is dangerous to health." He mopped his brow with a sleeve. "Jesus," he said again, "if staying fit was good for you it couldn't feel so bad."

"Ever tried eating less?"

"I'm a food junkie," Sherman confessed between a second onslaught of short breaths. "The only thing on earth I really fear is hunger." He rose unsteadily to his feet. "Okay, let's get this show on the road. My car's over there." It was a Ford parked by the opposite curb on freshly painted double yellow lines. A policewoman was pacing round it, preparing to write a ticket.

"What's wrong with here?" Avery asked. "Fresh air. Friendly natives with notebooks at the ready."

"Don't give me that shit," Sherman said with unexpected venom. "*You* talk in the open, *I* don't. An intelligence *aficionado* like you ought to know little details like that." He walked, weak-limbed, over to the car for a guileless tourist act he obviously did often.

"Is *that* what those lines mean? They're red where I

259

come from. Thanks for telling me, sweetheart, I'll never do it again. It's a wonderful city you have here, absolutely wonderful. And you English are so nice, I'm just laid back. Don't we just love it here?" he appealed to Avery, to enroll him in the deception. "We can't wait for our next visit." The policewoman hesitated and he stopped low over her to place a hand on a shoulder, a vast bird of prey hooding its catch. "We're staying at the Hilton," he confided. "You'd think for what we're paying they'd explain about parking restrictions."

The woman sighed and put her pencil away. It was a lousy act, Avery thought. Presumably the way he towered over her explained its success.

Sherman drove twice around the Marble Arch, his seat at the rearmost stop and his head against the roof lining.

"Do you fill out expense claims?" he asked, his eyes on the mirror.

"Sure I do."

"Then give me some advice, as one stranger in town to another. What's the category for purchase of a wrecked car? Do I put it under travel or unbudgeted capital items?"

Hell, that sounds ominous, Avery thought, but Sherman refused to say more.

"Let's find ourselves a quiet spot first," he insisted, and after one more trip round the arch made a dive through the traffic for the Edgware Road and proceeded north by an amazingly circuitous route, alternating between main roads and side streets, sometimes doubling back, continuing to stare into the mirror. To Avery, it was as overdone as the performance with the traffic cop, spy mania carried to extremes, and he settled back with an amused smile.

Eventually they passed Lord's cricket ground and turned into a car wash, the only decent car wash in the entire damned city, Sherman claimed. The brushes had to sound like wire wool scraping metal or it was a total waste of time. He muttered something to the attendant at the cash desk and juggled the wheels onto the tracks. They were carried forward into near darkness. Foaming water sprayed from all sides and the brushes scratched up the windscreen and began to grind their way over the roof.

"Hear that?" Sherman said. "That's what I mean."

Suddenly the track stopped with a jolt and the brushes fell silent but the water continued to douse the car as if in a tropical downpour.

"What do you know?" Sherman said slyly. "We seem to be stuck."

"Handy," Avery said. "Out of reach of cameras and mikes."

"Could be." Sherman half turned to face him. "It's been a busy couple of days for me. Three investigations into the life and times of the late Dr. Corrigan. Thanks to you, I've gone into the used-car business and pursued a yellow intelligence official, name of Ballantine."

"I make that two investigations," Avery said.

"I'll come to the third in my own time. Let's start with the expensively acquired Rover. I had our best auto mechanics take it apart, what was left of it. We were short of a hood and a door, and down to two wheels. Who cares, it was a steal at only five hundred pounds. Jesus, the agency's going to take *me* apart next. Know what we found?"

Avery shrugged, worried by the grim manner.

"Zilch, a big zero. I've got a real lulu of a mechanic's report on my desk. Subject one British Leyland car, it says. Condition slightly less than roadworthy. Missing a few components such as doors, which may or may not have been part of the original equipment when it left that well-known factory. Cause of accident, an accident." There was scorn in Sherman's eyes, or was it anger? "And a polite footnote, handwritten at the bottom. Please can we get back to lesser tasks now, such as modifying agency cars for surveillance?"

"Who asked you to buy the goddamn car!" Avery retorted. "That wasn't *my* idea."

"I guess I can charge it to experience," Sherman said, as if to himself. "I wonder if there's an experience column on the expense sheets?"

"Maybe Ballantine's people got there first, did you think of that? Maybe they removed the evidence."

"They didn't touch it."

"*What?*"

"It was held under wraps for two weeks but they didn't so much as wave a wrench at it."

"How do you know?"

"Because our mechanics at Chicksands say so, and they know what they're talking about."

"It wasn't an accident! I know it wasn't."

Sherman spoke as if alone. "Suppose this character Avery is right, I said to myself. Suppose we're missing something. So I send one of our field operatives prowling the coroner's office in Swindon and he gets me an unofficial copy of the autopsy examination. It makes interesting bedtime reading; thank God I'm not squeamish. Corrigan had as many fractures as a Ming vase, lesions and bruises galore, massive damage to the upper skull and what would have been fatal compression of the right frontal lobe. Note the 'would have been.' Actural cause of death is listed as coronary thrombosis. The guy was dead before his car so much as touched another vehicle."

"Do you believe that?"

"He was forty-six and I'm thirty-four, otherwise we had a lot in common. He was overweight, under stress, and drank too much. You ask *me* if I believe it, a fellow sufferer? Hell, I could feel the heart palpitations as I read the words."

"They're conning you," Avery said simply.

"Who?"

"I don't know who. Whoever did it."

"Look, jerk," Sherman sneered, "I don't intend to do my own autopsy as a double check. If you think I'm about to disinter an Irish body by dead of night from English soil, you've got another thing coming. It was an *accident,* got it? And there's not a shred of evidence that Corrigan's life was other than snow white. He made our computer system for two whole days before I came to my senses and had his files scrubbed off again."

The windows were opaque with condensation. The water beat a galelike tattoo on the roof. Sherman fished in a pocket for a photograph which he concealed in his hand as he considered it with an accusing stare.

"Let's move on to investigation number two, shall we? Subject, one George Ballantine. Nationality, British. Age, fifty-one. Marital status, divorced, no

263

children. I do a preliminary sortie on the computer and what do I find? That he's a department head at GCHQ. Do those cryptic initials mean anything to you?"

"No."

"Government Communications Headquarters. Based in Cheltenham. Pretty old English town, ghastly-looking establishment."

"And they do what?"

"What the name suggests. They handle all official communications for the British government. Scrambled phone links between ministries, diplomatic messages to the embassies overseas, that kind of stuff. Whitehall traffic, we call it. The idea is to get the good news to its destination without prying eyes having a peek."

Avery shook his head. "Somehow, I don't picture George playing carrier pigeon between government offices."

"They also *listen* at GCHQ. They monitor other people's airwaves and analyze for tidbits. They're real big in the listening business, my friend, with posts throughout Europe and the old Commonwealth."

"Intelligence, you mean? Yes, that figures."

"Put another way," Sherman said with emphasis, "Ballantine is in the same game as me but pulls a damned sight more rank."

Avery was handed the photograph, which he assumed to have been taken in the street with a telephoto lens.

"That's George," he confirmed. "You've captured the benign look perfectly."

"I'll spell it out for you. Ballantine works for GCHQ

and GCHQ buys electronic kit from Quantek. Ergo, Ballantine is a legit client of Quantek's. If he feels like keeping a beady eye on their comings and goings, where's the harm in it? When a minor defection occurs at a defense extablishment using a Quantek system, why shouldn't he organize a routine investigation to make sure his work isn't at risk? In his exalted position, I'd do the same."

"Now hold on. Are you trying to say that Corrigan just *happened* to drop down dead while Ballantine was trailing him? Some coincidence!"

"What I'm saying is that my boss, Henderson, gets to hear I'm checking out Ballantine and hits the roof! Protocols ignored, abuse of the host country and all the rest. Jesus." Sherman clawed mist from the windscreen to stare glumly into the mechanical rain, remembering the scene in Henderson's untidy closet of an office. "You're an overgrown college boy fresh in from Fort Meade," Henderson had screamed. "A dinosaur with a dinosaur-sized brain. What do you know of European field work yet! You're over here less than a year and you're barging into GCHQ territory, making tidal waves. I told you: take a sniff and report back, don't follow through. You'd better get used to singing soprano because when you leave this office your balls stay on my desk as trophies."

Sherman pushed his face so close Avery could feel the hot breath. "For a time, Henderson and Ballantine worked together like that in Berlin." He locked the fingers of both hands. "They listened together, swapped notes on traffic and finally fell out. Who knows why they fell out. I don't, I'm just off the plane from Maryland. But suddenly Henderson discovers one of his staff, yours truly, stalking Ballantine on his own home ground, taking secret snapshots from a moving car in Main Street, Cheltenham." He snatched back the photograph. "I leave the rest to your imagination. 'Who is this guy Avery?' Henderson yells at me. 'Why does he have to pick on me out of the thousand other suckers in the agency he could've rung? Whose fucking side is he on?' Which brings us to investigation number three." Sherman jabbed a finger viciously into Avery's ribs. "You, friend."

Avery backed away until he was against the car door. The water gurgled down the glass next to his ear; a trickle had found a way in and was dripping into a pool on the carpet by his feet.

"Your wife pointed us in the right direction," Sherman said, "and, boy, did she take some finding. She put us onto a very helpful character. Dr. Danziger, does that sound familiar? He hangs out in an expensive place in Topanga Canyon. Six bedrooms, a new Jacuzzi and a triple garage with triple Mercedeses to match. I should have gone in for his line of work instead of joining the agency. Shrinks do very well for themselves."

Avery closed his eyes. How do you explain a perfectly ordinary bout of overwork to a man like Sherman? Tell him it happens to one person in ten at some time or other? That it's no worse, no more permanent, than measles? Plink, plink went the trickle of water. It was as if the car was perspiring for him. He was deadly cold, too cold to perspire.

"Three months off sick last year," Sherman was saying. "A combination of marital problems and near-paranoiac dedication to work, isn't that right? An obsessive tendency to see boogiemen under the bed and in every computer system you get your mitts on. Christ, if only I'd followed my instincts. If only I'd done that bit of research first!"

"I thought medical records were private," Avery muttered lamely.

"You gave up any claim to privacy the minute you called Henderson." Sherman switched on the ventilation fan to clear the windows. "And don't give me that invaded-civil-rights look! Dr. Danziger saved your bacon. I had you figured for some weird kind of plant for a while there, trying to brew trouble between us and the British. But Dr. Danziger assures us no, no way would you do that. And do you know for why? Because according to him you're got that rare type of unswerving integrity which is the exclusive preserve of nut cases! So he sends his regards and suggests a long rest before you worry yourself back into a nervous breakdown." Sherman sounded a long blast on his horn. It reminded Avery of another he had once heard, interrupting a nightmare. He shivered; the car had the damp-feeling, damp-tasting cold of a crypt.

The brushes scraped back into life and the car shuddered, moving forward toward a gleam of daylight. Powerful air jets tidied the water on the hood into silver globules like ball bearings and hurried them away over the windscreen.

"Suspicion like yours is fucking contagious," Sherman said contemptuously. "I'm all set to have a quiet chat in the park when I run past a car waiting along the road with two guys inside. I go twice round the monument and it sticks tight to my bumper. It's

267

an Opel, a favorite of the Soviet field operatives over here. So I play a gentle game of hunt the thimble up the back streets and it's suddenly gone. If it *had* been a Q car I'd never have shaken it off that easily, yet I still feel the need to hide in here while I confess my stupidity. Christ Almighty, a guy like you could start an epidemic of nerves."

Three young blacks leapt on the car as they emerged, swabbing the body with leathers. A line of cars stretched from the entrance to the car wash, across the garage forecourt and a long way along the main road.

"You know my trouble?" Sherman said with regret. "I was a judo black belt in my carefree youth. My hands are lethal weapons. I've learned to control them so well I'm incapable of losing my temper. Are you ever lucky I'm so bloody controlled." He nodded to a nearby corner. "It's your turn for exercise, friend. There's a subway station over there."

Avery sat tight. "I found one more thing yesterday." He had no idea why he bothered to say it.

Sherman covered his eyes with a hand.

"A list of dates and times. Corrigan had it."

"Meaning what?" The question was put flatly, without interest.

"I don't know yet."

"You don't know yet!" Sherman mimicked parrot fashion, and he pressed heavily against Avery as he reached over for the door handle to throw the door wide. "Out, mister. I won't say it's been good knowing you."

Obediently, Avery left the car.

"I don't want to hear another damned thing from

you," Sherman cautioned. "If the Russians drop an H-bomb on Swindon, you tell someone else, okay? Try the Israelis, they'll believe any conspiracy theory going." He dragged the door shut and took off with a squeal, leaving a trail of wet tire tracks.

Avery stood staring after him until one of the black youths yelled for him to move; just behind, a car was leaving the wash.

"Thank you so much, Dr. Danziger, he thought. That's the last business you get from me, ever. Slowly, pensively, he made his way to the subway. He considered the possible truth of the autopsy report and he wondered whether Sherman had imagined the Opel and, if not, what it meant. But by the time the car doors hissed open all that mattered was that Sherman—the poor marvelous fool—had fumbled the catch and left the ball lying there for him to pick up once more. For which mercy, Avery thought, he would forgive the man every harsh word.

21

Franklin's motorcycle was back. It was propped in the front garden at 43 Mayfield Avenue, half across the steps. Avery knew it was the Kawasaki even before he pulled back the tarpaulin which hung over it like a shroud. A nice machine, an almost new 500cc twin cylinder with an iridescent blue tank. Conspicuous, you might say.

After ringing the doorbell, he turned to view the somber houses across the street. The steeply pitched roofs, the threadbare hedges, the sagging net curtains at the windows. All gray and dingy in the drizzle and encrouching darkness of a November evening. What the hell am I doing back here? he demanded of himself, as his eyes roamed the windows. God only knows. Clutching at straws again? Thrashing around in a quicksand of my own making? The Corrigan investigation is a dead end, that's for sure. What else *can* I do but come back to the beginning and have one final try. And this is where it all started, with Franklin's disappearance.

"Oh, it's you!" Valeria Ashton said. "The aggressive Mr. Gardner." She greeted him as she would a salesman, putting her hand on her hips and breathing a long, impatient sigh.

Now, he wondered, am I going to get away with a second visit? Have the heavies been to see her since I was here? Did she happen to mention me to them and set them diving for their notebooks, exchanging urgent glances? An *American* you say, miss? Are you sure? There are no Americans assigned to this case, not as far as we know.

He forced a smile and nodded down to the bike. "I see the wheels are back."

"It's a good job I ride," she replied sourly. "Do you know what they said, your friends in the Kent constabulary? We don't do deliveries! Charming! Well, are you coming in or not? I'm not standing our here all night."

She left him there to close the door.

"They phoned up last week," she threw back in the

270

dark hall. "A cocky young sergeant. 'Your boyfriend's bike is taking up room in our car park,' that was the gist of it. 'Let's face it,' he said, 'our errant Mr. Franklin is hardly going to be back for it himself.' Bloody charming," she said again in bleak judgment. "It's true what they say, we're well on the way to becoming a police state. Politeness costs nothing."

The flat was heavy with cooking smells. She saw him into a chair then went to the kitchen alcove, stopping at the curtain.

"I'm about to have supper. It's only spaghetti but you're welcome to join me."

Avery shook his head.

She stood there staring at him, shuffling her feet, playing with the hem of her sweater. "It's not news, is it? I've given up expecting news about him." Avery had wondered how long it would take her to ask.

"No, I'm sorry. I'm here because we're reopening the investigation."

"We? Which of the many possible *we's* would that be?"

"My people. The British seem happy enough with the Budapest angle but there are one or two aspects which bother us."

For his benefit, she glanced at her watch. "I've had a hard day at the fort and there's a program I want to see on the box."

"I won't be long."

"Famous last words," she said before withdrawing.

She was soon carrying a tin tray to the small dining table at the other end of the room. "If you don't mind doing the interrogation in the Ashton suite . . . ?" she said, beckoning with her head. "Famous for its fine

271

cuisine, exquisite decor and stunning panorama over Sevenoaks."

He joined her there to discover an enormous mound of spaghetti bolognese with an inviting homemade aroma, and an assortment of cream cakes to follow. Impossible, he thought. How do you stay so skinny?

She must have read his mind. "It's a man substitute, isn't that what the phychologists would say? Shoveling in the food to fill a vacuum in my life? Take it from me, Mr. Gardner, it is not the same thing."

"Have you had any word from Bob?"

"A long-distance phone call every day. Sometimes he talks for hours about Marxism, hours. How good things are on the other side, what a superior social system they have. The operator who puts him through sounds distinctly Slavonic, if that helps. You know, guttural and evil." She gave a lengthy sigh. "Oh, come on! Would I tell you!"

"So you haven't heard from him?"

"You know that very well." She dug into the spaghetti, assuming a hangdog expression.

"I thought he might have found some way of getting word to you. 'I'm all right, darling, don't worry'—something along those lines? It can't be difficult for him to arrange. A request in the ears of his new masters."

She ate in sulky silence, perhaps feeling he was trying to provoke her, to suggest how unimportant she must have been to Franklin. No, Avery thought, she's not pretending. There's been a total silence on the Franklin front.

"I came to ask you again about the day he vanished," he said.

"The story won't change."

"You never know. It might, just a little."

She glared and demanded, "Are you suggesting I lied!"

"No. But you were very upset when we met. Maybe the passage of time will have given you a different perspective."

In reply, she twirled strands of pasta under his nose then stuffed them into her mouth.

"I want to know whether anything about his disappearance bothers you," Avery said. "You've been reconsidering it, say, and there's a detail which doesn't quite add up. Anything, however small."

"Such as?"

Avery shrugged. "Well, his passport, for instance. You said he took it with him . . . ?"

"Yes."

"Was it up to date? Could he actually have used it?"

"As far as I know. Otherwise they'd have turned him back at the airport, wouldn't they?"

"I want to hear only what you know at firsthand, not assumptions. What else did he take? Shirts, suits, underwear?"

She nodded, plainly bored.

"And he didn't take any wrong clothes?"

"None of them were mine, if that's what you mean!"

"How about pyjamas? I always seem to forget mine when I travel."

"There were none to take, he never wore them." She smiled innocently. "He once said to me that men who wear pyjamas must have something to be ashamed of."

"Ha, ha," Avery said. "The clothes were packed in

273

what?"

"A small suitcase; more a carryall, really. The kind of bag that goes under an aircraft seat. You don't need to check them in."

"How did he get it on the motorcycle?"

"If you care to go out and look, you'll find a pannier with big rubber straps."

"Where would he have packed the Vulcan papers?"

"In the case, I should think." She ate more spaghetti and added, with a full mouth, "There were only a few files, they wouldn't have taken much room."

"Let's try a different tack. Can you think of anything he didn't take that he should have?"

"Me!"

Avery thumped the table in exasperation. "Try to help me, Miss Ashton. I'm on your side, believe it or not. I don't like the defection story either, it doesn't figure."

"She put down her spoon and fork, suddenly interested. "Why?"

"Why? Because too many people have gone out of their way to tell me how unimportant he was. If they're right, he had no reason to run, did he?"

"And what if I say, Yes, he left his favorite socks behind? Does that bring him back?"

Avery reached over to clutch her hands. "Anything, Miss Ashton," he pleaded. "Any damned thing."

She stared past him, gripping tightly. "He took the wrong razor," she murmured after a time. "Don't ask my why."

"Please explain . . ." Now he was doing the gripping.

274

"We both had safety razors. No fancy electric shavers, just good old-fashioned steel and soap." She glanced at Avery then quickly looked away, reddening slightly. "For legs and underarms in my case, I'm sure you've heard of the practice. Bob took my razor and left his behind, that's all there was to it. He was in a tearing hurry, I expect. That's why all the bedroom drawers were pulled out and the place was a shambles. He must have been in and out in minutes."

"Slow down a moment. Yours was one of those dinky lady shavers?"

"No, they're useless, stupid things. It was a Gilette, the same as his."

Avery left the table to stand at the window. Don't get excited, he told himself, not yet. It might be nothing, another dead end. He turned back to her and asked, "How did you know which was which?"

"I just did, can we leave it at that."

"No, we can't. I want to hear the whole story."

She pushed the food aside, no longer hungry. "It's kind of personal."

"Look," Avery said fiercely, "your underarms can be as hairy as a Portuguese sailor's for all I care. *I want to know!*" Hell and damnation, he thought, what is it about this poor bitch that she's so easy to shout at."

Her eyes widened. "It might be something like that," she admitted so quietly he barely heard it. "Do we have to go on with this? I wish I'd never mentioned it."

Avery sat at the table and took her hands again to reassure her, to apologize for his brusqueness. "I'll put it to you as simply as I can. Did Bob Franklin come

275

back here and pack that case? Or did someone else do it? A stranger who didn't know about the two razors? Now, are you going to help me decide which it is?"

She stared at him for an age but without surprise. Perhaps, he thought, the same idea had occurred to her. She had scarcely dared to entertain it. "We had an argument once," she said distantly. "Bob went to the bathroom to shave and the blade was blunt, his last blade. It was all my fault, he said, and as a matter of fact it was. He had to wait for the local chemist to open before we were able to leave for the fort. So we were late in. Little incident, big drama—you know how these things can be. Stupid woman, keep your hands off my gear. *My* personal gear. The next morning I discovered a shiny new razor waiting for me in the bathroom and there was a new golden rule to be obeyed without question at all times. My razor was to stay on the left of the shelf and his to the right. Anyway, some weeks later he had a blunt razor again, his fault this time. He went to use mine and found it all clogged up with hair. From unsavory places, do you see? All right to encounter in the bedroom at midnight but much too nasty to be near a male face at seven in the morning. Big drama again, he came on real heavy about it. From then on, he hid his razor from me in all manner of places. On top of the bathroom cabinet, behind the pill bottles." She searched Avery's face for his reaction. "This must sound very small-minded?"

"Go on . . ."

"I didn't realize what had happened at first. But a couple of weeks after he left I made a determined effort to pull myself together. I was in a mire of self-pity and had to snap out of it. Smarten yourself up, Valerie, I said. Go to the hairdresser's, get the silk blouse out of mothballs, make your legs smooth and enticing. That's what I intended. It was only then I found my razor wasn't in its place on the shelf. Neither of them was there."

"Show me," Avery said, getting up.

"It's only a shelf!"

"I still want to see."

The tiny bathroom was through a door just behind her chair. The ceiling sloped steeply; the room was presumably wedged under the stairs. The small bath was unpaneled, perched on bow-legged iron supports. To use it one would have to squeeze in under the veteran water heater which took up most of the wall above it.

"There," she said, pointing to a razor on a glass shelf over the sink. "That's his, got it? Mine was taken." She touched an aerosol of shaving lather. "There was one of these, too. That was gone. So was his toothbrush and the tube of paste."

"And you discovered the razor where?"

She crouched by the sink, crooking a finger to draw him down beside her. "Here." She reached under, to the back of one of the heavy metal brackets supporting the basin. "It was quite a search, I can tell you. For a while, I thought he'd taken both of them."

Avery tried the hiding place. Yes, there was just room to balance a razor there.

She laughed somewhat nervously at his bemused face. "I agree, it *is* crazy. You'd think it was a buried hoard of gold I was after."

"How would a stranger know which toothbrush to

take?"

"It wouldn't be hard to guess." She gave another strained laugh. "A sturdy brown handle next to a slimmer pink one? Real male-female role playing, isn't it?"

They returned to the living room where she tried the spaghetti, wrinkling her nose at how cold it had got. "Let's retire to the lounge, shall we?" she suggested. "The chef wasn't at his best tonight." From her ungainly armchair she asked, "Does the mystery of the razor help any?"

"It might." Avery was pacing up and down, too tense to sit. "The motorcycle was left at Lydd, right?"

"Yes, in the car park."

"With the key still in the ignition?"

"Of course not!"

"Then how were you able to drive it back?"

"Because he kept a spare in the bedroom."

"How many door keys does it take to get into this apartment?"

"Two. One for the front and one for the door behind you."

"I thought as much. Now, did Bob keep those keys on the same ring as the motorcycle key?"

"I don't know," she answered with a helpless shrug.

"Yes, you do, it's buried in your memory. All you have to do is dig for it. Picture him parking the bike downstairs, turning off the engine, coming up the steps to the door . . ."

Her eyes had closed and she was making twisting movements with a hand. The hand dropped as if to a pocket. "On a single ring!" She cried. "All together."

"Good." Avery went to the door and bent to the big

Chubb deadlock. There was another lock above it, and ordinary Yale. "Why all this hardware? Forgive me saying it, but you don't have much to protect?"

Her face flushed. "Some intelligence man you are! Bob kept secret files here, remember! He fitted that Chubb lock himself as a precaution. Suppose one of the local villains had broken in for the usual pickings, cash and a transistor, and ended up with defense files as a bonus! There would have been all hell to pay."

"Yes, that figures."

"There's a similar lock on the front door. Bob fitted that, too. He was good with his hands when he bothered."

Avery examined the door frame. There was no sign of forcible entry. He played with the Chubb lock, turning the key and watching the chunky tongue flick in and out. How easy is it for an expert to pick one of these? he wondered. God, I wish I knew.

"Do you mind explaining what's going on in that head of yours?" Valerie asked.

"In a minute." Avery sat facing her, on the settee. "Did any of your neighbors see Bob come back here that afternoon?"

"I haven't the faintest idea. I didn't ask. Do you think I went shouting the story down the street? *Bob Franklin's done a bunk to the East. Did you see him leave with the secrets?* Come off it!"

"But no one mentioned to you they'd seen him?"

"No."

"How about the motorcycle? Was that spotted outside?"

"It comes to the same thing, doesn't it?"

"Not necessarily. If a stranger had turned up on it

279

there's a fair chance he'd have been noticed, right?"

"I suppose so."

"So our mythical stranger can't take that chance. He doesn't dare bring the bike here."

"Please," she said in a little-girl voice. "Please explain."

"I give you the picture as I see it. Bob doesn't defect, he's innocent on all charges. It all starts when he happens to say the wrong thing to Dr. Corrigan down in Swindon. That brings the bad boys running and they decide they have to dispose of him. Or perhaps it's a ghastly mistake and he's accidentally killed. Either way they have a problem." Avery looked at her with concern. "Shall I go on?"

She nodded quickly, fearfully.

"Someone hits the panic button. A cleanup unit is dispatched here to make it look as if Bob has left under his own steam. It's a terrific cover story, if you think about it. I mean, who's going to search for a body when a man is believed to have defected?"

"What do you know?" she demanded. "What is it you're not telling me?" Her hand flew to her mouth. "Oh, God, you haven't found him, not dead?"

"No," Avery said, shaking his head. "It's a wild flight of fantasy which may, and I mean may, fit the facts. I agree with what you told me last time. The defection story doesn't ring true. It's got the security people fooled, but if you say it's out of character, I believe you."

"Does your version make any better sense?" She was confused, not knowing what to believe, what to *want* to believe.

"Let's stick with it a moment. If they follow my

280

reasoning about the bike, they can't risk bringing it here. There's no need to anyhow. The suitcase can be taken away in a car, on foot, any damned way. So one of the cleanup squad roars off to Lydd to leave the bike in a prominent place. Now, here's the interesting supposition. *Suppose they forget the door keys.*"

"Aah," she murmured.

"Motorbike man has them and doesn't realize it. Meanwhile his buddies have to get in here in a hurry. How do they do it?"

"Pick the lock, I should think."

"With that old busy-body watching from over there? A fully paid-up member of the senior citizens' surveillance corps?" Avery gestured over his shoulder to a high window across the street. He had noticed the old woman as he stood on the outside stairs, sitting in full view behind partly drawn muslin curtains.

Valerie peered out and laughed. "Old Winnie, you mean?"

"You can't miss her up there. She might notice a stranger playing around with the door, she might not. But again, they can't take the chance."

"She's got dreadful eyesight," Valerie said.

"They wouldn't know that. So the front door is out. Now what do they do?"

"Easy. Walk down the passage at the side of the house and into the garden. There aren't any gates."

"Is there anyone in the garden apartment during the day?"

"No. It's occupied by two blissfully married gays. They run an antiques shop in Tonbridge. They're both there during shop hours."

Avery was already on his way to the window at the

back of the room, pushing aside an armchair to reach it. The garden ran down to a church on the next street, a gloomy affair with a rusting crucifix at one end of a corrugated iron roof.

"Spiritualists," she said, joining him there. "I've often wondered what they get up to."

"So, no neighbors overlooking the rear. And an easy climb up to a convenient balcony."

"It is sort of vulnerable," she agreed. "That's one of the reasons I had the window fitted."

It was a modern, aluminum-framed window, obviously put there recently; pivoted at the top with two sturdy handles at the base to secure it.

Avery rapped on the glass. "Was this open or closed that day?"

"Closed."

"How can you be sure?"

"Because it always is when I'm out. It's a ritual before I leave each morning. Bob spotted how easy it would be to break in here and house-trained me."

Avery tried the handles and ran a finger along the close-fitting rubber sealing strip. "It wouldn't be easy to get in, would it?" he murmured sadly, shaking his head.

"Burglarproof," she said. "That's what the window people assured us. There was a dreadful, rotting old window here and we had to have it replaced. I keep saying I'll do the same at the front but I never seem to get round to it."

Avery caught his breath and dropped to his knees. He had noticed a small hole in the glass beside one of the handles. "Christ!" he muttered as he found an identical hole close to the other handle.

She knelt beside him. "But why?"

"Made during construction, maybe?"

"Don't be silly, holes let drafts in! Anyway, I'd have noticed them before. I'm sure they weren't there last time I cleaned the window."

"Two holes," Avery said. "Just big enough to push a strong piece of wire through. A length of wire with a hook at one end, say. How does that grab you? To jiggle open the handles the way thieves break into cars."

"Done with a drill?" She had noticed how perfectly round the holes were.

Avery pressed closer to the glass, feeling with the top of a finger. Each hole tapered slightly, larger on the inside surface than outside. The inside edge was finely splintered, as if by the entry of a bullet. A *bullet?* he thought. Surely not. He dove for the nearby armchair, tore off the cushion and dug in the recesses around the seat. He gave no answer when she demanded to know what he was doing.

"Yours, I believe?" He threw her a ballpoint pen then placed a ten-penny coin and a paperclip on the floor. "Ah!" He held a small metal sphere out to her in the palm of his hand.

"A ball bearing?" She rolled it to and fro, wondering why it was flattened on one side.

"An air pistol pellet. And I'm willing to bet neither you nor Bob ever used an air pistol in here."

She stared in astonishment before shaking her head.

"Then that's how they did it," he said, with barely suppressed excitement.

"A bit farfetched, isn't it?" she retorted. "I mean, his man comes here and can't get in but he just *happens* to have an air gun with him. No, it's ridiculous. I can understand a revolver . . . but an air gun?"

"An expert's tool for housebreaking," Avery said. "Let's be clear, whoever pulled this job *was* an expert. He'd have a leather case in his car, full of charming toys." I bet if I dared to ask Sherman about the air pistol stunt, he was thinking, he'd confirm it as a standard method of entry. He could probably say which country favored it, too. Quick, and quiet. Put the barrel against the glass and squeeze the trigger. Just a slight *phut* and moments later you're climbing in.

"I think I could do with some coffee," Valerie said, her voice suddenly husky. "How about you?"

"What a good idea." Avery was on his hands and knees in search of the second pellet. Not that it mattered whether he found it or not. One pellet was enough.

22

"Now what?" Valerie asked. She sat cross-legged on the floor in front of him. Her face was strained and her eyes red. Avery thought she must have cried quietly to herself in the kitchen although he had heard only the grumbling electric kettle.

"You'll say nothing about his, understand? It's your secret and mine until I find out more."

"Why didn't the Special Branch men see the holes in the window?" she queried plaintively. "Why did I have to go through weeks of not knowing?"

"Because they weren't looking. They had a preconceived idea of the facts, and the evidence seemed to support it."

"Stupid bloody men! I knew they were stupid. I told them Bob wasn't the type to defect."

"Do you trust me?" Avery asked.

She looked up a him with surprise. "Who else can I trust?" she said, as if questioning herself. After some thought she added, "Yes, I suppose I do now."

Avery took the handwritten list from his pocket, the list found in Corrigan's diary. "Then give me an honest answer about this." He passed the sheet to her. "Is that his writing?"

"Yes." She needed only a glance to confirm it.

"Have you ever seen that before?"

"No, never."

Read it!"

He watched her eyes move, across and back, slowly down the list.

"I've never seen it," she snapped.

"What does it mean, Miss Ashton?"

"They're dates . . ."

"I know that!"

". . . . And game times."

The words hit Avery with the force of a blow to the face. Christ, he thought, of course they are! What else could they be! Fool not to see it.

"How do you know?" he asked somehow controlling his voice.

"I don't actually *know,* do I! I'm simply guessing.

But since Bob wrote them down, that's what they must be."

"Did he ever talk to you about game times?"

"Constantly. And I'd turn on the box or open a book and politely suggest he shut up. Didn't I tell you that last time? I'm sure I did."

"So the times mean what? What's the connection between them?"

She read them again before shaking her head. "I can't say, not from memory."

"I assume there are records of past games at the fort?"

"Of course. A whole library of them. Binder after binder of computer output, going back to the day the system was installed."

"Then I want you to do something for me. Go through those files tomorrow, checking each of the dates and times on that list. I want to know what the link is, what weapons and tactics were being played. There *has* to be a connection. I want you to find it for me."

She frowned darkly at him, narrowing her eyes. "I'm sorry, I can't do that."

"Rules, you mean? The dear old Official Secrets Act?"

She nodded very seriously.

"Shall I go over it again for you?" Avery said grimly. "Bob Franklin wrote that list. Then he drove to Swindon, where he gave it to Dr. Corrigan. He promptly disappeared, never to be seen again. The same day, along come men with air guns to fake a defection."

"You say!" she retorted with sudden doubt.

"What's your clever theory, then?"

She hid her face in her hands. When she finally took them away it was to stare at him with a look of fever, with a strange, wild tiredness. "All right," she mumbled, then raised her voice to a nervous shout. "But if I get booted out over this, it's on your head. The bloody U.S. government can pay my pension."

"Good girl. Can you do it tomorrow? I'll phone you here in the evening."

"If that's what you want," she said submissively.

"Be very careful," he told her at the door. "They're dangerous men, whoever they are. They got Bob first, then Dr. Corrigan. Don't be seen searching those records."

"Dr. Corrigan?" She almost jumped.

He gave no explanation. Yesterday, he thought, I almost ended up convinced it was an accident. But not now, not after finding that pellet.

He took her hand and said, "Please be careful." He felt a need to repeat it. Thank God, he thought, I did my Sherman act on the way here, learning a trick or two from the expert. Up and down the side streets, around the London houses, catching a subway train and then doubling back to the Rover after making sure the coast was clear. If there *was* anyone on my tail—in an Opel or any other damned kind of car—he was long since shaken off.

Certainly, there was no Opel in sight outside. The street, when he surveyed it from the high front steps, was as quiet, as commonplace, as it had been on his first visit. For some unaccountable reason its innocence disconcerted him. It felt as wrong as finding a thief in a monastery.

23

Strewth, Valerie thought, whatever do they keep it all for?

She was in the D Branch archive, confronted by the sheer volume of the records. Every war game that had been played on Vulcan was there, preserved in the minutest detail. The computer listings were filed in heavy binders at least six inches thick, and each game required ten or more binders.

That's over five feet of shelf space per game, she thought. What in heaven's name is it all for? I suppose they feel a need to keep records of some sort but does anybody ever actually *look* at them? I never have, not till now. And I can't remember any of the other from the Command Room sloping off to delve into game history. Well, it's hardly what you'd call bedtime reading! It's a case of saving paper for the sake of it, that's what it is. The civil service all over, bless its cotton socks.

She was used to following the progress of games on a display screen. With a screen, you could choose the numbers you wanted, homing in on the incidents that interested you. There was no such selectivity about the printed records. Every single number spewed out by the computer was there. All densely packed together, hundreds of items to a page. Numbers, numbers, and yet more numbers. The identification codes for weaponry and vehicles, their locations on the map, their directions and speeds of travel, the amounts remaining of fuel and ammunition.

Oh well, she told herself, go to it, Val.

14th July. That was the first entry on Bob's list and

that turned out to refer to Game No. 13. She took down the binder which covered the state of play at 1200 hours, hefted it over to the reading table and flicked through the big pages.

Oh, yes, it bloody would be, wouldn't it! she thought. One of the complicated games. One of the controller's frantic Doomsday battles. Armor charging every which way. Several squadrons of air support units in action. Batteries of Red artillery pounding away, on the defensive. Oh, yes, it bloody would have to be one of those! Find the missing link among that lot. Needle in a haystack.

24th July. That was the next game in the series: No. 14. She examined the state of play at 2200 hours. No air support this time, not so much as a single gunship. Plenty of armor again but in formations quite unlike those of the previous game. Very little opposing artillery; in this battle Red was on the offensive and seemed to be relying on rocket launchers.

"Different," she murmured, puzzled. "Quite different."

And so it was with the next game. On her initial assessment there was nothing in common between the three battles. Except the quantity of numbers!

You're missing something, Val, she said to herself. Back to square one. Hey-ho.

And so back to the listings for 14th July.

She pored over the printout for more than an hour, trying to detect a pattern. There was none. Or if there was, it wasn't obvious. Tiny needle, she mooned. Blinking great haystack.

Maybe it isn't the state of play at 1200 which matters, she decided then. Suppose it's to do with the way the pieces move *next?* Now there's a thought. What happens at 1205?

She turned the page and the next sheet in the binder was blank. So what he next.

"Funny . . . ?"

The next page wasn't blank, not quite. It carried only a single word in the top left-hand corner: RESTART.

So what? Restarting the Vulcan system was a common enough occurrence. It happened every day, first thing in the morning. The computer was switched off overnight. Which meant it had to be switched on again the following morning before battle could recommence. *That* was a restart. So what?

All the same, she thought, that's some coincidence. I mean, a restart which just happens to follow one of the times on Bob's list . . .

She went quickly to the next game again, found the pages for 2200 hours, then turned over. Two blank pages in succession. Then a page with a single word. RESTART.

"Eureka!"

Help, had anyone heard her yell that? A quick look around: no. Thank goodness the place was deserted.

So, there *was* a connection. All the other games on the list would be the same. She already knew they would be, but checked to make sure. Yes, just as she thought. The times on the list were all points immediately prior to a restart of Vulcan.

Very fishy, she thought. Not to say creepy. Espionage and spooks and things that go bump in the night. Each evening the computer is switched off and we all go home. In the morning we turn up again and

Vulcan is restarted. *What happens in between?* Is something going on here at night? Is someone breaking into the fort to get his hands on Vulcan? Is that what Bob's list means?

She returned to the well of the Command Room—to the engine room, as the junior staff there called it. She switched on her display. Gosh, wasn't Major Colby doing well all of a sudden! He'd be unbearable over lunch. Good for a drink but utterly impossible.

It was not long after that when she was struck by the implausibility of her break-in theory. It wasn't that the fort was impregnable. What place was? No, that wasn't the point.

"Damn and blast."

Well, it had been such an exciting idea.

But it simply wasn't possible, she could see that now. For any one of those times it might make sense. For two of them? Yes, she might buy that, just. But for all of them? No, it wasn't possible, not remotely.

"Silly fucking numbers."

That carried in the Command Room. Blushing, she placed the list on her desk, shielded it with encircling arms and crouched low, her nose almost against the paper as she stared at the times. Not at the dates: that didn't matter. Just the times.

She smiled then. Had Bob noticed that about the times? Of course he had, that was the reason for the list. But I bet it took him longer to make the connection, she thought. Poor darling Bob, he could be so blinking slow. That's why he had to take documents home with him and put in so much effort out of hours. To keep up. Otherwise he got hopelessly behind with his work. No, I bet it took him a deal longer to spot it.

She replaced the paper in her handbag, pulled back her shoulders and started toward the dais. Big Brother land. Gosh, what do I tell God this time? she wondered. How do I persuade the controller to send me packing to the archives again?

Avery called as agreed that evening. From a telephone booth, a stack of coins at his elbow.

"I spun the controller a real yarn," Valerie said, talking a mile a minute. "About the computer calculations for armor-piercing rockets. I said they were badly adrift. I said the error probably went back several games. It really put the wind up him."

"So he let you check the back records?" Resourceful lady, Avery thought. I had a feeling you would be.

"*Let* me? He went as white as a sheet and *ordered* me to! What do you think of that? I was able to spend a morning in the branch archieves without a soul looking askance. So you needn't worry, Mr. Gardner. No hot breath on the back of my neck. Afterwards, I went back all contrite and said: sorry, my mistake, controller. You should have seen the look of relief!"

"What did you find?"

"Trouble was, I needed a second go at the records. So I played real dumb. I'd looked up the data for the wrong rocket launcher, that's what I said. There might still be an error. Bloody stroll on, he went berserk! Move your backside, young lady, and get cracking. Get back there and do your homework. Properly, this time. It was lovely. We're friends again now but it was touch and go, I can tell you. Much batting of eyelids on my part and looking coy. Wow, I don't want to go through that again."

Terrific, Avery thought. Tell me your life story while you're at it.

"*Is* there a connection?" he asked.

"I'm coming to that. They're all restarts of the system."

"The entries on the list?"

"What else?"

"Restarts? That happens after a computer shutdown, doesn't it?"

"That's right. Which means each morning as a rule. At first, that's what I thought it was. Just normal morning start-up procedure."

"And . . . ?"

"I got to thinking about those times. Twelve hundred hours. Twenty-two hundred hours. O-four hundred."

"I do have a copy of the list!" Avery said tetchily.

"What do you notice about them, then?" she countered.

"Not a damned thing. Why don't you tell me?"

"I'll give you a clue, shall I? We finish our war gaming each evening at establishment closing time. That's five o'clock. It doesn't matter where we've got to in the game. *Finis.* Down pens, on with coats and hit the road to the pub. That's life in the British civil service. Are they like that over in Washington?"

"Exactly like that. Get to the point."

"So the game time might be twelve fifteen when we shut up shop, that's the point, mister. Or four forty-five. Wherever we happen to be at."

"But not a precise, round time? Is that what you're saying?"

"Quick, aren't you?" she observed. "Yes, that's exactly it. I mean, now and then the system will be shut down bang on the hour, but the odds are against it."

"So where does that get us?"

"Well . . . that meant I couldn't be looking at normal morning restarts. And it was then I remembered the other reason we have for restarting."

She paused for so long that Avery had to say, "Don't keep me dangling, Miss Ashton. I'm not auditioning. Your dramatic potential cuts no ice with me."

"Computer failure," she said in reply.

"Eh?"

"Computer failure, that's the connection. Com-put-er fail-ure. Yes? The machine goes down. It gets repaired. Then we restart. See? I could kick myself. I mean, Bob was going on and on about it, except I didn't listen. About how unreliable Vulcan was. *That's* your link, Mr. Gardner. Those times were all points in various games when the computer suddenly went on the blink."

She waited while he thought about it.

"So you've got a crappy system," he said. "I'm not sure that gets me very excited."

"It will. There's more to come."

The phone *pip-pip-pipped* maniacally in his ear and he fed in another handful of coins.

"Why are you in a call box, by the way?"

"Because it's evening," he improvised. "My office is shut, like yours. And I'm halfway to the theater."

"Mmm." she was on her guard.

"Okay, we'll leave it till morning if you like. I'll call you from agency premises. That make you feel better?" Try that for size, he thought. See if you can sit on your story overnight! No way.

"Don't be silly," she said.

"Then give . . ."

"Well, it's that time factor again. That's what I noticed next. Twelve hundred hours. Twenty-two hundred hours. O-four . . ."

"Etcetera, etcetera," Avery cut in.

"Convenient, huh? The computer always failing bang on the hour? So I checked back through the operator's log. That list of Bob's was for all of the computer failures since the fourteenth of July. And they all happened precisely on the hour. Fishy, eh?"

"I'll need time to digest it."

"Hang on, there's more. Take the first game, the one on the fourteenth. The computer went down at twelve hundred hours, right? Know when that game started? The game time, I mean?"

"Tell me."

"At twelve hundred. At noon the previous day. That's a game day, of course."

"Jesus," Avery said.

"Now the next game. The computer went down at twenty-two hundred. Have a guess when *that* one started."

"The same time the previous day?"

"Clever man!"

"So it crashed after exactly twenty-four hours of war game . . ."

She whistled. "You do mental arithmetic, too? Is there no end to your talents?"

"How about the other games on the list . . . ?"

"What do you think? The same, exactly the same."

"Phew."

"Someone is sabotaging Vulcan, Mr. Gardner," she said with sudden soberness.

"So it would seem," he agreed.

Oh, no, they're not, he thought as he drove back to Lambourn. It can't be that simple. The machine goes down, the service guy comes along to repair it and then it's back in action again. So how long can it be down? For a few hours? A day at the most? It wouldn't be worth the trouble. That's inconvenience in my book, not sabotage.

All the same, the computer *is* crashing and it won't be due to a man with his finger on the OFF button. One of those system components is going on the blink with startling regularity. What can it be? A tape deck? Hardly. A printed circuit board?

"Jesus."

He almost drove off the road into a tree.

A printed circuit board.

Oh, you poor fool, Patrick, he thought. You even said it to me! You were pissed out of your mind and you let it slip in the car. How was I to know what you meant?

Vulcan is just a succession of board failures.

The Irishman's voice sounded in his mind, the words hesitant and slurred.

You knew about it then, Avery thought. Franklin had told you and you knew. Why didn't you confide in me? Hell, you might still be alive if you had.

He sat brooding in the cottage. It was cold and he had to draw a chair close to a radiator. No open fire tonight; he was too engrossed to bother.

His own earlier thoughts had come back to him.

The computer goes down. The service man comes to repair it. Then it's back in action again.

The service man! And what does he do, there at the fort? Replace the defective board, that's the usual procedure. And then what? Drive off with the old one, of course. Through the gates, past the guards and away.

24

"Lunch?" Avery said. "Why don't I take you away from all this?"

Barbara Young looked up from her typewriter and smiled. "On one condition."

"No talk of Patrick?" he guessed.

"No talk of Patrick." She added emphasis with a decisive nod.

"It's a deal. I had a pub meal in mind, something quick and simple. There's a phrase for it, isn't there?"

"A pie and a pint?"

"That's the one."

There wasn't much variety in the pubs around there. They were all much of a muchness, Barbara said as they drove off in search. Beams in genuine medieval fiberglass. Splodgy Axminster carpets like bad dreams. Pop music on draft. Still, if that's what he wanted, a taste of the high life in the steppes of outer Swindon . . .

The place they found was exactly as she had predicted. A stern-visaged fifties building with pretensions to Jacobean origins, a moat of asphalt, a wooden bench with a view only of a busy main road. An eccentric sign on a pole lodged in the asphalt, "Parking for patrons only. Fee for nonpatrons £10 a day." another beside it, "No Coaches."

They carried their drinks to a corner seat in bright red padded vinyl, as far away from the jukebox as possible. Beside the bar, a sallow youth was lazing away his lunch hour by shooting down Martians on a screen.

"Romantic," Barbara said.

Avery made an apologetic shrug. "Sorry. But it was too cold for another picnic."

"No, lover, I meant it. You and me together. Who cares about the crummy pub?" She reached under the table for his hand. "And thanks for the flowers. Correction, flower. I didn't think you'd remember, to be honest."

"It was the most magnificent rose in the park. I rejected hundreds before settling on that one."

"You *stole* it?"

"I didn't go for the selection in the shops. What else could I do? All's fair in love."

She giggled. "You're dreadful, Martin. Get me another someday, please?"

"Tomorrow, how about that? I'll raid every country garden in the area for the very best. Personally graded."

She moved closer, widening her eyes at him. Those changeable eyes, with a mood for every occasion. Even the color seemed to vary. "And take me to bed again."

"Okay," he said.

"Soon, Martin. Soon."

"When would you like?"

"There's no time like the present."

"*Now*, you mean?" A tempting idea normally, he thought, but he had other plans lined up for the afternoon.

She laughed with childlike glee. "I was thinking of tonight, actually. It happens to be a good evening for alibis."

Avery raised her hand and pressed it to his lips. "Done. Sealed with a kiss."

"Nice sort of contract," she said.

"There's a condition, though. Can I draw your attention to the small print?"

She went very rigid and demanded, "What sort of condition?" She moved away a little as she said it.

"I want you to do something for me, first."

She regarded him surgically. "Sex something, you mean? A novel kind of foreplay something, is that what you have in mind? Or would it be damned, blasted Quantek something again?" She already knew the answer from his awkward manner. "Oh, don't bother to reply! Quantek!"

Her voice had risen and the youth at the bar turned, drawn by the smell of an argument.

"Patrick was murdered," Avery said, very quietly. He hadn't intended to tell her, not just yet.

She froze.

"Shall I repeat that?"

She trembled her head, staring in anguish. "I heard."

"So if I seem to be obsessive, I have good reason."

"*Seem* to be! Oh, brother!"

"I'm sorry it gets between us like this."

For a long time she said nothing, fidgeting with her

299

handbag then she asked. "Murdered? How murdered?" Her tone was one of outright disbelief.

"In the car. I don't know how."

"But who would do a thing like that?"

"That's what I'm trying to find out. That's why I need your help tonight."

She gazed blindly across the lounge. "Tell me about it," she said, without emotion.

What do I say? he asked himself. That the autopsy report makes me out to be a fool or a liar? That I found two tiny holes in a window? That a computer is breaking down like it has one eye on the clock? Since when did machine failure in one county prove murder in another!

What would my father's advice be about this? he wondered. "Where's the smoking gun?" that's what he'd say. "The prosecution hasn't a leg to stand on without a smoking gun." And he'd be right; instinct isn't enough. I *must* have proof or I'm no more than the crackpot Sherman takes me to be.

"Tonight," he replied. "It will keep till then."

"No, damnit, now!"

"No. After you've done what I want."

"You use me, you know," she noted despondently. "You might be up to God-only-knows-what under my very nose yet you expect me to give you a helping hand."

"Patrick was murdered, Barbara. By person or persons unknown. I need one more piece of evidence, just one. Are you with me or not?"

"I believe you," she said with a labored nod. Then a baffled shake of the head and, "I don't believe you, it's impossible. Who would do that to him? Blast,

300

what does it matter?"

She knows in her bones I'm right, Avery mused, but she won't accept it. She can't. Death by accident is fine in its way, it's unfortunate but acceptable. But not murder, she won't have that. A murder would demean Patrick, her boss and her lover.

Good God, he realized as he read her misery, murder is lower class in this crazy country, for villains and workers only. *That's* what's bothering her. It doesn't happen to nice people over here, not to directors of companies—even if they drink like fishes and smash up government chairs. Come home with me, darling, I'll show you equal opportunity in action. Where I come from it can happen to anyone, from migrants to presidents.

He took her hand, stroking it as he spoke. "I'm a visitor to Quantek. I mean, that's my status there. So when we return I'll have to sign the visitors' book at the gate. The guard will give me a plastic badge. Later, when I leave, I'll have to return the badge and I'll be marked down in the book as having left the premises."

She waited, ill at ease.

"This evening, I want you to return my badge for me."

"*Me?* You're out of your mind."

"Why?"

"Why, he says! For a dozen reasons. For a start, I don't much look like Martin Avery, do I! Add to which, the guards on the gate know me."

"I've thought of that." A secret smile was playing across Avery's face.

"Oh, yes, I've got it. I wear a disguise, right? You're mad!"

"What you do is this," Avery said. "Tonight, you leave for home precisely at five. On the siren. The exit road is like Picadilly Circus in the rush hour then, with all those hardworking colleagues of yours reluctantly charging off pubwards. You mingle with the throng, as they say. You chuck my badge in through the gatehouse window. You don't stop. Do you see the plan? If we're lucky, the guard assumes it was me and checks me off his list."

"If *we're* lucky!" she repeated. "That's really comforting. What happens if I'm caught red-handed?"

"You bat your eyelids at the guards and look coy. I'm told it works wonders."

"Sexist twerp!" But something about the idea was making her smile. She lifted her face and closed her eyes. He accepted the invitation and kissed her.

"Where will you be going?" she asked in his ear. "All by yourself in there?"

"Uh-uh, no dice." He wagged his head solemnly then laughed. "If you don't know, they can't torture it out of you."

"Peter Hurst's office? Is that where you're headed?"

"No, you're not even warm. Shall I brief you on stage two of the operation now?"

She sat up abruptly. *"What?"*

"I'm alone in the factory, right? Night has fallen. You have to get me out."

"Oh, yes? Who supplies the green beret and grappling irons?"

"I'm damned serious!"

302

"So am I! What the hell do you mean, get you out!"

"Look at it this way. I could scale the boundary wire; it's only ten feet high. But I don't know what detection devices they've rigged up to it. So I might trigger an alarm, *savvy?* I might not but I can't take that risk. Which means I have to leave by the front door. And that means I need you again. QED."

"Me?" Barbara mumbled. "Me again?" She was dumbfounded.

"It's an old trick," Avery explained, "but I think it will work. You drive past the gate and stage a breakdown a short distance on. Wring your hands and act distracted. Lure the guards down to you. Lady in distress."

She gave it a great deal of thought.

"I want you there at eight on the dot," Avery said, gazing at her anxiously.

"Why eight?"

"The guards do their rounds at seven fifteen, flushing out the stragglers. That gives me the clear field I need and half an hour to do it in. Add a contingency and it brings us up to eight."

"Eight, then," she said, hardly believing her own words.

"And then we'll go on to the cottage, all right?"

"Oh, goody," she said sarcastically. "I get a reward for bad behavior."

Back at Quantek, he walked her to her desk, unclipped his lapel badge and presented it to her.

"After you stop, raise the hood and pull off two spark plug leads. Got that?"

"Yes, sir," she said with a jokey salute.

"Martin?" she called as he was part way down the

corridor. "Haven't you forgotten something?"

He turned.

"To synchronize watches," she said in a loud whisper, and her peal of laughter followed him away. Since leaving the pub she had decided to enjoy the escapade. Might as well be hung for a sheep as a lamb, she felt.

Avery went to the field service department, a down-at-heel building on the far side of Hurst Park.

"Hallo again," he said. He had been there that morning. Just looking around, getting to know the operation, he had said.

"Back so soon?" the service manager muttered. He tried to squeeze a friendly smile onto a harassed face but the effort was beyond him. He wore grimy brown overalls with the breast pocket stuffed to overflowing with pens and pencils. Rather like a chestful of military medals, Avery thought. A brave protector of the country's defense hardware. Christ, if only he knew . . .

"Is it all right if I have another look? If I just kind of *hover* for a while and get a feel for your staff's work?" Avery was standing sideways on to the man's desk. His breast pocket—where the visitor's badge should have been—was hidden by a hunched shoulder.

"Well . . . I suppose . . ." The man began to slip from his tall stool but Avery stopped him.

"No need to bother. I'll roam free if that's okay with you. Just to drink in the atmosphere. Fascinating place. That *is* okay, is it? Yes?"

One of several telephones on the desk began to ring. Even as the manager reached for it, another was starting to bleat.

"I'll leave you to it," Avery said, stealing away.

Every electronics factory has one: a storage place for empty cardboard boxes. The components which are purchased ready assembled from other suppliers arrived packed between wedges of polystyrene, in sturdy cartons. They are unpacked and tested—soak-tested, which means they are left switched on and running for days at a time to check their endurance. Meanwhile, the cardboard boxes have to be kept somewhere until the tests are over. The components are then packed back in them for reshipment as part of complete systems.

At Quantek, the room of empty boxes was at the back of the field service shed.

Avery stood by the door there, waited until he was sure none of the men was looking his way and ducked inside, out of sight. Then he made a cavity under a high stack of cartons and lost himself.

The building was dark and vacant when he emerged that evening, with the uncanny stillness peculiar to normally busy places when they are left to themselves. Like a closed department store, a deserted fairground, an abandoned film set. At ground floor level a large open area was crowded to capacity with Dexion storage racks and cluttered workbenches. Stairs led up to a gallery with boxlike offices.

Avery followed the beam of his flashlight over to the booth where they recorded the incoming calls requesting service visits, and tried the logs for July and August. Satisfied at the result, he moved on to the service manager's desk, where there was a different set of records: the service reports. The engineers completed a form for each of their visits to a customer, detailing the nature of the repair. Avery searched the file. He went through it again, form by form, and then again before giving up. Grim now, he chose a chair well away from the windows and huddled in it.

Someone was here before me, he thought. *Someone has taken the Fort Halstead reports. Every damned last one of them.*

It was just after seven thirty. With a shiver, he drew up his collar. The building was as cold as an icebox.

25

He heard the dog first, wheezing laboriously outside as it passed a window, straining on the leash. Then he heard the guard: heavy boots crunching over a patch of gravel.

He froze, holding his breath.

The steps moved on, along the side of the building. They faded but Avery remained immobile, staring in the darkness towards the distant door. Keep going, he willed the guard. Just keep patrolling, friend.

A key rattled in the lock.

"Hell!" Avery dived for the meager cover of a workbench. He had allowed himself to be caught almost in the open, marooned in the center of the big shed. An unwanted thought presented itself: is this Barbara's doing? Was I a fool to trust her?

Fluorescent lights cracked on, jabbing painfully at his eyes. Not all of the lights, just a bank of tubes close to the door. Peering under the bench, Avery could see the guard's legs framed in the doorway, an Alsatian beside them. It was a big brute, almost black, and its ears were pricked. It came slowly into the building, dragging the guard behind it, sniffing suspiciously.

Christ, Avery thought, am I upwind? Is there any such thing as upwind or downwind indoors? Christ, what a mess.

He lost sight of the legs then but could still hear the dog's insistent whine. The guard had regained the initiative and the dog's claws were scrabbling at the floor as it was hauled off somewhere.

"Kerm on, Niger," the man grunted. "Bleedin' move it."

Where in hell was he going? Avery wondered. He was reminded with sudden vividness of the game he had been forced to play as a child. When you can see your hunter searching, it's not so bad. You peer through the closet keyhole and watch him come, stopping all the while to look behind and under each piece of furniture. No sweat, you know how clever you've been in concealing yourself. But then he moves off to one side and you lose sight of him. . . . It's when you know he's there but you can no longer see what he's doing—that's when the glacial trembles start jolting the spine.

That stupid goddamned game again, he thought angrily. Why do I remember it at the most unlikely times? Why do I remember it ever?

There was a clatter of china and soon the burbling of a kettle.

Avery breathed freely again, barely able to believe his luck. He recalled having seen the impromptu

307

kitchen earlier in the day, at one end of a long worktable. He began to crawl forward on his stomach for a view of it.

The dog howled, pawing the floor.

"Oh, bleedin' give over," the guard shouted and he did something that resulted in a squeal.

Then Avery heard another voice which, just for an instant, caused the hairs to stand on the back of his scalp. It was a laughing voice and the laugh verged on hysteria.

". . . Ha, ha, ha. The chap from Or-leans is in the *water! What* a cal-amity. Just *look* at him, thrashing around in there. And Delft are *rom-ping* home now. In the clear. Playing their joker, too."

A television? Not a television set, surely? It couldn't possibly be, not in there. Avery resumed the crawl until he had sight of the dog again. But he couldn't see the guard now, not at first. He had to squeeze forward under the workbench before he was able to locate him.

Yes, it was a television, a monitor unit normally used for component testing. The guard had obviously discovered how to tune it for broadcast transmissions. Sly bugger, Avery thought. Look at him with his cup of instant coffee and his feet up, watching his private gogglebox. Some guard you turned out to be, the Lord be praised.

On the screen, people in huge clowns' uniforms were chasing a pantomime horse. One of the clowns tripped over his own enormous feet and toppled into a lake. *

". . . And there goes the last of the Frenchmen," the commentator chortled. "Oh, my *good-ness* . . .

308

what a *washout* for Orleans. They've run out of time. It's a *dis-aster* for the French."

The guard had anchored the leg of his chair over the loop in the dog's leash. The dog was sprawled full length with it front paws out, its head resting on them, ears still held high and twitching. It seemed to be staring balefully along the floor straight at Avery. With a yelp, it jumped up and pulled hard on the leash, whining frantically.

"Belt up!" the guard said, yanking it back.

In the cold light of the overhead tubes, the animal's eyes were blank white disks. Its lips were curled back and Avery could almost feel the sharp teeth just by looking at them.

It was 7:46. What time does this stupid program finish? he wondered. At 8:00, perhaps? That's too bloody late, I have to be down at the gate by then. Move it, for Chrissake, you square-eyed fink. The Russians are breaking in on the far side of the factory. Your country needs you there. 7:46 already. Oh, my God.

The dog dropped back onto its stomach, still watching, just moaning fitfully to itself now. It reminded Avery of a story Corrigan had once told him, that night in the car. A shaggy-dog story, the Irishman had called it. The one about Hurst and an Alsatian he used to bring to the office.

It's funny how irrelevant fragments flit though the mind when you're under pressure, Avery thought. Here I am quaking like a fucking leaf and I suddenly remember that. Not so irrelevant, though. A useful guide to character, you might say; another piece of the jigsaw dropped into place. Thank you, Patrick.

His watch said it was 7:52. The inane commentary rolled on. The costumes had become wilder and the antics more absurd. The whole program seemed to be about falling into the lake. Now they were falling off trapezes.

"*Splash!*" the voice said redundantly.

The guard was still jammed tight in his chair, on his second cup of coffee. A third cup was a surefire certainly. So, suddenly, was the midnight movie.

You're not going to go, are you? Avery thought with desperation. Not ever. Lazy bastard.

There was a telephone on the work surface just above his head and he eased up to take a look at it.

Thank goodness for that, he breathed. At least something in this Bleak House of a factory is up to date.

The telephone had push buttons. A conventional dial would have made too much noise.

He pulled it down to the floor beside him and the cord reached, just. He lifted the receiver, quickly clamping a hand over the earpiece to strangle the answering howl. Both hands were shaking badly. The dog had started snarling as soon as he made his move.

Now what? he asked himself. Have a guess, that's what. Choose any number from one to a thousand.

He was feeling ridiculously light-headed. It was nerves, of course; stress sometimes had that effect on him. Either he went as calm as Lake Placid or he became as out of control as a drunk. He never knew which it would be until it happened.

Which number will hit the jackpot? a voice said inside his skull. *All of them or none?*

Crazy, he thought in answer. Perhaps none of them.

333. Now there's a good number to start with. Try that for size.

He punched the buttons and the dog was off again, giving an urgent growl. Then a yelp as the guard leaned over the chair to cuff it.

Avery listened. *Nothing.* Wherever the extension he had dialed was ringing, it was well out of earshot. Damn! Oh well, if at first you don't succeed . . .

248. Nothing again.

109. Not a goddamned thing

177. Was that a sound in the distance this time? A lonely phone ringing in one of the nearby office blocks? Fat use that was with the TV going full bore.

". . . And now Turin are in trouble," the commentator squealed. "Have you *ever* seen a splash like it?"

It was 7:57. Where would Barbara be at this instant? Avery mused. Heading toward the factory? Damnit, she must be almost at the gate by now.

He tried another number, another, a frantic stream of digits.

Nothing.

Now hold things a moment, he told himself. You're being totally unsystematic. Calm down, Avery. There has to be a simple solution to this problem. What's the number on this extension here?

He peered at the dial. It was extension 511.

So we want one close to that, he concluded. But not too close. The idea was to get a phone ringing upstairs, not right behind him.

He tried 530. The number had a good sound to it, a lucky feel.

Suddenly, a phone was ringing from the gallery above, from one of the tiny offices.

Avery felt himself go limp. Sweat was pouring from his forehead and his hand was so wet he could hardly keep a grip on the receiver.

He let the extension above ring on and on. He no longer dared to look at his watch.

"Awl right, then," the man grumbled at last. "Awl bleedin' right. I'm coming, for Gawd's sake." His chair scraped noisily.

Don't leave the fucking dog! Avery prayed. Hell, why hadn't that possibility occurred to him before? A tug at the leg of an unoccupied chair . . . a quick bound . . . Oh, my God.

"Oy, move it, Nigger!" the guard yelled. The dog began a pitiful complaint, scratching helplessly at the floor as it was manhandled away, over to the iron stairs and then up.

"Four-legged friend!" the guard said amid chestly pants as he finally achieved the top step. "What a bleedin' laugh." He was still tugging, by the sound of it.

Avery had removed his shoes. The moment he heard the ringing tone stop, he charged silently for the door, flicked up the latch and tumbled out into the delightful cold of night.

By way of the shadows, he reached the gate—just as Barbara's elderly Renault came sputtering by. It must be well after eight by now, surely? He pressed the button on his watch. It was exactly ten past eight. Thank God for women, he thought.

He told her the story in the car. Well, most of it. He left out the part about the hidden microphones at Lambourn. Why damage female sensibilities? he reasoned. Why cause unnecessary distress?

Besides, they were headed that way now and why ruin a perfect end to the evening? It's a fact, he decided, with another attack of light-headedness: it's a fact that high stress is the ideal preamble to sex. I've noticed it before, it's the best damned aphrodisiac going. Christ, what kind of sex lives must bank robbers have?

Barbara cross-examined him expertly. Did the holes in the window *really* mean what he said? How incredible. Was he one hundred percent certain about those computer failures at the fort? Cripes, it sounded the most almighty conspiracy.

Yes, yes, yes. He was saying yes to everything. They were just coming into Lambourn village. When should he ask her not to talk about this at the cottage? How would he keep her quiet? By means of an excess of passion, possibly? Yes, that should do it very nicely.

"You still haven't dealt with tonight's little raid," she said. "Don't you think the getaway driver deserves some explanation?"

He squeezed her hand and said, "I had to find out if it was always the same service engineer who visits Fort Halstead."

"And is it?"

"No. Sometimes it's a guy called John Burton . . ."

"I know him. One of our old-timers."

"Sometimes it's a Paul Spooner."

She shook her head, not recognizing the name.

313

"And on one occasion it was yet another guy. I've jotted his name down in my notebook."

"Three different men," she said. "And one of them as sweet as they come and only a few years off retirement."

Avery nodded. "Which means it's not the service engineer who's pulling the stunt. I didn't see how it could be but I had to be sure. The dispatch clerk in field service obviously sends along whichever engineer happens to be free at the time the call comes in. And when he gets to the fort, the engineer simply follows the instructions in the service manual. A component has failed and he replaces it with a working unit. He's an innocent pawn, you might say. He won't have the vaguest idea of the important role he's playing in the enterprise."

"Martin!" Barbara said sharply, catching at his sleeve. "Will you *please* stop that. What bloody enterprise?"

Avery patted her thigh lightly. Take it easy, the action said. All in good time. "That system at Fort Halstead is having the hiccoughs with remarkable regularity," he replied. "So reason tells me it must be the same component which is failing each time, do you see my logic?"

"I think so."

"Which is why I wanted to see those service reports. The engineer writes down the identification number for the part he replaces. I badly wanted to have a look at that number. I've a pretty good idea which component is failing but I'd like to be certain."

"I don't see why that's so important."

314

"My guess is that it's a part with a small computer in it, a microprocessor." He spoke very quietly, watching her face.

"*Is* there such a thing?" she asked, turning to him in wonder. "One computer inside another?"

"Oh, yes. You bet your sweet life there is." Avery gave her a knowing smile. "That's what the Vulcan system is, a collection of computers all doing slightly different tasks. One big machine handling most of the calculations and four tiny ones to help out, to do what we call the housekeeping jobs. The people at the fort know all about it. They see it solely as a smart piece of design. God," he said as if to himself, "are they in for a nasty surprise."

"This one you're after . . . it's a *spy* computer?"

"That's what I'm assuming, yes. It's the only explanation that makes any sense. They're not after the defective part itself, Barbara. They're after the information stored in it. It's the neatest damned way I ever heard of smuggling secrets out of a defense establishment."

"But worth killing for? Killing two innocent people?"

"It rather depends what the secrets are, doesn't it? Someone obviously thought it was worth it."

She drew to a halt at the bottom of the private lane. The front door of the cottage was caught in the headlights, crooked under its tiled porch.

"What time must you be home?" Avery asked.

"Midnight, if possible. Half past twelve at the very latest."

"I'll need a lift back to my car—I left it behind the factory. I'll tell you the rest of my theory then, on the

315

way back." He sealed her lips with a finger. "Meanwhile, silence is golden."

"If I still want to hear it by then," she said. "I'll demand my money back."

26

The boundary of the site, running beside the main road out of Cheltenham, was protected by a high fence in the now familiar wire mesh, strung between concrete posts. Inside, pressing almost up to the fence, was a jumble of prefabricated huts which looked as flimsy as cardboard. The main buildings were set farther back on a strategic rise of ground—two identical office blocks with massive, gridded façades like the coops of a battery farm. Avery guessed there must be many underground levels buried beneath the grassed banking: built to survive an atomic attack. The sign beside the gatehouse had a military-style emblem, and the kind of bland lettering to be found in post offices. It said, "Government Communications Headquarters."

He turned the car and drove past for another look. This time he slowed to a snail's pace and tried to estimate the number of windows.

Whatever they were up to in there, he thought, it took plenty of people to do it. Four thousand of them at least, from his rough count of the windows; perhaps as many as five thousand. Far more than would be needed simply to handle official messages between ministries and to the embassies and consulates overseas. Far, far more. The intelligence work Sherman had mentioned wasn't a minor part of their business—it must be their main reason for being. GCHQ was an intelligence empire, probably the biggest in the country.

Oh, yes, he thought, it's the perfect home for dear old George. I always imagined he worked in a damned great ministry beehive like this.

A uniformed guard marched briskly to the car as it stopped at the entrance barrier. He made a circular movement with a hand, asking for a window to be lowered.

"Sir . . . ?"

"Mr. Ballantine, please."

"Got an appointment?"

"No, but he'll see me."

"Sorry, but there's no one of that name here."

For just a moment Avery was taken aback. Could Sherman have lied?

"Initial G," he said. "G for George. G as in government business of the greatest importance."

The guard snorted. "You can go through the alphabet for all I care. Makes no difference, there's no such person here."

"Take a look in your establishment directory, huh? You'll find him."

"I've no need to look. Move along now, sir. Don't cause trouble."

"Clever fellow, aren't you," Avery said. "A staff

317

complement of nearly five thousand and you remember every single name."

"Just turn the car," the guard said impassively. "You're on government property."

"Will you do something for me? There's a pub a mile or so along the road. Know the one I mean, the Malmesbury Arms? When I've gone I want you to get on that phone of yours. Tell the nonexistant Mr. Ballantine that Martin Avery will be waiting there, in the parking lot."

The man was beginning to lose his temper. "Push off! Now!"

Avery backed toward the road. "Did you get the name?" he called. "Martin Avery. And tell him it's urgent. I'm sure your quaint security procedures will let you do that."

Midmorning. Over an hour to opening time and the pub parking lot deserted: a playground for the wind to sculpt darting shapes from dried leaves and dust. A miniature tornado danced and spun in front of the Rover.

You're going to hate me for this, George, Avery thought with a wry smile. A hard drinker like you, having to sit here in sight of those locked bar doors. Sorry, but it wouldn't keep.

Within a matter of minutes, the Ford Granada entered slowly and drew alongside. Ballantine was alone. He wound down his window—the same George Ballantine, just as Avery remembered him. The round face which looked too smooth ever to need a shave. Those diamond-sharp eyes which seemed to belong to an altogether tougher face and threatened to see into

318

your very soul. The same antique suit as rumpled as an elephant's skin: with the window down, Ballantine draped his arm over the door, revealing a shiny elbow.

"I see they let you out," Avery began brightly. "It's like the Berlin wall back there. How the hell do you stick it, day in, day out?"

"The irrepressible Mr. Avery again," Ballantine said with a stage-managed sigh. "The security chaps at the gate are having kittens and I'm dragged out of a meeting to set matters straight. Oh, yes it *would* have to be you!"

"I've been doing your job for you," Avery said, smiling. "I figured it was time to tell you what I've found. Since you didn't leave me your phone number, what else was I to do?"

Ballantine tried an even more world-weary sigh. "Hop in, if you must. I suggest the front seat this time. Your usual place in the back would be a trifle unsociable."

Avery shook his head. "My territory, George. The way you people handle cars makes me nervous."

Ballantine sighed one more time then came round to the Rover.

"To tell you the truth, I hardly recognized you without the gang," Avery said as he took the seat beside him. "Where's the pet rattlesnake today? How come you're having to drive yourself?"

"Okay, laddie, fun time over. Let's hear what you have to say."

"You took some tracking down, know that? What if I hadn't been able to find you?"

"But you had expert help," Ballantine said smugly.

"Like from your new friends at the National Security Agency."

"Eh?" Avery was unable to hide his surprise.

"I've been up in London for a couple of days. When I got back here this morning, there was a note in my pigeonhole asking me to call a certain Joel Henderson. Heard of him?"

Avery responded with a desultory nod.

"We're old partners in crime, he and I. The nub of his message was that you were still doing some unofficial sleuthing behind my back—he felt I ought to know. He also owed me an apology, so he said. One of his operatives was injudicious enough to tip you off where I work these days. 'Avery will be camping out on your doorstep next, George,' that's what he said. 'With binoculars, a tape recorder and a cheap Japanese directional mike.' " Ballantine locked his arms tight and tucked his chin knowingly into his chest. 'So your arrival today is not exactly unexpected. My God, man, but you're predictable."

"I've got some information on Vulcan," Avery retorted. "I think it will come as a nasty shock."

"Why don't you go home, laddie? Back to the sun and the marijuana? Do something useful for once: become a dropout."

"You've never been prepared to explain your job to me," Avery said, "but I can make a good guess. You spend your days scouring intercepted radio messages, right? Sifting through a mass of information for whatever useful nuggets you can find. The same type of work as Henderson's section."

"There are similarities in what we do . . . yes, I think I can safely admit that."

320

"Except that he covers only London and your sources are farther afield. Your electronic ears are turned towards Eastern Europe."

"Very possibly."

"*Very possibly!* Jesus, why are you always so damned cagey! You're the main supplier of the Red data they use in Vulcan. Well, am I right or not?"

Ballantine studied a button on his waistcoat before nodding gravely.

"What resources have you got in your clandestine little empire? Eavesdropping stations in countries like West Germany? Mobile units for use whenever the Warsaw Pact countries mount a military exercise? A network of agents behind the Iron Curtain?"

"No!" Ballantine said emphatically, "not agents! I keep strictly to radio and telex monitoring. I never — but never — encroach on Red territory. It's a dirty business, running agents, not my scene at all."

"But the point is this: you'd be pretty damned sore if the people at Fort Halstead were careless with the results of your hard work? Presumably, an important part of the intelligence game is that the other side shouldn't learn exactly how much you know about them?"

"I'd say that's rather obvious."

"And you'd be even more upset if the fort was letting *British* secrets slip through their fingers?"

Ballantine shifted ponderously in his seat, turning to face Avery for the first time, his eyes revealing his sudden concern.

"Get to it," he snapped. "If you've something to say, let's have it. I can do without the prologue."

"You were one of the committee which drafted the specification for Vulcan?"

"Yes, you were told that."

"So you're familiar with the technical design of the system?"

"I'm not a computer expert as such but I know enough to get by."

"There's a piece of hardware called the terminal interface unit. Have you heard of it?"

"I believe so."

"Do you know what it does?"

"Ah, now there you have me."

"Then I'll enlighten you. Officially, its function is to control all those displays in the Command Room and the side rooms."

"Officially . . . ?" Ballantine said, frowning.

"There's a microprocessor inside that unit. A computer on a chip."

"You could be right. There are several in Vulcan. Four, if I remember correctly. Or is it five . . . ?"

"This one has its own store. A private memory, if you prefer the term."

"That comes as no great surprise. All computers need a store to be able to operate. Even tiny computers on chips."

"You're absolutely right, George. But this one has a suspiciously *large* store. In fact, it's several times larger than is necessary to control those displays."

"So . . . ?"

"Here's the reason why. Most of the time, that unit does what it's supposed to. But every now and then the microprocessor carries out some nefarious work on the quiet. It records the state of play at crucial points

322

in the game. *It's a little spy,* George, located where no country has ever managed to infiltrate a spy before. Am I getting through to you yet? It salts away the vital details of a game in its store and no one is any the wiser. After twenty-four hours of war gaming the store is full; that's as much information as it can hold. And here comes the clever bit. The microprocessor now indulges in a bit of malingering. It refuses to respond normally and all the displays go blank. What does it look like to Campbell-Jones and his staff? Like a perfectly ordinary computer failure, of course. So the call goes out for a friendly service engineer to come and replace it."

Ballantine was staring, his mouth open.

"You can probably work the rest out for yourself," Avery went on. "Once that unit has left the fort, it couldn't be easier. All our man has to do is connect it up to a special piece of hardware he keeps at the ready. It won't be complex—just a few control keys and a printer. Then hey presto!—he's printing the secret information smuggled out in that store. Weapons, tactics, the lot. It'll take ten minutes at most, at the end of which he scrubs the store clean to destroy the evidence. Then he returns the unit to the repair shelf where he found it."

"You can prove all this?"

"I wouldn't say *prove* exactly . . ."

Ballantine closed his eyes and moaned, "Here we go again . . ."

"It's been happening for months, George," Avery said, catching his arm. "I can tell you which games they were interested in. I can tell you the precise dates when those units were taken from the fort to the

323

repair shed at Swindon."

Ballantine practically jumped. *"Swindon?* You mean *Quantek?"*

"Well, where else? I can point you at the man behind it, too."

Tell me, Ballantine implored, raising his eyebrows in question. Then: no, don't, I don't want to hear. His face was like putty and he rubbed his eyes, lost for words.

"Let's guess, shall we?" Avery said, with a cunning smile. "He has to be high up in the company, a man of considerable influence. How do we know? Because he was able to get that spy unit designed into the system. Because he has the run of the factory, which is why he can pluck it out of field service at any time of his choosing."

"I know what you're implying and I don't like it one bit."

"I never imagined for one moment you would."

"Not Peter Hurst?" Ballantine said, wearily shaking his head. "The man who has everything . . . why should he turn to spying?"

"Presumably, that's the trademark of the master spy," Avery suggested. "He's the one man you'd never suspect, not in a million years."

"But Peter Hurst . . ." Ballantine murmured. "You've simply got to be wrong."

He was only mouthing the words, Avery could tell. Behind that expressionless face of his, the brain must be racing, testing the likelihood of the idea. You're more than half convinced, Avery thought: you won't admit it but you are. Let's see how you like the rest. . . .

He said, "His wife's name is Halina. An unusual name, don't you agree? Not exactly *English*."

"She's French. So what!"

"*Polish*, George. Halina is a Polish name. As a matter of fact, I didn't know either till I thought to check."

"So what!" Ballantine said again, uselessly.

"You might try digging around the roots of the family tree. Maybe you'll find close relatives still living in Poland, a basis for pressure to be put on Hurst. Christ, it's not *my* goddamned job to find the motive! It's time you and yours did some of the detective work round here!"

Ballantine fell into a troubled silence and began to fuss with the backrest adjustment to his seat, seemingly unable to get comfortable.

You're just a mechanic, Avery thought, a desk-bound technician. You probably know all there is to know about radio frequencies and message encryption and weapon statistics. But you don't understand *people*, do you? Didn't Sherman mention you were divorced? That's no surprise.

"There's more to come," he said. "And the rest of the evidence points the accusing finger in the same direction. Want to hear it?"

"Why not," Ballantine muttered remotely, still struggling with his thoughts.

"It seems there was an eager young scientist at Fort Halstead. Know the one I mean, name of Franklin? Unfortunately for him, he became interested in why Vulcan seemed so unreliable. He wasn't suspicious as such, he had no reason to be. Just curious, an enthusiastic computer expert faced with an unusual technical problem. I think he assumed he'd discovered no more than a design fault, an error in one of the computer programs. I'm convinced he didn't suspect espionage or he'd have said so to his girlfriend, Valerie Ashton, and we know he said nothing of the sort."

"And how do *we* know that?" Ballantine said dryly.

"Because we asked her, George."

"Did we, indeed!"

The raised twitching eyebrows made Avery grin. "Now, from this point on I have to guess his moves but my theory seems to fit the known facts to a tee. As I see it, Franklin was basically a nice guy. He admired Vulcan enormously, and the men at Quantek who designed it. Well, nice guys don't like to get men they admire into hot water, so what was Franklin to do? He probably decided that the right course of action was a friendly word in the ear of one of Quantek's top people. I can almost hear him: Psst! there's an annoying fault in the system you supplied. How about correcting it before anyone else notices? Plausible so far, George?"

There was only a grunt in reply: Ballantine was staring across the parking lot.

You're trying to get ahead of me now, Avery thought. Trying to figure the rest of it out.

He shrugged and continued: "But he doesn't have any contacts at Quantek, so who can he go to? Why not the technical director, Dr. Corrigan? The title sounds impressive . . . if you don't know the internal politics at Quantek. He's the top technical man, or so it appears, and this *is* a technical problem. Yes, the way I see it, Corrigan would have been the obvious choice. And note this, George. Franklin was posted to the fort after Vulcan was installed. So he wasn't to know Corrigan had been kept well clear of the project.

"Which brings us to that fateful Thursday, the day I first arrived at Quantek. Franklin hopped on his motorcycle and set off for Swindon on his errand of mercy. And that's when things began to go horribly wrong. *While he was in Corrigan's office, Hurst walked in with me and saw them together.*"

"But why should he recognize Franklin?" Ballantine asked quickly. "A nobody from a place he hardly ever visited?"

"I doubt if he did. I think something made him smell a rat—perhaps it was Corrigan's manner when he was disturbed, we may never know. Whatever, Hurst decided to find out who the visitor was. How? Well, he might have taken a peek at the visitors' book they keep at the main gate, that's only one of several ways. And there it would be in black and white: Name, Robert Franklin; Organization, RARDE. At the sight of which, I imagine Hurst flew into a panic and called his contact, the guy he passes the information to. 'I think my cover's about to be blown,' he said. 'For God's sake, take care of it. Bring in the embassy assassins if you have to !' "

"Steady on, old chap," Ballantine said. "Steady on. Just because I'm listening doesn't mean I accept all this. *Which* embassy?"

"That's your province, not mine. That's for you to find out."

"You really do have a remarkable imagination, Mr. Avery, I'll say that. Read a lot of Agatha Christie, do you? Fancy yourself as the fearless detective?"

"Hear me out, George," Avery said, looking hurt. "It all fits together perfectly, you'll see. The killer squad disposes of Franklin and fakes a defection . . ."

"Tell me something." Ballantine rested a hand on Avery's arm. It was a fatherly gesture, sympathetic even. "This hypothetical squad of yours—why would they go so far as to kill a man who suspected nothing? That's what you implied, isn't it? That Franklin had no reason to be suspicious?"

"The stakes were enormous, that's the point. Hurst had created a unique source of information—an electronic spy right at the heart of one of the country's top defense establishments. It had taken him two years to do it and the big payoff was yet to come. It was irrelevant that Franklin was only sniffing around the edges—he was getting too damned close for comfort."

"And then what, Mr. Avery?" Ballantine's eyebrows climbed into mocking half-moons. "And then Corrigan?"

"You got it. He presented Hurst with an almighty headache because the fake defection had unexpectedly backfired. You were personally involved now, correct? News of a defection at the fort, even a minor one, suggested a risk to your precious homework. You came running with the cowboys in tow, yes?"

Ballantine nodded silently.

"And you soon discovered that meeting between Franklin and Corrigan. So you and your boys were watching the doctor around the clock. You'd no real grounds for alarm yet; it was still routine surveillance.

But you took no chances and that's how we came to meet up outside the factory. Am I right so far?"

"As near as makes no difference."

"For all his failings," Avery said, "Corrigan had the brightest brain in Quantek, which is why Hurst never dared let him near Vulcan. He was the single greatest threat to the plot. Suddenly, what Hurst had always feared actually happened: Corrigan put two and two together and deduced Hurst was behind it. Do you remember that dinner we had at Hurst's?"

"I'm hardly likely to forget it in a hurry!"

"Corrigan as good as told Hurst he knew, and right under our very noses, George! He produced a microprocessor at the dinner table, remember?"

Ballantine stroked his chin, then murmured, "Yes . . . now you mention it."

"It was exactly the same model as the one installed in that spy unit. Corrigan was sure Hurst would get the message but for good measure he spelled it out. I don't recall his exact words but they were something along the lines: It's amazing what you can do with these little fellas. *And right in front of you, George!* Know what he was saying? 'I've worked out the whole story, Peter Hurst. But I'm not turning you in to the authorities, at least not yet awhiles.' "

"*Blackmail*, you mean?" Ballantine's sharp eyes bored into Avery's.

"Well, Hurst certainly assumed that's what it was. The moment Corrigan left the room, he made a grab for that computer and threw it on the fire. It was a mindless response, really. He wasn't disposing of evidence as such. I guess it just made him feel better."

"Corrigan was drunk," Ballantine said. "He was in no fit state for subtle games of that kind."

"Oh, he was drunk, all right. Which brings us to the dilemma facing Hurst. I suspect that if Corrigan had been the reliable type, Hurst might have gone along with it. Perhaps been extra nice for a while, given him a few more Quantek shares and a bigger role in the management of the company. Whatever was needed to buy time until the important war games start at the fort and the plan comes to fruition. Except that Hurst saw Corrigan as anything *but* reliable; he was volatile and unpredictable. As I say, that presented Hurst with an awful dilemma. He didn't give a stuff about Franklin's fate but he cared a great deal about Corrigan. He genuinely didn't want to order out the assassins for a second time."

"You can read his mind, of course!"

"It's the only possibe reason why Corrigan wasn't killed sooner!" Avery explained. "Franklin disappeared on the Thursday. Corrigan died the following Tuesday. That's five whole days, George. Five dangerous days during which he might have come running to you at any time. So what do we deduce? It's obvious, isn't it? Hurst didn't tell his embassy contact straightaway that Corrigan was a risk. For those five long days Hurst was praying he wouldn't be forced to have him killed."

"You're off the rails," Ballantine said, shaking his head sadly. "You're way out in orbit. Hurst *cared* about Corrigan, you say? That's not the Peter Hurst I know!"

"Are you familiar with partnerships?" Avery asked.

"Because I am. There's one kind: the guys who put on an affable front for the world and then sink the knife blades in one another's backs behind closed doors. I'm speaking of the other kind, George, the very opposite. The Quantek kind, the kind I saw as a kid at home. Men displaying mutual hate in public but actually harboring a deep-down respect they'd never admit to because they don't want to admit it to themselves. Hurst and Corrigan were like that. They hated working together but they were even more afraid of going their separate ways."

"Hmmph!" Ballantine snorted.

"I'm right, George, believe me. One of Hurst's first acts when I arrived was to try to introduce me to Corrigan. He *wanted* me to meet him because he thought it would help the sale. And I agonized over that, I can tell you. Was I wrong to suspect Hurst? Could he ever have brought himself to have Corrigan killed? For a while I actually thought not. And then I remembered a story I was told about Hurst and a dog, and that made it crystal clear. Oh, yes, he was able to do it, all right."

"A dog! Suddenly we have a dog appearing on the scene!"

"I won't repeat the story," Avery said soberly, "it isn't important. The point is this: Hurst has a cold streak in him, an unusually callous side under that friendly exterior. The way I see it, a man who could put down a favorite pet because it no longer looked attractive could do exactly the same to a fellow human. Does that sound farfetched?" Avery had seen the look of disbelief clouding Ballantine's face. "It shouldn't. In an odd kind of way that's what Corrigan had become to Hurst, a pet of sorts; an extravagance like his racehorses. Corrigan clung to his job solely on Hurst's whim. He could still be an asset at times: the colorful company character with the ready wit and the eloquent tongue. His mistake was to overplay his hand at dinner that night. Suddenly, he wasn't fun anymore and Hurst had him destroyed, put down."

Ballantine snapped his fingers. "Just like that, eh?"

Avery echoed the action to confirm it. "Certainly, George. It was easy enough. Franklin's disappearance was officially hushed up, don't forget, which means Corrigan had no inkling anything had happened to him. When he had a call purporting to come from Franklin he assumed it was genuine. It *bothered* him, of course it did. A guy he'd met only once suddenly suggesting a meeting way out on a highway, of all places? It bothered him so much he almost changed his mind as he was driving. Do you remember? That turn back, the long stop to think things over, then the decision to see it through? I've come this far, he reasoned, why not find out what it's about. And we were right there behind him in your car. They were taking a terrible risk."

"And they, whoever they are, did what to him?"

"Don't ask me. *You* couldn't solve that one, how am I supposed to!" Avery sank in his seat, closing his eyes as if exhausted. In truth, he felt suddenly sick. "Not the pleasantest of tales, is it?" he said, articulating his thoughts.

"Nor the likeliest I've ever heard," Ballantine offered with a pronounced sniff.

"I'll admit that; it's circumstantial evidence only. But you *can* get proof."

"I fail to see how."

Eagerly, Avery sat up again. "By catching Hurst in the act, of course. The next time there's a computer failure at the fort, just mount a twenty-four-hour watch on the field service department. Then when Hurst comes to collect that interface unit, you pounce. You'll be able to lock him up and throw away the key. I doubt if you'll ever get a charge of double homicide to stick, but so what! Spying carries a far longer sentence these days, doesn't it?"

"I'll need to do my own investigation first," Ballantine said noncommittally, "to corroborate your version. Hell's teeth, man, a story like that *needs* double checking."

"Naturally."

"If we find that you're right . . ."

"There's no if about it, George."

". . . *If* you're right, Mr. Avery, we'll take whatever action seems appropriate. You can depend on that." Ballantine shook hands, preparing to leave. "Extraordinary," he murmured to himself, looking Avery over. "Quite extraordinary."

"You know the saddest part of the whole saga?" Avery said as an afterthought. "Corrigan would never have squeaked, never. Hurst didn't have a damned thing to worry about."

Ballantine frowned heavily. "You're being inconsistent. You said a minute ago he was unpredictable." He released the half-open car door and a gust of wind caught it, blowing it wide against the stops.

"No, I said Hurst *regarded* him as unpredictable. The point is: poor old Corrigan never suspected he was in danger. All that mattered to him was that his lifetime partner was a spy. And know what, George? Know what effect that had on him? He hit the bottle again. He'd been on the wagon for months and suddenly he was drinking like a fish. He spent days just mooning around, staring into space—I saw him at it and didn't understand at the time. The knowledge that Hurst was a spy cut deep, but he still respected the man, more than anyone else he knew. I'm as sure of it as I'll ever be of anything. Hurst had nothing to fear from him, not a goddamned thing."

"Friendship, is that what you're saying? Honor?"

"Both. Maybe something deeper, even."

"Balls!" Ballantine said angrily. "Utter balls! They were like Kilkenny cats, those two, at one another's throats on the slightest provocation! And as for Corrigan . . . My God, he was a shell of a man. Don't imply *honor*, my lad, not to him! Don't insult my intelligence!"

"My word," Avery said, startled by the outburst. "Take it easy."

"Well it's stuff and bloody nonsense," Balantine said, digging in a trouser pocket; "the craziest thing I've ever heard." He pulled out a handkerchief and mopped his brow. "For all I know, the whole story's nonsense. Who knows what to believe with you."

Avery seized his arm, gripping hard. *"Get him, George!"* he growled through his teeth. "Just get him. I don't like what he did to that poor Irish bastard. Get him for me, would you?"

Ballantine stared at the show of emotion then tucked the handkerchief away and left the car. "We'll see," he said, bending. "Meanwhile, don't muddy the water. I shan't thank you if you tip Hurst off with any more of your amateur sleuthing."

"You've got a damned nerve!" Avery retorted. "Who's been doing all the work while you and the cowboys sat on your asses!" But he managed a limp smile. "Okay, I'll give you a free field from here on in. Make sure you use it. Just as long as you get the bastard."

He watched Ballantine walk to the Ford: short and tubby, rolling as he went and leaning more than was necessary into the blustery wind, like a sailor struggling across a deck in a gale. Avery watched him settle into the driver's seat, very stiff and upright, and start the engine.

A long stare from him as the car moved away. A cautious halt at the road then a turn and he was heading slowly back to the establishment.

No wonder you need Mulholland, Avery thought. You wouldn't catch a tortoise, left to your own devices.

27

The long-handled wire fork that hung beside the fireplace was for making *toast!* How quaint, how very English. Why had it taken him so long to realize that? Sitting cross-legged on the hearth, Avery speared another slice of bread and held it out to the flames.

He looked around the living room, watching the long shadows climb the walls to the beamed ceiling. If you forgot the hidden microphones the cottage was still quite a place. Outside: the soft, mysterious sounds of the country. Inside: the old pictures and guns, the leatherbound books, the fine furniture, the Persian carpets. He knew quite a lot about those carpets now—a search in one of the books had shown how to distinguish between the ornate borders: the two in here were Kashans and there was a hundred-year-old Kerman in the upper hall.

A few more days, he thought wistfully, then back to Los Angeles. He'd miss England and all this; wasn't that crazy?

After finishing the toast, he reached for his pocket Dictaphone. One more spurious report for Hurst's benefit, a final comment on how terrific Vulcan was proving to be. Keep the suspect in blissful ignorance.

"Memo to Larry Brokaw," he began. "Visit to Quantek, England. Week four. I am now confirmed in my opinion that Vulcan is a quite outstanding system. Meetings with the design team this week focused on the features for overall game control by the Command Room staff . . ."

His eyes wandered to the side wall, just above the telephone, and he smiled. In a few days' time Brokaw would be hearing the real story at last. Sorry, Larry, but you're not going to like this. Take a seat by the pool and a long, refreshing look at that sunset of yours, then brace yourself. I'd forget the military market if I were you, and stick to office systems. Guess what you nearly sold to the Pentagon . . . !

Later that evening, the doorbell rang and he found Barbara there, looking like an Eskimo in an anorak with a halo of imitation fur around her face. He drew her into the hall for a lively embrace. She returned the caresses for a while then unexpectedly bit hard on an ear.

"*Ow!*"

"Business before pleasure," she said with a cheeky smile. "Since you weren't at Quantek today I've had to chase you here."

"This is a *working* visit, Barbara?"

"Fifty-fifty." She put her mouth against his cheek to whisper, "That dodgy part you were so interested in—it's called a terminal interface unit." Then she frowned and asked herself, "Have I got that right? Don't worry, I've written it down somewhere."

Avery stared, speechless.

"Well?" she asked. "Is that the one?"

"Come again . . . ?"

"Is that the one you thought? You said you could guess which it was."

He caught her arm and spun her to the door. "A drink, Barbara? How about a pub? There's one in Lambourn I keep meaning to try."

"But there's always plenty of booze here," she

337

protested. "Don't say you've finished it all?"

"You drive," he said, hustling her toward the Renault. "It'll save me getting my car out."

Let's hope that bloody hall isn't bugged, he thought.

She struggled with the remnants of a synchromesh to get noisily into second. The gear lever was typically Gallic: a cranked tube protruding from the dash, which she pushed and pulled and twisted with effort.

"Well . . . ?" he asked.

"I told you, it's called a terminal interface unit. You're not the only detective round here."

"How did you find that out?"

"Simple, darling. I asked."

"*You did what . . . !*"

"I said—I asked. And don't get so cross, I only asked John Burton."

"*Who?*"

"The service engineer—you know, the old-timer I told you about." She reached down to touch Avery's hand. "Come on, Martin, you said youself the engineers weren't involved, so it was quite safe. Besides, he's a sweet old dear. I wasn't taking a risk."

"You *asked* . . ." he said, shaking his head in amazement, and then had to smile at the thought. "Well, if that doesn't beat all. What a lady!"

"Easier than burglary," she said.

"I guess it is."

"And there's more where that came from."

"Meaning?" he asked, apprehensively.

"It'll cost you a Dubonnet and lemon to find out."

"Is that a reward or punishment?"

"Hush, you," she said. "I happen to like it."

On the edge of the village, she slowed at the first inn and gave him a questioning look.

"This'll do fine," he agreed.

It was small and Spartan, with bare, scrubbed floorboards and a coalfire burning in an old-fashioned iron grate. A group of elderly men in baggy tweeds were playing darts—they stopped and fell silent to watch them enter and cross to the bar. The game only began again when Avery had bought the drinks and chosen a high-backed wooden bench in an opposite corner.

"Okay, let's hear it, lady . . ."

"Those service sheets—you know, the ones you said Peter Hurst removed to cover his tracks? They *weren't* taken, Martin."

"But they must have been! They sure weren't there when I searched last night."

She nodded, her dark eyes shining with excitement. "That's right, they were never there."

Avery was confused. "Who says so?"

"John Burton says."

"*You asked him that, too?*"

"Why not?"

"Jesus!" Avery exclaimed, covering his face.

"The service sheets are always left where the parts are repaired. That's the standard procedure—so the repair staff know which work to carry out."

"I know that!"

"Usually repairs are done at Quantek." She paused, watching him.

"How do you mean . . . *usually?*"

339

She smiled, delighted at her superior knowledge. "Apparently, some customers do their own repairs."

"But that doesn't happen at the fort, does it!"

"Ah, they're special," she said, and the smile became a tantalizing grin. "In their case, repairs are carried out by what's called a designated third party. It's an unusual arrangement but not the first time it's been done, so John Burton says."

"Did he happen to say who this third party is?"

"Your friends at GCHQ, of course!"

"But that's ridiculous!" Avery said.

She shrugged. "The service engineers don't see anything odd in the setup because there are several of our computers at Cheltenham and GCHQ insist on doing all their own repairs. It's such a top-secret establishment that nobody, but nobody, gets past the front gate."

"I fail to see the connection with the fort," Avery said, completely lost.

"The argument is that it makes economic sense for GCHQ to do the repairs for another defense establishment while they're at it. But they don't have a fleet of service vans, so Quantek does the fetching and carrying."

"You're absolutely sure that's where the units are taken?"

She nodded contentedly. "John Burton confirmed it. The engineer leaves the faulty part at the gate with the completed service sheet."

Avery stared into this glass. "And the named contact there is . . . ?"

"George Ballantine. Who do you think!"

"Christ Almighty!" Avery swore, "and this morning I told him everything I know. Everything." He searched the bar wildly, examining the faces, looking toward the door.

She didn't share his alarm. "But don't you see, Martin, it means you were wrong! There's nothing shady going on, nothing to worry about."

"*Then why didn't Ballantine say that!* Why didn't he explain that the parts are taken to Cheltenham. He just sat there and listened to me, then went off muttering that he'd take care of it. No, Barbara, it's worse than I thought." Avery took a deep slug of his scotch. "I don't know what it means yet but it's infinitely worse."

"Oh, cripes," she said helplessly.

"Ballantine!" he exclaimed, striking his forehead with the heel of a hand. "But *why*, Barbara? Why? Why on earth would he spy on his own ministry? *He's just stealing back the same information he gave the fort in the first place!* He can get any goddamned fact he wants about those war games simply by asking! It makes no sense, none of it does anymore."

"It does seem pretty crazy."

"But I was wrong about Hurst, that much is clear."

"Oh, *I* knew last night," she said. "The minute you told me."

"Thanks, sweetheart," he responded bitterly. "Thanks a million for saying so."

She nibbled his ear and murmured, "Well if you will make love like that, don't expect me to have the clearest of minds afterwards. But it could never have been Peter Hurst. He isn't clever enough, don't you

341

see? He's a smarty-boots businessman who can twist most people around his little finger but he isn't clever. And I don't like him, not one bit, but I'd never see him as the type to have someone killed. He's too soft, that man. Too soft, and none too bright."

"I need another drink," Avery said. "How about you?"

"I'm fine." She shrouded her glass with a hand.

When he returned from the bar with another large scotch, she said, "I did something else, some more detective work. Don't be angry again."

"It's not anger," Avery said, with a gentle shake of the head. "I'm sorry if it seems like that. It's sheer frustration, more like, and aimed at me not you."

And it's fear, he thought. Has that occurred to her? I may have been wrong about Hurst but there are still two dead people to account for.

"I looked at the visitors' book, Martin."

"At the main gate?" He was past surprise, now.

Yes, I said I was back-checking some old appointments and they let me go through it without turning a hair. I tried October the twentieth, the day you first came." She paused until his eyes bid her to continue. "You signed in just after eleven: Mr. Avery to see Mr. Hurst. Not long after, Robert Franklin signed in: he was seeing Patrick, well we know that. Then there were a handful of visitors attending a sales presentation—they don't matter. And just before twelve your friend showed up, the one and only Mr. Ballantine: to see Mr. Hurst, according to his entry in the book."

"But *I* was with Hurst! There was no sign of

Ballantine." Avery racked his brains, thinking back. "Hurst was due at a meeting in London, if I remember. He tried to off-load me onto Patrick but there was that silly quarrel and he ended up leaving me outside—by your desk, Barbara. Then he left. You've got to be wrong."

"No. I cross-checked with Agnes, Peter's secretary."

"Jesus Christ! Is there *anyone* in Swindon who won't know about this by the time you've finished!"

"Just listen, you," she said, poking him firmly in the ribs. "I did it carefully, got that? With my customary finesse. And *I* wasn't the one who blurted the whole thing out to the number-one suspect."

"What did Agnes say?" Avery demanded.

"That Ballantine gave Peter a lift to London. End of mystery. They were both due at the same ministry meeting and he offered to pick Peter up on his way through from Cheltenham."

"And saw Franklin's name in that book . . ."

"He must have done, Martin. It's in bright green ballpoint, as a matter of fact, and enormous capital letters—RARDE, like it was up in lights. There's no way he could've missed it."

Avery quickly finished his drink. "Take me back," he said.

"So soon? I like it here."

"Just do it!" He caught the glint in her eye and remembered to add, "Please . . . ?"

They sat in the car outside the cottage. It was a coal-black night with low, scurrying clouds hiding the moon and stars. He thought again how remote the cottage was; for some reason one noticed that especially at night.

"Your husband . . ." he said.

"Jim, his name is."

"Does he look like me?"

She laughed. "What a funny question."

He seized her hand and demanded, *"Does he!"*

The laugh died in the instant. She flicked on the courtesy light and examined his face, turning it first to one side then the other. "Do women fall for similar types, is that what you mean? Some people think so."

"Barbara!"

She sighed and said, "You don't have much in common. He's forty-seven and balding, if you must know. Bags under the eyes most days, horn-rimmed glasses to add some dignity, and a sagging waistline. Once—maybe—there might have been a slight resemblance but not anymore." She snapped off the light and confessed in the darkness, "So now you know. Perhaps that's why I have this uncontrollable urge to rape visiting Americans."

Avery was broodily silent.

"Why did you ask, Martin?"

"It doesn't matter."

"I'd still like to know. It's an odd thing to ask, especially now."

A car passed on the lane above the cottage and he could see her small face illuminated by the sweeping beams of the headlights. He cupped it in his hands.

"Because, my love, I have a nasty feeling I may need a passport tomorrow that isn't American and doesn't have 'Avery' written on it. Now do you see? I may have been wrong about Hurst, but not about Franklin and Patrick."

"Don't!" she cried, biting her knuckles.

The headlights were suddenly gone, hidden by a bend in the lane. Avery bent forward, peering anxiously through the windscreen to where they should reappear again at any second. When they did not, he wound down his window.

"Cut the engine!"

She obeyed without question. There was no sound of another car — just the wind buffeting the trees.

He kissed her solemnly. "Do a couple of things for me, would you?"

"If you want . . ."

"Go home, like now. Straight home, understand? Don't stop for anything or anybody and drive like the wind."

"In this old crate!"

"Just go, okay. Know the phone number here?"

"Of course."

"Dial it when you get back. Don't say anything, just let it ring three times then hang up."

"Why?"

"Do you need me to spell it out for you? I want to be sure you've made it home all right."

She stared, wild-eyed. "And you . . . ?"

"You're safer without me."

"Martin!" she said with a suppressed sob, throwing herself on him. He held her briefly then pushed her away.

"Tomorrow, can you get in to work without this car?"

"I've had to do it before."

"I might need it—they know the Rover. Leave it outside your house. Leave the keys here." He pulled down the sun visor to show her where.

She nodded, her body beginning to shake.

If she doesn't go now, he thought, she never will. "And make it a normal day at the office," he told her. "Understand? Take it easy, smile a lot. Act as if you haven't a care in the world." He kissed her fondly. "See you again someday, huh?"

"Promise . . . ?"

"I promise."

He left the car, opened the front door of the house and switched on the hall and porch lights. Then he stood on the lawn, clearly silhouetted against the light, waving as she drove away. He watched the beams of the car climb up as if into the black night sky before swinging down again and along the lane, turning, vanishing then reappearing, dwindling until they were finally gone, halfway to Lambourn. No headlights followed. The other car—if there was one there on the Downs road—stayed where it was.

In the living room, he charged for the telephone. What the hell was Sherman's number? 9832? Or was it 9382? this time the stupid man had better believe the story. Stupid great oaf! If only he'd listened before.

He lifted the phone and dialed, then stared at the handset and frantically jiggled the cradle.

The line was dead.

"Oh, my God," he breathed, and cold fear began to take him over, gnawing at his nerves. Shivering, he moved to the fire, holding his hands to the welcome warmth. As he went to get more logs from the basket, his eyes lifted, to the antique guns on the wall.

Maybe, he thought. Maybe . . .

The Boer War rifle felt heavy in his hands as he aimed the long barrel shakily at his reflection in an ornate mirror. There was no ammunition and it probably wouldn't fire anyway. But they won't know that, will they? he told himself.

The icy fear had a numbing effect on his mind. Like, he imagined, it would on a man about to freeze to death.

28

The car came two hours later, slowly down the hill and onto the forecourt. Avery turned out the living room light, then lifted the sash of one of the windows and pushed the rifle barrel into view. Blinded by the full headlights, he shaded his eyes, unable to see what make it was or who was in it.

The exhaust condensed in a thick cloud around the car, drifting like smoke across the bright beams. The engine was too warm to have been started nearby: it spun smoothly, with a quiet tick-over. The other car must still be up there.

For fully a minute there was no movement, so Avery leveled the rifle against the glare, at where he guessed the driver to be. At that, a door opened and was gent-

347

ly closed again. He heard the crunch of footsteps on the gravel; then a figure came to the front of the car—dark and featureless against the striated light, like a flat cutout, a black hole.

"There's no need for that," Ballantine said. "Not fire arms."

"You're right on schedule," Avery replied. "My God, but you're predictable."

Ballantine came a fraction nearer, casting a giant shadow over the lawn. "You're not a well man, Mr. Avery, that's all I've come to say. I've been talking to Henderson again and he mentioned your medical history. It's all clear now, these wild ideas of yours. You have my full understanding, I promise you." He took two more steps forward, extending a hand. "Look, put that down, there's a good chap."

There was an uncertain edge to his voice. You're wondering where I got the gun, Avery thought. If a man points a rifle at you, you don't stop to think whether it's loaded.

"You've got a problem I don't envy, George," he said. "If I suddenly turn up full of lead in a morgue, even Henderson and his fat sidekick will begin to suspect I was telling the truth. *No, hold it there!* No nearer!"

"The saints preserve us," Ballantine murmured. "The man's gone way over the top." Then, more loudly: "You're wrong, you know. I've been looking into your story. There's a simple explanation for everything. Look here, why don't I come in to tell you? It's blasted cold out here."

"*Stay put!* And tell those cowboys up on the hill to

348

stay where they are . . ."

Ballantine uttered one of his long-drawn sighs. "Cowboys? Which cowboys?"

"You know what I couldn't figure out?" Avery said. "Why there was so much action going on around me. Shall I repeat that, George? Around *me*. Jesus, was I slow! You turn up at Quantek the very day I do, and Franklin vanishes the same afternoon. Next, we meet over dinner at Hurst's—for no good reason, just an introduction to friendly old Goerge, the ministry warhorse. The following day I find you and your posse on Corrigan's coattails. One day later, there you are again—at the crucial moment when he's biting the dust. And I get loaned a cottage, only to find it's bugged from floor to ceiling. A long string of coincidences, you might say. Too bloody long—real life is never like that. Except they *weren't* coincidences, were they? There I was thinking I was simply a spectator, watching the action from the sidelines. Like hell! *I was the main event, wasn't I, George?* You arranged to give Hurst a lift that first day because you couldn't wait, you had to find out what kind of man Brokaw had sent over. This whole sordid saga happened because of me."

"Paranoia," Ballantine said, shaking his head with regret. "That's what it is."

"You were never after those secrets at Fort Halstead. That was just a dress rehearsal! You had to be sure the scheme would work. You had to discover the likely flaws first and get rid of them so the real thing would run like clockwork."

"And what real thing would that be? Do put the

349

gun down, there's a good chap. You don't look as if you know how to handle it."

"Uncle Sam," Avery said. "An electronic spy buried deep in the Pentagon. You're nothing if not ambitious."

Was it his imagination, or did the dark shape suddenly become very still, rooted to the spot?

"You know what I assumed at first?" he continued. "That it was some harebrained British intelligence stunt which got out of hand. You know the problem better than I do: the Americans don't tell you half the information they have on the other side, and you return the compliment by playing the same two-faced game. That calls for plenty of ingenuity and my first guess was that clever George Ballantine had come up with exactly the right scheme. Bypass the official liaison channels altogether—put a bug in the Pentagon. That would be quite an intelligence coup, eh? You could discover what information they really have on the Russians, over there in Washington. You could learn about the offensive European strategies they've prepared and somehow forgotten to mention to NATO. Yes, I almost convinced myself that was the answer, George. It would be in the best traditions of the intelligence game, all in the interests of a healthy alliance! Of course, it would have to be a strictly *unofficial* scheme, a little private enterprise on your part, but it seemed to make sense."

Hunching his shoulders, Ballantine thrust his hands deep in his overcoat pockets and stamped his feet.

"What do you think of it, George? Let's have your expert view on the logic of a sick mind . . ."

There was no reply. Ballantine stamped again, scattering the drifting exhaust fumes like dust.

"And answer came there none? As you like." Avery shrugged privately in the seclusion of the room. "The trouble with that theory was the two killings. I mean, that's a weird establishment you work for — a stranger could take it for a damned great mental hospital if there wasn't a sign outside to say otherwise — but I'm sure even they draw the line at murder . . . especially of nice guys from another department of the same shop. So you see my reasoning? You can't be doing this for the British, officially or unofficially. And you sure as hell aren't doing it for the United States!"

"As a matter of fact, I'm in the pay of the KGB," Ballantine said derisively. "Why did it take you so long to work that one out?"

"Well, it speaks!" I was beginning to wonder. *Did you hear that, you guys?*" Avery shouted. "*George just confessed.*" You're getting light-headed again, he rebuked himself. For Chrissake, take a firm grip, calm down!

"Well, do I get to come in now we've got that off our chest?" Ballantine asked, making a move. "It's bloody brass monkey weather."

Avery answered with a threatening jerk of the gun barrel, forcing a hasty retreat to the car.

"And then there are the microphones," he said. 'One upstairs for the careless pillow talk and one by the phone. By the phone, George, did you hear that? Let's eavesdrop on what this fellow Avery is privately reporting to his boss . . . does he like the system? . . . is he getting suspicious yet? Well, you couldn't ask for a phone tap, not officially. What reason would you give? Oh, you're on the Moscow payroll, all right. And in a very useful position too—probably even a unique position, like your little electronic spy. You've spent years patiently working your way up the establishment ladder, I should think, to take charge of monitoring East European communications. That's quite a job, a damned sight more important than it sounds. Versatile too, in your skilled hands. You can let the fort have just sufficient information to keep them happy. What do you do with the rest, the really big stuff that would get through if you weren't in the driving seat? Put it in the shredder? As a bonus, you liaise with American intelligence over here, keeping your finger firmly on the pulse. And then there's the gilt on the gingerbread: you can let your paymasters know how effectively they're scrambling their defense communications. Better tighten up security, you can say, we're learning too much lately. You want to see the heap of data we collected last week from that exercise in the Baltic . . ."

"Very pat," Ballantine observed. "You'll almost have me believing it."

"You shouldn't have got greedy, though. That was your undoing. If you hadn't cast your avaricious eye on the Pentagon, you'd never have been rumbled. But you found yourself appointed to that Vulcan specification committee, wasn't that how it happened? Boy, you couldn't believe your luck! You suggested that they include some microprocessors in the design. Tongue in cheek, was that, George? Just trying it on? Except that they went and did it, exactly as you asked."

And you fell out with Corrigan over precisely that issue, Avery realized even as he spoke. *That's* what the disagreement was about at the ministry, those two years ago. Corrigan couldn't see any reason for having that oversized store and he tried to get it dropped. Poor Patrick, why couldn't you keep your head, ever? Why was your life one long argument?

Ballantine folded his arms, leaning back against the radiator. "This morning it was Hurst, and now it's my turn. Who's next on your list? The archbishop of Canterbury?"

"I was wrong about Hurst. I doubt if he's even involved. You don't need him to be. Just flatter him every once in a while, act the big client and pull a few strings—he'll do whatever you want."

"Tell me something, Mr. Avery. I assume you believe all this rubbish. So why are you telling *me* of all people? If I'm what you think, I mean?"

"Because I've no alternative, George. The way I see it, if you'd gone on thinking I suspected Hurst, you'd have tried to pick me off. Quietly, of course, and cleverly. But quickly, before I had second thoughts on who was really behind it. Well, I already know so you can forget that. I want to do a deal."

"Let's have it . . ."

"I've told no one else. Not Hurst, not Brokaw. No one."

"A trifle unwise of you to say so, one might think," Ballantine mused.

"No, that's basic to the deal. You've lost the sale to the Pentagon, you're going to have to accept that. There's going to be no Vulcan in my country, leaking

353

our secrets to the East. But that's as far as it goes. I don't have to tell Brokaw the real reason for not signing that licensing agreement. I can say there are severe reliability problems with the system."

"I don't follow . . ."

"What tricks you get up to over here are no concern of mine. That's a headache for the British, and frankly I don't give a damn. You can play your silly spy game to your heart's content—I doubt if it affects the balance of power one jot. So here's what we do. You call off those cowboys up there. I catch the first west-bound plane out of Heathrow in the morning. And there's an end to it, George. I won't ever mention your private arrangement with Moscow, not to anyone."

"And that's the deal, as you put it?"

"Straight down the line."

"Why don't I enter into the spirit of this for a moment. Just for the fun of it, shall we say? Aren't you forgetting something? *Get the bastard, George*—that's what you shouted at me this morning, snatching my sleeve and your eyes like a madman's. What kind of fool would trust your silence after that!"

Damn and blast! Avery thought. Still, it was worth a try.

"And I wish you wouldn't insult my intelligence, Mr. Avery. I wouldn't have faked a defection, not if it was up to me. That's the flaw in your stupid story. I would have pushed that young man off his motorbike at high speed, got it? Left him dead by the side of the road and no questions asked at the fort."

Ballantine was suddenly gone, lost somewhere behind the glare of the car's lights. Avery heard the driver's door click open.

"I'll tell you what, Mr. Avery. Why don't you drop in at GCHQ in the morning? Tell your tale to some of my colleagues. I'd rather like that. Dull old George Ballantine, that's how they see me. Works too hard for his own good, drinks a mite too much, doesn't exercise anywhere near enough these days. Yes, do that for me, would you? You'll do wonders for my image." The voice was suddenly angry. "In fact, do any damned thing you like. But on your own head be it. I've done my best with you and I'm washing my hands of the whole crazy business. Tell the neighbors, I don't care. Phone the police if you want, I don't give a fuck. Have them throw a protective cordon around the area if it makes you feel better."

"The phone's dead, George," Avery heard himself say.

"Is it, now? Well, hard bloody luck!"

The door slammed. The engine was revved. The car was turned laboriously, backward and forward in the forecourt—making a meal of it—and Avery could see at last that Ballantine was alone. Then it moved away up the hill. It didn't stop as he expected in the lane above: the headlights were finally gone exactly where they should, just where Barbara's had vanished on her way to Lambourn.

Avery closed and secured the window, drawing the curtains. He put the gun aside and stood close to the fire, swinging his chilled hands and stamping his feet as Ballantine had done.

That was too damned easy, he thought: the guy simply leaving like that. What's going on around here?

Ballantine pulled in a quarter of a mile short of the village. Beating his hands against his sides, he walked back along the dark lane, stumbling at times against the uneven grass border. He swore under his breath as a stray twig from a hedge tore at his cheek.

The BMW was parked off the road, through a five-barred gate and well hidden in a thickly wooded copse from any passing traffic. The lights of the cottage were in clear view below, immediately through the screening trees.

He rapped on the passenger window and Vladek wound it down.

"Do it," he said. "He won't be any trouble."

"You chose a fine bloody night!" Vladek said. His breath misted and hung in the air.

"Did you hear what I said?"

"I heard."

"Is there a back way out of that place?"

De Freitas was at the wheel, a pair of binoculars trained on the cottage. They had enormous front lenses, and a cable ran to a battery pack on the back seat.

"Do me a favor!" he said, looking pained.

"I'm off, then," Ballantine said. "I've got a deuce of a head, one of my migraines. It hasn't been the best of days."

"Terrific!" Vladek sneered.

"Listen, laddie," Ballantine said, pushing his face close. "Listen, trigger-happy Mr. Vladek. A simple motorbike accident and we'd be in the clear. But you had to overreact and put a bullet in that chap Franklin. So you can clear up this fucking mess; it's

356

one of your own making.

"What about the woman?" de Freitas asked. "Mrs. Young?"

Ballantine held up crossed fingers. "I think we're clear on that front. Nothing we've taped gives me any cause for concern. But I've got Mully watching her, just to be sure. He's on channel seven if you need him." He gave a minimal nod of the head then picked a cautious way back through the undergrowth, into the night.

"Jammy bastard!" Vladek swore, with the window safely closed. "Going off to bloody bed! Can't you run the engine, just for a minute or two? How about some heat in here?"

"You want to get warm," de Freitas said, "you take some exercise."

He lifted the glasses again and aimed them at the cottage, noting with satisfaction how exposed it was, how far it was on all sides from cover. A light came on in the kitchen and he watched Avery enter, begin to grind some coffee, then glance to the window and cross quickly to pull down the blind.

The image was as clear as if it were daylight. Just a trifle fuzzy, as if seen through gauze.

29

It was a wintry dawn when it came, colorless and cold. Imperceptibly, the sky lightened from black to a steel gray. Pale, distant shapes tantalized the eye like mirages, never quite materializing then vanishing again, taken back by the passing night. Then suddenly they were there: trees and hedgerows and a hillock, rising from a slowly dissolving swamp of ground mist. The rutted fields looked as hard as granite under a crust of hoarfrost.

Avery let the living room curtain drop back and climbed the stairs to the bathroom to look dolefully into his sleepless eyes, sunken and bloodshot as they stared back at him.

This is exactly the way he wants you, he thought. Exhausted and beginning to question your judgment. Off guard.

In the kitchen he poured the last of the coffee down the sink—it had been a night of endless black coffees—and found he couldn't face breakfast either. So he returned aimlessly to the living room, kicked the fire into a final burst of flames and went for a stiff measure of whisky.

But he couldn't keep away from the window. He raised the curtain again, just at a corner, to gaze up the facing slope. There was the hedge running beside the lane, bobbing and turning, broken in places, impenetrable in others. There could be no car concealed behind it, he was sure. Perhaps farther along, where the lane curved away before dropping out of sight over that low ridge? And the copse up there, what of that? The trees were bare against the sky but there were plenty of them and close together; around their trunks brambles tangled into a dense thicket. Behind the trees the ground dipped to a small clearing, by the look of it. Yes, there might easily be a car hidden up there, assuming there was a way in from the lane. Damned if he could see it, though.

He walked back to the liquor cabinet for more whisky: not too much, just enough to fill the aching void in his stomach. Then he sat in one of the deep leather club chairs, staring absently at the embers in the grate, now glowing dimly under a spreading mantel of ash. Outside, the rooks were stirring in their tiny wood, croaking in the damp air and crying plaintively to the absent sun.

Barbara, he thought suddenly: what of her! Had she made it back safely? Suppose he was destined never to know . . . Odd to discover he cared so much. Odd that he cared yet this was the first time he'd stopped to think of her . . .

A sudden sound from the roof made him jump, his heart beating madly against the walls of his chest. *Damned birds!* One of them had flapped clumsily down to the eaves, scrabbled for a toehold on the gutter and sent moss and twigs cascading down a drain pipe.

. . . And odd to realize how much sympathy he had for Corrigan, a man he'd barely known. Patrick, you were nothing but a great overgrown child, he mused, a man who bared your soul for all to see. Barbara is amusing because she chooses to be, but you played the clown because you *had* to. And the more desperately you tried to reach out to your fellow men—to entertain them, to impress them—the more vulnerable you became. God, I know what that's like. I, more than anyone, understand that feeling.

What a way to die, Avery thought then, brooding on the prospect of his own imminent death. Surrounded by others on a busy highway yet totally alone. Imprisoned in a metal coffin.

Remembering the accident again, he shivered and sought comfort in the scotch. *Accident!* The hell it was. The car suddenly out of control, hitting that truck and plowing into the highway divider. And then those flying sparks, the sound of tortured metal, the engine hood breaking lose . . .

Does metal feel pain? he wondered stupidly. That's all I could see: the Rover being torn apart. I saw the death throes of a car but not Corrigan's, yet he was in it, just in front of us.

The car! he thought in horror. My God, I was out of the cottage for almost half an hour last night, in that pub in Lambourn. *But the car was still here!*

It was a large garage. Typical of Hurst, it was better decorated and more lavishly equipped than any guest would ever need. There was a smart cobbled floor and spotless white walls hung with garden tools as lovingly arranged as works of art. At one end, a large work-bench was stocked with yet more tools, for the house and the motorist.

Avery paced slowly round the Rover, touching it, stopping to bend and stare underneath. *Exactly the same model as Corrigan's.* He knelt and reached under to a small dark pool below the engine, felt the

360

stickiness and sniffed at his fingers. It was only oil and not much of it. Probably there for ages; all cars leak a little oil.

With great care he eased the key into a lock, bracing himself as he turned it. Not on the driver's side—he entered by the passenger door.

Why are you so shit scared? he demanded of himself. They're not going to blow you up, they can't. But he still felt the need to do it that way, moving stealthily.

Lying across the seat, he peered under the steering wheel then up behind the dash at the multitude of thin colored wires. How could one tell if any of them had been disturbed? You couldn't, he realized, not with a tangle like that.

In a drawer of the workbench he found a coil of wire and took it back to the car, where he delved under the dash again. The red wires running up to the steering column must be the ignition circuit—attaching wires from the coil to bridge it, he ran two lengths back into the house: across the hall and into the living room, closing the doors as he went. He bit on the plastic sheath to bare the ends, took a long prayerful breath then touched them. Distantly, there was the rasp of the starter motor. He touched them again and again, watching the blue sparks, until the cold engine finally fired. A minute's wait to be sure it was safe then he broke the circuit and returned to the garage.

With the hood raised, he gazed gloomily at the engine. Just another car engine, he thought: a mess of leads and pipes and hoses. And me a guy who doesn't

361

even change his own oil. Who knows what the cowboys might have done!

He looked it over, fighting his way through the snaking ignition leads to check that all was as it should be. There seemed to be plenty of brake fluid in the reservoir, he noted. Damn! What else was one supposed to look for?

He slid on his back under the car and searched the bottom of the engine then around the insides of each of the wheels. Nothing, absolutely nothing. You're wrong about this, he told himself. A man like Ballantine doesn't pull the same stunt twice. He wouldn't dare. Even Sherman would have second thoughts about another car accident.

Back in the living room, he reached again for the whisky decanter, hesitated, then raised the glass stopper slowly to his nose. It smelled of whisky—what the hell else should it smell of! But he left his tumbler empty, all the same.

George, you sly bastard, he thought from the depths of the chair: you're as cool as they come. You weren't following Corrigan that last day to investigate him—you were there to make sure he died according to plan, to see the job through to completion. And suddenly there was Martin Avery climbing into the back seat! A close shave to end them all, one might think. But what did you do? Nothing much—that seems to be your style, your stock-in-trade. A double-take, a momentary loss of nerve, but you soon came to your senses; enough for a quick caucus meeting with Mulholland out on the pavement, away from my hearing. I can almost hear you, George. "Don't panic,

Mully. This can work to our advantage. Keep him watching the cafeteria while the lads in the BMW get at that Rover and fix it good and proper. No cause for alarm, eh? Avery, bless him, has just turned up to give us an alibi."

"Damn!" Avery shouted, as he shot from the chair. "It *must* be the fucking car!"

He walked around it again, three times. No, four. Another exhaustive search of the interior, another anguished stare at the engine. Then down on the cobbles again, flat on his back and under. It was the same as before: cables, brake lines, fuel feed pipe, suspension, steering gear. Oil and congealed mud everywhere. Not a sign of tampering.

So don't drive the car, he told himself. Who says you have to drive the goddamned car!

But then what? They get you some other way . . . ?

Now he began to wander about the garage, a man in a daze. Fingering the garden hose, staring dumbly at the lawn mower, picking up a portable inspection light from the workbench and idly swinging its heavy-duty cable.

Why not? he thought then. Just one last look . . .

So he plugged in the light and extinguished the overhead bulb. Then he plunged the light into the engine bay and a layer of oil and dust showed up clearly, covering everything in sight. There were smudges on the cylinder head . . . well, he'd touched that. And a smear on the air cleaner . . . yes, he'd handled that, too.

He moved the light toward the rear of the engine, close to the bulkhead to the passenger compartment.

Then he stared and lowered it farther, to highlight the dusty film. *There were marks on the ventilation trunking*. He ran his finger across . . . yes, recent marks. And *he* hadn't made them, he was sure.

A quick dash back to the bench for a screwdriver and he was unfastening the union to look into the trunking.

Fixed with adhesive tape to the inside wall was a capsule—made of gelatine; the kind that heat would dissolve. It was filled with colorless liquid . . .

The clock on the side table gave the time as 6:25. Jim Young was sound asleep, the air reverberating in his hairy, flared nostrils like the bass notes of an organ. Barbara slipped quietly from the bed and out of the room.

"Well, you're a sight, and no mistake," she told her reflection in the bathroom mirror. "What *does* he see in you?"

She doused the pale face in cold water and that brought some color to her cheeks but made her nose red and shiny.

"Mata Hari?" she said, putting her head to one side to gaze sorrowfully at the nose. "Some bloody hope!"

She switched on the light at the dining end of the downstairs room and it flashed and faltered, sputtering to itself before coming on, harsh and white and far too bright. She hated that fluorescent fitting. As she moved a pile of fourth form exercise books to one side to clear the table she stared crossly up at it. Why could that man never find time to replace it with something decent, a normal bulb in a nice silk shade? Cripes, she thought, why do *I* have to do everything round here? Full-time secretary, housewife and super-sleuth.

At the sound of food, the poodle shook itself on the rug in the bay window at the front of the house, stretched, then came over to rest its head on her knee.

"I need you," she told it, her mouth full of cornflakes. "For once in your lazy life you can do something useful."

The avenue was deserted, the street lights still on; streaks of silver were beginning to rend the sky. Pulling up the hood of her anorak, Barbara closed the front door quietly and let Raffles drag her to the gate.

She knew every car in the street—every one that should be there. Turning left and not looking back, she let the dog set the pace, a slow procession along the pavement from tree to lamppost to tree. Past her decrepit Renault 4 and Jim's slightly more respectable Renault 12. (She sighed at the peeling sticker still in the back window: "Gilbert and Sullivan's *Iolanthe*. Walcote Road School. 16-18 September.") Then past the Richardsons' Allegro, going rusty at the bottom of the doors, just as Jim had forecast. Next, the Keegans' smart new Lancia—where *did* they get the money? Jim would ask on Sunday mornings. Not for the car, that comes with the job; I mean the cash for all that car polish. Bet they change the air in the tires once a week while they're at it!

"That's right, Raffles," she murmured. "Pee on the silly hubcap."

She wanted to turn, to look back along the street, but somehow stopped herself.

Up to the corner then along by the shops. Harry, the newsman, was up and about like a lark, getting ready for 7:00: a single light showed in the window and a shadow was moving somewhere at the back, behind the rows of greeting cards.

Another left turn, into a street just like hers: the same three-up, two-down semis set cheek by jowl, the same stunted trees, the curbs on both sides a sea of similar Austins and Vauxhalls, Datsuns, and Mazdas. We're an offshore colony of Japan out here, she thought sadly as she gazed at the cars. Jim's right about that.

"Come on, Raffles," she called, whistling up some speed. She added, under her breath: "They won't be waiting round here, will they!"

The next side road ran alongside an open field which none of the houses faced. A stop while the dog christened a tree trunk, then a brisk walk to the corner, where she pushed her hands deep into her pockets and ambled again, a housewife interested only in the neighbors' curtains.

Hello . . .

That was one she'd never seen before—the Opel a few cars this side of the house. It *was* an Opel, wasn't it? One of those Manta coupes Jim drooled over? The dream car for when he got his headship. Metallic silver, he even knew the color it would be. Second-hand, of course.

That'll be the day!

She was staring up at the Rileys' as she passed it, at the half-painted window begun over the holidays two years ago and destined never to be finished. But she saw the man trimming his fingernails at the wheel of the Opel. And the soft-brimmed hat on the seat beside him. Like bloody Al Capone.

366

Cripes, she thought, that'll be one of Martin's cowboys. What did he call him . . . ? George's pet rattlesnake, *that* was it!

Our Lady in Heaven, now what do I do?

30

Avery first thought of the loft only as a possible hiding place. He had forgotten what was up there . . . clean forgotten.

He was systematically working his way through every room in the cottage in search of a safe place—looking into cupboards, however small; peering under the larger pieces of furniture. It needn't be for long, he thought, just for a matter of minutes if all went well. At least, that was the assumption, the perhaps forlorn hope. Then, as he crossed the upper landing to inspect the smaller bedrooms, the hatch in the ceiling caught his eye. Ah yes, the loft . . .

Standing at the top of the access ladder, he switched on the light and glanced around, assessing his chances. A number of possibilities came immediately to mind: behind those tea chests stuffed with unwanted papers, behind the lugubriously gurgling water tank, in the deep shadows under the far eaves . . .

Why even hide? he thought then with an unintended shrug. If they think to come here looking, the game's up anyway.

Hurst's abandoned playthings were scattered about, just as he had seen them last: the rackets, the golf clubs, the clay-pigeon launcher, a dusty cricket bat. It might make a useful weapon, that bat. A damned sight easier to swing than the butt of an ancient rifle!

"My God!"

He was suddenly staring at the launcher, hypnotized by it. Without seeming to make the decision to move, he found himself climbing in and stumbling over the joists to where it lay. It was badly rusted, sure, but there must be grease downstairs in the garage. And that spring looked mighty powerful . . .

How far does one of these damn things fire? he wondered. Then, as he began a fevered search of the surrounding loft: what do the clays look like and what sort of boxes do they come in?

He eventually found an almost empty box under a pile of junk in a corner. There were only three of the saucer-shaped clays inside and two were so badly cracked they must surely disintegrate as soon as they were fired. Still, one should be enough. One *had* to be enough.

It would help some, he thought grimly as he carried the launcher down to the hall, if you'd fired one of these before.

"*Acton!*" someone whispered mysteriously in Vladek's right ear.

He was dozing fitfully under an inadequate car blanket, wondering in his moments of wakefulness whether he would ever feel his fingers and toes again.

In his mind, he was huddled on the edge of a drifting ice floe, his shoes off and beside him, his bare feet dangling in a black and freezing Barents Sea. Then that single word penetrated his subconscious.

Why Acton? his dulled brain asked. That nasty inner suburb of London, a hinterland of factories and mean houses. This is Siberia, not bloody Acton.

An elbow was jabbed painfully into his ribs.

"Eh? Wasat?"

"I said, wonderboy, we have action at last."

Vladek forced open his eyes, to see de Freitas nod ahead through the windscreen, then reach over to the back seat for the binoculars.

In the hollow below, the garage door of the cottage had just been swung open from the inside. Even as he looked, a stream of white vapor issued from the Rover's exhaust and soon the car was reversing out.

"You cold?" he asked, massaging his thighs.

"A bit. Not much."

"You naturally cold-blooded or something? That the secret?"

"You're great with a shooter," de Freitas said, "but you're no all-rounder."

"Meaning you fucking are. . . ."

"I get by, wonderboy."

Below them, Avery maneuvered the car as close as it would go the the front door, then got out and opened the hatchback. He returned to the cottage through the garage, closing the door behind him. Overhead, a solitary rook was silently circling, fingering the sky.

Vladek drew in his breath sharply as the circulation began to return, sending a pain searing up his leg.

"Thermal underwear," de Freitas said with a smug grin. "Simple when you know how. Long john pants and long-sleeved vests. Gear for arthritic old men, got it?"

"Terrific!" Vladek said miserably, and he reached under his jacket to his shoulder holster for his Makarov 9mm. It felt good in his hand, reassuring. It was an old gun, yes, but the newer Stechkins were clumsy great things, nearly twice as heavy with a full magazine. They certainly *felt* twice as heavy.

Avery reemerged carrying two travel bags which he packed in the trunk. As he closed the hatch and went back into the house, Vladek tracked him with the gun, making clicking noises with his tongue.

"Put that away, for Chrissake!" de Freitas implored.

Vladek obeyed with a scowl but kept a hand tucked under his coat, over the holster. He seemed to draw warmth from it.

"Come on, Yank" de Freitas said, after some minutes.

"*Is the engine still running?*" Vladek grabbed his arm.

"Jesus!" Quickly, de Freitas leveled his glasses at the exhaust. "No. No, thank God."

"But it'll be warm under that hood. It *was* running."

"Not for long. And that's a twenty-minute capsule at normal running temperature. So take it easy, Vlad. He'll be out any time now."

"What if he isn't?"

"Look, the guy's about to leave, isn't he? Coat on,

370

cases in the car. He'll be out."

"What's the dissipation rate of that stuff?" Vladek asked, still worried by the inactivity.

"VX-three? From a stationary car? Hours, mate. Bloody hours."

Avery left the cottage with a decisive slam of the front door, climbed into the car and started the engine. He began to reverse toward the lane but stopped with a jerk and was instantly out again, his bewildered face partly turned to the copse as he went through his inside pockets, as if in search of tickets or a wallet. Then, with the engine still running, he let himself back into the house, leaving the door ajar.

He sat on the stairs, the launcher primed and ready beside him, and glanced up to the grandfather clock on the landing. It was almost 8:40.

Now, he thought, how long should I give it? Ten minutes would drive me bananas, but these characters are professionals. So let's say fifteen. Yes, fifteen minutes and their nerves will be strung as tight as violin strings.

The minute hand moved with excruciating slowness to 8:50. By then, his own nerves were in poor shape. But hang on awhile longer, he told himself. The pendulum swung ponderously to and fro above him, its steady beat seeming to mock him as it reverberated through the hall. *Tick, tock. Tick, tock.* It was a familiar sound that had become part of his life over the past few weeks. Suddenly, he hated it. Outside, he could hear the faster note of the car engine. And they can hear it too, he thought. At least, they'd better be able to.

371

But what do I do if they come down too soon?

8:51 now. Stick it out, he thought, gritting his teeth. Give it the full fifteen minutes. The full treatment.

It was, quite simply, the longest quarter of an hour of his life. Perhaps there had been occasions in his far-off childhood when time had hung in similarly dreadful suspension—on wet Sunday afternoons in winter, or that unaccompanied visit to see a dying, unloved uncle in hospital; no doubt he'd think of others later. But now, as the hand finally jerked up to 8:55, his mind went blank.

He seized the launcher and ran down with it to the back door and out onto the small rear terrace. Ducking under a window he went as close as he dared to the corner of the house farthest from the copse. The rookery was what . . . fifty meters away? Would the thing actually carry that far? With a silent prayer, he aimed at the trees with their dark, broodily squawking shapes, and pulled the lever.

"I don't like it," Vladek said. "Twenty minutes and nothing. It doesn't feel right."

"Fifteen," de Freitas said. "Fifteen minutes, okay? And shut up. I'm trying to think."

His hands were gripping the binoculars so tightly the knuckles showed white. With each passing minute, he was swinging them ever more erratically over his target area: from the side lawns to the back garden, past that up to the nearest hedge, at the boundary of the field which dipped down behind the cottage. It must be all of forty yards to that hedge and open all the way. But was that a ditch beside it, running the length of the field? A possible escape route if Avery could make it there? No, he reassured himself yet again, not a chance. But still he stared through the glasses—from the cottage to the field and back again to the cottage, agonizing. Fifteen minutes!

There was a noise from below. Breaking twigs, he thought: the sound of someone crashing through undergrowth. It was instantly drowned. The sky seemed suddenly black with rooks—turning, diving, their hoarse shrieks echoing from the Downs behind.

"No!" he said, catching his breath. "No!"

"Oh, yes!" Vladek yelled, leaping from the car.

De Freitas chased him to the edge of the copse, seizing his arm to drag him round. "I was *watching!* I saw nothing. Got that, *nothing!*"

"Tell me, then . . . if you were down there, where would you run to?"

De Freitas released the arm. "Those trees . . ." he admitted lamely.

"Right!" Without another word, Vladek ran down to the lawn, drawing his gun. Crouching low, he made for the Rover, peering through the windows to scan the front of the cottage. Not that the guy was there any more.

The bloody gas! he thought then, and sprinted for the cover of the porch, rolling the last few yards—anything to put as much distance as possible between him and that car with its still-running engine.

He kicked the front door wide. The hall inside was empty. He turned, to find de Freitas tearing across the lawn toward him, bent almost double, his Stechkin in his hand.

"You try the back," Vladek said.

"No guns, remember. Not unless you have to."

"He's got a fucking rifle!" Vladek spat over his shoulder as he entered the hall.

He crossed to the nearest door and listened: all seemed quiet and still inside the room. Shielding himself with the wall, he reached for the handle and threw the door wide. There was still no sound. He spun into the doorway, knees bent, his arms outstretched, both hands gripping the Makarov.

It was the kitchen: he should have known that. A look told him it was deserted, with nowhere to hide.

Moving silently, he crossed the hall to the other side. That must be the door to the living room. He eased toward it, pressed against the wall . . .

He froze on a sound from behind him and began to rock back onto his heels, ready for a rapid spin turn . . .

"De Freitas," a voice called from beside the stairs.

Vladek closed his eyes thankfully and took a deep breath.

"The back door was open," de Freitas said, coming over. "Wide open."

"I told you, he's fled the coop." Vladek opened his jacket to holster the gun, intending to give chase over the fields. Even as he did so, there was a noise from the living room. It was slight but unmistakable: the sound of a chair scraping on a wood floor.

"*Cover!*" Vladek whispered, flattening himself to the wall beside the door.

De Freitas moved quickly out of direct line of fire, back to the stairs and up several steps, his gun aimed over the banisters at the door.

They heard the chair again, well inside the room. It must be over by the far wall, Vladek thought. And if a guy moves a chair while he's holding a rifle, he's in trouble . . .

Seizing his chance, he burst into the room. He could see immediately it was empty. For perhaps a second or so, his eyes took in what he assumed to be a pocket dictation machine, scraping to itself where it lay in front of the fireplace. Then everything went black. He choked and keeled over, and as he fell his finger tightened on the trigger. A single shot hit the ceiling.

De Freitas had lost sight of Vladek as he smashed the lock with a flying kick and leapt into the room. He stiffened in horror as the shot rang out, then went as slack as a jelly: he knew the characteristic bark of a Makarov.

"Vladek?" He was sweating profusely.

Now there was the sound of footsteps from deep inside the room.

Silence.

"Vladek . . . ?" he called again.

His answer was another footstep from the far end of the room, just one, rather muffled.

He padded down to the door. As he approached it obliquely, he saw outstretched feet on the floor just inside and recognized the rubber-soled shoes. His instincts failing him for the moment, he moved a few more paces toward the body, using the open door to shield him from the rest of the room.

Then he was blind and unable to breathe. He

seemed to be walking but had no idea whether he was still upright. He felt his knees crumbling and his heart racing as if it were out of control. And then no more . . .

31

Ballantine began to suspect that something might be wrong before he reached Lambourn. He tried the radio one last time and still got no response from the BMW. Of course, they could be in pursuit of Avery and out of range, but he didn't like it, not one bit. His head felt fuzzy again and his brain dull: the migraine was like a storm cloud hanging over him, threatening to break at any minute. He cranked down the window to take a cold blast of air full in the face.

Fifty grand, he thought dismally. Fifty grand for getting that system successfully into the Pentagon. Nothing for trying. And that bastard of an American was hell-bent on screwing it up.

He switched channels and Mulholland's voice answered, "Delta."

"Alpha," Ballantine said. "Had any word from our friends on five?"

"Not a peep, Guvnor, not recently."

"Last time was when?"

" 'Bout three this morning, I should think. We exchanged miseries, as they say. That character Vlad wasn't too happy with you, I'll tell you that for free."

Ballantine was turning out of Upper Lambourn, onto the twisting land leading to the Downs. "Where are you?" he asked.

"Still outside the bint's place, and bored to tears."

Ballantine glanced at the car clock: nearly nine thirty. "Shouldn't she be at work by now, at Quantek?"

"Well, she isn't, take it from me. I reckon she's expecting someone. Keeps coming to the window and looking out."

"I don't like it," Ballantine said, and the incipient sickness spread. He felt it behind both eyes, deep in the pit of his stomach, even affecting his knees. "Stay put, understand? Eyes peeled."

"Anything wrong?"

"I'll let you know," Ballantine muttered, putting the phone down.

From the lane, he saw the roof of the cottage first, tucked into its fold of Berkshire downland. Next, through a break in the hedge, he caught a brief glimpse of the Rover, standing in front of the garage. He became positively alarmed then. It hadn't been out last night—de Freitas had forced his way into the garage to fix it! So what was it doing in the drive now? *What was it doing still here?*

He pulled onto the shoulder beside the gate and made into the small wood at a trot, at what in his book passed for running these days. Fifty grand, he was thinking again as the breaths came short and fast. For God's sake be there, chaps. Be there, watching.

He stopped dead in his tracks on entering the clear-

ing: the BMW was obviously empty, both doors wide
open. As he approached it with trepidation, the view
opened up to the hollow below and he could see the
exhaust vapors spreading low across the lawn from the
Rover, and the open front door to the house.

He sounded the car horn, saw no movement and
gave a second, longer blast. He had to remind himself
of the prize, to resist the temptation to run: fifty
grand and early retirement; endless hours in the
garden at last. And of the penalty for failure: who
wants enforced retirement to a pokey *dacha* by the
Black Sea!

For minutes on end he stared at the cottage, trying
to clear his head, trying to summon the resolve to go
down, and when he finally moved it was slowly, with a
weary resignation. At every step he expected to hear
the words, "Hold it there, George," and see that
bloody rifle barrel poke out of a window. But they
never came, and to his astonishment he found himself
at the door, unchallenged.

He tried a wary, "Hello . . . ?" It sounded
incongruous calling in like that, standing on the front
step as if he were a brush salesman, but what else was
one to say? He tried again, a bolder "Hello . . . ?" and
heard no sound from within.

For a reason he was later never able to explain to
himself, he felt suddenly threatened by the gaping
door and the silent hall beyond, and he shied away to
look in fear through the adjacent window, pressing his
face against the cold glass.

Fools! That was his first and only thought on seeing
the bodies. Fools! I had Avery trussed and plucked for

you and all you had to do was roast him. Oh, you fools.

Exactly how it had been done didn't matter; it was obviously the VX-3. Which meant, he reasoned, that the Rover must be safe. So he went to it and switched off the engine, and an uncanny peace settled over the cottage with its lush green lawns and flowered borders. Then it was like a bloody cemetery, he thought with a shiver: what with those two bodies in there. And he sat on the edge of the car seat, his feet on the grass, his mind working furiously. Above him in a now blue sky, two rooks fought a strident feud round the elms and over the stubbly cornfield.

He found a heavy flint in one of the flower beds. With his handkerchief clamped tightly over his mouth and nose, he smashed in a living room window. It had been a small capsule; the room was large and the door must have been open to the outside for some time. The gas should have dispersed by now but he was taking no chances. Still holding his breath, he reached in for the window catch and threw up the sash. Then he retreated to the comfort of the car. His eyes, he noted, showed no sign of streaming and didn't sting in the least. But did that actually mean anything? He wished he knew more about VX-3.

After fifteen minutes, he felt it was safe to enter. Stopping in the living room doorway, he took a cautious sniff before breathing normally. Bothering to sniff was stupid, he realized immediately: if there was still any of the nerve gas in the room he would have been dead by now whatever he did. With a moody shrug of the shoulders, he moved in to inspect the two dead men.

"Fools," he said again, with outright contempt this time as he saw their guns. There lay Jaroslav Vladek: Polish-born, a naturalized Englishman for many years, a car dealer from one of the better parts of south London. Beside him, Rupert de Freitas: to all appearances English through and through, a free lance writer of independent means, with a mansion flat in Kensington. Neither with a trace of a criminal record, with any reason for the police to do other than touch their caps and murmur, "Sir." Yet both had chosen to carry Soviet army standard-issue handguns. My God, he thought in amazement, what do they teach these lads in the Kursk Academy these days! The guns went into the capacious pockets of his heavy overcoat and he removed the holsters from the bodies and slung them over an arm.

Now, he thought, where's that damned capsule, if there's any trace of it left? The search was short; he knew it had to be somewhere warm: by the fire or close to one of the radiators.

"Bastard!" he swore as he saw where Avery had put it. A piece of Scotch tape was stuck to the face of one of the radiators; it arched slightly at the center where the capsule had been. Carefully, he peeled it off into his handkerchief, which then joined the Makarov in a pocket.

He began to hurry himself, now. The Dictaphone on the floor clearly meant something— he'd listen to the tape later and find out what. For the moment, it followed quickly into the same pocket as he walked back for a closer look at the bodies.

Vladek's features were frozen into a terrified star

380

and his skin was drained of color. Ballantine felt the face gingerly: it wasn't what he'd call warm but it was still far from cold. Dead for little more than an hour, he guessed, although only an expert could say for sure. But only an hour or so: thank God for that.

The hand flapped loosely on Vladek's wrist when he raised an arm. He put his foot against the elbow and jerked back until he heard a bone snap—he didn't care which one. Then he rolled the body onto its side and took a vicious kick at the lower chest, feeling the ribs crack under his toe.

De Freitas was the same: not yet cold, not yet stiff. He broke an arm again and aimed a mighty kick at a kneecap.

Then he took an atlas from the book shelves, choosing it because the spine was only an inch or so thick—about the thickness of the edge of a hand—yet it was big and heavy. He slammed it with great force down onto the windpipes of both men, dusted it off with a sleeve and returned it to the shelf.

Next, he pushed over a chair, broke a table lamp and disarranged a carpet, before taking a final look round to be sure he'd missed nothing of importance. Then he left the house, closing the front door behind him.

From a call-box in Lambourn, he dialed police headquarters in Swindon and asked for the CID.

"Listen carefully," he said hoarsely, "I'll only say this once," The voice he chose sounded terrible, even to him, but the police would probably expect something of the kind.

"Sir . . . ?"

381

"I was with two mates, doing a job on a country house. Are you listening?"

"Where are you calling from, first?"

"*Listen!* This American came down and caught us at it, we thought the bloody place was empty. A raving luntic, some kind of karate nut. I was lucky to get away. He killed the other two. *Killed them,* did you hear?"

"Killed, was that?" The detective-sergeant might have been noting the loss of a dog.

"Russet Lodge, Upper Lambourn. That's the place I mean."

"I've got that. Now . . ."

"An American, I'm sure he was an American. Raving fucking madman."

"Can we go over that first part again? There were the three of you, is that what . . ."

"A hint, copper," Ballantine said. "He left his car behind and scarpered on foot. I saw him. In the middle of bloody nowhere. I suggest you check on any stolen cars around there." He slammed the receiver down and drove quickly away.

"She's still here," Mulholland confirmed over the radio. "Saw her at the window again a few minutes ago."

"Stay right where you are, then. I want him, Mully. I want him so bad I can't tell you."

"Avery?"

"Of course, fucking Avery."

"What's gone wrong?"

"Later. I'll fill you in later," Ballantine said, signing

off. Not over the air, laddie, he thought. Have some sense or you'll end up like the others.

At a village somewhere—he no longer knew or cared where—he stopped at another telephone booth and called a London number which was etched in his memory.

"Yes . . . ?" the familiar, accented voice answered. They had never met.

"Traffic Light," Ballantine said.

"Green," came the answer.

Quickly, Ballantine explained what he'd done.

"We could've removed those bodies," the contact said coldly, after a long pause for thought. "For what reason you have to advertise in neon lights a mile high?"

"How many men could you put on the streets at an hour's notice?" Ballantine countered. "To cover airports, main railway stations, seaports . . . ?"

"Twenny, Serty. Who knows exact numbers."

"All looking for a man they wouldn't recognize for sure if they saw him face to face! *Now* do you see?"

"Okay, so you rope in the police and *they* catch him. What comes next?"

"It's up to you to make sure you know the moment they pick him up. You can do that, I presume?"

"It can be arranged, yes. It depends where, what force."

"And then you wipe him out, and damned quick. You've got people who can do that? Better than the clowns you provided last time?"

There was another long pause: heavy breathing in Ballantine's ear. Not prepared to wait, he said, "I may have to bale out in a hurry. Get that escape route ready in case."

"Pity, after all this," the voice said, without feeling.

"As you say . . . a pity." It was the only reply which came to mind.

Right outside the call-box, Ballantine was violently sick in the gutter. Perhaps there had still been a trace of VX gas in the room. More probably, it was delayed reaction to what he had done to those bodies. His mouth tasting foul, he turned the car for London.

He had spent a whole weekend recently planting daffodil bulbs in his small parcel of English countryside — that was his immediate thought and it stayed with him for the entire journey and then as he sat in a strange, bare flat, waiting for news. Would he ever see them bloom?

32

"Thanks, Nutcracker," Avery said.

He dismounted and gave the horse a grateful slap on the rump. You're no Silicon Chip, he thought: but you were a damned sight better over the rough. Hack or not, you're all right by me.

He was without baggage, with only his wallet and passport and a few oddments stuffed in his jacket pockets. It had taken over an hour by back lanes and bridle paths, and even using an ordnance survey map found in the cottage he had more than once missed his way. But he was finally here—over the next field and beyond that far hedge was Sylvia Avenue: Barbara's home.

He removed the saddle and harnesses from the horse and pushed them into hiding in a shallow ditch.

"Have a nice day," he said, and a heftier slap sent the horse trotting away over the field. He found a place in the hedge where the local children had beaten a path through, and squeezed out onto the road.

He strolled across the nearest end of the street first, looking up to where he expected the Renault to be, and frowned when he couldn't find it. By a parallel street, he went to a far end and glanced down again as he slowly crossed the intersection. Again, there was no Renault, not that he could see. Yes, there were plenty of parked cars and it might be among them: one of those many roofs. Perhaps last night Barbara had been unable to find a free space outside the house and had parked it farther down the street. But it wasn't where it should be and that gave him an uneasy feeling. Barbara had promised to leave it at the house and she wasn't the type to break a promise.

He doubled back down the side road and started along Sylvia Avenue itself; slowly but not so slowly as to attract attention. He reasoned that if anyone was watching the house they would naturally face the other way, toward the shops, expecting callers to come from that direction. The nearer he got to number 22 the more certain he became that her car was gone.

"Hold it," he cautioned himself, stopping.

385

He had noticed the Opel because it was so much newer than the other cars in the street, smarter. Then he saw the man slouched at the wheel. Seeing only his back, Avery had no idea who he was, but the fact that someone was sitting outside was enough. He patted his pockets thoughtfully, turned this way and that as if undecided, then strode back the way he had come, to the corner and out of sight.

That's just great, he thought: she saw the bird dog waiting out there and took the car with her to draw him away. A brave try, even if it failed. Or maybe she took it with her as a signal, a warning of danger. Smart thinking.

Yes, that's just great, Barbara, he thought bitterly: except what do I do now for fucking transport!

There was the character in the Opel, watching the house. There would be another guy at Quantek to keep an eye on her every move, incidentally covering that single way in to the parking lot! And where else would they be? At the local railway station, for sure. Hell!

By the side street, Avery returned to the shops. Past a newsman and a butcher, a hardware store and a tiny florist's little wider than a corridor, past a pet shop with fluttering, twittering cages crowding the pavement.

There was a telephone booth outside a small post office and he waited, pacing from one side to the other, glowering in through the glass as a woman worked her way down a conspicuously placed stack of coins. As he moved round to the side she was facing, she would shift position to look the other way, somehow never quite seeming to catch his eye.

He leaned against a lamppost, hands deep in his trouser pockets for warmth, wishing he'd stopped at the cottage long enough to unpack his overcoat from the Rover. But that thought had been far from his mind as he'd run full-tilt down those stairs from the attic, out of the back door and away over the fields. And on reflection—although it didn't make him any less cold to realize it—perhaps the stableboy would have been less ready to accept his word that the ride was by arrangement with Hurst if he'd arrived in an unsuitable city coat.

Another coin clanked into the box. Avery sighed and stared listlessly across the road. There was a garage facing, with petrol pumps and a small showroom of new cars behind. He watched a car enter, and the driver fill the tank then go into the main building to pay at the cash desk. The keys were left in the car!

What if . . . ? Avery found himself thinking. What if . . . ? but the idea was so absurd he forced it from his mind.

Eventually, many minutes later, he was in the telephone booth at last. He called Quantek. No, the operator said, there was no reply from Mrs. Young's extension.

"Has she been in this morning?" Avery asked, with rising concern.

"Come off it, love," the operator said. "How should I know, with the number of people we've got here!"

But she *wasn't* there: Avery was sure of it as he put the receiver down. She and that damned car of hers were somewhere else — God only knew where.

On an impulse, he raised the receiver again, holding it to his ear as if listening, but only as a means of staying in the call-box for a while longer — to observe the garage without being too obvious about it. He timed several drivers as they came and went. Half a minute. Yes, he could rely pretty safely on each car being left unattended for at least half a minute. And none of the drivers thought to remove the keys. Several, most obligingly, even left the door open.

Later, Avery was to think of it as an awful, real-life comedy of errors — when, that is, he could bring himself to think about it at all. It was the kind of situation that could happen, in the telling phrase, only to him. More correctly, he would remind himself seriously, it might have happened to anyone in the position he now found himself in. The question was: would anyone else have got themselves in that position in the first place?

He had spent some time in the kiosk, staring unremittingly over at the garage, continuing to time drivers, wondering whether to choose a fast, expensive car or a more mundane one that would be harder to trace, wondering how long it would be before the alarm was raised, trying to guess what the English police did in cases like that: did they go in for road blocks over here? It was only then that he thought to look at the new cars in the showroom: a line of gleaming Peugeots with other cars ranged behind. Perhaps there was an easier way . . .

An elderly man insinuated his way into the view, wanting the phone. Avery began to mouth meaningless words into the receiver, turned around as the woman had done to draw him away, then spun back.

A test drive, why not? A chauffered ride in comfort
out to a deserted stretch of country, a sharp blow to
the salesman's head. . . . Avery gulped at the
craziness of his own thoughts. It must be, he felt in his
own defense, a late reaction to the events at the cottage. Who could think straight after going through all
that? Quickly, he moved his head to see round the
waiting man, who was back again.

Another car drew up at the pumps. An Austin, was
it? These English saloons still tended to look all the
same to him. It was a family four-door, anyway:
ordinary-looking and not especially fast. Ideal for his
purposes. The driver topped up the tank and went
into the building to pay, his keys still in the ignition.

"It's now or never!" Avery told himself, and he left
the booth and began to cross to the garage. But he
hesitated even then, halting in the middle of the road
so that a passing car hooted and swerved.

Why not *just* the test drive? he wondered at the
curb: a compromise, a kind of free lift out of the area.
Simply say, "Thanks for the ride, friend," and jump
out.

He stopped beside the Austin, his hand on the door,
and stared at the new cars again, agonizing over the
decision. "Test Drive the New Renault 18 Estate," a
sticker in the window invited. Behind those Peugeots
were some Renaults: he could see them properly now
he was closer.

"Jesus . . ."

He was suddenly looking to the side of the building
for the first time, to the alley which ran beside it to

the rear, and then to the sign on the wall: "SERVICE-Peugeot-Renault."

No, he thought: she wouldn't have. Would she? What a stupid, wonderful woman.

The foreman came over wiping greasy hands on an even greasier rag.

"Did Mrs. Young leave her car here this morning?" Avery asked.

"Ah, you'll be Mr. Avery," the man said.

Avery's knees nearly gave under him. But they felt even worse an instant later when the man added, "She didn't *leave* it, though. Not to speak of."

"*What?*" Avery steadied himself on a vast Peugeot estate, the size of a small bus.

"We *collected* it, sir. Wouldn't start, that's what she said." The foreman led the way between close-packed cars. The damp shed with its grimy overhead panes reeked of gas and stale oil. "Couldn't find anything really wrong, though," he said, giving a broad wink as they came to the Renault, still coupled to a tow truck. "I mean, nothing a new engine wouldn't fix. There were two spark plug leads off, that's all. Can't imagine how."

"What happened this morning?" Avery asked.

"Didn't she say?"

"Not really."

"Know her well, do you?"

"Fairly. Her and Jim."

The man shook his head affectionately. "A regular visitor, our Mrs. Young. Something's always going wrong. But she usually brings it in herself, won't have with tow charges, not as a rule. Gets the husband to

390

hitch it to his car rather than have us do it. Hang on . . . I'll unhook it for you." He disengaged the tow chains and rubbed his hand down his blackened overalls. "Calls us this morning and says it won't start. Would we come and get it, very urgent? This was the very minute we opened! Well, if it hadn't been her and just round the corner . . . know what I mean? Went meself. Collected the keys at the house and she says, very haughty: take it away and fix it. I won't have you doing it in front of my neighbors, my husband's a schoolteacher. I ask you, caring about neighbors! Still, women and cars . . . get it all the time." Now he shrugged. "As I say, it was only the leads come adrift. Right as rain now. And by rain I mean a nasty downpour, get my meaning?"

"She was at *home?*" Avery said, bewildered.

The man nodded, pulling bunches of keys from a pocket and searching cardboard tags for the right ones.

But of course, Avery thought: with the car here and that guy still outside—where else *could* she be! Why hadn't that occurred to him before?

"How much?" he said.

"Tow charge for no distance to speak of? A quick look under the bonnet? Let's call it a fiver, as it's her."

Avery gave him ten pounds, then collapsed into the driver's seat and was only able to drive away when the man's curious stares finally became too much to bear.

He called Barbara an hour later, with some forty miles safely put between him and Swindon. Forty lumbering miles and the engine threatening to overheat at any minute—he didn't in the least care.

391

"Hello," she said, her relief so total it was the only word she could get out.

Avery matched it with a similarly flat, "Hello . . ."

"You're all right then, Martin. I'm *so* pleased."

"It wasn't exactly uneventful, but I'm okay now."

"I can't say how relieved I am you've called." She was briefly silent, perhaps holding back tears. "I've been looking out the window nonstop, praying you'd think to call. *Don't come, Martin!* That man's outside, the one you called a rattlesnake."

"Mulholland?"

"Yes, him."

That explains the Opel, he thought. Probably great for highspeed pursuits but lousy for surveillance—far too noticeable. Yes, that's Mulholland all over.

"What do you mean, don't come?" he said.

"I'll tell you where to pick up the car," she said.

He stifled a nervous laugh. "I've got it already, Barbara!"

"*My* car?

"The same. I collected it from the garage."

She needed some time to think before saying, "But, darling, the idea was, you called me *first!*"

"*What?*"

"I mean . . . how did you know, how did you guess . . ."

Put that way, Avery could find no convincing answer except to suggest, "Perhaps we think alike." He wanted to swear at her suddenly, to let off steam, to ask how the hell he was supposed to know she was still at home with the car gone . . . but somehow he stopped himself. She *had* tried, for Chrissake. And perhaps it was true: they did think alike, a little.

"A suggestion," he said kindly. "Call the police, huh? Say there's been a suspicious character lurking outside your house for . . . how long?"

"Oh, hours. Five, six."

"They'll get him off your back."

"I knew I was letting you down," she said, "but I was afraid to go out with him there, terrified. And Jim's no use in situations like this. All I could think of was to get the car away for you."

"That's okay," he said as gently as he could. "It worked out, didn't it?"

"Have you looked in the glove compartment?" she asked, to redeem herself. "In that tin box Renault *calls* a glove compartment?"

"No, why?"

"Remember what you were asking last night, about me and Jim?"

It escaped him for the moment.

"About whether we fall for similar people . . . ?"

"I didn't exactly put it that way, Barbara."

"I've left his passport in there," she said quickly. "And a spare pair of his specs."

"You've done *what?*"

She laughed shyly. "It's nine years old, that passport. I'd forgotten that. When someone asks what your husband looks like, you don't think how he was nine years ago, do you?" Her voice was suddenly strangely sad. "He's changed, Martin, changed a lot in that time. I hadn't realized how much." Then she forced another, brighter, laugh. "You might just make it, you know, with those glasses on and your hair

393

combed back. But you'll be as blind as a bat. He can't see a hand in front of his face without them."

Avery felt as stunned as if he had been struck. It was the whole thing, he cold hardly believe it: the car, the passport, even the goddamn glasses! She was a walking miracle and he wanted to tell her so.

But she cut into his thoughts before he could form the words.

"I'm glad you got out of that cottage," she said with understated simplicity.

It was mutual admiration, he realized then: we like one another for what we actually are, a partial reflection of ourselves—not for what we wish we were. And doesn't that beat love any time, ordinary love? The kind of relationship I have with Laura?

Somewhere in his memory he seemed to recall thinking just such thoughts once before, watching another couple and envying them—but he couldn't quite remember who or where.

It also beats love, he thought, because we both know when to stop. We would stop now anyway, even if I wasn't going. And—my God—isn't that the greatest, most precious thing a man and a woman can ever do for one another? Go, before the memories turn to regrets.

"I'll call you," he said.

"Please . . ." she said.

You're damned dumb, he told himself as he drove away: leaving a woman like that.

No, you're not, he decided a while later.

It was a debate he had a feeling would never be resolved.

Epilogue

The ferry to Cork churned its way slowly out of Pembroke Dock and turned for the open sea. The great refinery of Milford Haven sprawled along the facing Welsh coastline, jetting orange plumes from its pencil-like chimneys. The sky was an overcast gray, with that hidden brightness peculiar to seascapes—a sense that there was immense light somewhere behind the low, drifting clouds. The sea was almost black, rolling sluggishly, hinting in its turn at hidden darkness, at immeasurable depths. Gulls followed the ship like beggars, waiting for scraps from the galley, hitching a lift on the upcurrents from the funnels, their wings barely moving.

Avery saw all this from the stern rail, taking the breeze and spray on his face. He stayed there until the coast receded and was lost in mist and distance. Until, as he preferred to think of it, Britain became first a small island in its cold sea, then a smaller one, and was finally gone. Perhaps, he thought, it had looked like that to an earlier generation of Averys, migrating from a different English port all those years ago. Had they felt the same? That knowledge of dangers left behind, not the slightest sense of regret, the certainty they would never return? Had they felt as relieved as he did now?

His hand rediscovered the glasses in a pocket and he smiled. On seeing the English passport, the harbor officials at Pembroke had scarcely glanced at him. There had been several police there, engaged in inspecting the passports of other nationalities, but he had simply passed them by. Driving the car up the ramp and into the hold had been difficult—as Barbara had said, the glasses were for appalling vision—but he had somehow survived. Cork next, he thought. Then a leisurely drive to Shannon Airport, and home. How much of the story he'd eventually tell Brokaw, he hadn't yet decided: that would keep for the plane journey. But Larry had asked for Quantel to be turned on its head and he'd got exactly that.

And what of George Ballantine?

I'll say nothing of him, Avery thought, I don't need to.

There was, he felt, a fortuitous symmetry to the whole business. Two deaths on one side—that was counting Franklin and Corrigan as ranged on the side of good—and two in retribution on the other. Done by their own hand, in a way, with their own gas turned against them. And then there was that electronic spy—discovered like so many human spies must have been before it because it was just too regular in its habits, because it sneaked out the secrets in the same way every time. There were no loose ends to speak of; they had tied themselves. Leave well enough alone, he thought. Enough is enough.

No, George, he mused, I don't have to do a damned thing about you except let you stew in your own juice for a day or two. When you realize I've gone you'll dive for cover. Say hello to the Kremlin for me.

The seagulls were suddenly dropping down to the wake like Stukas, and their shrill cries reminded him of another, similar sound he had heard that morning. It was like music in his ears.

THE GUNN SERIES BY JORY SHERMAN

GUNN #1: DAWN OF REVENGE   (594, $1.95)

Accused of killing his wife, William Gunnison changes his name to Gunn and begins his fight for revenge. He'll kill, maim, turn the west blood red—until he finds the men who murdered his wife.

GUNN #2: MEXICAN SHOWDOWN   (628, $1.95)

When Gunn rode into the town of Cuchillo, he didn't know the rules. But when he walked into Paula's Cantina, he knew he'd learn them.

GUNN #3: DEATH'S HEAD TRAIL   (648, $1.95)

With his hands on his holster and his eyes on the sumptuous Angela Larkin, Gunn goes off hot—on his enemy's trail.

GUNN #4: BLOOD JUSTICE   (670, $1.95)

Gunn is enticed into playing a round with a ruthless gambling scoundrel— and playing around with the scoundrel's estranged wife!

GUNN #8: APACHE ARROWS   (791, $2.25)

Gunn gets more than he bargained for when he rides in with pistols cocked to save a beautiful settler woman from ruthless Apache renegades.

GUNN #9: BOOTHILL BOUNTY   (830, $2.25)

When Gunn receives a desperate plea for help from the sumptuous Trilla, he's quick to respond—because he knows she'll make it worth his while!

GUNN #10: HARD BULLETS   (896, $2.25)

The disappearance of a gunsmith and a wagon full of ammo sparks suspicion in the gunsmith's daughter. She thinks Gunn was involved, and she's up-in-arms!

GUNN #11: TRIAL BY SIXGUN   (918, $2.25)

Gunn offers help to a pistol-whipped gambler and his well-endowed daughter—only to find that he'll have to lay more on the table than his cards!

GUNN #12: THE WIDOW-MAKER   (987, $2.25)

Gunn offers to help the lovely ladies of Luna Creek when the ruthless Widow-maker gang kills off their husbands. It's hard work, but the rewards are mounting!

Available wherever paperbacks are sold, or order direct from the Publisher. Send cover price plus 50¢ per copy for mailing and handling to Zebra Books, 475 Park Avenue South, New York, N.Y. 10016. DO NOT SEND CASH.